1901: Black educator and reformer Booker T. Washington is invited to lunch at the White House by President Teddy Roosevelt. The same year sees the publication of Washington's now-classic memoir, *Up From Slavery.* (The Bettman Archive)

1903: Brothers Orville and Wilbur Wright test their first machine-powered airplane on December 17, near Kitty Hawk, North Carolina. The Wrights make four successful sustained flights, the longest lasting 59 seconds. (The Bettman Archive)

1904: St. Louis, Missouri, is host to the World's Fair. The exposition boasts the largest use of electrical lighting and the largest collection of automobiles in the nation's history. The American public is also first introduced to the ice-cream cone.

1905: American football's ugliest season sees 18 deaths and 159 injuries, according to a report in the *Chicago Tribune.* President Roosevelt summons representatives from the Harvard, Yale, and Princeton teams to the White House to caution them about "brutality and foul play."
(Culver Pictures, Inc.)

1908: William Jennings Bryan is nominated as the presidential candidate of the Democratic Party at the national convention in Denver. This will be Bryan's third pursuit of the presidency—and his third defeat. (Western Heritage Museum)

1909: Teddy Roosevelt leaves the White House after seven years in office. His presidency has seen the breakup of major industrial trusts, the passing of the Pure Food and Drug Act, and the acquisition of the Panama Canal. (The Bettman Archive)

THE AMERICAN CHRONICLES
DECADE ONE

DAWN OF THE CENTURY

ROBERT VAUGHAN

BANTAM BOOKS
NEW YORK · TORONTO · LONDON · SYDNEY · AUCKLAND

DAWN OF THE CENTURY

A Bantam Domain Book / February 1992

ISBN 0-553-29249-8

Published simultaneously in the United States and Canada

Bantam Books are published by Bantam Books, a division of Bantam Doubleday Dell Publishing Group, Inc. Its trademark, consisting of the words "Bantam Books" and the portrayal of a rooster, is Registered in U.S. Patent and Trademark Office and in other countries. Marca Registrada. Bantam Books, 666 Fifth Avenue, New York, New York 10103.

PRINTED IN THE UNITED STATES OF AMERICA

OPM   0 9 8 7 6 5 4 3 2 1

This book is lovingly dedicated to
Margaret Woods Allen
whose affection, kindness, and support
mean more than I can ever repay.

PROLOGUE

The World's Fair Special hurtled south through the rain and the Illinois cornfields. For just over five hours the train had clipped off the miles at the rate of one a minute; now it was nearing the end of its journey. Behind lay wet tracks gleaming softly in the gray morning light and coal smoke lingering in the warm air. Ahead lay Eads Bridge across the Mississippi, then a double-track railroad tunnel that led into St. Louis's Union Station.

Two hundred and six passengers had boarded the nine coaches in Chicago at three o'clock that morning. Now they began preparing for their arrival—collecting their belongings, buttoning their jackets, and waking their children. The quiet anticipation of the journey was building into a great excitement, for at the cost of only twelve dollars, each man, woman, and child on this train had purchased a round-trip ticket to the future and back. They had come to St. Louis to see the Centennial

Exposition of the Louisiana Purchase, better known far
and wide as the World's Fair.

The official purpose of the fair was to commemorate
the Jefferson Expansion; the actual purpose was to
celebrate the arrival of the twentieth century and the
promises it held in store for all mankind. It was Friday,
May 6, 1904, and an editorial in a St. Louis paper that
very morning read:

> Our city is like unto the new age. It is modern in
> every way, humming with industrious energy and as full
> of hope and promise as the century we have so recently
> begun. All St. Louisians, indeed, all Americans can take
> pride in the fact that the greatest of all World's Fairs has
> been impressively opened and is being attended and
> praised by persons of the most important stature.

The train roared over the bridge onto the Missouri
side of the Mississippi River, then plunged into the
darkness of the tunnel under Washington Avenue. For
eighteen city blocks it ran under the center of the city,
finally emerging on one of the huge network of tracks at
Union Station.

Outside, a forest-green Victoria carriage, pulled
along by a team of high-stepping, matched grays, turned
west onto Market, the street side of Union Station. The
hollow clopping of prancing hooves made a staccato beat
on the glistening wet pavement as the driver maneu-
vered the carriage through the traffic, then brought it to
a stop under the Union Station porte cochere. The
passenger was carrying a newspaper under his arm as he
stepped from the covered carriage.

"*Abwarten Sie, Herr Petzold?*" the coachman asked.

"*Nein,*" Thomas Petzold replied. "Don't wait. I'll
take the streetcar back to the office."

"But the rain. *Ist nicht gut* an important man like
you get wet."

"It's okay, Otto, I'll be all right, *danke,*" Thomas
said, smiling at his own and Otto's mixture of languages.

"Sehr gut, Herr Petzold." Otto snapped the reins, and the team of grays pulled away.

A rather smallish man of thirty-one, Thomas Petzold had a high forehead, close-set gray eyes accented by pince-nez glasses, and an oversized nose. If one had only photographs to go by, one might think him quite unattractive. But those who were around him all the time were so caught up by his wit and vitality that they never really thought of him as a homely man.

Though he had come from Germany only ten years earlier, Petzold could speak nearly accentless English. But the high proportion of German-speaking immigrants in St. Louis made a German accent and the ability to speak German a decided asset. Because of that, Petzold had developed a chameleonlike ability to tailor his form of speech to fit the need, reverting to either German or a German accent when it was advantageous, but most of the time speaking English with the same flat Missouri twang as the other business leaders of St. Louis.

Heading into Union Station, Petzold passed through the golden entrance arch, under the mosaic-glass window, then climbed the great staircase to the Grand Hall, from whose sixty-five-foot-high vaulted ceiling hung an enormous, heavy chandelier. At all hours of the day and night the marble floor of the Grand Hall teemed with humanity: men and women moving to or from trains, children laughing or crying, and redcaps scurrying about under the burden of passengers' luggage. On one of the arcades overlooking the Grand Hall, a group of mustachioed men—all identically dressed in red-pinstriped white shirts, red bow ties, and red sleeve garters—were singing what had become the fair's anthem, "Meet Me in St. Louis, Louis."

The Chicago and Alton World's Fair Special was just pulling into the station, and as it arrived, Petzold could feel the floor rumbling underfoot. With other things on his mind, though, he was hardly aware of all the bustle and activity as he continued up the stairs to the relative quiet of the third floor, where the offices of all the railroads that served St. Louis were located.

Until just over five months before Petzold had been a reporter for the German-language *Westliche Post*. Then on a cold, wet day in January he had stood with a small group of people at the steps of the St. Louis courthouse to attend a public sale of the bankrupt *Evening Standard*.

There hadn't been many bidders. A handful of the paper's employees who had remained loyal had been there, hoping that someone would see something in the defunct paper worth buying and thus save their jobs. But none of the major newspaper owners of the city had shown up. To a man they had believed *The Standard* was dead and were perfectly willing to let it be buried.

They had had every right to think the newspaper was beyond salvage. Deeply in debt and its credit exhausted, it had been steadily losing circulation. And the physical plant had been in worse shape: Type was badly worn, the flatbed press was continually breaking down, and the building itself was in danger of collapse. There had been so little interest in buying such a disaster that Thomas Petzold had bought the building, equipment, circulation list, and Associated Press membership for his opening bid of five hundred dollars.

He had offered jobs to all the employees who wanted to stay, but he had changed the name of the paper from *The Evening Standard* to *The St. Louis Chronicle*. At the first meeting of his staff he had pledged that his new paper would "be a servant of the people, would oppose all fraud and corruption wherever it might be found, and would champion truth and principles over prejudices and partisanship."

A glutton for work, the new publisher had won the immediate loyalty and admiration of every one of his employees. He had made them feel as if they were a part of the paper, that they had a vested interest, beyond mere employment, in the newspaper's triumphs.

From the very first issue *The Chronicle* had been exciting, provocative, even shocking; a quality of sensationalism had caught the interest of all who read it. Circulation had grown by leaps and bounds, and in less than half a year *The Chronicle* was a threat to the major newspapers of the city in daily numbers.

When the editor of one of the other newspapers had realized that *The St. Louis Chronicle* was rapidly gaining ground on the majors of the city, he had accused Thomas Petzold, in print, of "crass sensationalism bordering on the obscene." Petzold had made no excuses. In his own editorial he had replied, "I believe that *The Chronicle* has, in addition to the obligation of informing its readers, the right to amuse and entertain them as well."

What Petzold hadn't said but was proving in his daily operation was that he also believed *The Chronicle* had the right and the obligation to become St. Louis's most successful newspaper. Today he was taking a step that he believed would help him reach that goal.

His first stop at Union Station's third-floor suite of offices was at the St. Louis and San Francisco Railroad, better known as the Frisco Line. By telephone earlier today he had arranged a meeting with General B. F. Yoakum, the president. As Petzold was already becoming one of St. Louis's most notable figures, he was recognized immediately by Yoakum's receptionist and ushered into the General's private office the moment he arrived.

The St. Louis and San Francisco Railroad did not go to San Francisco; it never had, and it never would—though that had been the original intention when Missouri endowed the line with 1.2 million acres of land and one million dollars in bonds. But marauding bands of outlaws had so terrorized the line during the Civil War and in the years immediately following that the line went into receivership. The bankrupt line was ultimately purchased and reorganized by a group of investors represented by General Yoakum, and he had surprised everyone by announcing that he wasn't even going to try to reach San Francisco.

Yoakum greeted Petzold warmly, then offered him a chair and a Havana cigar. The newspaperman sat in the former, and when he accepted the latter, the general prepared two of them by snipping off the ends with the elaborate silver-plated model guillotine that perched on the corner of his desk. He held a match first to his visitor's cigar and then to his own before sitting back in his chair, surrounded by a cloud of aromatic smoke.

Petzold admired the gold-plated model of an engine and tender—flanked by tiny flags of the United States and the Frisco Railroad—that sat on the front of Yoakum's desk. This was the impressive desk of an important man, for the publisher knew that in America, presidents of railroads and captains of industry were more powerful than were the titled nobility of Europe.

"I'd like to thank you very much, General, for agreeing to see me," Petzold said, opening the conversation.

"I must confess, Mr. Petzold, that I've been looking forward to meeting you. I think it's amazing what you've accomplished with your paper in such a short time. People are always talking about your stories, you have very good pictures, and I've been most impressed with your editorials."

"Thank you for the compliment."

"That isn't a compliment, Petzold, it's a statement of fact. Compliments are for ladies who wear ostrich feathers in their hats. Now, what is all this about?"

"General Yoakum, I have a proposition that I believe you'll find very interesting."

A piece of loose tobacco leaf stuck on the tip of Yoakum's tongue. The railroad man pulled the cigar away to spit it out before he replied, "Then by all means let me hear it."

Petzold smiled. General Yoakum was a man who got right to the point, and he appreciated that. "My staff tells me your trains carry an average of seven hundred and fifty passengers per day. Is that true?"

Nodding, Yoakum replied, "Yes, I would say that's a pretty accurate figure."

"With that in mind I have come here to suggest a new service for your passengers. I think you should provide free copies of *The Chronicle* to everyone who rides your trains."

"Is this a onetime thing, a promotion of some sort, or do you mean every day?"

"I mean every day, General." Petzold held his cigar over a polished brass ashtray and bumped off an ash.

Yoakum clasped his hands together and leaned forward, resting his elbows on the edge of his desk. "That sounds like a damn fool thing to do," he said, the cigar clamped between his teeth. "Why would I want to do that?"

"I know about you, General Yoakum. I know how, when you bought this railroad, you abandoned the idea of going west to the Pacific and instead set about spanning the midcontinent from the Twin Cities to the Gulf of Mexico. And I know how, at first, there were many on your board who thought you were wrong."

"Wrong? Mr. Petzold, there were some who thought I was downright blasphemous," Yoakum said with a laugh.

Thomas laughed with him. "Quite so. And yet, under your direction this railroad has not only recovered, it has prospered, doubling in passengers, tonnage, and track mileage. That is true, is it not?"

"Yes, I'm happy to say, it's true," Yoakum answered, beaming proudly.

"Then you and I are alike, General, for we have each taken businesses that were failures and made successes of them. And, because we are alike, I know what you feel and how you think. And I know that once I explain it, you will understand the wisdom of providing the service of newspaper delivery to your passengers. Not only is it good public relations on your part, but news of our city will also be projected to all areas of your route. People will read of the exciting events going on here, not just during the World's Fair, but all the time, and they'll make plans to come for a visit. And when they do visit St. Louis, General, they'll ride on your trains."

Yoakum narrowed his eyes as if in deep concentration. Finally he smiled. "I have to admit, Petzold, your idea has merit. Visitors spend money, and that's good for the merchants. I'd not only be generating passenger revenue, I'd also be doing a good thing for the city."

"Exactly," Petzold agreed.

"What would you charge me for seven hundred and fifty newspapers per day?"

The publisher examined the fiery tip of his cigar for a long moment. Then he looked up at General Yoakum with a sly smile. "For you, General Yoakum, I will charge nothing."

Yoakum's mouth and eyes opened wide in shock. "What? You will *give* me the newspapers? But I don't understand, man. Why would you make such an offer?"

"Simple," Petzold replied. "Besides the Frisco Line, there are twenty-one other railroads that serve St. Louis. I intend to—"

Yoakum interrupted him with a peal of laughter. "Why, you clever old fellow, you!" he exclaimed, still laughing. "I understand now what you're going to do. You're going to tell the others that I am already using the newspapers on my trains . . . and that will force them to make *The Chronicle* available on theirs as well."

"Precisely," Petzold confirmed. "The price to you, General, is nothing. But you must promise not to tell anyone else the terms of our arrangement."

General Yoakum put his hand across the desk and took Thomas Petzold's in a vigorous handshake. "Mr. Petzold, you have a deal . . . and a partner in your bamboozlement. Now would you like a suggestion? Go see the KATY line next. I'll telephone Bill Crush and tell him you're coming. I'll also tell him what a good thing this will be for the city. With the Frisco and KATY lines both taking your papers, no other railroad would dare refuse." He picked up the telephone, cranked the handle, then when the operator came on, spoke into the mouthpiece. "Central? Get me one nine two nine." He cupped his hand over the mouthpiece and looked at his guest. "My God, Petzold. Do you realize you could increase your circulation by more than five thousand papers per day if all the railroads take you up on this?"

"Yes, and more importantly, extend the reach of *The Chronicle* to far beyond the city limits of St. Louis."

"What a brilliant idea you've conceived!"

"Thank you," Petzold responded modestly.

"Hello!" the railroad magnate abruptly shouted into the phone. "Hello, this is General Yoakum from the Frisco line. I would like to speak with Mr. Crush, please." While he was waiting, he resumed his conversation with Petzold. "You know, in the short time since you started *The Chronicle*, you've shown the other newspaper people of this city what a fierce competitor you can be." He chuckled. "I certainly hope you have no interest in the railroad business."

"Only that the trains run on time and get me where I am going," Petzold said.

"By the way, when do you start supplying us with your papers?"

"Oh, we started that this morning," the publisher answered with a smile. "I took the liberty of having today's newspaper delivered to your passengers."

"You mean you did this even before you had my permission? What if I'd said no?"

"You are a very intelligent man, General Yoakum. I knew you wouldn't refuse the offer."

"You don't say. I— Oh, hello?" he called back into the phone. "Mr. Crush? General Yoakum here. There's a gentlemen coming over to see you, a Mr. Thomas Petzold. Yes, the newspaperman."

CHAPTER ONE

The rain stopped before eleven; then the sun came out, so that by late afternoon it was the kind of soft, warm spring day that poets extol. On the center lawn at St. Louis's Jefferson College, in a plaza the students called the quad, young men and women lolled about, enjoying the sun, the flowers, the fragrant grass, but most of all the end of classes for the week and the upcoming weekend.

When Jefferson College opened its doors in 1853, it had very modest goals. Its founder and first president, Henry R. Spengeman, had established the all-male college named after Thomas Jefferson to "teach the English and dead languages, mathematics, mechanics, art, natural and moral philosophy, history, and the principles of the Constitution of the United States."

Henry Spengeman had been honored with a bronze statue of him, sculpted by Rodin in the style of his "The Thinker." Done at a scale three times life size and mounted on a large, concrete pedestal that had a brass plaque reading, IN MEMORY OF PROFESSOR HENRY R. SPENGEMAN, OUR BELOVED FOUNDER AND FIRST PRESIDENT, 1853–1881, the sculpture had the professor sitting on a chair, resting his chin on his right hand, while in his left he held a book. Those who could remember the professor said it was a typical pose.

The pedestal-mounted statue sat right in the middle of the quad and was set off by large, white-painted stones that formed a circle some one hundred feet in diameter. This was known as Statue Circle, and it was hallowed ground.

Jefferson College was still an all-male school; therefore the women present on the quad were guests of their male escorts. Some of the women were students at Mary Lindenwood, the women's college in nearby St. Charles. Enough commuter trains ran between the schools that weekend visits were easily arranged between the campuses.

Near the great bronze statue a group of four seniors were enjoying the privilege of their class. As upperclassmen they were authorized to be inside of Statue Circle, though the exact position of these particular young men—at the pedestal itself—was the most elite of the elite. Unlike the area inside Statue Circle, the pedestal wasn't reserved by tradition but had been staked out at the beginning of the school year by these four who, by dint of their popularity, social position, athletic ability, and academic achievement, had established themselves as the crème de la crème of the senior class. They called themselves the quad quad.

The obvious leader of the quad quad was Bob Canfield, a good-looking young man with well-chiseled features, dark hair and eyes, and a runner's chest and legs, all on a six-foot frame. A miler, he had that very day won an intercollegiate meet with his best time ever. The other three were also varsity trackmen: David Gelbman, another miler, and sprinters Terry Perkins and J. P. Winthrop.

Only two weeks of school remained, and the entire

student body was feeling a sense of importance—the seniors because they'd be graduating, the juniors because they'd soon move into the exalted position of seniors, and the two lower classes because they'd be moving up.

At the moment there were no women with the quad quad, though Bob was expecting Connie Bateman on the next train from St. Charles. Connie, a student at Mary Lindenwood College, happened to be the daughter of William Bateman, the current president of Jefferson College. Though not officially engaged as yet, Bob and Connie had what was called "an understanding."

"What do you think?" Terry Perkins asked, holding up his sketch pad. "Have I captured the essence?" His pale-blue eyes sparkled with amusement, but his muscular, well-proportioned body almost seemed ready to challenge a less-than-favorable response.

"Let me see," J.P. answered. The tall, black-haired youth stood and struck a pose like that of Professor Avery, the art instructor. With his left arm across the body, his left hand cradling the right elbow, and his right hand on his chin, he narrowed his eyes and studied the picture. "Oh, my good fellow, do you really think you have captured the essence with this abysmal collection of lines and smudges?" he asked, perfectly duplicating the professor's sibilant voice. "Your trees have no symmetry, your flowers look as if they are made of wax, and your stream is running not downhill, but up. Oh, and tell me, Mr. Perkins, have you perhaps made a discovery that our noted astronomers have missed? Not one, but three suns in our solar system? For, dear boy, that is the only way one might explain your source of light."

Bob and David laughed, though through his laughter, David squinted his deep-blue eyes at his friend and asked, "You're being a little hard on him, aren't you, J.P.?"

"Do you want these lips to say what these eyes do not see?" J.P. quipped. "Mr. Perkins, I must tell you, you represent no threat to Winslow Homer; however . . ." He let the last word hang.

"However?" Terry asked hopefully.

J.P. smiled. "However, I think you'll be able to pull a 'gentleman's C' in Professor Avery's class."

"Alleluia," Terry said, running a hand through his light-brown hair and breathing a sigh of relief.

The others applauded, for though they had all successfully completed their final art assignment, Terry's two previous attempts had been rejected as "unsatisfactory."

J. P. Winthrop was the best artist of the group and the most critical judge. If he guessed Professor Avery would give a C, then Terry could relax.

"Well, Terry, it's beginning to look as if when the rest of us walk across these hallowed grounds to receive our sheepskin, you'll be with us after all," David said, though in truth, even if Terry's submission was not accepted, there would be no danger of his not graduating. Like the others, he had maintained a very high average in all his classes.

"Yes," Terry said. "My honor is saved."

"It would've helped if you'd chosen a simpler subject," David suggested. The blond-haired youth shook his head slowly. "The Garden of Eden is not a logical subject for someone with your limited abilities. Why did you choose such a theme?"

"I was trying to play it smart," Terry answered. "I figured since no one knows what the Garden of Eden looks like, no one could say my idea was wrong. What I should've done is draw a lot of tree stumps, like Bob." He turned to the leader. "What did you call it again?"

"'The Naked Swamp,'" Bob answered.

"I don't understand it," Terry complained. "Here I try to draw something beautiful, like the Garden of Eden, and it takes me three times before Professor Avery will accept it, while you draw an ugly bunch of tree stumps, and you get an A your first time out. Who can explain it?"

"I can explain it," J.P. said. "Bob got an A because he deserved an A. The harsh reality of a swamp, empty save for the stark stumps repeated again and again, the stillness of the water, the loneliness of the sky . . . Why, his picture was the work of genius."

No, Bob thought to himself, it wasn't the work of genius. And he was no artist. But in this case he did know his subject, perhaps as well as anyone alive. "The Naked Swamp" was in fact the sum total of his heritage.

He was from Sikeston, a small town in southeast Missouri that was sometimes called swampeast Missouri, for the entire bootheel of the state was covered with swamp. At one time it had also been covered with trees, and those trees had been the Canfield source of income. For three generations now the relative affluence of the Canfield family had been based on the sale of hardwood timber.

Jack and Green Canfield, Bob's father and grandfather respectively, had bought thousands of acres of swampland in the years following the Civil War, sometimes paying no more than a dollar fifty an acre and ten cents per tree. After getting control of the land, they would send in a team of woodcutters to bring out the timber.

The woodcutters worked from small boats, cutting the trees and leaving high, denuded stumps behind. The demand for hardwood lumber was insatiable, and for forty years business had been very profitable. But the business was nearly finished now. The demand was as great as ever, but forty years of gathering the lumber with no means of reforestation had exhausted the supply. And the intense harvesting had left hundreds of thousands of acres of ugly swampland, studded with stumps and infested with mosquitoes and cottonmouth snakes. Bob's family now owned one hundred fifty thousand acres of such land.

"Hello, the cars from St. Charles have arrived," Terry said, interrupting Bob's thoughts. "And there is Miss Bateman."

The quad quad looked in the direction of the commuter station and saw perhaps a dozen people coming down the hill toward the campus. One of the more strikingly beautiful of the new arrivals was Connie Bateman.

"Would you mind telling me, please," David asked in a long-suffering tone of voice, "what a woman like Miss Bateman sees in our friend here that she doesn't see in me?"

"Oh, nothing more than good looks, a sparkling personality, intelligence, athletic ability, wealth, and class," Terry answered.

"Okay, I'll concede all that. But what else?"

The others laughed.

Connie reached the bottom of the small hill, then started across the quad toward the statue. Though the seniors vigorously defended the sacred ground of Statue Circle against all underclassmen and outsiders, women friends of Jefferson College seniors were allowed inside. As Connie moved through the underclassmen and their young women, they made way for her like the sea parting for Moses. Reaching the perimeter, she stepped lightly over the ring of white rocks and, smiling brightly, approached the quad quad.

Connie was a very pretty woman with a profusion of auburn hair—one long roll of which hung coquettishly over her left shoulder—eyes that were nearly green, and a delicately molded, upturned nose. She was chic, haughty, and graceful, just like one of Dana Gibson's models brought to life . . . and of course that was exactly the look she was trying to capture.

"Oh, my, look!" Terry said, pointing at Connie's clothes. She was wearing a white shirtwaist and a blue skirt that accented her wasplike waist, then fell softly over her hips and close enough to her legs to suggest their form. Like many college women, Connie was wearing a "walking skirt," which was short enough to expose her ankles. Though such attire was permitted for "sporting wear," it was not generally acceptable as truly proper dress, and many restaurants and clubs would have asked her to leave, had she shown up in such an ensemble.

"In order for a lady to be deemed properly dressed," a tongue-in-cheek article on etiquette in *The Jeffersonian*, the college's newspaper, once explained, "an observer must be kept in total mystery as to a female's means of locomotion. To be proper, neither a woman's feet nor her legs should ever be seen; therefore, she must appear to glide across the ground as if God had provided her with wheels."

However, it wasn't the short length of Connie's skirt that had caught Terry's attention. It was the colors.

"Look at what she's wearing—blue and white! My dear young lady, need I remind you that our colors are red and green? You are wearing the colors of Westminster. You dare to defile the sacred Statue Circle attired in the colors of another institution?"

"If you wish, David, I'll come to the lady's rescue," J.P. offered. "I'll slash my wrists and dye her dress red with my own blood."

"That wouldn't do any good," David pointed out. "You're a Winthrop. Your blood is blue, remember?"

J.P. shrugged and smiled at Connie. "I'm sorry, Miss Bateman. I *did* make the offer with all good intentions, but I'm afraid David is quite correct. Alas, we Winthrops are all blue-blooded, and were I to bleed on your dress, it would only make matters worse."

"Nevertheless, I am grateful for your gallant offer," Connie said, laughing. "And I'm sorry I couldn't come to the meet today, but I had an exam in English Lit. How did the quad quad do?"

"Bob took the laurels in his event, while David came in second," J.P. answered. "Terry was second in the one hundred, and I was third."

"Oh, it sounds as if you all did well. I do wish I could have come," Connie said, clapping her hands in delight.

Across the quad in his office on the third floor of Spengeman Hall, the current president of Jefferson College, Professor William T. Bateman, walked over to the window, automatically adjusting his tie and straightening his jacket as he did so. It was late afternoon, but he was a man of such meticulous neatness that though he had worn his suit all day, it still looked early-morning fresh.

Standing at the open window, he looked through the screen at the sunlit, familiar scene laid out below . . . the white circle around Henry Spengeman's statue, the academic buildings fronting the grassy square, and the azaleas in full bloom on the hill near the commuter station. Professor Bateman often stood here, looking out over his domain much as a king might survey his realm.

Below him, the groups of strolling or sitting students and their guests were enjoying moments that for the rest of their lives would form some of their most pleasant memories. Professor Bateman knew that though these students would go on to other things, be it careers in the professions or business, they would always have these moments.

He thought himself distinctly blessed by the fact that his own memories were multiplied by the collective memories of all his students. He was a part of this college, and it was a part of him. He could not deny it without denying his own existence; its well-being was his well-being.

And that well-being was now threatened.

For the last two years enrollment of incoming students had decreased. The drop had been small enough so as not to raise too much of an alarm among the Board of Regents, and Professor Bateman had explained it away as being the result of the school's tightened academic standards.

"If we truly are to be competitive with Harvard, Yale, and the other finer schools of our country, then we must keep our academic standards high," he had told the board. "Now, while this will attract the top-quality students, it will also frighten away the more marginal ones, and our enrollment may experience a slight decrease. However, I am certain that we will be able to make up the difference shortly, and as our reputation grows, so will the applications for enrollment."

Despite his assurances, a new problem had recently developed. Missouri's four normal schools had had their designations changed to teachers' colleges. But while primarily specializing in turning out teachers, these state institutions now offered four-year college degrees at a fraction of what it would cost to attend Jefferson—and the state teachers' colleges were open to men and women.

Professor Bateman had been looking over the tentative enrollment for next year's class and was shocked to find an alarming drop in admission applications. He could no longer placate the board by telling them enrollment would come back. Something was going to have to be done to *get* it back. He couldn't lower tuition, but he did have another idea. However, implementing it would require a change in the original charter, and in order to bring that about, he was going to have to convince the Board of Regents to go along with him.

His plan was to make Jefferson College more attractive to prospective students by, when classes began next year, opening the doors to women as well as men. He was also going to propose that the school broaden its educational offering and be redesignated as a university. That would require an expenditure of more money at a time when decreased enrollment put operating funds at an all-time low, but in the professor's mind that was the only way to save the school.

For a few moments Professor Bateman allowed himself to dream about what the campus of Jefferson University might be like at the end of the twentieth century, if his plan proved successful: The campus would be crowded with great new academic buildings, bursting with students, and enjoying a reputation as "America's Oxford." And in a corner of his dream was a small concrete monument with a modest brass plaque, commemorating William T. Bateman as Jefferson's savior and one instrumental in its early guidance.

But first he would have to convince the Board of Regents that his idea was sound.

On the northwest corner of Spengeman Hall was a concrete pit with a narrow staircase of ten steps leading down to a basement entrance. The open door at the bottom of the steps revealed a room that was impeccably clean and orderly, the occupant of this room believing that slovenly living habits were the sign of a slovenly mind. The bed was made up, the extra pair of shoes were well shined, the table had been cleaned off, the supper dishes had been washed and put away, and the book its owner had been reading had been placed to one side.

The book came from a shelf full of textbooks from the various courses offered at Jefferson College. At first glance they appeared no different from any other textbooks, but closer scrutiny disclosed that each of them had been painstakingly repaired with reconstructed binders, reassembled pages, and patched covers.

At the top of the steps, leaning against the iron-pipe railing that protected the unwary from falling into the pit, a tall, well-built young man with skin the color of cocoa looked out over the quad. He was Loomis Booker, who at twenty-three was just a couple of years older than any of the students of this college, though he generally thought of them as much younger than himself.

It was six years now since Loomis had come to St. Louis from Alexandria, Virginia. He had left home in the middle of the night, with all his worldly possessions rolled up in an extra shirt plus the four dollars that his teary-eyed, terrified mother had placed in his hands.

Loomis's grandfather had been a slave, and he had often told the young Loomis stories of the underground railroad and how the slaves used it to escape from the South, similar to the flight led by Moses four thousand years before. When Loomis thought of it, he couldn't help but compare his own rapid departure from Alexandria with those escapes made by slaves fifty years earlier.

Loomis's own flight had been the result of a game played by young white men who, after getting drunk, thought it would be great entertainment. The game had been called "nigger-bashing," and the rules had been quite simple: After equipping themselves with a club about the size of a baseball bat and mounting horses, the white youths had gone about bashing the head of any black they happened to encounter.

The game had been played before, and while they never intended to kill anyone, accidents did happen, and so far three black men had died. Since it was a very popular game and a number of spirited white youths played it, the police hadn't been sure who was actually to blame for the deaths, so no arrests had been made— though there had been a strong admonition in the paper against such "callous and ungentlemanly behavior."

But boys will be boys, after all, and it was just a little harmless fun, the prevailing local attitude had it, so when a half-dozen young men had gotten intoxicated while celebrating the twenty-first birthday of one of their group, nigger-bashing seemed like a perfect way to cap the evening. With whoops of exuberance they'd left the party and rode out to find their first victim.

Loomis Booker hadn't played the game right. He had ducked the first four boys who came toward him, and that was acceptable. He had warded off the fifth with his arms, feeling a numbing blow where the bat struck, and that, too, was within the rules. But when he had grabbed the club of the sixth rider and jerked him from the saddle, that was definitely against the rules. And when the rider had fallen on his head, cracking it open, that was a violation of the highest order.

The serious injury to one of their number had a sobering effect on the remaining riders, who immediately turned their attention from Loomis to their injured companion. When they had picked up their friend to ride away, the limpness of the man's body told Loomis that the youth might well be dead. He had hurried home and informed his parents of the incident, and they had been terrified that the police would be coming for him at any moment. The idea that he might plead self-defense had never occurred to them. Loomis was black; the injured—possibly dead—man was white. The only option open to Loomis had been to leave Alexandria forever that very midnight.

After a year of toiling wherever he could find work, then moving on to another city when he couldn't, Loomis had wound up in St. Louis. While reading the "Want Directory" of the *St. Louis Post-Dispatch* he saw an ad that interested him:

FURNACE AND HANDYMAN WANTED. Colored man as general man about place. Inquire at Jefferson College. Five dollars per week and room.

There had been other jobs for "colored men." One, offering work as a laborer, had paid as much as twenty cents an hour, an extremely good wage. But Loomis had seen only the job at Jefferson College, wanting that position more than he had ever wanted anything in his life, because he had wanted to be on a college campus.

From his earliest years, Loomis had had a thirst for knowledge that his father always insisted was unnatural for a man of color. Natural or unnatural, that hunger for learning was real, and Loomis had seen the job at Jefferson College as the opportunity to satisfy it.

He had gotten the job, and since arriving on campus six years before, he had set about fulfilling his ambition for an education. Although the college was for white students only, Loomis Booker began "stealing" an education for himself. He hadn't stolen any of the textbooks; he had salvaged them from the trash after they were thrown away. But he had stolen the knowledge the books contained.

Few of the students and even fewer of the faculty knew about Loomis Booker's program of self-education. Bob Canfield had found out about it during his second year, and ever since that time, Bob had been helping Loomis by bringing around assignments so Loomis could develop his own curriculum. The help wasn't all one-sided. Bob discovered early on that Loomis was a good man to study math with, and together the two had worked out some difficult math equations.

Though Loomis lacked any official confirmation, by self-study and determination he had already completed the disciplines for three degrees. Having no piece of paper to reward him for his efforts, he had to be satisfied with learning for learning's sake, and he kept quiet about what he was doing for fear that if the wrong people found out about it, he might be forced to leave.

Loomis didn't want to leave. He knew it was incongruous for him to love this school that was, by charter, for young white gentlemen only. But he loved Jefferson as much as any student who had ever gradu-ated, and he felt as much a part of it as any student or any member of the faculty. Listening to the men's chorus singing "Golden Leaves on Jefferson Ground" or any one of a half-dozen other melodic college songs, he could actually feel a lump come to his throat. He cheered lustily for the "Bears" on the football field or the cinder track, feeling elated when they won and sad when they lost.

Sometimes late at night he would sit on the railing at the entrance to his small basement room and stare out across the quad at the moonlit statue of Professor Spengeman. Though he would never say anything about it to anyone, Loomis could almost believe that, on occasion, the statue was visited by the spirit of the professor. And he knew that, regardless of the charter and the rules of the school, the professor, wherever he was now, would approve of Loomis's ambition. It was almost as if Loomis could hear Spengeman say, "Now that I've had time to think things over, Mr. Booker, I no longer believe that the pigmentation of a man's skin should deny him the right to an education."

Loomis's thoughts were interrupted by the whistle of the KATY *Flyer* as it left St. Louis, headed for Kansas City. The KATY track passed just south of the school, shielded from the campus by a densely treed area. Since the train left Union Station at a quarter to seven and it took some fifteen minutes for it to come this far, Loomis knew it must be about seven o'clock. With a sigh he reluctantly abandoned his vantage point to return to his room. It was later than he'd realized, and he'd promised himself that he would read at least four more chapters before he went to sleep.

CHAPTER TWO

On board the KATY *Flyer*, one hundred seventeen passengers settled in for the trip. Some chose the dining car, where tonight they were served a choice of breaded veal cutlet with tomato sauce, chicken à la king on toast, or fresh gulf fish fillet with potatoes, fresh vegetable, coffee, tea, or milk, all for twenty-five cents. A portion of pudding, cake, pie, or ice cream could be had for five cents extra. Many of the passengers had eaten at the Harvey House in Union Station before they left, though some had bought one of the sack lunches that were for sale at the depot for ten cents. Today's sacks contained a cheese sandwich, a boiled egg, and an apple.

Just over one hundred copies of *The St. Louis Chronicle* had been placed on board the *Flyer* before its departure, and though one or two papers were subsequently taken off at intermediate stops, most of them would make it all the way to Kansas City. There, many of the passengers would hold on to *The Chronicle* when they boarded the various trains to points west, sending copies of the newspaper toward Dallas, Albuquerque, Phoenix, Denver, San Francisco, Portland, and Seattle. In Seattle one paper would even wind up in the sea bag of a deck officer of the *Edward Sewall*, a giant four-masted steel windjammer bound for Hong Kong.

One of the newspapers eventually turned up on the *General Joe Jack*, a local train on the Chicago and Burlington line in Northern Wyoming. Looking for some way to pass the time between Newcastle and Gillette, a salesman noticed it in the luggage rack over his seat and began reading it. Fascinated by stories of the World's Fair, the drummer tucked the paper under his arm when he got off the train in Gillette and boarded the stage-coach for Oshoto, where he then left it on the counter in Dunnigan's General Store. Dennis Dunnigan set the paper aside without bothering to read it, though he would remember it a few days later when he needed some wrapping paper to protect the glass globe of a kerosene lantern he had just received.

At cock's crow Eric McKenzie, fifteen years old but tall enough and mature looking enough to pass for eighteen, came out of the bunkhouse. His sandy hair tousled and his blue eyes still filled with sleep, he went into the barn, then soon came back out, leading a team of horses over to a wagon. Spring came late in the high plains country of northeast Wyoming, and while it would be warm enough later in the day, it was still early-morning cold. Though Eric was wearing a denim jacket and flannel shirt, he could feel the chill cut through to the bone. The horses, not at all pleased to be taken from their warm stalls, obstinately jerked their heads up and down as the youth began slipping on their harnesses.

"Come on, be nice," Eric told them. "Another couple of hours it'll be so hot, you'll wish you had some of this cool back. Now, stand still."

As if understanding his words, the horses stood quietly until he had them hitched to the wagon.

The sun—blood-red and not yet painful to the eyes—rested just on top of Devil's Tower, several miles to the east, as if dotting the "i." Between Devil's Tower and the bunkhouse lay sixty-five thousand acres of rangeland, fed by the Belle Fourche River that shimmered in the morning sun like a twisting strand of molten gold. The bunkhouse was part of a compound in the middle of that rangeland, along with a cookhouse, a smokehouse, a barn and corral, a granary, a machine shed, and an unpainted outhouse for the cowboys. A two-story, white-frame gothic main house complete with turrets, dormers, a big bay window, a screened-in porch, and a painted outhouse sat opposite the bunkhouse, and between them was a two-and-a-half-acre garden, irrigated by an Aeromotor windmill in the corral that also pumped water into the trough for the livestock; the cookhouse and kitchen of the main house each had their own hand pumps. This spread was the Flying E Ranch, owned by Rodney Ebersole, a sixty-five-year-old Englishman who had come to America thirty years earlier.

Finishing with the team, Eric went into the cookhouse, coming back out moments later carrying a sandwich of biscuit and side pork for his trip. Walking over to the wagon, he put the biscuit on the seat, then climbed aboard and picked up the reins. He heard the screen door pop shut on the bunkhouse, and when he looked in that direction, he saw Jake Quinn and Marcus Parmeter just heading for breakfast.

"Eric, you ain't left yet?" Marcus called, still tucking his shirt into his pants.

"I'm leaving right now. I'll see you two at noon."

"Boy, don't you go gettin' liquored up in town, now, you hear me?" Jake called to him.

"Yeah, and not only that, you stay away from Susie," Marcus warned.

"Susie? You mean the woman that does the cleaning at Dunnigan's? Why should I stay away from her?"

"Why? Boy, I'm tryin' to look out for you, is all. You know, that thing of hers has been known to slam shut tighter'n a snappin' turtle. If you was to be on top of her when that happened, it'd take two men an' a small boy to pry you loose."

Eric laughed. "Well, in that case I'll sure try to behave myself," he said, releasing the brake.

"Behave hisself," Jake scoffed as he and Marcus stepped up onto the porch of the cookhouse. "Hell, that's the only reason Ebersole sends him to town, 'cause he don't do nothin' *except* behave hisself."

"Well," Marcus said, "that's what happens when you send a boy to do a man's job."

Eric knew that the teasing was in good spirit; Jake and Marcus were his two best friends. Considerably younger than they, or anyone else on the Flying E for that matter, Eric was a good worker who always held up his end no matter what the job. He was also quick to give a hand to a friend, and he could be depended on in a pinch. That was all a man needed to win acceptance out here, and though Eric often came in for good-natured joshing about his age, Jake, Marcus, and the others regarded him as their equal.

But they were right about Ebersole choosing Eric to go because he didn't get into trouble. He stayed away from the small room that Dunnigan had attached to his store where the cowboys could buy liquor and, though not quite a saloon, was the closest thing anyone had to a bar without having to go all the way into Gillette.

Jake and Marcus had forfeited their right to make the supply run because they each had gotten liquored up their last time into town. Jake had not only gotten drunk, he had picked a fight with the town constable and was thrown into jail. That little episode had cost Ebersole fourteen dollars, the price of Jake's fine. And though Marcus, who had gone next, had stayed out of trouble, he came back to the ranch so drunk that he couldn't work for the rest of that day and wasn't worth much the following day, either.

By contrast, when Eric was sent, he went straight to the store, picked up the supplies, and came straight back. Impressed, Ebersole announced to everyone that from then on only Eric would be allowed to go into town for supplies. But since the others assumed Eric took no pleasure in the trip, they didn't actually resent it that he could go and they couldn't. They had had their fun, and if they were paying the price now, they figured it was worth it.

The trip into Oshoto would take about an hour and a half, but far from minding and contrary to what the others believed, Eric enjoyed it, for it afforded him the opportunity to read one of his books without being subjected to teasing. Eric could read because he had had six years of schooling, most of it provided at home by his mother, who had once been a teacher. Because Eric could read, he was somewhat unique on the Flying E.

Ebersole had been delighted to learn that Eric could not only read but seemed to have a real hunger for it. The Englishman owned an excellent personal library, and he was most generous when it came to letting the youth borrow his books, taking great pleasure in having someone he could discuss them with. He could scarcely wait until Eric was finished to launch the dialogue.

"What was your impression of *Uncle Tom's Cabin?*" he would ask. "You know, a war was fought to settle the question of slavery. How do you feel about colored people?"

"I've never seen a colored person," Eric would reply. "But I can't see how a person whose skin is a different color should be treated any differently than somebody whose eyes are a different color. Jake and I have brown eyes, you and Marcus have blue eyes, but we aren't always fighting because of it."

"Oh, Eric, you can't just make a statement like that and be done with it," Ebersole would say. "You have grossly oversimplified the issue."

Ebersole seemed to be happiest when Eric's opinion would differ from his own. When that happened, he would advance his own theories with great relish, argue his points with logic and precision, then lean back in his chair with a pleased smile on his face as Eric rebutted. The stronger Eric's points were in rebuttal, the happier Ebersole would be, and Eric firmly believed that the rancher often chose the opposite side of a question, even if he didn't believe it, just for the pure fun of debate.

To keep the conversations more stimulating, Ebersole had drawn up a reading program for Eric. In addition to Harriet Beecher Stowe, Eric had read from the works of William Shakespeare, Sir Walter Scott, Miguel de Cervantes, Jonathan Swift, Nathaniel Hawthorne, Mark Twain, and Charles Dickens. The Dickens books in Ebersole's library had all been personally autographed by the author, and when Eric saw Charles Dickens's name written in a bold hand on the flyleaf of one of the books he was reading, he felt a sense of absolute awe.

"Can you imagine what it must be like, Mr. Ebersole, to be a writer, to have your words printed in a book? It would be like . . . like talking to the ages," Eric had said.

Ebersole had chuckled. "Talking to the ages. Yes, I suppose it would at that. Well, you're a bright enough young lad, Eric, with a wonderful facility for words. Perhaps one day *you* will write a book."

"But how could I?" Eric had asked. "I'm just a cowboy."

"You're just a cowboy, Mark Twain was just a riverboat man, and Charles Dickens pasted labels on bottles of shoe polish. Where do you think writers come from? They have to come *from* the people to be able to relate *to* the people," Ebersole had answered. "Ah, lad, I can't begin to tell you how much I envy you. You have a good mind, a marvelous sense of self-discipline, and a most commendable ambition. Think about it. The marvels of the world and this wonderful new century are out there, just waiting for you."

Eric recalled his conversation with Ebersole as the team plodded along steadily on the road to Oshoto. Was Ebersole right? Could an ordinary person really become a writer like Dickens or Twain? Especially someone with a background like Eric's?

The youth was only twelve when his mother and father had contracted pneumonia and died in a Montana blizzard. It being midwinter, Eric had been snowed in and unable to go for help. The ground had been too cold to bury them, so Eric moved them to the barn and wrapped them in a tarpaulin. While the frozen bodies of his parents had waited in the barn for the spring thaw, Eric had spent the time just trying to survive.

When neighbors came to call that spring, they were shocked to find the twelve-year-old boy living there alone. He had cut his own firewood, hunted and cooked his own food, and even fought off an attack by a starving, frenzied pack of wolves.

Well-meaning people had put Eric in an orphanage, but within a year he ran away and went to Wyoming, where he convinced Ebersole's foreman that he was old enough to work. He had been a cowboy ever since, and though he enjoyed the work, liked the people he worked with, and had practically adopted Ebersole as a father, he knew that this wasn't all there was to life. He had run across a phrase in one of the books that described what he felt. He had a "divine discontent" for more.

The rutted road abruptly became Oshoto's rutted main street, and the young cowboy pulled his mind back to the task at hand: getting Mr. Ebersole's supplies. Only nine buildings made up the whole town, and Dunnigan's General Store was nearly as big as the other eight combined. That was because Dennis Dunnigan kept enlarging his establishment. Starting out with a store, he had built a small addition to house a bar, another for a barbershop, then two rooms out back to provide the only thing Oshoto had in the way of a hotel. The result was a rambling, unpainted wooden building that stretched and leaned and bulged and sagged until it looked as if the slightest puff of wind might blow it down.

Dunnigan was sweeping the porch when Eric stopped the wagon out front. A large, balding man with a bushy red beard, Dunnigan was wearing an apron that may have been white at one time, and as the wagon drew to a stop, he scratched and smiled broadly at Eric. A nondescript yellow dog was sleeping on the front porch, so secure in his surroundings that he did nothing more than briefly open his eyes at Eric's arrival.

"Hello, Eric. How's Mr. Ebersole?"

"He's doing well, thank you, Mr. Dunnigan." Eric set the brake and tied off the reins, then reached into his shirt pocket. "I have a list of the things he needs."

"You was the one that come the last time, wasn't you?"

"Yes, sir, I was."

Dunnigan scratched his beard and looked back to the east, as if looking for someone else.

"Yeah, well, the thing is, I was sort of expectin' maybe Jake or Marcus would come this trip."

Eric laughed. "Mr. Ebersole said he wasn't going to send them anymore because they got drunk last time."

"Ah, it was nothin'," Dunnigan said with a wave of his hand. "Just a couple of boys havin' a good time is all. What's the harm? And they spent good money with me." He sighed. "Well, never mind. Come on in. I'll start filling Mr. Ebersole's order."

Eric climbed out of the wagon and stepped up onto the porch. He leaned down and patted the dog's head, then followed Dunnigan inside. The interior of the store was patterns of shadow and light. Some of the light came through the door, but most of it was in the form of gleaming dust motes illuminated by bars of sunbeams stabbing through cracks between the boards.

Dunnigan's cleaning woman, Susie, was on her hands and knees in the back of the store, using a pail of water and a stiff brush to scrub the floor. She looked up at Eric and brushed a strand of pale brown hair back off her forehead. Her eyes were gray and one of them tended to cross, and when she smiled, there was a gap where one tooth had been knocked out by a drunken cowboy. Jake had once said of her, "She ain't much of a looker, but she's all we got."

"Did you come by yourself, boy?" Susie asked.

"Yes."

"That's too bad. I was hopin' maybe Jake or Marcus'd be with you." Shoving the pail to one side, she got to her feet, revealing that she had tied up her skirt to keep from getting it wet. That had exposed her legs all the way above her knees almost to the bottom line of her bloomers.

Eric had never seen a woman's legs before, but one time in Ebersole's library he had found an art book with paintings of naked women. He remembered how, discovering them, his breath had come in short, hot gasps, and he had looked around quickly to make sure no one had seen him. He felt the same way at this moment, and his eyes cut away in quick embarrassment.

Susie laughed. "Why, what's wrong, honey? Ain't you never seen a lady's legs before?" She hiked her skirt up even higher, and when Eric looked again, he could see the lace on the front of her bloomers.

"No ma'am," Eric answered.

"Well, these here ain't no different from your legs, honey, except maybe they're a little softer." She walked over and grabbed Eric's hand, then placed it on the inside of her thigh, high above her knee. "See what I mean?"

"Yes, ma'am," Eric replied. He felt his face burning, and his tongue had thickened so that he could scarcely talk.

"Susie, for God's sake leave the boy alone. He ain't ready for you yet," Dunnigan called from one of the shelves, where he was busy assembling the goods on Ebersole's shopping list.

"I'm just trying' to get him interested in buyin' me a drink, is all," Susie countered.

"Why, I'd be pleased to buy you a drink, ma'am," Eric responded.

Susie smiled broadly. "There, now, you see? That's all I wanted from the boy," she said to Dunnigan. Then to Eric, "Honey, you come with me out here to the bar."

The bar smelled of sour whiskey, stale beer, and other smells that Eric couldn't identify. Susie went around behind the counter and took out a bottle of whiskey. She used her teeth to pull the cork, then poured herself a glass. "Sure you don't want some of this?" she offered.

"Uh, no, I better not. Mr. Ebersole wouldn't like that very much."

"Oh. And if Mr. Ebersole don't want you to do somethin', you don't do it. Is that it?"

"Yes, ma'am."

"Are you a good boy, Eric?"

Eric didn't know exactly where the conversation was going. He had a feeling she was teasing him, but he didn't know about what or why.

"I don't know," Eric mumbled. "I guess I try to be."

"Well, I'm good, too, honey." She laughed. "You just ask Jake or Marcus how good I am."

"Eric," Dunnigan called from the store area. "I got Mr. Ebersole's order all ready for you to put in the wagon. The lantern chimney's wrapped in paper, but you need to be careful with it. Maybe you should carry it up on the seat with you."

"All right," Eric called back. He started toward the store, but Susie stopped him.

"Wouldn't you like to see how good I am, honey? It won't cost you too much, and we can use one of them rooms in back."

Suddenly Eric realized what Susie was saying. She was a whore! He hadn't know that before now. He'd read about such women, had heard the others talk about them, but he didn't know he'd ever seen one. A big grin spread across his face.

"Oh! I . . . I didn't know that about you."

"You didn't know what?"

"That you were a . . . available." He amended what he was going to say because he didn't know how she would react to the word, and he didn't want to hurt her feelings.

"Honey, I'm always available, if the price is right," Susie quipped.

"Does it really snap shut sometimes?" he asked.

"What? What are you talking about?" Susie asked.

"I heard that sometimes when a man was on top of

a lady, she could snap shut on him and keep him trapped there for hours."

Susie whooped with laughter. "Where'd you ever hear such a thing?"

"From Marcus."

"Well, that Marcus, he ought to know. I figure he's laid on top of enough women."

"Has that ever happened to you?"

"Honey, it ain't never happened to me before," Susie replied, chuckling lewdly, "but if it ever was to, I couldn't think of nobody I'd rather have in the saddle than you. What about it?"

Eric thought about it for a moment and nearly took her up on it. He had never been with a woman, though that wasn't something he'd admit to the others. But he suspected they knew he was still untried, and he was afraid that if he went back into the room with Susie this morning, they would, somehow, be able to read it in his face when he got back. If they did, their teasing would be unmerciful, and he didn't think he was quite ready to take that.

"Not yet," he said. "Maybe next time."

Susie put her foot on a coal scuttle and pulled her skirt up as high as it would go, then ran her hand down her leg slowly, seductively. "Honey, there ain't nothin' says you couldn't try it now an' then do it again next time," she suggested. Gesturing, she added, "That ain't somethin' you're likely to wear out."

Blushing, Eric hurried over to pick up the supplies.

The lantern Eric had picked up at Dunnigan's was for the bunkhouse, and late that afternoon Jake began assembling it. Eric noticed that the wrapping protecting the chimney was a newspaper from St. Louis, and he picked it up and began reading an article about the exposition. It was the first time he had ever heard of the World's Fair, and the more he read, the more fascinated he became.

"Boy, what's got you so quiet over there?" Jake asked.

"He's prob'ly still thinkin' about Susie," Marcus answered from his bunk, where he sat cleaning his pistol. He looked up. "That it, Eric? You wishin' you'd took a go with Susie?"

"Maybe he did," Jake suggested.

"Naw," Marcus answered. "If he had, we'd know it by now. A fella get's his ashes hauled, he can't keep all that quiet about it."

"You ain't answered my question, Eric," Jake said. "What is it you bein' so quiet about?"

"I'm just reading this newspaper," the youth answered distractedly. "It's all about a World's Fair that's going on in St. Louis."

"What's a World's Fair?"

"It's a place full of the most marvelous things."

"Why don't you read some of it to us?" Marcus suggested. Neither Jake nor Marcus could read, and though they were somewhat sensitive about that around strangers, they were quite open about it with Eric and often asked him to read things to them.

"All right," Eric agreed. "Listen to this story about electric lights." He began reading, "'When the switch was thrown a great wave of electrical light swept over the big festival dome, deluged the Cascades, flashed over the bridges of the south lagoon and broke into a thousand ripples over the Education Building and Electricity Hall. It flashed here and there like vivid lightning, leaving myriad clusters of light in its wake. It pressed out in a thousand tongues, skirting the water's edge, running up and down walls, whirling through circles, and bringing brilliancy out of the night.'" He looked up from the paper. "Doesn't that sound magnificent?"

"You ever seen any of this here electricity?" Jake asked as he continued to work on the lantern.

"No," Eric admitted. "But I'd sure like to."

"They got some down in Gillette," Marcus put in. "Leastwise, they did the last time I was there. Course, they might have run out by now."

Eric laughed.

"What's the matter? What're you laughin' at?"

"You don't run out of electricity like you run out of coal oil."

"The hell you don't," Marcus replied. "There was two electric lanterns hangin' outside the door of the Silver Dollar Saloon. One of them was burnin', and the other wasn't. When I asked why it wasn't burnin', the bartender said it was burned out."

"Yes, but that doesn't mean it had run out of electricity," Eric tried to explain.

"You ever seen it?" Marcus challenged.

"No."

"Well, I have, so who are you to tell me what it means?"

"I've read how the incandescent bulb works."

"The inca— The what?"

"The electric lamp. I've read how it works."

"Yeah, well, never mind all that," Jake interjected. "Read some more about that fair."

Eric read several more articles, specifically searching out those that held the most wonder: a story about automobiles, another about a special train that traveled from Chicago to Cincinnati at an average speed of over seventy miles per hour, and even one about sending a telegram without wires.

"Now, hold it!" Marcus said. "You're makin' all that up! There ain't no way you can send a telegram without wires!"

"No, I'm not making it up, Marcus, I promise. It's all right here."

"Have you read how that works?"

"No. I've never even heard of it before," Eric admitted.

"Lord, lord, wouldn't you like to go to St. Louis to see some of them wonders though?" Jake mused.

"Why don't we?" Marcus proposed.

"How?"

"Well, the spring roundup's done, all the calves are branded. Mr. Ebersole could let us go for a couple of weeks. That'd be enough time to get to St. Louis and back."

"What do you think, Eric?" Jake asked. "You want to try it?"

"Yes," Eric said. "I guess I'd rather be in St. Louis now than anyplace else in the world."

"Then, by God, let's go."

Graduation day was a test of endurance for the seniors of Jefferson College. Their schedule would be full from the moment they got out of bed till that afternoon, when they would don the academic robes for the ceremony awarding them their degrees.

The dormitory washroom was bustling. Young men set out an array of grooming devices for their morning ablutions, honing straight razors on leather strops, working up lather in china mugs, and stretching and contorting cheeks to get the closest shave possible. Pomade was put to the hair and mustaches, while liberal doses of after-shave cologne scented the air with all the spices of the Orient.

Bob Canfield, like every other senior on this day, was wearing a dark blue jacket with the school crest embroidered in gold thread on the left breast pocket. Only seniors on the day of graduation or those who already held degrees from Jefferson College could wear the crest, which was a shield divided by three horizontal bars bearing an open book. Above the bars were three stars, representing the stars in the United States flag. Below the bars were three fleurs de lis, the armorial emblem of the kings of France, representing St. Louis's French background.

Bob's white trousers were neatly pressed, his shoes well shined, the detachable shirt collar in place, and the bow tie knotted perfectly. If he had learned nothing else during his four years here, he told himself, he had at least learned to knot a bow tie, something he never wore before coming to Jefferson College.

"Mr. Canfield," an upperclassman had addressed

him on Bob's first day on campus, "I don't know what type of backwoodsmen populate Sikeston"—the senior had incorrectly pronounced the first syllable *sicks* rather than *sykes*—"but here in the city we are gentlemen, and we will wear appropriate attire. Appropriate attire, Mr. Canfield, means a bow tie."

Bob had stood before the mirror in his room that night until after ten o'clock, learning the proper way to knot a bow tie.

He smiled at the memory as he hurried across the quad. Dew nestled in the grass like scattered diamonds, its prisms catching the early-morning sun and sending thousands of tiny bursts of color to dazzle the eye, and Bob stayed on the white gravel walk so as not to wet his shoes. Reaching Spengeman Hall, he went down the steps of the concrete pit at the northwest corner of the building, then knocked on the door.

When Loomis Booker answered the knock, a broad smile spread across his face. "My, my, Mr. Canfield, you do look imposing."

Bob gasped in surprise, thinking the same about Loomis. He was used to seeing the man in his work clothes, denim coveralls and a flannel shirt. Now, however, the janitor/handyman wore a charcoal-gray suit, white shirt with starched collar, a black tie, gray silk vest, spats of the same shade gray as the vest, and shining black shoes.

He stepped back to admire his friend. "Mr. Booker, I have never seen you so finely attired."

"This is a special day for you seniors," Loomis said, "and I wanted to dress in your honor."

The smile left Bob's face, and sadness came over him. "It isn't right, you know," he said. "This day should be just as special for you. You've done more than enough work to qualify for a baccalaureate. I think you should apply to take the final exams, then request a degree."

"No!" Loomis said quickly, putting his hand out to grab Bob's arm. "Please, Mr. Canfield, don't say such a thing! Don't even suggest such a thing! You could get me fired!"

"So what if you are fired?" Bob asked. "Mr. Booker, whether you have a degree or not, you're an educated man. Do you think it's appropriate for a man of your intelligence and education to be working as a janitor and furnace stoker for five dollars per week?"

"It's honest employment," Loomis said defensively. "I do my work well, and I'm paid in accordance with the agreement I entered into when I accepted the position. I see nothing dishonorable in it."

"But you could do so much better."

"Really? Well, let's see. I've made a particular study of transportation management—but you and I both know that the only real position in the railroad industry that would be open to a gentleman of my color would be as a porter. There are some colored firemen, but none of them can ever hope to become engineers. Suppose I applied to one of the riverboat companies? The only positions available to me would be as stevedore or steward. Now, while I grant that these, too, are honorable positions and would probably pay more than I'm making here, I wouldn't have the opportunity to continue my study."

"But if there's no reward for your study, why do you do it?" Bob asked.

"Mr. Canfield, do you believe your education here has been worthwhile?"

"Yes, of course I do."

"Given the choice of having a degree from this institution without the education or having an education from this institution without the degree, which would you prefer?"

"I would prefer the education without the degree," Bob said with a sigh.

"Exactly. The education is my reward. And under the circumstances, it's reward enough."

"I guess I see your point," Bob said. He sighed again. "Still, as we go through all the ceremonies and celebrations today, it'll seem damned unfair to know that you are as deserving to wear this crest as any graduating senior here, and yet you are left out."

"You took a class in philosophy, Mr. Canfield," Loomis said. "We studied together, remember?"

"Diogenes, looking for the honest man," Bob replied, smiling. "How can I ever forget?"

"Did Diogenes or Plato or Socrates, or anyone else for that matter, ever say that life was fair?"

"No, I guess not," Bob conceded. "But when I walk up to get my degree, I'm going to feel that part of it is yours."

"Damned right it is," Loomis said, laughing. "Especially the calculus part."

He looked behind Bob. The campus was filling up with blue-and-white-clad seniors, all very aware of the gold crest on their jackets and walking taller today because of it. They were hurrying to a prayer breakfast, the first event of an event-filled day.

Nodding toward them, the janitor said, "You had better go on now, Mr. Canfield. Your big day is starting."

Bob reached out and took Loomis's hand. He squeezed it very tightly, then put his other hand over it. "Mr. Booker, whether you realize it or not, you've been an important part of my education, and I thank you most sincerely."

"It's been a pleasure, Mr. Canfield. A real pleasure," Loomis replied softly.

Giving Loomis a small salute, Bob retraced his steps to the center of the quad, then headed for the dining hall, where the men's glee club, minus the graduating seniors, sang at the prayer breakfast. The perfect blend of their voices, strong and pure, had always moved Bob anyway, but when they concluded their program with the Jefferson College alma mater—"Golden Leaves on Jefferson Ground," to the tune of the old folk song, "Aura Lee"—he felt a big lump in his throat. He stared at his plate, hoping no one else would see that his eyes were filled with a sheen of tears. Bob needn't have worried. Had he looked up, he would have seen that all the other seniors were having the same response.

Bob would miss this place that had been his home for the last four years and that now felt more like home than his real home did. He would miss everything about it, especially the rest of the quad quad, and he admitted to himself that while excited, he was also a bit scared about what the world—and his future—held for him.

When the southbound train stopped at the Frisco depot in Sikeston, Missouri, at 1:38 the next afternoon, Bob Canfield, his newly issued degree safely packed away, stepped off onto the brick platform and looked beyond the depot at his hometown. It was a Saturday afternoon, and the community was filled with the out of towners who came to Sikeston on this their "go into town" day. The men gathered to discuss pigs and corn and mules, while the women gossiped as they attended to their weekly shopping. But it was the children who were the most animated. Faces scrubbed clean, their eyes were wide in eager anticipation as they planned how they would spend the five cents they'd been given for their great adventure. It was a look into the past, for Bob could remember how his own excitement had built toward the end of each week over the prospect of getting into town on Saturday.

"Hey, Bob! Bob!" a young voice called, and he looked around to see his brother, Billy, running to greet him. Billy was considerably younger than Bob, coming along as a surprise addition to the family nine years ago. Billy had the same dark hair and blue eyes as Bob, though with the added attraction of a spray of freckles across his nose.

"Hello, Billy. Where's Pop?"

"He's waiting in the auto," Billy replied. "He sent me to meet you."

"Did you say he's waiting in the *auto*?"

Billy smiled broadly. "Yep, that's what I said. It's a Packard, with a twenty-two-horsepower engine. Wait till you see her, Bob. She's really a beaut!"

"I'm sure it is, Billy, but I wish he would've brought a wagon. I'm finished with my schooling, and I brought everything home with me. I really have a lot of luggage."

"Don't you worry about that," Billy said. "It's a touring car. It'll carry as much as any old wagon, I'll guarantee."

Bob laughed. "Oh, you guarantee, do you? All right. Help me with the luggage, and we'll see just how grand this new machine is."

Billy ran down to the express platform and got a small cart, then pulled it up to the larger cart waiting beside the baggage car that was being filled with luggage. "I see your stuff," Billy shouted. "You've got the green-and-red Jefferson pennant stuck on every one."

"Yes," Bob said. "I found out four years ago that they make it a lot easier to find your luggage when there's a big pile at the railroad station."

"I'll remember that when I go to Jefferson College," Billy said.

Bob laughed. "Well, that'll be a while yet."

"We read in the paper about you winning the intercollegiate track meet," Billy said. "You did the mile in four forty-three. Wow! I'll just bet that's the fastest in the whole world!"

"Not quite. If it was, I would've entered the Olympic Games they're having in St. Louis this year. My time isn't even the fastest in the country."

"But you won the intercollegiate meet," Billy protested.

"That was only between colleges from the west," Bob explained. "There are runners from Colgate, Yale, and Harvard who are faster."

"Have you ever raced against them?"

"No."

"I'll bet you could beat them," Billy said firmly.

They had been loading the small cart as they spoke, and now they pushed it around to the other side of the depot. This was Prosperity Street. Glancing at the Jefferson Hotel on the corner, a big, three-story, red-brick building, Bob could remember thinking as a very young boy that this must be the biggest building in the world. Running east from the hotel were two blocks of stores, shops, cafés, and saloons, beckoning to the

Saturday visitors packing the sidewalks. The street was crowded with several dozen horse-drawn rigs and one larger green automobile that Billy pointed at with pride.

Bob's father was sitting in the big overstuffed bench seat in the back of the Packard. Just in front of his big seat were two smaller chair-type seats that faced aft, so that five people could be accommodated in the passenger section of the car. When the canvas top was raised, only this section of the auto would be covered. The driver, who sat on the right-hand side, and the front-seat passenger would remain exposed to the elements.

A black man, wearing a tan duster, a matching cap, and a pair of goggles, sat importantly behind the wheel. Spotting Bob and Billy approaching with a loaded luggage cart, he got out of the auto and took the cart from them. Attached to the rear of the Packard was a great square trunk, its lid secured by two wide leather straps. The driver began loading Bob's luggage into the trunk.

"Hello, Pop!" Bob said, hurrying over to his father. "This is quite a welcoming committee."

"Do you like it?" Jack Canfield asked. "I just bought it three weeks ago." He smiled. "I must admit, this seat sure makes the seven miles between home and here a damn comfortable ride."

"Mom never mentioned it in her letters."

"I told her not to tell you," Billy said. "I wanted it to be a surprise."

"Well, it's a surprise all right," Bob declared, running his hand over the shining green hood. When the driver returned to the front of the car, Bob suddenly recognized George Summers, a man who had worked for his father for as long as Bob could remember. "Why, George!" he said, smiling broadly and reaching out to take the driver's hand. "I almost didn't know you in that getup."

"Yes, sir, Mr. Bob, this is some getup, all right. It truly is," George said.

"So, you're driving, are you? I would've thought you'd be too old to learn a new trick like this."

"I'm the only one on the whole place that your papa lets drive this machine," George said proudly.

"How's your family?" Bob asked. "How's Pearl?"

George's youngest, Pearl, was a month younger than Bob. As small children, unaware of racial and sexual differences, the two had been playmates. But as they grew older and these differences began to assert themselves, they played together less and less frequently until, eventually, their special relationship ended.

Pearl had grown into a very pretty and very bright young woman, and though he would never admit it to anyone, barely even to himself, Bob had wondered a few times in his life if perhaps, in a different place and a different time, he and Pearl might . . . but his thoughts were never more articulated than that. And since he had met Connie, the thoughts didn't even occur anymore, though he still maintained an interest in Pearl's well-being.

"Pearl's doin' just fine, Mr. Bob," George said. "Just fine, thank you."

Bob got into the back seat with his father, while Billy climbed in the front seat, where he would sit alongside George. George walked to the front of the car, gave the crank a twist, and when the engine popped and sputtered into life, hurried around to hop behind the wheel. Squeezing a couple of honking sounds from the rubber bulb at the rear of a brass horn, he put the Packard in gear, and they were off.

"Faster, George, faster!" Billy shouted excitedly.

"Lord, Mr. Billy. If we go any faster, we're gonna be flyin'," George admonished.

"Faster!" Billy said, laughing and bouncing up and down in his seat. "Faster! Bob wants to get home as quick as he can!"

The new graduate was only one hundred fifty miles and, by train, one day away from St. Louis, but tonight, sitting under a large elm tree in the backyard, watching the flickering fireflies that seemed like tiny golden stars come to earth, Bob felt as if he had left one world and entered another. And in a way he had. The quad quad, the athletic meets, the songs of the glee club, the late-night cram sessions, all that was over. It was just one day in the past, but it was spinning into eternity with every passing second—a time that had been so important and would never be again.

Bob wondered where the others of the quad quad were and what they were doing. J. P. Winthrop, he knew, was going back to New York, so he probably wasn't home yet. David and Terry both lived in St. Louis, though on opposite sides of the city. Terry wanted a job with one of the newspapers in St. Louis and would probably be making the rounds next week, trying to find a position. He didn't know what David had in mind—not even David knew what he had in mind.

And what about Connie? Connie had cried last night after the graduation ball was over, but Bob reminded her that Sikeston was only a day's trip away.

He thought of Loomis Booker. He was going to miss Mr. Booker much more than he had thought he would. He and Loomis had often studied together, and there was some truth to Mr. Booker's joke that the calculus part of Bob's degree belonged to him. But it wasn't just the study he would miss; he would miss the man and the conversation.

Loomis Booker was an enigma to Bob. Not just because he was very closemouthed about his background, but because Bob, who had known black people his entire life, had discovered that he didn't know them at all. Mr. Booker was as different from George as night from day.

"Why do you find that strange?" Loomis had asked, when Bob mentioned it.

"Well, it's just that I thought I knew colored people," Bob had started to explain, but Loomis cut him off with a wave of his hand.

"Don't you see what you're doing, Mr. Canfield? You're saying you know colored people as if we are one entity. George is colored and I am colored, therefore we must be alike. William Bateman is the president of this college. Is he like the motorman you meet on the Bellefontaine car? President Bateman is a very educated man, and the motorman is a rather simple man, but both are white."

Bob had laughed. "I see what you're trying to say."

"I suspect that you genuinely like George, don't you?" Loomis had asked.

"Why, yes. I've known him all my life. He's like part of the family."

"And though you and I are most particular to call each other Mr. Booker and Mr. Canfield, I believe that a certain bond of friendship has developed between us as well, has it not?"

"Yes, of course it has."

"But even you, with a good heart and a genuine fondness for George and for me, are guilty of racial prejudice."

"No, I—"

Again Loomis had interrupted. "Hear me out. Your prejudice isn't a prejudice of the heart, and therefore I don't fault you for it. A prejudice of the heart is brought on by hate, and that can never be corrected. Yours is a prejudice of the mind, and that *can* be corrected."

"What do you mean?"

"Simply this, Mr. Canfield. You look at us and see nothing but a unifying color. Snowflakes have a unifying color as well, but they're quite different from one another. We are like those snowflakes. We are individuals, with individual characteristics. Some colored people are educated—not as many as whites, of course, because it's much more difficult for us to get an education—and some are not. Just remember, not all fat folks are jolly. And not all colored folks love watermelon."

"I'm sorry," Bob apologized. "I won't make that mistake again."

"Yes, you will," Loomis retorted. "You white people are all alike."

Both men had laughed at that.

"Bob? Bob, are you out here?" Jack Canfield suddenly called.

At the sound of his father's voice, Bob's thoughts of the campus slipped away. "Yes, Pop, I'm over here by the elm tree."

Out in the swamp Bob could hear the frogs calling to each other and a night bird's shrill cries hanging in the heavy air. It was late enough in the evening so that the ugliness of the stump-studded, brackish-water landscape was covered by a veil of black.

Jack Canfield, coming from the house and walking toward Bob, seemed to materialize out of the darkness. He was carrying a bowl, and he told his son, "Your mama made some ice cream. She figured you might want some. I reckon it's been a while since you had any homemade."

"Homemade ice cream would be wonderful. Thanks, Pop."

"Are you glad to be home?"

"Yes, of course."

"But you've been to see the elephant, so it's going to be hard for you to settle back down to living in the swamp," the older Canfield stated.

"What?"

Jack laughed. "That's what your Uncle James always used to say. Anytime someone would go see something glorious, he would say they had gone to see the elephant. And, of course, he believed that there were so many things to see out in the world, that no one could possibly be satisfied with what we have back here."

"He was right and wrong," Bob said.

"Meaning?"

"There *are* many glorious things out there in the big world," Bob explained, "and I'm *not* satisfied with what we have here. But that doesn't mean I want to leave."

"What *does* it mean?"

"It means I want to change things," Bob replied.

Jack sighed. "Who doesn't want to change things?" he asked. "When I was a young man, just after I married your mama, this was the most beautiful country you could ever imagine. I wish you could've seen it then, son. There were hundreds and hundreds of cypress trees, every one of them so tall they seemed to touch the sky. And elm and river birch and silverleaf poplar and dozens of other varieties so numerous, I can't remember the names of all of them. The swamp was full of game, too, and the sky was thick with birds. But the best thing was the people. They were always happy. Men would go out in their flatboats to fell the big trees, the sawmills were going full steam, and stacks of freshly cut lumber would pile up on every corner in town to be shipped out by train or riverboat to places all over the country. For a while there we were producing more hardwood timber than anyplace else in America. This place was alive then."

Jack was quiet for a long moment, and Bob knew that his father was seeing again the scenes of his younger days. Finally Jack sighed, then smiled sheepishly, as if suddenly aware of the long silence and feeling the need to fill it.

"Of course there are no trees left for the lumber mills, so the good days are over. For us, too, I'm afraid."

"The good days don't have to be over," Bob suggested. "We can farm."

Jack shook his head. "Too many folks are trying to do that as it is. Small high places here and there— Sikeston Ridge, Crowley's Ridge, those are the only areas not covered by water nine months a year. There are too many farmers and not enough land."

"We have one hundred and fifty thousand acres of land," Bob said.

Jack laughed. "And no more than thirty acres of it dry. You know what the rest of it's good for, don't you?" he asked. "Its only purpose is to help hold the world together."

"Pop, my geology professor at school says that the land down here, our land, has the best farming soil in the entire world. It's delta land, enriched by nutrients deposited by the Mississippi River. And he said this is especially true of the swampland."

"He said that, did he? Well, did he say how the hell a person could go about farming under water?"

"No, but—"

"Well, then that's the end of it, isn't it?"

"No," Bob said again, adding resolutely, "we're going to get rid of the water, Pop. We're going to pump all this water out of here, and when we do, we'll have the most productive farming country this side of the Nile."

"It can't be done," Jack said. "There've been people talking about that as long as there've been people here. There's no way you can pump all the water off one hundred and fifty thousand acres of land. My God, boy, that would be enough water to fill that canal they're digging down at the Isthmus of Panama."

"Pop, before I left St. Louis, I saw some of the wonders of the World's Fair. They had engines of incredible horsepower, marvelous electric motors, wireless telegraphy, telescopes that let you view the moon's surface as clearly as if you were taking a stroll across the lunar landscape, and engineering feats that'd astound you. What it taught me is that twentieth-century man can do just about anything he wants." Bob spooned up the last bit of ice cream from his bowl, then pointed out into the blackness. "This swamp *can* be drained and farmed, Pop. We'll just have to figure out a way to do it, that's all."

Jack reached up and stripped off a few leaves from a branch of the elm tree. He rolled them in his fingers for a moment, then looked at his son. Inexplicably, he smiled. "You know, son, after the war it was me who talked your grandpa into buying up all this swampland and taking out the trees for lumber. He thought it was a damn-fool stunt, but he told me that time had rolled around so that it was my turn to call the shots. He went along with my decisions and supported me in everything I did till the day he died. I reckon that's the way things ought to be. If you think you can figure out some way to drain this land and make it worth something, you go right ahead. I'll back you with everything I got. Only remember, your little brother has a stake in this, too."

Bob grinned broadly, then got up from the bench and hugged his father tightly. "Thanks, Pop," he said. "I won't let you—or Billy—down."

CHAPTER THREE

It was midmorning by the time the *Empire State Limited* backed into Grand Central Station, and even the squealing of the train as it came to a stop didn't wake J. P. Winthrop.

"Mr. Winthrop? Mr. Winthrop, sir, the train is in the station!" a voice suddenly called, knocking on the closed compartment door. J.P. opened one eye as the knock sounded again, harder this time, and the persistent voice—which the young man now recognized as the porter's—repeated, "Mr. Winthrop?"

Groaning once, J.P. raised himself up on his elbow and pulled the shade aside to look through the window. Another train was just a few feet away, separated from his by a narrow, brick-paved walkway that was crowded with detraining passengers. They walked briskly toward the main station through wisps of steam that drifted out to tease them.

"Mr. Winthrop?" the porter called again, rapping on

the door so loudly this time that J.P. was certain the knock could be heard all up and down the length of the car.

He unfolded his tall frame from the berth and crossed to the door. Opening it, he stood in the doorway in his undershirt and drawers, yawning and running his hand through his tousled black hair, his dark eyes still filled with sleep. "Arrogantly handsome" was the way a girlfriend of Connie's had once described him, and when asked what arrogantly handsome meant, she explained that he was "good looking as if it were his right to be good looking and as if he couldn't understand why everyone else wasn't equally as good looking."

At that precise moment a man, his wife, and their little girl came down the corridor, struggling with the luggage they had kept in their own roomette. Seeing a grown man in his underwear, the child laughed and pointed. "Oh look, Mommy, it's just like the story, *The Emperor's New Clothes*. That man hasn't got anything on."

"Don't look at him, Gloria," the mother said stiffly, reaching down and turning her daughter's head away.

The father stepped quickly between J.P. and the girl. "Sir, really! You should have more decency than to expose yourself to a lady and an innocent child," he scolded indignantly. He hurried his family along the corridor toward the door at the end of the car.

"Do you mean to tell me you've never seen a man in his drawers before?" J.P. called after them. When he saw the porter smiling, he asked, "What does he mean, 'I exposed myself?' Why, in college I ran on the track team in a uniform that exposed far more than this."

"Yes, sir," the porter said, chuckling.

"What time is it?"

"It's nine o'clock, Mr. Winthrop. We're in New York, and all the passengers got to get off here."

"How much time do I have?"

"Not long. In just about a half hour we're going to be takin' on new passengers. But I have to have this compartment all cleaned up and ready to go before that."

"All right, I'll get dressed," J.P. said.

"Very good, sir." The porter smiled again. "By the way, do you feel all right this mornin'?" he asked.

J.P. put his hand to his forehead. "Well, now that you ask, I do have a headache."

"Yes, sir, I expect you do," the porter said. "The way you and those other college boys was carryin' on in the club car last night, I expect you is bound to have one mighty big headache."

J.P. frowned. "Carrying on? Oh, yeah. The boys from Penn." His frown turned to a smile. "I forgot about that. We sang a lot of fight songs and had a few drinks, I believe."

The porter laughed. "No, sir. It was the other way 'round," he corrected. "You sang a *few* songs and had a *lot* of drinks."

"Did we, uh, do any damage or make fools of ourselves or anything like that?"

"No, sir. You was all fine gentlemen, and the only damage you did was to yourselves. I expect those other boys got headaches about as big as the one you got this mornin'."

"I certainly hope so. I would hate for it to get back to any of the quad quad that I let a bunch of guys from Penn outdrink me. Don't worry. I'll be ready in a few minutes," J.P. promised.

"Yes, sir. Thank you, sir."

As soon as the door was closed, J.P. pulled down the small wash basin, then looked at himself in the mirror. He stuck his tongue out and examined it closely, almost surprised to see that it looked the same as always. He could have sworn that it would be covered with fur. Smiling ruefully, he reached for the toothbrush and powder, and inside of ten minutes, he was washed, shaved, and dressed, wearing his blue blazer with the gold crest.

Packing up his kit, he stuffed it into his overnight bag and left the train, walking briskly along the platform and into the waiting room of Grand Central Terminal.

• • •

Ellen Winthrop stood waiting expectantly. Spotting her handsome son, she waved and called, "Pierpont, I'm over here, dear."

Turning at the sound of his mother's voice, J.P. smiled at her across the terminal and hurried over to embrace and kiss her.

"Hello, Mother. I could have hired a cab. You didn't have to come meet me."

"I know I didn't have to, but I wanted to. You know, you didn't come home at Christmas, and it's been nearly a year since I saw you."

"I wrote you why I couldn't come home. I was in charge of the art for our Christmas pageant."

"Yes, and St. Louis is just too far away for you to come home when you have only a few days off." Ellen sighed. "Why on earth you chose to go to some obscure little college in St. Louis, of all places, I'll never know. Especially when you could have gone to Harvard or Yale or even Columbia, right here in New York."

"Jefferson College is a very fine school, Mother, with an excellent reputation. And as for being obscure, it's becoming better known all the time."

"Yes, well, your father went to Harvard, and his father before him. You know, your grandmother Winthrop was very disappointed that you didn't go there, too."

"Maybe that's exactly why I *didn't* want to go to Harvard," J.P. said.

"Pierpoint, you mustn't say such things," Ellen scolded.

"Why not? Now, Mother, you have to admit, it hadn't exactly been 'Over the river and through the woods to grandmother's house we go,' with us and Grandmother Winthrop, has it?"

Despite herself, Ellen laughed. "I guess not," she admitted. "Let's summon a redcap for your baggage, then hurry home, shall we? We've so much to talk about—and plans to make for your future."

"How is Grandmother Bristol?"

"She's fine. She didn't feel quite up to making the trip down to the station to meet you, but that's just age. Actually, she's doing very well and is waiting for you at home."

"You're looking well, Mother. As pretty as always," J.P. said as he picked up the small suitcase again and gave his claim check to a nearby redcap who then hurried to get the baggage.

"Thank you," Ellen replied automatically. She had been receiving compliments on her looks for her entire life, and now she scarcely heard them, even when they came from her own son.

In her youth Ellen Winthrop had been a woman of such stunning beauty that all conversation would stop when she entered a room, because every man present would turn to look at her in unabashed admiration. Now nearly fifty, Ellen was still a woman of uncommon handsomeness, tall and slender, with deep brown eyes and a face as smooth of wrinkles and free of blemishes as it had been in her youth. Her nose was delicately formed, her cheekbones were fashionably high, and her lips needed only the lightest application of lip rouge to be rose-petal red. Had it not been for the gray streaks in her hair, she might well have been taken for a woman twenty years younger. She could have dyed the streaks out—she knew that many of her friends did—but she left her hair alone, not even aware that the streaks of gray, contrasting so sharply with her otherwise youthful appearance, managed to somehow enhance the overall image.

Unlike most women her age, Ellen was looking forward to the time when maturity would begin to dim her beauty, which she knew could be as much a curse as a blessing. All her life people had gravitated toward her because of it. As a young girl she had learned that a pretty smile and a pleasant word could make things go much easier for her. But she also discovered that it was a two-edged sword: For every person who was attracted by her beauty, another was repelled by it. As a young

woman she had found that many women were jealous
and almost openly hostile if she came near their beaux or
husbands, no matter how innocent the contact might be.
It was as if they regarded Ellen as one of the Sirens of
Odysseus, a woman whose mere presence was intolera-
ble because her seductive beauty could not be resisted,
even by the most principled of men.

That was exactly what Opal Winthrop had thought.

Opal was the grande dame of New York's upper
crust, joining her own sizable fortune to the Winthrop
millions. When her son had reached marriageable age,
she realized that his wealth and position in society would
make him one of the most eligible bachelors in America.
Therefore she had laid plans, like a queen mother, for
her son to marry well, and she was always on the lookout
for a gold digger, which was what she had considered
Ellen Bristol to be.

"Everyone knows," Opal had told all her friends,
"that Ellen Bristol is trading on her beauty to improve
her own position. It is disgraceful, and I hope every
eligible bachelor is made aware of that girl's scheming."

Ellen hadn't exactly been running from poverty.
Her father had made a good deal of money during the
Civil War as a blockade runner. Louis Bristol hadn't
been a patriotic blockade runner whose ships carried
guns or medicine to the beleaguered South. What he
had traded was silks, wines, and other items of a like
nature that the luxury-starved wealthy of the South
were willing to pay quite handsomely for, and it made
Louis Bristol a relatively affluent man. His fortune had
been nothing like those of the Vanderbilts, the Goulds,
the Morgans, or the Winthrops, but he had been
wealthy enough to skirt the edges of society—as close as
he could ever get, since the source of his money had
made him a pariah among the New York and Newport
set.

Despite her father's persona non grata status, Ellen
Bristol's beauty managed to open doors that otherwise
would have been closed. The same women who had
secretly feared her beauty also openly solicited her as a

decorative ornament for their parties, and it was at one of those parties that she had met Doyle Winthrop.

From the moment Doyle met Ellen, his mother had feared the worst. Then, in a self-fulfilling prophecy, Opal Winthrop's son fell in love with the very girl his mother had warned the others about. When Doyle had asked his parents if he could present Ellen to them, they begged him to forget about her. When he had persisted, they told him she would not be welcome in their home.

Doyle had married Ellen despite his parents' disapproval, and, as a result, they refused to accept her as a daughter-in-law, which meant they no longer accepted Doyle. In addition to refusing to receive them in their home, Doyle's father, Arthur, had changed his will, leaving Doyle with nothing but a twenty-thousand-dollar trust fund and a fashionable, if not posh, two-story brownstone on Twenty-sixth Street, near the Jerome mansion.

Arthur died shortly after his son's marriage. Because of his early and unexpected death and the fact that he and his son had not reconciled, the will he had changed the day after Doyle and Ellen were married was the will that was probated.

In the meantime Ellen's father had made a series of disastrous investments that left him absolutely penniless. Unable to face bankruptcy, Louis Bristol closed himself in his study one evening, put the barrel of a .44 Colt in his mouth, and pulled the trigger. Ellen's mother had had nowhere to go, so Doyle and Ellen brought her to the brownstone to live with them. Ellen was expecting a baby, and Doyle thought it would be good for his wife to have her mother with her.

Tragically, Doyle contracted typhus and died the same month J.P. was born. Because she had lost her husband and then so quickly after that her son, Opal had softened somewhat. She had a grandson now, and she didn't want to be completely shut out of his life. But as she had still not received Ellen socially, she was left with no way to communicate with her except through a lawyer, proposing an arrangement that was still being followed.

J.P. was the sole heir to the Winthrop money. Opal offered to pay Ellen a very generous yearly stipend, provided she not marry again until J. P. was at least twenty-one. In so doing Opal had hoped to ensure that J.P. be raised with no male influence diluting the Winthrop genes.

Having no other source of income and a son and a widowed mother to take care of, Ellen had accepted Opal's offer. Included in the arrangement was the stipulation that J.P., who had been named John Pierpont after J.P. Morgan, a distant cousin, would be brought to see his grandmother at least once a week. Ellen had complied with that stipulation, and the two women had always been coolly correct with each other, their relationship not improving one whit over the years.

That afternoon at lunch, J.P. entertained his mother and Lillie Bristol with tales about the World's Fair. He had bought many souvenirs there, and he now brought these out to show. One that particularly interested them was a picture of a tribe of rather wild-looking natives.

"Who are these quaint little people?" Ellen asked.

"They are called Igorots, an aborigine tribe from the Philippines," J.P. explained. "An entire village has been created for them—grass huts, trees, streams, all reconstructed just as it is in their home. They go about living their daily lives, totally ignoring the thousands of people who pass by every day to gaze at them."

"It must be horrible for them," Ellen said.

"It doesn't appear to be. They seem to be able somehow to shut everything out, as if they weren't in the middle of a city thousands of miles from their origins." He laughed. "Of course, there *have* been a couple of problems—such as, they were made to wear pants."

Ellen laughed with him. "Yes, I can see where that might be a problem."

"And some busybodies have made a fuss over their diet."

"What is their diet?"

"Dog."

"I beg your pardon?" his grandmother said, aghast.

"Dog," J.P. repeated. "It seems that the main staple of their diet is dog, and some people were shocked to see the animals taken from a pen, slaughtered, dressed and cooked as casually as if it were chicken being prepared."

"Well, I should hope so," Ellen declared, shuddering in revulsion. "It would be awful to see something like that."

"Mother, if people don't like to see it, they should simply go on to some other exhibit," J.P. countered.

His mother chastised him. "Pierpont, surely you can't approve of such a thing?"

"It's the way they are, Mother," J.P. said, shrugging. "As far as I'm concerned, we had no right to bring them over here in the first place. But since we did, we have no right to interfere with their diet."

Ellen diverted J.P. onto other, more appealing aspects of the fair, making the ground more comfortable through the remainder of lunch. Lillie excused herself shortly afterward to take her afternoon nap, and Ellen then informed the maid that she and her son would take their coffee in the parlor.

The parlor was stuffed with settees, divans, ornate tables, and armchairs, and Ellen and J.P. seated themselves on facing settees as the maid brought in a tray of coffee and sugar cookies. J.P. continued to tell stories of the fair, then switched to anecdotes about Jefferson College and the quad quad.

"You boys were together for the entire four years of school, weren't you?"

"Yes, Mother. I'll never have better friends than they are. I shall miss them greatly."

"What about David Gelbman?"

"What about him?"

"He's Jewish, isn't he?"

"Yes, he is."

"Did he fit in well with the other boys?"

"Mother, I can't believe this! You are anti-Semitic? Uncle Levi, the administrator of Grandfather Winthrop's estate, is Jewish."

"He isn't actually your uncle," Ellen corrected.

"I know he isn't my uncle, Mother, but I have called him that for my entire life."

Ellen nervously touched her hair. "Dear, please don't misunderstand me. I didn't mean my remark to be taken as one of antagonism toward Jews. Goodness knows Mr. Friedman has certainly treated us wonderfully all these years. I was just curious, that's all. As you know, there are many Jews here in New York, and over the years I think Jews and Gentiles have managed to get along quite splendidly. But away from New York, in a place like St. Louis, for example, where there probably aren't very many Jews, I am interested in how they're accepted."

"In the first place, St. Louis isn't exactly a small town in the country. It's the fifth largest city in America. And I assure you, David's family isn't the only Jewish family in town. Be that as it may, the fact that David is a Jew never became an issue—certainly not among the members of the quad quad. And I can't believe that you would think that it would be."

"Pierpont, the Jews are wonderfully industrious people. But you must realize that they have a history of being a persecuted race. Right now they're being forced out of Russia and other parts of Europe and are coming to America by the thousands. And even in New York they've not all found a haven. Surely you've ridden down Mott or Hester streets and smelled the stench, heard the noise, and seen the squalor? Jewish immigrants are crammed into that area like sardines in a tin; mothers, fathers, children, grandparents, uncles, aunts, and cousins are all crowded into one tiny apartment. It must be unbelievably miserable to live there, and yet bad as it is, it's apparently better for them here than it is in Europe, for still they come."

"Believe me, David doesn't live like that. I've been to his home. It is much larger and much nicer than this one. His father owns Gelbman's Department Store—that's a very big and very successful emporium in St. Louis."

"Yes, well, I'm sure he was a very good friend to you, dear, as were the other boys. But you'll be making new friends through your business contacts. Which reminds me, Grandmother Winthrop expects you for dinner tomorrow evening. She is giving a party and has invited several of the most successful bankers and investment brokers. I think the idea is for you to choose one of them. Or for one of them to choose you."

"I don't need Grandmother Winthrop to find a job for me," J.P. said testily.

"Pierpont, heaven knows your grandmother and I have had a lifetime of differences. However, I am convinced that she is truly sincere in her efforts to find the best possible position for you. And don't forget, she still wields a great deal of power in this city."

"I'm sure she does," J.P. said dryly. "But I already have a position. I'll be working with J. P. Morgan."

"Mr. Morgan?" Ellen smiled broadly. "Why, Pierpont, that is absolutely marvelous! But of course your grandmother will be thrilled to hear that news! Where will you be working? In the bank or in his investment house or with one of his companies?"

"As an assistant art curator," J.P. answered.

"As an assistant *what*?"

"Art curator. He buys a great deal of art, and he wants me to work with his curator to search out new collections and help catalogue those collections he's already assembled. We've exchanged several letters about it, discussing it in some detail."

"Dear, surely you can do better than take care of a few pictures for him! And you wouldn't even be in charge of that; you would only be an assistant. Perhaps if you let your grandmother speak to him, he would find a more suitable position for you. After all, you *are* named for him."

J.P. held up his hand. "Mother, don't you understand? I love art. This is the position I asked for. This is exactly what I want to do. And we aren't talking about a few pictures; we're talking about one of the world's most magnificent collections of art."

"You mean this is to be your life's career?"

"Yes, Mother, that is exactly what I mean."

Ellen breathed a long sigh. "Your grandmother won't understand this, Pierpont. She won't understand it at all." She shook her head. "The truth is, *I* don't understand it." She looked at her son for a long moment, then suddenly smiled. "You know, your father had a stubborn streak. And it's a good thing, too. If he hadn't, we would've never been married, and you wouldn't be here."

"Perhaps," J.P. said. Then, grinning, he added, "However, the latter event could have occurred, even if the former had not."

Ellen stared at her son, her surprise evident. Then she picked up a silk pillow from the settee and threw it at him. "Pierpont, you have become cheeky since attending that western school, and I want you to know that I don't approve." But her sharp words were undercut by her laughter.

Today was what Terry Perkins hoped would be his first day as a journalist, the career he'd decided to pursue. Standing at the top of the stairs leading to the offices of *The St. Louis Chronicle*, he tugged down the jacket of his three-piece suit that somewhat masked his powerful and athletic body, smoothed his light-brown-almost-blond hair, wished briefly that he didn't have the smattering of freckles across his nose that he felt made him look far too youthful and not nearly authoritative enough, and straightened his tie. Taking a deep breath, he stepped into the corridor.

The newsroom and administrative offices were on the third floor of the Chronicle Building, which was being renovated and was adorned with signs begging visitors to excuse the inconvenience. Outside the building workers scrambled over the façade on scaffolding to paint, point the brick, and replace damaged window frames. Inside, a great deal of work had already been completed, and Terry looked around the reception area at the leather sofas and chairs for the use of visitors, a large clock standing against one wall next to a rather ornate umbrella stand, and several highly polished brass spittoons.

The freshly painted walls of the front office were decorated with framed, history-making newspaper front pages from the past, starting with old eight-column pages in five-and-a-half-point type with very small headlines at the top of each column and ending with modern-style six-column pages and eight-point type with big, brassy headlines spread all across the page. Though the older front pages were from other newspapers, the latest front page on display was from *The Chronicle* itself, telling of the World's Fair. In huge, sixty-four-point type the headline blared: GREATEST OF ALL WORLD'S FAIRS, IMPRESSIVELY OPENED.

A high, frosted-glass partition separated the receiving part of the office from the working part. From beyond that wall Terry could hear the clacking of typewriters and the periodic jangle of telephone bells. Someone shouted urgently, "Copy!" and Terry felt a sense of the excitement of a newsroom in operation.

Terry knew the history of *The Chronicle*, how Thomas Petzold had bought the failed *Evening Standard* just six months ago and performed a near miracle in revitalizing it. That was why he wanted very much to work for this newspaper, and while working as editor-in-chief of *The Jeffersonian* during his senior year at college he had prepared himself for this day.

Terry had written to Petzold a few weeks earlier, requesting a personal meeting as soon as classes were completed. The publisher had answered that he'd be glad to meet with him and advised him to stop by his office at his earliest convenience. Terry had graduated on Friday; this was the following Monday—and he would have come Friday if there'd been time after the graduation ceremony was completed.

He walked up to the desk of the receiver. The word "receptionist" was being used more often now, but the sign on this man's desk read, "Mr. Fitzhugh, Receiver," making it clear that this man, who appeared to be about fifty, preferred the traditional title. When the man continued to be absorbed in something he was reading, Terry cleared his throat to attract his attention.

Mr. Fitzhugh paid no attention to him, so Terry cleared his throat again. When the man still didn't look up, Terry spoke.

"Excuse me, sir."

"I know you're there," Mr. Fitzhugh said. "Just a moment, if you please."

Terry stood quietly until at last the man glanced up. Fitzhugh wore rimless glasses that bisected his narrow face, and his plastered-down hair looked artificially dark.

"Now, what can I do for you?"

"I wish to apply for a position with the newspaper," Terry replied. "I have a letter from Mr. Petzold, suggesting that I stop by to see him."

Without a word in response Fitzhugh got up from his chair and walked over to a filing cabinet to pull out a form. Handing it to Terry, he instructed, "Fill this out and leave it with me when you're done. I'll file it away, and when there's a need for a new employee, you'll be considered."

Terry took the form and looked at it for a moment, then back at Fitzhugh. "Uh, excuse me. I'll be happy to fill out your form, but I'd like to meet with Mr. Petzold."

"Mr. Petzold does not meet with every prospective employee," Fitzhugh announced haughtily.

"But I have a letter," Terry insisted.

"That doesn't matter," Fitzhugh responded. "You see this sign on my desk? It says 'receiver.' Now, one of the jobs of a receiver is to keep people from bothering Mr. Petzold."

"I don't want to bother him. I want to ask him for a job."

"That's what this form is for."

"But this form doesn't say anything," Terry complained. "It has room only for my name and address and any previous employment. It doesn't take into account my education or the fact that I was editor of my college newspaper or that I received a letter of commendation from the president of the college for an article I did on the future of education in the twentieth century. How can you possibly evaluate my worth from this?"

"Do you want to fill out this form or not?"

"I want to speak with Mr. Petzold."

"I told you, that is not possible."

With a frustrated sigh, Terry took the form.

Fitzhugh pointed to a table. "There are pens and inkwells there. You may fill out the form and leave it with me, or you may take the application with you and post it at a later date."

"Thank you," Terry grumbled.

He walked over to the table and sat down. This wasn't going at all the way he had planned, and he was trying to think of some way to convince the clerk to let him in to see Petzold.

Suddenly there was a commotion from the newsroom side of the frosted-glass wall. "You can't find out? What do you mean, you can't find out?" The loud and demanding voice could be heard easily over the jangle of telephones, the clatter of typewriters, and the murmur of men at work. The entire office then fell ominously quiet, making the voice seem even louder as it angrily continued, "I am the publisher of *The Chronicle*. I speak with the voice of the people. When I send a reporter to find out which city councilman is going to be indicted and why, I expect him to come back with the answer!"

"But, Mr. Petzold," a quieter voice of another man responded, "I have tried every way I know to find out. It simply can't be done. Those grand jury transcripts are sealed up tighter than a drum. It's a very closely guarded secret."

"By thunder, Mr. Jenkens, I pay you well to find out those secrets, no matter how closely they are guarded," Petzold rejoined. "Now, you get back down to the courthouse and find out who the councilman is, why he is being indicted, and when the indictment is coming down."

"But I have an appointment to interview the World's Fair president, Mr. Francis, at ten. I don't see how I can do both."

"Try," Petzold ordered.

"Yes, sir," the reporter answered.

Terry finished filling out the application, then took it back to Fitzhugh's desk.

"If anything comes open, your application will be considered," Fitzhugh said, accepting the form. "Along with the others."

"How many others are there?"

"About twenty, I think."

"I see," Terry muttered.

The dreams and plans he had made for a career in journalism began slipping away like air escaping from a deflating balloon. He felt empty and numb. While he stood there, a rather chastised-looking man came from behind the partition and walked quickly over to the door. His hat was on, and he was carrying a tablet and pencil. Suddenly, Terry got an idea.

"Is that Mr. Jenkens?" he asked the receptionist.

Fitzhugh, who had gone back to reading the paper, looked up just as the man was leaving. "Yes, it is," he answered. "Why do you want to know?"

"No particular reason," Terry replied. "I've read some of his stories. They're pretty good."

"I'm sure he would be thrilled with the evaluation, especially coming from a college graduate and the former editor of a college newspaper," Mr. Fitzhugh remarked.

Ignoring Fitzhugh's sarcasm, Terry rushed down the three flights of stairs to the street, where he saw the reporter striding toward the courthouse, looking resentful. Moving quickly, Terry ran over to a parallel street, then cut across to the courthouse, dodging the pushcarts, grocer's display trays, newsstands, and pedestrians, his mind racing as fast as his feet. His idea, if it worked, might get him the job immediately; if it failed, it'd no doubt forever ruin his chances of working for *The Chronicle*.

Reaching the courthouse before the reporter, Terry waited just inside the door until he saw Jenkens coming up the steps, and then he hurried out to meet him. "Are you Mr. Jenkens?"

"Yes, I am. Why? Who are you?"

"I'm a messenger," Terry lied. "Mr. Petzold just called from the newspaper office. He said he's changed his mind. Forget about the story here, and keep your appointment with President Francis."

"Well, that's more like it," Jenkens said. "I went to a lot of trouble to set up that interview with President Francis. I don't think he'd appreciate it if I were late."

"No, sir," Terry said. "Oh, there's a trolley coming now. You can catch it, if you hurry."

Jenkens shouted his thanks at Terry, then ran quickly down the steps and out into the street to board the electric trolley car that would take him out to the fairgrounds for his interview.

Smiling, Terry pivoted and went into the building. A half-dozen people were in the circuit clerk's office when Terry reached it a few moments later. He had taken a bold step in sending Jenkins away so he could get the story himself. Now he had to produce.

"Look here. We have deadlines to meet," someone was saying to a harried-looking court clerk, and his words were echoed by three others. All four men were wearing hats, and cards sticking from their hatbands identified them as members of the press. "When are you going to give us the information?" the same reporter asked.

"I'm sorry, gentlemen," the badgered clerk said from behind his counter. "The prosecutor has left specific instructions that no information be given out at this time."

"At this time? Then, pray tell, at what time *will* it be given?" demanded one of the reporters.

"I'm sorry, gentlemen. There's nothing I can do," the clerk said again.

"Yeah, well, being sorry doesn't write our copy," one of the reporters grumbled.

Terry felt a sinking feeling in the pit of his stomach. If these hard-nosed, experienced newsmen were getting nowhere, what made him think *he* could get the story? He had let his enthusiasm and anxiousness override his common sense. Now he would not only not get the job, he would wind up making a fool of himself as well. He didn't even have anything to identify him as a reporter.

"Yes, sir, can I help you?" the clerk asked, addressing Terry and obviously glad for the opportunity to move away from the members of the press.

"I'm a reporter," Terry said, and even as he spoke the words, they sounded like a mockery.

"Thank goodness they finally sent us a replacement," the clerk said. "Did Judge McHenry send you down? Well, no matter. Our regular reporter has taken ill, and we must have the minutes of the grand jury certified."

"What? No, you don't—"

"Go on back there to the prosecutor's office," the clerk continued, oblivious to Terry's denial. "You'll find the transcript of the notes already typed. All you have to do is compare the typed pages with the notes the court stenographer took."

Suddenly it all became clear. Because Terry wasn't wearing a press card, the clerk thought he had meant a court reporter, not a newspaper reporter. That mistake was going to allow him to look over the very material he was down here to see. What luck!

On the other hand a degree of danger was involved. If he were caught making an unauthorized perusal of the court documents, he could be found in contempt of court and perhaps even be sent to jail.

"Young man!" one of the newsmen called. "Young man, I'm with the *Post-Dispatch*. As soon as you're finished reading those notes, could I have an interview with you?"

"And could I as well? I'm with *The Globe*," another reporter asked.

The clerk came around from behind the counter and stepped between Terry and the assertive reporters. "He has no authority to release information," the clerk said.

"Authority? Who cares?" one of the reporters exclaimed. "When he reads those notes, he'll have the information we need."

"Would you please get on with it?" the clerk asked Terry, exasperated and anxious to get the reporters out of his hair.

That settled it. Terry smiled at the clerk. "Very well," he said. "Where are the court notes?"

"In there." The clerk pointed to a door. "You won't be disturbed."

"Remember, I asked for the interview first!" the *Post-Dispatch* man shouted as Terry went inside.

Closing the door behind him, Terry looked around the room. It was a legal library, with walls lined with books and a long oak table surrounded by red leather chairs dominating the center of the room. On the table was a stack of typewritten pages and a stenographer's tablet. Terry was supposed to compare the typed transcript with the notes in the notebook, but when he looked at the notebook, he saw that it was all in shorthand. He couldn't read shorthand!

Wait a minute, he thought. What difference does that make? He wasn't here as a court reporter to certify the documents for the court. All he had to do was read the typed transcript; it would have everything he needed for his story. He'd read the typewritten report as quickly as he could, then leave.

Fifteen minutes later, with the who, why, and when information that Petzold wanted, Terry slipped out through the back door of the library. He had not given his name to the clerk, and if he was lucky, by the time the clerk came back and found him gone, the man would have already forgotten what he looked like.

Pleased with having pulled off such a coup, Terry hurried home and quickly composed his story on his new typewriter. That done, he returned to the Chronicle

Building, taking the stairs up to the third floor three at a time.

"You again?" Fitzhugh asked coldly. "What can I do for you now?"

"Would you be so kind as to inform Mr. Petzold that Terry Perkins is here to see him?"

"I will do no such thing," Fitzhugh snapped.

"Tell him," Terry insisted, "that Terry Perkins has the story about the indictment of the city councilman. The who, the why, and the when," he added, speaking loudly enough so that Petzold would have to be able to hear it.

"Would you please leave?" Fitzhugh ordered.

At that moment the door to Petzold's office opened, and the publisher stuck his head out. "Who is Terry Perkins?"

"I am Terry Perkins, sir," Terry said. "Perhaps you remember me? I was the editor of *The Jeffersonian* this year, and I wrote you a letter."

"Oh, yes. The college boy."

"Yes, sir."

"And you say you have information about the indictment of the city councilman?"

"Yes, sir. I've already written my story, sir," Terry said, holding it out toward Petzold.

"Yes, well, I'm most impressed, but, Mr. Perkins, I've already sent my Mr. Jenkens to get the story." Petzold turned to go back to his office.

"Excuse me, sir," Terry called to him. "But Mr. Jenkens won't be getting the story."

Petzold stopped and turned around. "Oh? And what makes you so sure of that?"

"I, uh"—Terry cleared his throat—"I met him at the courthouse and told him that you had called the court with a change of orders. I told him you wanted him to go immediately to the fairgrounds and interview President Francis."

"Young man, just who do you think you are?" Fitzhugh demanded angrily. "That is the most deceitful—"

"—and enterprising idea I've heard today," Petzold put in, interrupting Fitzhugh's tirade.

"But you don't understand, Mr. Petzold. He was here when you were discussing the assignment with Mr. Jenkens. He even asked me to identify Mr. Jenkens for him. He took advantage of the situation."

"No, *you* don't understand, Mr. Fitzhugh," Petzold responded. "But then, I wouldn't expect you to. You are a receiver, not a reporter. A reporter, you see, must be inventive if he is to be successful. Young man, come into my office and let me read what you have written."

"Yes, sir!" Terry agreed with a grin.

Connie Bateman was home for the summer, but it was almost as if she hadn't been away. Although she had left her father's house and moved into the dormitory on the campus of Mary Lindenwood College in St. Charles, she had visited the Jefferson College campus many times during the year. That wasn't unusual, for numerous Mary Lindenwood students took the trolleys to Jefferson for weekend activities such as football games, dances, and other events. What made Connie's circumstances unusual was that Jefferson's campus had been her home for many years. And if Professor Bateman's plan was adopted, Connie wouldn't be going back to Mary Lindenwood at all this fall but would finish her education right here at Jefferson.

That idea appealed to her, though she couldn't help but be a little frustrated by her father's timing. Had he instituted this program last year, she would have been able to be here in time to share at least one year with Bob Canfield.

Professor Bateman's plan to convert Jefferson College to Jefferson University and to include women depended on unanimous approval by the Board of Regents. If only one man voted against it, the entire plan would have to be abandoned, for it could only be instituted if the charter was changed, and the charter could only be changed if there were no dissenting votes.

The Board of Regents was meeting this afternoon to consider the proposal. As was often the case, especially when school wasn't in session, the meeting would be held in the dining room of the residence of the president. Professor Bateman had asked Connie if she'd help him prepare for the meeting.

Though it was the middle of the afternoon, the venetian blinds were closed, so the dining room was all dark shadows when Connie went in. When she walked over to the west wall and began opening the blinds, alternating bars of bright light and dark stripes splashed onto the oak dining table. On this tiger-striped surface Connie lay pencils and ashtrays before each chair, then put a pitcher of cold lemonade and several glasses on the buffet. She had just finished preparing the room when voices in the foyer signaled the arrival of the board members for the meeting. Connie's mother had died when her daughter was twelve, so from an early age Connie had been pushed into occasionally serving as her father's unofficial hostess. Because of that, most of the members of the board had known her since she was a young girl, and as they came into the dining room they smiled and spoke to her. One or two made the obligatory remark as to "how grown-up" she looked now. Connie suppressed a laugh. She was nineteen years old. She *was* grown-up.

Excusing herself, Connie closed the door behind her to allow the men to conduct their meeting. Then she went immediately to the upstairs parlor to sit by the open heat register. She had learned many years ago that if the registers were open in both the dining room and the upstairs parlor, she could hear what was being said. As a matter of decorum she never listened in . . . unless she had a more than passing interest in the purpose of the meeting. Today she had more than a passing interest. She very much wanted Jefferson College to open its doors to women, not just so she could attend, but so any woman who was qualified could. Perhaps it was because she had not had the gentle influence of a mother during her formative years, but

Connie had never been able to accept the inequality of the sexes.

The meeting had already started by the time she reached the upstairs register, and she sat quietly, listening to the proceedings.

"Let me get this straight, William," one of the regents—Connie believe it was Mr. Fiddler—was saying. "At a time when the college is losing money and our coffers are running dangerously low, you want to spend more money?"

"Yes."

"But don't you think that's a little foolish? It seems to me that we would better serve this institution by finding ways to cut back on our expenditures. The athletic programs, for example. Let us cut out football and baseball and track."

"That is precisely what we should not do," one of the other board members said. "The athletic programs of the college are what help to make our name known and thus attract new applicants. And isn't that the problem now? We have too few applicants?"

"A quality education is what our students want, not football."

"Gentlemen, gentlemen, please," Professor Bateman said, interrupting the discussion before it got any more heated. "You are right, Harold. Our applicants are seeking a quality education. But James is also right. The athletic program makes us known to prospective students. I believe the education one gets at Jefferson is superior to that of any other institution in the state. Indeed, if I may be so bold, it is superior to any school west of the Alleghenies. The problem is, the number of disciplines a student may pursue is limited. Therefore, we must offer them a wider range of courses—we must redesignate ourselves a university, and we must admit women."

"Assuming we become a university, must it follow that we allow women to attend?" Harold Fiddler wanted to know.

"This is the twentieth century," the professor explained. "Times have changed drastically since Professor Spengeman established this school in 1853. More and more women are seeking a higher education. If we keep our doors closed to them, we are denying the existence of half the population. We must go forward, not backward, for I assure you, gentlemen, if we begin applying austerity measures to this institution, it will soon cease to exist."

"Next, I suppose, you'll be wanting to open the door to the coloreds?" Fiddler suggested.

"No. As a practical matter I realize that allowing colored students in would be counterproductive. However, I sincerely believe that before this new century is completed, we will see qualified colored students on our campus as well as on campuses all across this country. And I believe that is as it should be."

"That will never happen. They have their own schools. Why, in this very state there is Lincoln University," a new voice said. Connie wasn't sure who this speaker was.

"Yes, there is Lincoln," Professor Bateman agreed.

"Bateman, what do you know about Loomis Booker?" Fiddler suddenly asked, and, in the upstairs parlor, Connie gasped and leaned forward to listen more attentively. Bob had shared Loomis's secret with her, that he was, using the janitor's own words, "acquiring a purloined education from Jefferson." But she had never breathed a word of it to anyone, not even her father.

"What about Mr. Booker?"

"Surely, President Bateman, you know what he is doing?" Fiddler asked.

"He is acting as our furnace stoker, janitor, and handyman," Professor Bateman replied. "He is the best we've ever had in that position, and he is doing it all for seven dollars and fifty cents per week. Gentlemen, we just raised his salary this year. Surely you aren't suggesting that we cut it back to five dollars again. That isn't going to save us any money, and we will lose an outstanding worker."

"No, I'm not talking about the money he makes,"

Fiddler said. "I'm talking about the classes he's taking. What do you have to say about that?"

"As far as I know, he isn't taking any classes."

"That's not what I've heard," Fiddler said. "I've heard that if any student in this school has a problem they can't solve, they can go to Loomis Booker and he'll help them. And I'm told that he has a complete library of our textbooks in his room."

"Yes," Professor Bateman said. "That is true. But he pulled those books out of the trash after they had been discarded as no longer usable. He then patched them up to make them usable again."

"In other words, he stole them," Fiddler said.

"No, he did not steal them. He salvaged them. There is a significant difference."

"But he is partaking in the educational process of our institution," Fiddler complained. "In my book, that's the same as having coloreds enrolled. How's it going to look if someone thinks we have niggers here?"

"I assure you, Harold"—the professor's voice was cool—"that any education Loomis Booker has obtained has been achieved by his own self-study. I find that commendable in any man, and I refuse to see how that could, in any way, reflect unfavorably upon this institution."

"Yes, well, nevertheless, I think we ought to keep quiet about it. I wouldn't want this to get out."

"I believe Mr. Booker has always been most discreet about it," Professor Bateman said. "In fact, he and I have never discussed it at all, and I'm not sure he even knows that I know what he is doing."

"Let's get back to the subject at hand," James Boyd insisted. "If we change from a college to a university, how much will it increase our budget?"

"By at least fifty percent," Professor Bateman answered. "But that's in the short run. In the long term the idea would attract enough new students to offset the increase in cost, and, in fact, start us growing again."

"And if we stay as we are?"

"Assuming we don't grow, we can operate for four or

five more years. If we continue to lose students, three or four."

"Then the way I see it, gentlemen, we have no choice," Boyd said to the others. "We must either adopt President Bateman's plan for growth or face the fact that this school will soon cease to be. I put that in the form of a motion."

"Second."

"All in favor?" Professor Bateman asked.

Connie listened with bated breath.

"Harold, your hand is not up. Are you opposing or abstaining?" the professor asked.

"What difference will it make?" Fiddler groused.

"If you abstain, the measure will carry. If you vote against it, the measure will fail."

There was a long, pregnant pause. Then Fiddler said quietly, "I'm abstaining."

"Gentlemen, the motion is carried," Professor Bateman said in a strong, vibrant voice. "I thank you for your vote of confidence."

Connie closed the heat register and walked over to look out one of the upstairs parlor's front windows, across the street toward the hilltop campus. From the time she had learned that women couldn't attend Jefferson, when she was still just a little girl, she had been resentful. She would have to be resentful no longer. But, she decided, for her father's sake and for the sake of the school, she had better be prayerful.

"The alma mater," she said aloud with a smile. "Now it'll have to be rewritten."

CHAPTER
FOUR

As Eric McKenzie, Marcus Parmeter, and Jake Quinn led their saddled horses out of the corral, Marcus—letting some of his excitement out—took a playful swipe at Eric, knocking his gray Stetson off. Eric grabbed the hat before it hit the ground and put it back on. In addition to the hat, Eric was wearing the clothes he always wore—cotton work shirt, denim trousers, and boots. He had a denim jacket for protection against the cool mornings and evenings, but it—along with two other shirts, two other pairs of pants, a change of underwear, soap, tooth powder and toothbrush, and a comb—was packed in the small carpetbag now hanging from his saddle pommel. Jake and Marcus were dressed the same as Eric was, and their carpetbags were packed with the same gear, though theirs included a razor, shaving brush, and mug. All three were wearing pistols that they intended to leave with the liveryman in Newcastle, where they would board their horses while they took a train to St. Louis. They were going to the World's Fair.

The threesome had just mounted up when the screen door at the back of the main house slammed shut, and when they looked toward the sound, they saw Rodney Ebersole coming toward them through the garden. He trod carefully on the freshly turned soil to avoid stepping on tomato plants that were now at shoe-top level. Waiting for their boss, the cowboys reached down to pat the necks of their animals who, saddled and bridled, were anxious to get going and were dancing about and tossing their heads nervously.

"So, lads, it's off on your great adventure, is it?" Ebersole asked. His precise, rather clipped English accent was as pronounced now as it had been the day he'd arrived in America, a freshly discharged lieutenant from Her Majesty's Royal Guards.

"Yes, sir," Eric answered.

"Mr. Ebersole, we all want to thank you for givin' us the time off to do this," Jake said.

"Nonsense. The work's all caught up; the time is yours to use as you please. I believe Eric said that your plan was to ride to Newcastle and catch the train there?"

"That's right."

"Have any of you ever been to Newcastle before?"

"No, I don't reckon," Jake replied, sheepishly. "Truth is, ain't none of us've never been nowhere before."

"What route have you selected to Newcastle?"

"Oh, there ain't nothin' to gettin' there," Jake said. "We'll just ride south till we reach the railroad, then follow it east."

"That's a sound plan to be sure, but there's a much easier way," Ebersole suggested. "Easier and about five hours shorter, I would imagine. Would you care to hear it?"

"Sure," Jake said.

"Start your journey from the Belle Fourche, here on the ranch. When you get to the first fork that goes east from the river, follow it. It will lead you in a southeasterly direction all the way to Newcastle. By proceeding along this tributary, you should quite easily raise Newcastle before nightfall."

"Want us to bring you back a souvenir from the World's Fair, Mr. Ebersole?" Marcus asked.

"Thank you, but that won't be necessary, Marcus," Ebersole replied. "All I really want is for the three of you to have a good time and stay out of trouble." He pulled his wallet from his back pocket. "Now, here is a little bonus. Fifty dollars for each of you," he said.

"Fifty dollars!" Eric exclaimed.

"It's not much, but . . ."

"Why, it's an out-an'-out fortune, Boss," Jake declared, smiling broadly.

"You three lads have served me faithfully and well, and this is just a small way of showing my appreciation."

"Thanks, Mr. Ebersole. Thanks a lot," Eric said as he accepted his fifty dollars. "This is very nice of you."

Ebersole reached up and put his hand on Eric's, then squeezed it tightly. "Eric, you are like a son to me; you truly are. I want you to have a good time, and I think the World's Fair will provide you with some wonderful experiences." Suddenly his countenance changed. "But I have this unshakable feeling, this feeling that—" Ebersole broke off and looked away. During the silence, the windmill in the corral, answering a breeze, creaked and swung into the wind. The thirty-six blades whirled into life, and the piston began rattling and clanking as the pump started its up-and-down motion. Still, Ebersole did not finish his sentence.

"Mr. Ebersole? Are you all right?" Eric asked.

"Yes, lad, of course I am," Ebersole finally replied. He squeezed Eric's hand again, then turned to walk quickly toward the house. "You fellows take care of each other," he called back over his shoulder.

"Marcus, Jake, did you see Mr. Ebersole's eyes?" Eric asked in surprise. "There were tears in them. He was crying!"

"He's a good man," Marcus said quietly.

"But he was crying. Why do you think he was crying?" Eric wanted to know.

"Eric, sometimes it's best not to pry into what a man's feelin'," Marcus suggested softly. "Come on, let's go." Clucking at their horses, the cowboys began their long journey.

Using Ebersole's directions, they began following the fork that ran southeast from the Belle Fourche River. They had gone scarcely four miles when the fork ran dry. That didn't slow them down too much, for there was still a deep enough cut in the creek bank that made it quite easy to follow, so they continued their trek. The farther they went, though, the harder following it became. In some places there was only the suggestion of a creek bed, and in many places there wasn't even that.

The creaking of saddle leather and the jangling of the bits was nearly drowned out by the sound of hooves striking stone as they continued to trail the creek bed, often discernible only by the pattern of pebbles arranged by water when a freshet had filled the stream.

They rode for the better part of the day, not even leaving their saddles to eat a lunch of ham and biscuits that Cookie had insisted on packing for them. Before them the plains stretched out in folds of hills, one after another. As each ridge was crested another was exposed, and beyond it lay another still. The dusty grass gave off a pungent though not unpleasant smell when crushed underfoot by their horses. They plodded on.

"How are we possibly supposed to know where to go now?" Marcus finally asked. "There ain't hide nor hair of that old creek bed we been followin'. That is, the one we been *tryin'* to follow."

"We need to go right through here," Jake said, pointing slightly to the southeast of their trail.

"And just how would you be knowin' that?"

"Simple," Jake replied, smiling. "I just asked myself where I'd go if I was a creek. And I'd go right there, through that little cut."

"What makes you so sure?"

"Well, you ever seen a creek run *up*hill?"

Eric laughed. "Marcus, I do believe he has a point."

Marcus unhooked his canteen and took a long drink. Capping it again, he grumbled, "Yeah, well, I'd feel a lot better if we could find us some *real* sign of the creek. I don't much like the idea of wanderin' around out here, who the hell knows where."

"But we can't really get lost," Eric observed. "Even if we lose the trail entirely, we can head south until we find the railroad just like we'd planned to do in the first place."

"The boy's right," Jake said. "Now, quit your bitchin' and come on. I'd kind of like to get to town before dark."

"You ain't goin' to find no town before dark, I promise you that," Marcus muttered.

A short while later they got their first glimpse of the town they had been looking for.

"Well, now, lookee there, Marcus. What do you suppose that might be up there?" Jake asked dryly.

Marcus glanced at his friend, who was eyeing him triumphantly, but said nothing.

Obviously not willing to let it alone and determined to get a rise out of his partner, Jake waited a moment or two, then said, "Yep, for all the wanderin' around in the vast, uncharted wilderness, I reckon we happened to stumble onto someplace by accident. I just wish I knew what the name of that town up there might be." He nodded sagely. "'Course, it could be we got ourselves lost and that ain't nothin' but one of them things you see in the desert. What do you call it, Eric?"

"A mirage," Eric answered.

"Yeah, a mirage. You reckon that's a mirage up there, Eric? Or could it be—"

"All right, goddamnit! It's Newcastle!" Marcus finally blurted out, interrupting Jake's teasing. "What the hell, you think maybe me and Eric couldn't have found it without you?"

Clearly satisfied that he'd finally gotten the reaction he wanted, Jake laughed. "Marcus, I don't think you could find your cock in the dark if you had a map and used both hands," he said.

Marcus laughed with him. "Well, I don't need to find it, if I got me a gal to find it for me."

"Like Susie?" Eric quipped, getting into the game with the others.

"Yeah, like Susie."

"Personally, I don't find Susie all that attractive," Eric said. "I think you two are crazy."

"Well, now, hold on there, boy. Don't you go puttin' Susie down, if you ain't tried 'er. You tell the boy, Jake. Now, is Susie really all that bad?"

"I'll admit that she's at least better than a hole in the mattress," Jake said, laughing.

They rode on in silence for a while longer, and then Jake spoke again. "Will you boys look at the size of that town? It sure as hell puts Oshoto all to shame, don't it? How big you reckon this place is, anyway? You think it's got a thousand people in it?"

"I wouldn't know, but there's a lot of folks here. You can tell that just by lookin' at the place," Marcus replied. "I mean, look at it. It's three or four times as big as Oshoto. This here's a real town. Oshoto ain't no more'n a store and a handful of scraggly old buildin's."

They made their observations about Newcastle while watching it grow steadily closer. It had risen suddenly, like an apparition in the desert, but it was some time after they first saw it before they actually arrived. And, just as the clear, thin air played tricks with the visual distance, the natural bowl in which the town nestled was acting as a megaphone, so that certain distant sounds reached them as well.

They could hear the trill of a piano . . . the high shriek of a woman's laughter . . . a crying baby . . . a barking dog. Somewhere in the town a drayman was working his team, and his whistles and shouts floated out to them.

"Damn if this here ain't downright spooky," Jake said after a while. "It's been lookin' like we wasn't no more'n a mile away from it for the better part of an hour, but we ain't gettin' no closer. I'm beginnin' to wonder if we're ever gonna get there."

"We'll get there," Marcus said. "What do you say, soon's we get into town we go find us a whorehouse? A big one, where they got maybe eight or ten gals, and we could line them up against the wall and take our pick. And no sharin', like we got to do with Susie."

"Sounds fine by me," Jake said. "What do you say, Eric?"

"Well, I . . . uh, I'm just thinking about the money, is all. Don't forget we have to have enough to board our horses, get a train ticket to St. Louis, and still have enough for hotels both here and there."

"Yeah, but Mr. Ebersole give us that fifty dollars apiece that we wasn't countin' on," Jake said. "Now, with what we already had, seems to me like that ought to be enough to get us a good café supper, get us drunk, get us a whore, and still have enough left over to go to St. Louis and take a look at all them wonders."

"You want to know what I think?" Marcus said. "I think the boy's a little bit scared."

"Scared of what?" Eric challenged.

"Scared of bein' with a woman," Marcus said. "Admit it, Eric. Don't you get all scared and start makin' excuses everytime we talk about maybe it bein' time for you to see what bein' with a woman's all about?"

"Leave him alone, Marcus. If he don't want to do it, he don't have to. But Eric, you don't mind if me and Marcus find us a woman, do you? I mean, we ain't had nothin' but Susie for so long."

"And we ain't had her in a while," Marcus put in, laughing. "Not since Ebersole give up on lettin' us get into Oshoto."

"Yeah, it's been near two months now for me," Jake said.

"Anyway, a man's got to have his ashes hauled ever now and again or else he'll just go plumb loco. You'll learn all about that when you get older," Marcus continued.

"All right," Eric agreed.

"Do you mean all right, you don't mind it if me and Jake get us a woman, or do you mean all right, you're gonna come along with us?"

Despite himself, Eric laughed. "All right, I'm going to go along with you," he said.

"Whooeee!" Marcus shouted, reaching out and knocking Eric's hat off, then, laughing, tousling Eric's hair. "Jake, you mark my words. After today, Eric's gonna be pesterin' us somethin' terrible to take time out for a woman."

"What kind of women do you like, Eric?" Jake asked.

"I don't know. I never stopped to think about it. I mean, a woman's a woman, isn't she?"

"No, a woman ain't just a woman," Marcus scoffed. "There's all different kinds. I don't know, maybe you ought to let me pick out this first woman for you," he suggested. "I mean, seein' as you ain't got no experience, you're liable to make a mistake your first time in the saddle that could just mess you up good from now on. They say things like that is what makes some men not do too good with women. So, how about it? You want me to pick one out for you?"

"No, thank you. I'll pick out my own. If I'm going to make a mistake, it'll be my mistake," Eric said. "I have no intention of letting you choose for me."

"All right, all right," Marcus said, holding up his hand in surrender. "I was just tryin' to be of some help, is all. I mean, wasn't I the one who picked out your first horse for you? And didn't I do a good job?"

"Yes, you did," Eric agreed. "But I don't think a horse and a woman are the same thing."

"Maybe they're closer'n you think. I mean, when you stop to think about it, what are you lookin' for anyway? Somethin' to climb up on and ride, am I right?"

Jake laughed. "Marcus, that's real gentlemanly, the way you treat your women with such respect. Thinkin' of them as horses."

"Hell, Jake, I treat horses with respect," Marcus quipped.

The others laughed, and in unison, without saying a word, the threesome spurred their horses, anxious to reach their destination as quickly as possible.

Newcastle was laid out like a cross. The vertical bar ran north and south, with the end of the street leading into a trail that finally disappeared out in the high plains. The horizontal bar of the cross ran east and west, parallel with the railroad track. Approaching the town from the north, Eric and his friends passed a cluster of private dwellings, and in an empty field near the houses a baseball game was going on among a dozen or so boys. As Eric rode by, he twisted in his saddle to watch. The players were about the same age as he, and for an instant, though the thought passed so quickly he was hardly aware of it, Eric felt a sharp sense of having missed out on something in his life. He couldn't hold on to the feeling though, because he didn't even know what it was he'd missed.

Beyond the houses was a high-steepled church, and beyond that, a mortuary. When they reached the commercial part of town they saw a man standing on the corner of a wooden porch in front of a bootmaker's shop. The man was wearing a three-piece suit, and a gold watch chain stretched across his vest.

"Let's get some information from that fella over there," Marcus said. "Hey, friend," he called. "Where's the whorehouse in this town?"

"I beg your pardon?" the man responded, a shocked look on his face.

"The whorehouse," Marcus repeated. "Where's it at?"

"I assure you, sir, if there is such an establishment in Newcastle, I am not a habitué," the man replied, drawing his jacket together indignantly, then walking quickly to put some distance between himself and the three cowboys.

"Well, goddamn, mister, you don't have to get into a piss soup about it," Marcus called after him.

Eric and Jake laughed loudly.

"Marcus, I have to hand it to you," Jake said. "You've got a real way with strangers."

"What the hell is a habitué?"

"Damned if I know. Ask Eric. He's the educated one."

"I don't know," Eric admitted. "I've never heard the word before."

"Yeah, well, if that fella ain't one, whatever it is, it's probably somethin' I'd like to be," Marcus muttered.

"Why don't we find us a saloon?" Jake suggested. "We could maybe get us a drink or two, then find out where's the best place to eat. And I'm sure the folks in the saloon'll know where the whorehouse is at."

"Yeah, well, the only thing is, most saloons has got their own whores," Marcus said. "I was wantin' me a real whorehouse, with red curtains and gold-framed mirrors and the like."

Nonetheless, they pulled rein in front of the first saloon they came to a block farther down and tied their mounts at the hitch rail. Giving the place a quick assessment as they stood out front, they pushed their way through the batwings and strode up to the bar, catching the bartender's eye.

After ordering beers for each of them, Marcus again posed his question.

"Ain't nothin' exactly like that in Newcastle," the bartender answered. He pointed toward the stairs. "But we got a top floor here with private rooms and beds, and three whores that look as good as any you find in one of them fancy places like you been goin' to."

Jake laughed. "We been goin' to?" he said. "Hell, mister, we ain't been—"

"—to one of them places in a long time," Marcus interrupted. "We worked the winter up on the Flying E. Reckon you heard of that. That's Rodney Ebersole's ranch."

"Don't know as I have," the bartender admitted. "But that don't mean nothin'. Excuse me. I got another customer." The bartender drifted down to the other end of the counter to serve a patron who had just stepped up to the bar.

"Jake, don't go tellin' him we ain't been to no fancy whorehouse," Marcus hissed. "He'll tell the whores here, an' they'll figure us for some dumb rubes from the brush."

"Goddamnit, Marcus, we *are* dumb rubes from the brush."

"Well, we don't have to tell everybody about it. Quiet, he's comin' back this way."

"Anything else I can do for you gents?" the bartender asked when he returned.

"Yes, could you suggest a good place to eat?" Eric asked, taking a sip of his beer, then wiping the foam off his upper lip.

The bartender looked at Eric as if seeing him for the first time, and then he looked back at the other two men. "This here one's just a pup. He's kinda young to be runnin' with you two, ain't he?"

Marcus's eyes narrowed menacingly. "You ever hear of a fella used to be down in the New Mexico territory, name of Billy the Kid?"

"'Course I have," the bartender answered.

"Then maybe you remember that by the time he was this boy's age, he'd done killed hisself ten men. When somebody told him he was awful young to be doin' that, he said he was old enough to get the job done. Now, how old do you think a person has to be to get somethin' to eat and find hisself a whore?"

"I guess . . . old enough to get the job done," the bartender replied, nodding slowly. He pointed through the window. "Right over there, across the street, there's a place called Delmonico's. I reckon that's as good a place to eat as anywhere you'll find in town."

"Thanks," Marcus said. "We're goin' to go eat now, and then we're going to come back for some serious drinkin' and to have us a run at them whores. Don't you let 'em get away."

"Don't you be worryin' none about that," the bartender said. "They won't be goin' nowhere. They'll be here all night."

"So will we, mister," Marcus said, grinning broadly. "So will we."

The threesome left their horses at the livery stable a few doors down, then headed into the restaurant. Their orders came quickly, and the two older cowboys wolfed down their meals.

"You plannin' on eatin' the rest of them taters?" Marcus asked Eric. When Eric shook his head no, Marcus took the youth's plate and shoveled the few uneaten potatoes off onto his own. Marcus had spent the whole meal instructing Eric in the proper techniques of "whoring," as he called it, and he now told him, "You're probably figurin' you should have you a real young whore, maybe someone about your own age. But if you was to do that, you'd be makin' a big mistake."

"Why would that be a mistake?" Eric asked.

"Because if she was that young, she wouldn't be knowin' a whole lot more about it than you, for all she was a whore," Marcus explained. "What you need to do is find yourself the oldest one over there. See, that way, there ain't no kind of way she ain't never been rode and no kind of man she ain't never throwed. Besides, the older the whores get, the younger they like their men. An old whore would be a real good one for breakin' you in."

Jake laughed. "Marcus, you're as full of shit as a Christmas goose, you know that? Don't go listenin' to him, Eric. He's just tryin' to make sure *he* gets the youngest and prettiest one for hisself."

"You gonna eat the rest of your steak?" Marcus asked.

By way of an answer, Eric forked the rest of his steak off his plate and onto Marcus's.

"You're wrong, Jake. I sure don't want the prettiest one," Marcus went on, carving off a large piece of meat. "You see, that's another thing about whores." He stopped to swallow before he finished his observation. "The prettiest ones, now, they think their good looks is all they need. What you want to do is to get you one that's just a little bit ugly. Most of them that's ugly know they're ugly, so they'll kind of go out of their way to treat you right. Of course, every now and again you're likely to get you one who's ugly, but she don't know she's ugly. Them's the worst kind, 'cause they figure they're pretty enough for looks to get them by, and they don't try none at all. An ugly woman that thinks she's pretty and don't try—now that's the worst kind."

"Marcus, it's too bad you can't write none," Jake said. "You could put all that down in a book. Eric, you ought to just follow this son of a bitch around with a pencil, writin' down everything he says. Hell, I'll bet there ain't nobody in the country knows as much about chasin' whores as Marcus here."

Eric laughed, then slid the uneaten portion of his pie to one side.

"Boy, what is wrong with you?" Jake asked. "You give Marcus all your taters and most of your steak, and now you didn't eat no more'n one or two bites of your pie. Are you feelin' all right?"

"Sure, I feel fine. I guess I'm just not hungry, is all," Eric said. Though he wouldn't tell the others, he had butterflies in his stomach just from thinking about being with a woman for the first time ever.

When they returned to the saloon after their meal, the three whores were working the tables for drinks, and the bartender told the visiting cowboys that none of the women could go upstairs before eight.

"Well, then, we'll just sit over at that table there and have us a few drinks while we're waitin'," Marcus said.

The bartender chuckled. "Yeah, that's the whole idea."

During the time they were waiting, Marcus and Jake talked about the women they'd known. Marcus, of course, had known the most—or at least he knew the most stories. Eric wasn't sure which. Eric was relatively quiet the entire evening. He'd tasted hard liquor once or twice before and didn't like it, so he wasn't drinking it now. He nursed a beer, while Marcus and Jake had two or three whiskeys each.

Eric had been watching the women work the customers for drinks, and he already knew which one of them he wanted. In fact, he'd made up his mind that if he didn't get her, he wasn't going to go upstairs at all. Though none of them looked under thirty, the one he had picked out seemed to have a softer smile and a gentler disposition than the others. Somehow she seemed less threatening to him. He had heard one of the men call her Penny.

"I take Penny," he told his friends. It was the first comment he had made in several minutes.

"Penny?" Marcus said. He twisted around in his chair and looked toward the three women. "Which one's Penny?"

She was sitting in the lap of a big, bearded man, twisting the hair of his beard around her fingers.

When Eric pointed her out, Marcus nodded. "She looks like she might be a good one for you. Which one of them other two do you want, Jake?"

"The one in the green dress."

"Damn," Marcus said. "Look how skinny she is. That'd be like pokin' it through a knothole in a board. Hell, she ain't even got no titties."

"Maybe so, but that's the one I want," Jake insisted.

Marcus grinned broadly. "Well, then this is workin' out just right, cause I like them with a little meat on their bones, and that gal over there in the blue'll suit me fine. Look at the size of them tits. You know, if a fella was to fall down in between them, he'd like as not smother before he could get hisself excavated."

At eight o'clock the woman in blue came over to the table where the three men had been sitting patiently for just over an hour. "LeRoy says you fellas want some company tonight," she said.

"You said it, honey," Marcus confirmed.

"First, we must get the unpleasant business of

money out of the way. Our company will cost you gentlemen a dollar and a half each, or three dollars for the whole night."

"I reckon we'll take about three dollars' worth, apiece," Marcus said.

"Oh, my. Big spenders are you? Well, I'm sure we'll have a wonderful time." The woman smiled. "My name's Amy."

"Amy, I done laid a claim on you," Marcus said. "My pards has chose up the ones they want, too. Jake there, he wants the skinny little gal in the red dress, the one that ain't got no tits."

"That's Sara," Amy said. "And she has tits, honey, though I must confess, I have seen larger ones."

"And Eric here wants Penny."

"Have you ever been with a woman before, honey?" Amy asked Eric.

Eric felt his cheeks burning in embarrassment. "No, ma'am," he answered, barely mumbling the words.

"Then you've made a wise choice," Amy said. "Penny's real good with young boys who're doing it for the first time. It's almost as if she has a calling for it."

Amy signaled the other two, and they came over to the table to stand beside her. She steered Sara toward Jake and Penny to Eric.

"Penny, this little sweetheart is one of your specials, if you get my meaning," Amy said.

"She means he ain't never done it before," Marcus added, and Eric felt his cheeks flush again.

Penny reached out and took Eric's hand in hers. She smiled, and Eric saw a few lines around her eyes that he hadn't noticed before. Perhaps she was older than he thought, older even than the other two. He liked her eyes, though. They were bright blue, and they were clear and deep and somehow not quite as hard looking as Amy's and Sara's eyes.

"There's no need to embarrass the young gentleman," Penny admonished Marcus. "We're going to do just fine."

"Well, shall we go upstairs?" Amy invited.

"Unless you're wantin' to do it right down here on the table," Marcus said. "I'm that ready I'm about to bust."

"Well, we certainly don't want that, do we?" Amy said, laughing. "Come on, ladies, I do believe these gentlemen are badly in need of our services."

Amy and Marcus led the way, Jake and Sara followed, while Eric and Penny brought up the rear. Aware of the other men in the saloon and knowing that *they* knew exactly why he was going upstairs, Eric thought he could feel the eyes of all of them burning into the back of his neck. But as they reached the first landing he happened to glance into the mirror hanging behind the bar, and it didn't appear as if anyone in the saloon was paying the slightest bit of attention to him and his friends. He was surprised by that, but it did make him feel a bit less embarrassed.

When they reached the second floor, Amy opened a closet door and reached in to get towels for all of them. To her consternation she found none, so she called down to the other end of the long hall. "Mary! Mary, where are the clean towels?"

A very stout, very plain-looking woman stepped out of a room at the other end. "They're down here," the woman said. "I brought them in from the line and folded them; I just haven't got around to putting them in that closet yet. You can come down here and get them if you need them right now."

"Mary, we don't want to come down there and get them," Amy replied sternly. "I thought we had an understanding, a division of labor, so to speak. We fuck, you keep us supplied with clean towels."

"All right," Mary said. "I'll bring some right down."

"Thank you." Amy turned to the men. "I tell you, ever since Mary came off the line she's been just real mean-spirited. She used to be one of us, so she knows we have to have a lot of towels in this business."

When the towels were brought, Penny took one, then, putting her hand on Eric's arm, led him into one of the rooms. Eric's stomach was in his throat, and his heart was pounding so hard he was sure Penny could hear it. The palms of his hands were sweating, and he rubbed them on his pants leg.

Penny shut the door behind them, then lit a single candle. She turned and smiled at Eric as she began stripping out of her clothes. Eric watched spellbound as first the smooth skin of Penny's shoulders was exposed. Then she turned so that he saw only her back as she removed the rest of her clothes. Calling on all the tricks of her professional experience, she used a shadow here, a soft light there, a movement to hold her body just so. As if by magic, she seemed to lose so many years in age and gain so much in mystery that she became fully as sensual a creature as anyone Eric had seen in any of the art books in Rodney Ebersole's library. Finally, raising the corner of the sheet, she managed to slip into bed using the shadows in such a way that he wasn't sure whether he had seen anything or not.

"Are you going to keep your clothes on?" Penny asked with a laugh that was musical, tinkling.

"No, of course not," Eric said.

She folded the corner of the sheet back, inviting him into bed with her, and showing herself from one breast all the way down to one side of her hip. He got the tiniest glimpse of a black, triangular patch of hair before she readjusted the sheet. He inhaled quickly, then began undressing.

"Oh, my, look at that," Penny said, when Eric was completely nude.

"I'm sorry," he apologized.

"Honey, the time to apologize to a woman is when it *doesn't* do that. That's the way it's supposed to be."

Eric slid in under the sheets. She reached over to touch him and her hand felt like both fire and ice contained in the same entity.

"Should I—" Eric started, but Penny shushed him, much as one would a small child.

"You just let me take care of everything, honey," she said. "It'll be all right. Trust me."

Under Penny's skillful guidance, Eric experienced

all the pleasures and explored all the mysteries his curious, fifteen-year-old mind could contemplate and his body could accommodate. He smiled as he had a thought: He had come into Newcastle a boy; he would be leaving it a man.

David Gelbman's family lived in a twenty-two-room brick house on Lindell Boulevard in one of the most fashionable parts of St. Louis. The house had steam heat, three marble baths, the latest in plumbing, and a kitchen icebox that took up one entire wall. The icebox was unique in that the blocks of ice were loaded from the back porch so that the iceman need never come through the house and drip water onto floors and carpets. It was also convenient, because the iceman could service the box even if no one was home. However, with four servants in residence, there was never a time when the house was completely unoccupied.

David had once asked his father if he didn't think the house was a bit ostentatious.

"If, God forbid, we were ostentatious only for show, I would say you are right, this we do not need. But if it is for business, it is sometimes good to make a big show. Unlike your big words, this, perhaps, you cannot learn in your fine school, but only in the school of life."

Chaim had then gone on to explain to his son how the house, indeed how his entire lifestyle, was used to make a statement about the success of Gelbman's Department Store. That way, he had said, it could impress—or even intimidate, if necessary—customers, suppliers, and competitors.

David wasn't sure how intimidation of a customer might be good for business, but he trusted his father's business sense. He had good reason to. Chaim Gelbman had come to America 45 years ago, a poor immigrant who had nothing but his business acumen and his skills as a tailor. When the Civil War broke out, he had tried to enlist in the Union Army but was turned down because of weak eyes. Denied the opportunity to serve his new country as a soldier, he had followed the army around, repairing old uniforms, making new uniforms, and building a reputation as one who did quality work at a fair price.

After the war, Chaim had settled in St. Louis and opened a small tailor shop. Over the years that small tailor shop grew into Gelbman's Department Store. Now Gelbman's newspaper ads boasted that it was "St. Louis's largest and finest," though two other stores, Famous on Broadway and Morgan and Barr's, which took up the entire square block between Sixth and Seventh and Olive and Locust streets, made the same claim. David had once decided with amusement that obviously they couldn't all be the largest and finest, though certainly they were all large and fine. Most of his father's success had happened before David was even born, and throughout David's entire life he had been the beneficiary.

Today was no exception. The Gelbmans were celebrating David's graduation with a "small" dinner party for a "few" friends, and the large formal dining room was glittering with all the proper accoutrements of success. Gold-rimmed bone china plates were cradled on larger silver plates, while an almost absurd array of silver knives, forks, and spoons spread out on both sides of the settings. The crystal and china gleamed golden from the flames of the long white tapers clutched by three elaborate silver candelabras that augmented the glowing incandescent-bulbed wall sconces and chandelier.

A quieter family celebration had taken place a few days earlier, one more meaningful to David than this one. Both father and son had worn yarmulkes, and Chaim had said prayers. It had been a solemn occasion, and David had felt closer to his father then than at any time since his bar mitzvah.

There was one thing David could appreciate about this dinner, though: Terry Perkins was among the guests. It was the first time David and Terry had seen each other since graduation, and they caught each other up on what they were doing. They began sharing stories about some of the antics of the quad quad, and by the time everyone was called in to dinner, the two graduates had the other guests in stitches.

Twenty-six people sat down at the long, lace-clothed oak table to a dinner of turtle soup, lobster mousse, and roast lamb. The table buzzed with talk. Some of it was about the World's Fair, but the exposition had dominated the St. Louis newspapers and the dinner table and/or parlor conversations of St. Louisians for so long that many people were beginning to search for other subjects. Sitting at the far end of the table, David heard only snatches of several conversations so that he was picking up something like an auditory kaleidoscope—enough for patterns to be discerned, but not enough for a full picture of what was being said.

"They've finally begun work on the Panama Canal. I never thought they'd ever actually get it started."

"Cy Young didn't let a man reach first base—not one man. It was a perfect game, mind you, a perfect game."

"Oh, it'll be Roosevelt again, you can count on that. T.R. will not only get the nomination, he'll be elected."

Immediately after dinner all conversation was halted by the bell-like sound of a silver spoon tapping on a crystal goblet.

"And so now, ladies and gentlemen, may I have, please, your attention?" Chaim asked.

Everyone looked toward him expectantly.

Chaim held his glass up. "For my wife, Golda, and for me too, God has blessed us this day. When I first came to this country, it was as a poor immigrant, with only the schooling that would let me write, read, and work a little math."

"A *lot* of math you could work, Chaim," someone said, and everyone around the table laughed.

Chaim grinned and looked at his son. "Well, at least we know I can add and multiply," he rejoined, a response greeted with laughter. "But there has always been in my heart an old-world respect for an educated man. When Golda and I were blessed with a fine boy, I made a promise to God. What did I promise, you ask? I will tell you." Chaim stopped, took a deep breath, then smiled sheepishly, as if ashamed of the emotion he was close to showing. "The promise I made," he continued, "was that, God willing, one day I should be in a place like this, surrounded by friends such as are here now, and I would lift my glass to my fine and educated son and say"—Chaim gazed at David—"*L'Chaim!*"

The guests all touched goblets, setting off a cheery ringing, like chimes. Chaim left his chair and walked over to embrace David, who, while somewhat embarrassed by the public display, accepted it graciously. There was a light round of applause, and then Chaim looked over at Terry, who, like David, seemed slightly embarrassed by everything. "And, to this man who is the friend of my son, I say also, *L'Chaim.* To life!"

Again the goblets clinked, and the guests drank to the second toast.

"Dad, you aren't going to hug Terry, too, are you?" David quipped. "Because if you are, I'm going to be very jealous."

"So, him I will not hug," Chaim said, laughing.

The guests were soon ushered into the spacious living room, and the celebrants broke into small groups to either catch up on old times or make new acquaintances. David mingled with his guests for a while, then caught Terry's eye, and the two of them retreated to the solitude and relative quiet of the front porch.

They sat on the porch swing, watching the traffic going by. Because of the fair, there were many more automobiles in town than there had ever been before. The young men began calling out the makes, keeping count of how many different models they could identify.

"I'd like to see Bob's father's auto," Terry said. "I got a note from him the other day, asking whether I'd gotten the newspaper job, and he mentioned that Mr. Canfield's bought a big touring Packard."

"Let's ask him to bring it up here," David suggested. "A big automobile parade is supposed to take place in two weeks. There'll be more automobiles in St.

Louis on that day than have ever been gathered at any one place before."

"Good idea. We'll write him a note and ask him to come," Terry said. "Besides, it'll be good to see Bob again—far more so than his father's car."

"You don't like automobiles?"

"Oh, I like the idea of building a machine that will go that fast, but what good is it? In a city you can't go any faster than a horse can travel, and a horse is much more dependable—to say nothing of being cheaper."

"I guess you're right. Oh, by the way, I read your story about the St. Louis Grays and the St. Louis Cardinals baseball teams last week. How did you get into sports reporting?" David asked. "Your first story was about a city councilman being indicted. That's quite a different subject altogether."

"Yes, it is," Terry agreed. "And that was what got me the job. But in order to keep the job, Mr. Petzold gave me a challenge. He told me I'd have to find a need of the newspaper's that only I could fill. I suggested sports."

"Tell me, did he embrace your idea in the beginning?"

"I must say that though he's not a sports enthusiast, he did agree that there was a need, and he decided to give me a chance to see if I could fill it. The article on the Grays and the Cardinals was my first."

"Let's see, what was it you said?" David mused. "Oh, yes." As if reading, he intoned, "'I do not see the Cardinals or the Grays finishing in the first division this year, unless the Cardinals improve greatly upon their hitting, and the Grays find two more pitchers and someone to replace the incompetent Anderson at the first baseman's position.' Well, that was quite a good story, but I don't imagine either team was prepared for such honesty in sports reporting," David said.

"Mr. Petzold told me not to make the sportsmen appear glorious. He said, and I quote, 'Our readers have as much right to expect the truth to be told on our sports page as on any other page, and I find little that is heroic in the ability to strike with a length of wood a horsehide-covered sphere sufficiently hard to propel it a considerable distance. I mean, what is the point? Someone else must then run and retrieve the ball, must they not?'" Terry laughed. "I told him that *was* the point, but I'm not sure he understood. He doesn't have much regard for our national pastime."

"But are you satisfied to be a sports reporter?" David asked.

"It isn't what I want to do for the rest of my life," Terry admitted. "But it is helping me to learn the ropes. And I enjoy going to the games and being able to interview the players and coaches. It will do until something more interesting comes along. What about you? Are you going to work for your father?"

"Yes," David said. "I'm sure I will . . . though not right away. I'm not quite ready to start selling ladies' shirtwaists just yet."

"What *are* you ready for?"

"Travel."

"Travel? To where?"

"I think I'd like to go to Europe," David replied. "I'd like to see the 'old country' and maybe even look up a few relatives."

Terry grinned. "You mean, have yourself an adventure?" he asked.

"Yes, that's it exactly. I'd like to have an adventure."

CHAPTER FIVE

A fly landed on Eric McKenzie's face, and though he brushed it away, it returned. It came back a second time and a third, until finally the irritation of it penetrated Eric's sleep and he was forced to open his eyes.

For a moment he didn't know where he was. This certainly wasn't his bed and this certainly wasn't the bunkhouse. Then he remembered what had happened the night before, and he turned his head to see a woman in bed with him. She was on her back, her head was turned away from him, and the bed covers had slipped down from her left shoulder, allowing Eric to closely examine her exposed breast, which was lighted by a beam of sunlight stabbing between the bottom of the dark-green shade and the edge of the window sill.

Penny's position had pulled her breast nearly flat so that the globe of flesh Eric had seen last night—and had made a thorough exploration of—was now just a gentle curve that was topped by a taut nipple. Quietly, and gently enough so that Penny wasn't aware of what he was doing, Eric lifted off the cover, then rolled it all the way down to the bottom of the bed. With her body fully revealed, the youth was able to see in person, for the first time in his life, a totally nude woman. He lay with his elbow bent and his head resting on his hand, studying her for the longest time, when knocking sounded loudly on his door, making him jump.

"Eric! Eric, come on! Wake up and come out of there!" Marcus shouted. "Someone's done stole our poke!"

Springing out of bed, vaguely aware that Penny was now stirring, the youth flung on his clothes and bolted out the door, still buttoning his fly as he confronted his friends. "Are you sure, Marcus? Jake, he isn't kidding me, is he?"

Jake shook his head. "No, kid, he ain't. I got restless and went down to the livery to check on our horses, and I got no farther than one foot in the door when the liveryman told me we was robbed. So I turned right around and come back for you two." Grabbing Eric's elbow, he propelled him down the hallway. "Let's see what we can find out."

The threesome raced down the stairs, their boots clomping noisily on the stairs, and ran out of the saloon and up the street. Eric's head was spinning by the time they reached the stable.

The liveryman was standing in the doorway, obviously expecting them and looking defensive. "I can't tell you no more than I already told you," he said to Jake.

"Well, tell us again," Jake ordered.

"Like I said, I come in this morning and I seen clothes laying all scattered over the ground. At first I didn't know where they come from, then I seen them three small carpetbags and remembered that you fellas was carryin' 'em last night. They was open and empty and tossed over to the side there."

"Mister, I had one hundred and twenty-three dollars in that bag," Marcus growled. "And my pards here had that much or more. I thought you was supposed to look out for things that was left here with you!"

"Horses and saddles," the liveryman retorted. "This ain't no bank. You ought to've had more sense than to leave money here. What do you think that sign is for?" He pointed to the wall, which displayed a large painted sign declaring: THIS ESTABLISHMENT RESPONSIBLE FOR HORSE AND TACK ONLY! NO OTHER VALUABLES TO BE LEFT HERE!

"Eric, what's it say?" Jake asked.

Eric read the sign aloud, then groaned. "Oh, this is all my fault. I didn't see that sign last night."

"No, it ain't your fault," Jake said, putting his hand on the boy's shoulder and squeezing it gently. "Like the man said, we should've had more sense than to leave our poke here."

"Mister, it looks like we won't be boardin' our horses here after all," Marcus said. "So I reckon we'll just take 'em and our clothes and get on home."

"I'm sorry about that, fellas. I'm really sorry," the liveryman said. He waved toward the barn. "Go on back there and get your animals. They already ate this morning, but I won't charge you for it."

"Thanks," Jake said.

Dejected, the three cowboys reclaimed their clothes, saddled their horses, then rode out of town, heading north back to the Flying E.

"Some adventure we had," Jake said dispiritedly.

"Well, at least Eric had him a woman," Marcus remarked. "There's somethin' to be said for that."

"Yeah? Well, I hope she was good, Eric, 'cause she cost you over a hundred dollars. And, boy, I wouldn't give a hundred dollars to spend the night with Anna Held."

"Who?" Marcus asked.

"You know, that real good-lookin' woman we seen in that magazine about show gals," Jake said. "Eric was readin' it to us one day."

"Oh, yeah, I remember. Say, there was another one in there I liked," Marcus said. "What was her name? Maxine?"

"Maxine Elliot," Eric said.

"Yeah, she was some looker all right—but I wouldn't give a hundred dollars for her, either. Who wouldn't *you* give a hundred dollars for, Eric?"

"The President's daughter, Alice Roosevelt," Eric answered, caught up in the game. "She's beautiful."

"My, my, the President's daughter?" Jake asked. "Okay, so how about Ethel Barrymore?"

"Sarah Bernhardt?" Marcus asked.

"Lillie Langtry?" Jake added.

"Lillie Langtry?" Eric repeated disdainfully. "She's old!"

Marcus laughed. "So was that woman you was with last night, but I didn't see you turnin' *her* down."

Jake began laughing too. "And not only that, you paid over a hundred dollars for her."

"Hell, we all did!" Marcus said. "And there wasn't a pretty one in the bunch!"

Now all three were whooping with laughter, and they had to wipe away the tears. The laughter died down, but it didn't entirely disappear because one of them would say something, perhaps no more than a single word or even a funny groan, and they'd all start laughing again. Finally, after several moments of silence, Marcus spoke.

"I tell you what's botherin' me more than just about anythin' else," he said, "And that's goin' back to Mr. Ebersole with our tails tucked in between our legs, tellin' him we didn't get no farther than Newcastle before we got ourselves robbed like a bunch of green-horn tenderfoot dudes from the East."

"I'm not lookin' forward to facin' him with that neither," Jake said. "What about you, Eric?"

"Losing that money so easily, it makes it look as if we weren't grateful for the bonus he gave us," Eric answered.

"Well, to hell with it!" Marcus exploded. "I don't know about you boys, but I ain't going back like this!" He abruptly reined in his horse, and Eric and Jake stopped as well to keep from riding away from him. They looked back at him, their saddles creaking as they twisted around.

"Well, just what do you plan to do?" Jake asked.

"I set out to go to St. Louis to see the wonders, and by God I'm gonna see the wonders."

"You're gonna ride that horse all the way to St. Louis are you?" Jake asked. "'Cause if you are, you'll have its legs wore down to stumps by the time you get there."

"No, I'm not gonna ride this horse all the way to St. Louis," Marcus answered, mimicking Jake's question. "I'm goin' on a train, just like we planned." He smiled. "And what's more, I'm goin' first class."

"Well, if you got an idea about how to do that, I wish you'd tell Eric an' me, 'cause we'd sure like to go along with you."

"I was hopin' you'd say that," Marcus said. "'Cause, you see, I *do* have an idea. And it's gonna take all of us to do it." He grinned. "Boys, we're gonna hold us up a train."

"We're gonna *what*?" Jake exclaimed.

"We're gonna rob a train."

"Have you taken leave of what little sense you ever had?" Jake snapped.

"Don't worry about it. Hell, it'll be as easy as fallin' off a log," Marcus insisted.

"Easy? You're talkin' about holdin' up a train the way Jesse and Frank James and boys like that used to, right?" Jake asked.

"Yeah. The only difference is, the James boys did it so many times that they got real famous for doin' it. I only want us to do it one time . . . just to get the money back that we got stole from us. Hell, there ain't nobody knows us around here, and we ain't never done nothin' like this before, so there ain't no way they're ever gonna know who it was."

"Well, there's a good reason why we never done it before," Jake said. "Seems to me like folks could get theirselves killed doin' stuff like that."

"Not if we're real smart with it," Marcus countered.

"If we're real smart with it, we won't be doin' it in the first place," Jake argued.

"Eric, you ain't said nothin'," Marcus said. "What do you think about this idea?"

Eric had been listening in absolute shock. His friends were discussing the idea as if it were a real possibility, and he couldn't believe what he was hearing. "Marcus," Eric said quietly, "yesterday you accused me of being afraid whenever you started talking about women. I denied it, but I guess I was a little. But now you're talking about holding up a train, and let me tell you, I'm not just a little afraid, I am scared out of my mind! I hope you aren't serious!"

"Oh, yes, I'm serious all right. And I know how to do it so that nobody gets hurt—nobody on the train and especially not any one of us. I guarantee it!"

"And just how can you guarantee it?" Jake asked. "What is this plan you got?"

"Jake, why are you asking?" Eric asked. "I can't believe you're even asking about it. Don't listen to his plan! Can't you see that that'll just encourage him into thinking we're interested?"

Eric's only chance to diffuse this crazy notion was by appealing to Jake. Sure, Jake also sowed a fair share of wild oats, but he was generally more sensible than Marcus and had managed to keep Marcus out of serious trouble before. The fact that Jake now seemed to be showing some interest in Marcus's plan was more than frustrating to Eric, it was frightening.

"Well, I must say that I *am* interested," Jake replied. "At least enough to hear him out. Come on now, Eric. It won't hurt none just to listen to what he's got to say."

Eric let out a long sigh of defeat and turned his head away to stare off into the distance. Marcus, encouraged by Jake's interest, started his explanation, and Eric could tell by Marcus's words and tone of his voice that, in the cowboy's mind, the proposal had already won acceptance. Marcus was now beyond trying to talk Jake into doing it and was merely explaining how it would be done.

"It'll be a snap, Jake. All we got to do is pick us out a water tower that's not near a town or nothin'. Then we wait for a night train to come along. We don't even have to do nothin' to stop it, just wait for it to stop for water. It bein' a night train, all the passengers'll be asleep, so none of 'em will be any problem. Now, when the train stops, we knock on the door of the express car and get them to open the door. All them express cars got safes, and you got to figure that every one of 'em's got at least three or four hundred dollars in 'em. The folks inside the express car won't be expectin' nothin', 'cause train robbers don't generally bother with that little amount of money. And they ain't gonna put up no fight where they might get themselves hurt over somethin' that small. Hell, boys, it'll be easy as pie."

"You know, I've got to admit, Marcus, that sounds like somethin' we might be able to pull off," Jake said. "They say the simplest plans is the best. What do you think, Eric?"

"I think it's a simple plan, all right. And anyone who'd do it would have to *be* simple. Jake, will you listen to yourself? Do you know what you are saying?" Eric groaned.

"I'm sayin' maybe we ought to think about this," Jake replied.

"No."

"Eric, what's the harm? Who's going to get hurt? What's a few hundred dollars to a big railroad company?"

"Yeah, it's not like we was stealin' from some person," Marcus said. "I mean, this is a big company we're talkin' about, not some poor cowboy who's worked hard for his money. This ain't at all like what was done to us."

"I'm against it," Eric said, but even as he said the words, he knew he had already lost the argument.

"I'll tell you what, Eric. You don't have to go with us," Jake said by way of compromise. "Me and Marcus'll do it by ourselves. You can wait somewhere for us, and we'll come back with the money, and then we'll go to St. Louis, just like we planned."

"Yeah, that's all right with me," Marcus said. "As far as I'm concerned, you can get a full share just like you was in on it with us."

Eric felt a cold chill run down his back, and he took a long, slow breath.

"No," he finally said, speaking so quietly that they could barely hear him. "If you two are determined to do this . . . I'm going with you. I remember Mr. Ebersole's last words to us were, 'You boys take care of each other.' I don't see how we can all take care of each other if you're off robbing trains and I'm hiding in the dark somewhere."

Marcus grinned and slapped Eric on the back. "Well, now!" he said. "Well, now, that's the way it should be—all three of us together!"

"Who're them fellas in that story you was readin' to us one day?" Jake asked. "Them three that was all for one and one for all?"

"The Three Musketeers," Eric said.

"Yeah, that's us," Jake said. "The Three Musketeers!"

"St. Louis, lock up your women!" Marcus shouted. "Eric McKenzie is comin' your way!"

Though Eric felt with every bone in his body that this was wrong, he couldn't help but laugh at the antics of his two friends.

Had it not been for the vindictiveness of his grandfather's will, J. P. Winthrop would have been a member of New York society's Four Hundred, a figure supposedly stemming from the guest list of a ball given by Mrs. William Astor and one suggested by Ward McAllister as representing "everyone, and the only ones, worth knowing."

Mrs. Astor, who was always and only called Mrs. Astor, as if the name itself were a title, was the undisputed center of the Established Order. Working out from this center, like a series of concentric circles, were the other luminaries—the Vanderbilts, Guggenheims, Stillmans, Billingses, Warrens, and Mrs. Stuyvesant Fish. Though not truly royalty—which American democracy supposedly frowned on—they took on the trappings of royalty, and as a result anyone who had the ear of a personage of the inner court could move freely through that court.

One such person was Harry Lehr, a rather pasty-faced man in his forties who had an acid wit and rapier tongue. Lehr could deliver insults with remarkable skill, coming close to, but never quite stepping over, the line that would incur anyone's wrath—at least, no one who counted. His outlandish remarks titillated and delighted the guests at parties, and it became almost an honor to be on the receiving end of one of his barbs. His position as court jester had been made when he greeted a diamond-covered Mrs. Astor one day by saying, "My God, Mrs. Astor, you look like a walking chandelier."

For a moment there had been a gasp of horror. But Mrs. Astor found the remark funny and she laughed. Soon the entire party was convulsed with laughter, and Harry Lehr's position was assured.

J.P. did not belong to one of the inner circles, but, like Harry Lehr, he did enjoy a certain degree of entrée, partly due to the Winthrop name and partly due to his favored position with J. P. Morgan, and he had been one of those invited to the ball given by Mrs. Astor that opened the summer season. Ward McAllister's pronouncement notwithstanding, there were four hundred fifty, not four hundred, guests at the ball, and it tended to serve as a watershed for those who were members of society and those who weren't. Those who were found themselves on a constant barrage of guest lists, not the least reason being that party givers who were not themselves members of the Four Hundred could enhance their own standing by having as guests at their affairs people who were.

J.P. used his access to such affairs in his work for Morgan. A casual comment overheard at a morning coffee, an afternoon tea, or an evening ball would sometimes lead him to a piece of art, or even to an entire collection, suitable for Morgan's acquisition.

J.P. actually abhorred these social events, and he was convinced that everyone else found them just as dull. But the idea wasn't to be entertained, merely to be present and to be seen, so that one could be invited to another boring party and be seen . . . so that one could be invited to still another.

It was at one such afternoon tea at the Waldorf Astoria, given by Mrs. Astor, that J.P. caught sight of Lucinda Delacroix. She was sitting daintily on the edge of a chair, holding a demitasse and tilting her head just so, as if hanging on every word of the old gentleman speaking to her. A shaft of light stabbed in through one of the enormously high windows, catching Lucinda in its beam. It fired the gold in her hair, made sparkling emeralds of her eyes, and gave her skin the almost translucent glow of pink marble.

J.P. remembered the last time he had seen her—at the end of summer, four years ago, on the beach at Newport. He had been about to leave for St. Louis and Jefferson College, she for Europe and the Grand Tour. They had both been eighteen then, and they had been in love . . . or, at least, they thought they were. They had taken long walks together in the salt air, sat on porch swings and shared secrets, and slipped away in the blue-velvet nights of the endless garden parties of the summer to find sheltered, shadowy corners where they could neck.

Lucinda had promised always to love him, and J.P. had promised to write faithfully. They had tried to keep their promises, but J.P.'s letters sometimes took three months to catch up with her, and on those times he had been back in New York, she was gone. He had made friends in St. Louis, she had attended parties in Paris, they both grew older, and their magic summer slipped far behind them to become part of another time and another life.

As J.P. continued to stare at her, Lucinda put her

hand to the back of her neck, as if feeling unexpected heat there. Finally, she turned to look toward the source, and when she did, she saw him. For a fleeting moment there was confusion on her face, as if she was trying to sort out who this person was and why he was familiar. Then there was surprise and recognition. When J.P. saw that she remembered, he smiled and bowed his head. She returned his smile and raised her demitasse to him.

Several minutes passed before they found the opportunity to speak to each other. Bored, he was making a close examination of a potted fern when she came over to ask if he liked potted plants.

"Not particularly. They need remarkable attention, and they play host to a host of insects. If I had been God, I would have made the entire potted-plant world out of silk."

Lucinda laughed, and the sound of it—light and lyrical, like the tinkling of a wind chime—struck such a familiar chord that J.P. could almost believe the past four years had rolled back, and they were once again young and in love at Newport.

"I wrote," he said.

"Twice. And I answered, both times."

"A year later."

"The letters were six months in transit," Lucinda explained. "How was college?"

"Educational. And Europe?"

"Enlightening."

J.P. laughed. "My, but haven't we acquired a most sophisticated patter."

"Oh, quite," she replied, joining him in laughter. "Isn't this a wonderful party?"

"Lovely. I'm having a great time, aren't you?"

"Smashing."

"Do you think we could leave?" she asked.

"How about a ride through Central Park?"

"I'll just get my parasol."

Taking her by the elbow, J.P. escorted her across the ballroom floor and out to the cloakroom. Lucinda retrieved her wrap and her parasol, and the twosome hurried to the front door, determined to elude any fellow guests.

At a signal from the doorman, J.P.'s driver rolled up in the Winthrop carriage, an elegant brougham with a wreathed "W" in gold leaf on the door. The driver started to get down but J.P. held up his hand, indicating that he would see to himself and the lady.

"Just take us for a ride in the park," he instructed as the two of them slipped inside. The brougham had two facing red-velvet bench seats, and propriety might have suggested that they sit across from one another, but J.P. slipped into the same seat as Lucinda, and she made no protest.

Cobblestoned Fifth Avenue was crowded with vehicles, both commercial and private, and noisy with the clopping of hooves and the whir of iron-rimmed wheels. There was also the chug of gasoline engines as an occasional automobile picked its way through the traffic. Each time one of the autos overtook the carriage, the begoggled driver would squeeze the rubber bulb of his horn to announce his passage. Driving north, they passed under the long shadows of the three towering church steeples that dominated the avenue; Brick Presbyterian at Thirty-seventh Street, Fifth Avenue Baptist at Forty-sixth Street, and Collegiate Reform Church at Forty-eighth Street.

After entering Central Park they rode for nearly two hours, filling each other in on the previous four years. Lucinda told of all the castles she had visited in Europe and of the dizzying view of Paris from atop the Eiffel Tower. J.P. had her laughing at his stories about the quad quad and spellbound by his descriptions of the wonders on display at the World's Fair.

Dismissing the driver just before six, J.P. asked him to inform the two Mrs. Winthrops that J.P. wouldn't be back for dinner and that he would take a cab home. Then he and Lucinda found a small, intimate restaurant on Central Park South. After dinner they crossed the street and sat on a park bench under the trees and watched the city light up for the night.

"They say that Manhattan is so brightly lighted by electric lights at night that if one were standing on the moon, they could see the glow," J.P. said.

"I don't like all the electric lights," Lucinda complained. "They're so white they take the color away."

"I agree. There's something to be said for the soft light of kerosene and gas. Then one could always find a dark corner; now it's more difficult."

"And why would one want to find a dark corner?"

"Has it been so long?" J.P. asked. "Have you already forgotten the times we sought out the darkness?"

Lucinda smiled up at him. "Maybe I haven't," she replied, and as she spoke she moved so that her lips were just a breath away from his.

J.P. laid his fingers on Lucinda's cheek. Holding them there for a long moment, looking into her eyes, he could see again the beautiful, tempestuous girl of his youth; yet he could also see the world traveler, a young woman of social grace and charm who could sit on a sofa to discourse with Mrs. Astor not as a child summoned into her presence, but as a lady of the court.

"Well, are you going to kiss me, J.P.? Or are you going to sit there for the rest of the evening holding my head as if you were afraid it was about to tumble from my neck?"

J.P. moved his lips to hers. He felt her mouth open slightly, and, almost involuntarily it seemed, his own lips parted. The tip of her tongue darted in out of his mouth. It was cobra quick and shocking and thrilling, all at the same time. J.P. felt a charge of sexual excitation course through him like an electric jolt, and he opened his eyes in surprise.

"What . . . what kind of kiss was that?" he asked.

"Did you like it?"

"Like it? Yes! But it nearly drove me wild."

Lucinda laughed, again like the tinkling of a wind bell. "It's the first time I've been able to use it. My girlfriends in Paris told me about it. It's the way they kiss their lovers."

J.P. grinned. "As they say, *vive la France!*"

In a small house on the edge of the swamp just outside Sikeston, Missouri, Pearl Summers lay naked on the bed. Her right knee was raised, and she was looking past it toward the window. She had just finished making love, and a tiny drop of semen had fallen on her thigh. She could see it glistening in the soft light from the moon that hung in the midnight sky. Warm and contented and still coasting down from the eddying currents of pleasure she had experienced just moments before, she climbed out of bed and walked over to look through the window.

Her lover, Boyd McMullen, propped himself up on his elbow on the bed behind her. "What are you lookin' at out there, Pearl?" he asked.

"The fireflies," she answered. "There are as many of them down here as there are stars in the sky. A million golden lights, winking on and off. They're beautiful."

"They can't be no prettier than you are, just standin' there like that," he said.

"Come here. Look at them with me," she invited, smiling over at him.

Boyd got out of bed and padded barefoot across the wide planks of the cabin floor. The house, now deserted except when they used it as their hideaway, had once belonged to a lumberman, and every plank in it had been milled locally. Boyd looked through the window, and as he did so Pearl moved behind him and put her arms around him, pressing herself against his naked back. Her breasts were flat against him, her wiry public hair was pushed into his tight buttocks. She clamped her hands around his chest.

"That's why you wanted me over here," Boyd said. "You didn't want me to look at fireflies, you just wanted an excuse to get hold of me again."

"That's right," Pearl said, laughing. "You're my prisoner now. You can't get away, no matter how hard you try. This is a double-lock grip that I learned from Bob Canfield."

"What else did you learn from Bob Canfield?" Boyd asked.

"Oh, lots of things. He was my friend."

"Did you learn how to please a man from him?"

Boyd's words stung, and Pearl released her grip, then turned and walked back toward the bed.

"Why did you say that?" she asked, the tone of her voice reflecting the hurt and anger his comment had caused.

"I don't like Bob Canfield," Boyd replied, turning to look at her. "And when I think of him with you, I get jealous and angry."

"In the first place, he's never been with me," Pearl said. "And in the second place, what right do you have to be jealous? Are you planning on marrying me, Boyd McMullen?"

"Now, Pearl, why would you even ask that question?" Boyd asked. "You know how things are."

"No, I don't know how things are," Pearl replied. "Maybe you'd better tell me."

Pearl knew exactly how things were, but there was something about this moment, about this relationship, that made her want to push the issue to the extreme, to experience the pain of hearing the words that she knew he would have to say.

"Pearl, be fair."

"Be fair? Be fair?" Pearl repeated in an angry voice. "Suppose you just tell me about being fair, white boy. Tell me about having a hunger for more schooling than six grades, which is all a colored girl can get around here. Tell me about laying with your man at night in a deserted little swamp cabin, then mopping the floors at his bank the next day and not even being able to look at him when he happens to walk by."

"Pearl, my father owns that bank. Can you imagine what folks would think—what folks would *do*—if they knew that Boyd McMullen was sportin' with a colored girl? Why, I'd be the laughin'stock of this entire town.

Folks would take their money out in droves and put it in the Matthews bank."

"Sporting? Is that what you call this? Sporting?"

"Well, sure. What would *you* call it?"

"How about calling it love?" Pearl asked in a quiet, almost pleading, voice.

Boyd stuck out his hands toward her and let out a long sigh. "Now, wait a minute. Hold it. Just you hold on there. Would you please tell me where the hell you got the idea to call this love?"

"Where'd I get the idea? You told me, that's where I got the idea."

"You ought to know better than to believe everythin' a man tells you when he's layin' in bed with you. I mean, we've had some fun, sure, but in love? You're a big girl, Pearl, and a very pretty one. Do you think everyone who took you to bed loved you?"

"Since you are the only one who ever took me to bed, and since I thought you did, I would have to say yes," Pearl replied.

Boyd started to laugh, then stopped and stared at her for a long moment. "Pearl, you're serious, aren't you?"

Pearl's throat was too tight for her to speak now, so she just nodded her head.

"Well . . . well . . . goddamnit, girl! What the hell were you thinkin'? Were you thinkin' maybe you and I could get married, just like that?" He snapped his fingers. "Don't you understand? My father owns the bank in this town. One day, *I'm* going to own it, and then my son, and then his son, and then his son! I couldn't marry a charwoman, for God's sake. Even if you weren't a colored girl, even if you was white, we couldn't get married. I have to marry someone who has the proper social connections and breedin'."

"The proper breeding? Is that all that matters? The proper breeding? Well, why don't you go see Mr. D. L. Clayton? He breeds mules. I'm sure he could find you a suitable broodmare somewhere," Pearl said.

"I can see right now that I've already let this get too

far. I didn't have any idea anythin' like this would ever happen. I mean, I have friends who've taken their pleasure from colored girls, but, goddamnit, none of 'em ever started talking about love. I thought colored girls liked fuckin'. Get dressed, Pearl. Just get your ass dressed, goddamnit! I'm going to take you back home!"

"You don't really mean home, do you?" Pearl asked coldly. "What you really mean is you'll take me back to the head of the lane. Don't forget, your carriage can't be seen out at the Canfield place. Someone might start asking questions."

"It's where I've always dropped you," Boyd said.

"Yes, I know." Pearl reached for her dress and began to slip it on over her naked body. It was almost funny: Less than five minutes earlier she had been feeling warm and contented; now she felt cold and empty.

Boyd cleared his throat. "Uh, listen, Pearl, in light of all this, maybe it'd be better if I, uh, fired you. I mean, I'll pay you to the end of this week, but don't bother comin' into the bank anymore. It wouldn't be right. I'll get another cleanin' woman."

Livid, Pearl turned and faced him. "It's easy enough for you to get another cleaning woman, but what about me? Where do I get another job?"

"I'll help you find a place to work. I'll put the word out; I'll tell some of my friends about you."

"About how good I am in bed, you mean?"

"Well, if you didn't get the wrong idea about things, it probably wouldn't hurt to be nice to whoever your new boss is."

"No, sir, thank you just the same," Pearl snapped. She slipped into her shoes and started toward the door.

"Hey, wait a minute," Boyd said, hopping around on one foot while trying to get a shoe on the other. "I'm not dressed yet."

"Don't bother. I'm going to walk."

"But it's five miles, through the swamp."

"I don't care," Pearl called over her shoulder as she walked through the door.

"Pearl! Pearl, goddamnit, wait! Wait a minute, will you? You're takin' this all wrong!"

"You go to hell, Boyd McMullen!" Pearl shouted as she ran toward the edge of the swamp.

It took Pearl over two hours to reach home, making her way by the light of the moon and fueled by anger and shame. When she finally walked across the front yard of her house, her feet hurting and her arms and neck covered with mosquito bites, she felt great relief. Suddenly she froze in fear. Something moved in the dark shadows on the porch.

"Pearl?" her mother's voice called softly into the night. "Pearl, is that you?"

"Mama?" She began to breathe again. "Mama, what are you doing sitting out here on the porch in the middle of the night?"

"No, girl, I'm the mama. I'm the one asks the questions. Now, what're you doin' comin' home at this time? You've been up to no good, I can tell that."

"Oh, Mama," Pearl began. Then she took a deep breath, and though she tried to hold the crying back, she couldn't. The sobs spilled over, and the harder she tried to stop, the harder she cried.

Clemmie Summers held her arms open and Pearl rushed to her, sinking to her knees in front of the rocking chair and letting her mother take her into her arms. Clemmie held her close and rocked her back and forth, just as she had when Pearl was a baby, patting her gently on the back and clucking soothingly at her.

When Pearl's crying subsided, her mother spoke. "I know it's about a man, darlin'. There ain't nothin' can make a grown woman cry like this except a man. But what I don't know is who?"

"It's Boyd, Mama," Pearl said softly.

"Boyd? Baby, I don't reckon I know anyone named Boyd."

"Boyd McMullen, Mama."

"Boyd McMullen? No, I don't reckon—" Suddenly Mrs. Summers gasped and held Pearl at arm's length so she could look her straight in the eye. "Lord, child! You ain't been layin' with some white boy, have you?"

"Yes, Mama, I have," Pearl murmured.

"Girl, are you pregnant?"

"No, Mama. I'm not pregnant."

"Thank the Lord for that." She pulled Pearl back to her bosom and began rocking her again. "Child, who else knows about this?"

"I don't know," Pearl answered. "Just Boyd, I guess."

"Well, he ain't likely to go blabberin' around that he's been layin' with a colored girl, and that's a good thing, because we sure don't want your papa to find out. He can't ever know nothin' about this, baby. You hear me? Your papa can't ever know nothin' about it."

"All right," Pearl agreed.

"And to make sure he don't ever find out, we've got to get you out of here."

"How? And where will I go?"

"Child, maybe the Lord's smiled down on you after all. Mr. Bob and young Billy are goin' to St. Louis, and they want to take that fool automobile instead of the train. They're leavin' tomorrow mornin', and your papa is goin' to be drivin' that machine for them."

"But what does that have to do with me?"

"Just today Mr. Bob asked your papa, did he think you'd like to go to St. Louis and work as a housekeeper for the man that's the head of that college where he went for his schoolin'."

"What did Papa answer?"

"He said you was workin' for Mr. McMullen at the bank." Pearl's mother chuckled. "Then Mr. Bob, he said, 'Pearl ain't goin' to be satisfied workin' down there. She's smarter than any one of them McMullens.'"

"Bobby said that?"

"Girl, where you get off callin' him Bobby? He's Mr. Bob to you," her mother said sharply.

"Mama, we were raised together," Pearl protested.

"He always called me Pearl, I always called him Bobby."

"It wouldn't be smart for you to do that now."

"I can't call him Mr. Bob. I'd feel like a hypocrite. Suppose I call him Mr. Canfield?"

"A hypocrite? Lord, baby, you do know some words. But, I reckon it would be all right if you call him Mr. Canfield." She brushed Pearl's hair back from her face, then used her apron to dry Pearl's tears. "I told your papa I thought you ought to take the job the gentleman in St. Louis is offerin'," she said. "That why I'm sittin' up like this, waitin' for you to come home. I won't like it, my baby bein' so far from me, but you're too smart to stay here. It ain't good for a colored girl to be as smart as you . . . not in these parts and in these times. So I think you should go to St. Louis and take that job."

"Oh, Mama!" Pearl exclaimed, smiling. "Oh, Mama, I think going to St. Louis would be the most wonderful thing that could ever happen to me!"

"Then you'll go?"

"Oh, yes, Mama! Yes, I'll go!"

The older woman let out a long sigh, then patted her daughter a couple of times on the head before she stood up. "Your papa tells me it's going to be a hard trip. It ain't goin' to be like ridin' a train. They've got to find roads for that machine, and that might be hard. So, I reckon you'd best be tryin' to get a little rest."

"But I'll have to pack my things," Pearl argued.

"I'll pack them for you, darlin'," her mother said. "I won't be gettin' any sleep this night, anyway. I was plannin' on gettin' up early enough to fry up some chicken and make some potato salad and baked beans for you all to take in a basket. Don't know where colored folks'd get a chance to eat, makin' a trip like that. And young Billy, he said why don't I just make enough for everybody?" She chuckled. "That boy sure does like my baked beans."

Pearl gave her mother a long hug. Finally she found the words to speak. "Mama, I love you. There's no daughter on this earth ever loved her mother more than

I love you. And I'll never be able to repay you for all the things you've done for me."

"Baby, you just try and make a fine life for yourself up there in that big city. That's all the payin' back your mama is ever gonna want or need."

CHAPTER
SIX

The mournful whistle of the approaching train brought home to Eric McKenzie exactly what he and his two friends were about to do as they sat their horses in a ditch at the bottom of the track bed. Under dripping trees, in the dark of night, with a cold rain spitting in his face, Eric tried one more time to talk the other two out of it.

"Listen, Marcus, Jake, I don't think we've considered the real consequences of this," he said. "We've had some fun thinking about it, sure, but it . . . it'll mark us as outlaws for the rest of our lives."

"Not if we don't ever do it no more," Marcus insisted.

"Eric, it's a little late to be bringin' that up now, don't you think?" Jake said. "You should have told us before if you wasn't in favor of doin' this."

"Goddamnit, Jake, I've been telling you from the moment Marcus came up with this crazy scheme."

"And we told *you* that you don't have to go through with it," Marcus said. "Now, if you're all that squeamish, why don't you just ride over there in the dark and see if you can't find yourself a sugar tit or somethin' to suck on while me and Jake pull the job?"

"Go easy on him, Marcus. He's just a kid," Jake said gently. "It's all right, Eric. If you don't want to do it, you don't have to."

Eric sighed. "I reckon I'll go through with it," he said resolutely.

"You sure?" Jake asked. "'Cause we can't have no more doubts now. It's too late for that. We're down to the nut cuttin'."

"I'm sure."

"Good man," Jake responded, and he reached over to squeeze Eric on the shoulder. "See there, Marcus. He's never let us down before; we ain't gonna have no worries with him."

"Never thought we would have," Marcus stated. "Always did say Eric was the best man on the Flying E, and that includes you and me."

The loudness of the whistle indicated the train was much closer now, and the steadily increasing noise made Eric's horse stamp its foot restlessly. Eric reached down to quiet his animal.

"Okay, boys, here she comes," Marcus said, the excitement of the moment creeping into his voice. He laughed. "Ain't we somethin'? Bet them James boys never pulled off a slicker holdup."

"We ain't pulled it off yet," Jake reminded him.

"We're about to. Pull your kerchief up over your nose and let's do it." Marcus said.

Eric stood up in the stirrups of his saddle and looked toward the approaching train. The headlamp was in view, its beam looking like a long, yellow finger stabbing the steadily falling rain and the puffing steam sounding like the gasps of some fire-breathing monster. As if to add to the illusion, glowing sparks were whipped away by the black smoke cloud that billowed up into the wet night sky.

"Get your guns out," Marcus ordered. "Soon as it stops for water, we'll go up and rap on the door of the express car. In five minutes we'll be ridin' away from here with three, maybe four hundred dollars in our poke."

Vented steam and squeaking metal sounded as the engineer began braking the train. Finally it rumbled and rattled to a halt, with the tender poised just below the water tank. All the coach cars were dark, the passengers undoubtedly asleep just as Marcus had said they would be. That was good. Even though Eric had no experience in robbing a train—or anything else—he was intuitive enough to realize that the greatest danger would come from the unexpected, and were the passengers awake, the unexpected could happen at any time.

"We didn't make it here none too soon," Eric heard the fireman tell the engineer as the crewman crawled out onto the tender. "I'll bet you there ain't enough water left in this tank to work up a good spit." The lid banged hollowly as the fireman dropped it open, then swung the spout over.

Eric shivered, knowing it was not from cold.

"Here we go, boys," Marcus whispered. "Eric, you stay down here at the bottom of this ditch while me and Jake ride up and bang on the door. Soon as they open it, you fire a shot off in the air. That'll make 'em think we got maybe five or ten more out here in the dark. They'll probably pee in their pants, but you can bet they'll give us the money bag. I'll toss it down to you, you throw a few more shots in the air to keep them scared, and then we'll get the hell out here." He grinned. "Simple."

Eric nodded, and Jake and Marcus slowly rode their mounts up to the top of the berm, making as little noise as possible. Down at the bottom of the gravel-covered embankment, Eric pointed his pistol straight up in the air and waited, his hand sweating.

Suddenly he heard Marcus rap sharply on the door of the express car and call, "Hey! Hey, open up in there!"

Eric glanced quickly toward the tender, but it was obvious that the fireman had heard nothing. The man's attention was on the water pouring into the tender, making such a roar that it covered all other sounds. And the engineer in the cab, surrounded by escaping steam and popping safety valves, seemed to be taking a catnap, as oblivious to the drama being played out below him as was the fireman.

The pulse pounding in Eric's ears, he watched as the express-car door slid open, a narrow wedge of light growing to a large gap. A man appeared in the gap and looked outside. "What is it? What do you want?" he called into the darkness.

"Okay, let her go!" Marcus shouted, and Eric pulled the trigger. The flash of light from the blast painted the side of the express car orange, and the vivid scene seemed to be frozen in Eric's brain for his most minute inspection.

"Throw down your money!" Marcus called.

"My God, it's a holdup!" the man in the doorway shouted. "How did they know?"

"Drop!" a loud voice called from farther back inside the car. The man in the doorway belly flopped to the floor.

"What the hell is—" Marcus started to yell, but the loud roar and bright flash of a shotgun interrupted him. Eric saw Marcus tumble backward out of his saddle. His face was shot away.

"Oh, Marcus! Oh, my God!" Eric shouted in a voice very nearly a scream.

"Let's get out of here!" Jake yelled. He managed to get his horse turned just before the second shotgun blast. With that blast came a spray of blood, bone chips, and brain matter, exploding from Jake's head as he went down.

Terrified almost to the point of hysteria, Eric jerked his horse around and kicked it. The horse, as frightened by the shots as Eric, needed no encouragement and raced toward the rear of the train.

"There's another one and he's gettin' away!" somebody shouted. "Shoot 'im, shoot 'im! Shoot the son of a bitch!"

"I used up both barrels! I gotta reload!"

"Oh, Jesus, Jesus, Jesus!" Eric heard himself crying

out, but if asked, he couldn't have said if it was a prayer or an oath. He heard a couple of windows sliding open on the train, then a shot—not a shotgun, but a pistol. He didn't know if it was one of the guards in the express car or a passenger who happened to be armed and wanted in on the action.

When Eric reached the end of the train, he kept going. The train was westbound, and Eric was heading east. He was reasonably sure the guards wouldn't have horses on board the train, but he couldn't take the chance. He kept his mount going at a full gallop for as long as he could to make certain that, if the trainmen did have horses, he would have some distance on them before they managed to get going.

Several miles farther, when the train was well out of sight, he pulled his horse into a dense copse of trees and let it catch its breath. He could feel the animal's pulse pounding fiercely, and he was afraid that its heart might burst. Swinging down from the saddle, the youth began walking the horse around to cool it down, talking soothingly to it all the while.

"You got me out of there," he said. "You got me out of there. Good boy, good boy."

With his own immediate danger over, Eric's thoughts went to Jake and Marcus, both of them lying back there with half their heads blown away.

"It wasn't supposed to be like this!" he shouted at the top of his voice. "Dammit, Marcus! Damn you to hell!" Then he repeated quietly, "It wasn't supposed to be like this." He put his arms around his horse's neck. "We were going to St. Louis," he said, his voice breaking. "That's all we were going to do."

Eric sank to his knees, then fell onto his stomach. Cradling his head on his arms, he sobbed ceaselessly. Finally, his energy spent, he tucked his legs up, curled into a ball like a puppy, and fell asleep.

Because he, Marcus, and Jake had been to Newcastle just a couple of days ago, Eric was afraid he'd be recognized there if he went back, so when he started riding again early the next morning, he continued eastward. The next town east was Wall, which, like Newcastle, was a railroad town, but Wall wasn't much larger than Oshoto. Eric's horse was limping by the time he rode into town, and when he stopped at the livery, the stable man walked out to take a look at the animal.

"Got problems with your horse, son?"

"Yes, sir," Eric answered. "And I've got a long trip, too. I, uh, I'm heading up near Pierre, to see my folks."

"Let me take a look here," the hostler said, picking up the horse's lame foot. "You say you got folks near Pierre? I used to live over that way. What's your name?"

"Eric—" Eric started to give his last name; then, afraid that the law might somehow know his name by now, he decided to come up with a new one. But his mind was virtually blank, and the only thing he could think of was Twain, as in Mark Twain. "Twain," he finally said; then, because he was afraid that wouldn't sound right, he added, "—bough."

"Beg your pardon?"

"Twainbough," Eric said. "My name is Eric Twainbough."

"Hmm. Don't reckon I ever knew no Twainboughs. Interestin' name, though." The hostler smiled. "Kind of classy soundin', ain't it?"

"Yes," Eric said. "I've always liked it."

"Well, Eric, there ain't nothin' wrong with your horse except he's got hisself a stone bruise. Three, maybe four days without ridin' him and he'll be all right."

"Three or four days? I can't wait three or four days."

"Why not? Someone in your family bad sick?"

"Uh, no. It's, uh, it's my mom's birthday."

"Well, tell you what," the liveryman said, looking at the horse. "I don't have no horses for sale right now, but there's a fella owns a ranch about five miles north of here. I'll give you fifty dollars for this one; maybe you can find one for that up there."

"It isn't my horse to sell," Eric said. "He belongs to Mr. Ebersole, the man I work for back in Oshoto."

"Well, then, looks like you got no choice but to wait around."

"What will you give me for my tack?"

"Hmm," the liveryman said, stroking his chin. "It's a workin' saddle, nothin' fancy 'bout it. But I can see you been takin' good care of it. I guess I could go thirty-five dollars."

"Make it twenty-five," Eric said, "and see that this horse gets back to Mr. Ebersole, and we have a deal."

"Done," the man said. "Come on inside and I'll count out the money."

As Eric waited for his money, a heavyset, gray-haired man came into the livery office. He was wearing a town constable's badge.

"Hello, Charley," the liveryman said. "Be right with you."

"Hello, Phil. Who's this young fella?" the constable asked.

"His name is Twainbough," Phil said. "Me and him is doin' a little business."

"Where you from, boy?"

"He's from up near Pierre way," Phil answered for him. "Why you askin' so many questions? I ain't ever seen you so curious."

"Yeah, well, maybe you don't know, but the west-bound was held up last night," the lawman said. "Or, I reckon I should say some fellas *tried* to hold it up. Two of them got theirselves killed, an' another one got away."

"Tried to hold up the train, did they? What'd make 'em do such a fool thing like that?"

Charley chuckled. "Could be they thought they were goin' to get away with the half-million dollars the train was carryin'."

"A half-million dollars?" Eric gasped.

"Yep, a half-million," Charley answered. "That's

sure a lot of money, ain't it? I reckon that's temptin' enough for a man to think about. But when you figure how many guards is watchin' over a money shipment like that, you got to know it ain't goin' to be easy."

"You said two of them was killed," Phil said. "Who was they?"

"Don't nobody know, yet," the constable replied. "From the way they were dressed and the calluses on their hands and all, they appear to be just ordinary workin' cowboys. That's what's got everyone so confused. How did them cowboys find out about the half-million-dollar money shipment? Nobody was supposed to know. That shipment was so secret that the railroad didn't even tell any of the law about it."

"No idea at all who it was?" Phil asked again.

Charley shook his head. "Nope, and it's goin' to be hard to identify 'em. They was both shot at near point-blank range in the head with a shotgun. You got any idea what a load of double-aught ten-gauge shot can do to a man's head from ten feet?"

Eric turned away from the two men and hurried quickly over to a stall, where he started throwing up.

"Boy? Boy, are you all right?" the constable called to him.

"I reckon this kind of talk could make some folks a mite queasy," Phil suggested.

"Yeah, I reckon it could," Charley said. "Oh, one thing. Somebody in the car thought they heard the robber that was out in the dark call one of the others Marcus. You know anybody by that name?"

"No, can't say as I do," Phil said.

"Well, they've sent wires out to lawmen all over the state, askin' us to check with the ranchers in our neighborhood to see if they had a cowboy named Marcus workin' for 'em, and if he's missin' now. If he is, then we'll likely have our man, and the rancher could probably identify the other one that was killed and the one that got away. That's why I'm here, Phil. I need to borrow your buggy to ride out to the ranches. My lumbago's been actin' up so bad lately that there ain't no way I can ride my horse."

"Sure thing, Charley. Let me get this boy his money and I'll be right with you. Eric?" he called.

Eric, who was still standing in the stall, was fighting back tears. He didn't look around when Phil called, so Phil walked over to him.

"Here's your money."

"Thanks."

"Son, are you all right? Your eyes is waterin' up somethin' awful."

Eric forced a grin. "It's because I threw up," he said. "My eyes always water when that happens. I'm sorry. You must think I'm just a big baby, acting like this."

"Yeah, well, if you ask me, the constable is an old coot, comin' aroun' talkin' like that in front of decent folks. You got nothin' to be ashamed of, son. There ain't no decent folk likes to hear about blood and gore like that." He put his hand on Eric's shoulder. "You take this money and you go on to your mama's birthday and have a nice time. I'll get the horse back to your Mr. Ebersole for you."

"Thank you," Eric said. He stuck the money in his jeans pocket, then, with a smile toward the constable, headed out of the stable.

"Hey! How you plannin' on gettin' to Pierre?" Phil called. "It's a good hundred miles."

"I'll walk," Eric answered over his shoulder as he stepped outside. He thought quickly, then added, "I can make it in the same three or four days I'd be waiting for my horse to heal, so this way I'll be home before I'd have even gotten started."

In truth, Eric had no intention of going to Pierre at all, saying that merely to mask his real intentions. He walked only as far as the depot and, when nobody was looking, hid in an empty boxcar standing on a side track.

When an eastbound freight finally came through on the main track at nine o'clock that evening, Eric climbed down from his hiding place and darted across the gravel and rails of the yard. Running alongside the train, he matched his speed to that of the slow-moving freight until an empty boxcar with a partly open door came by. He hopped up onto it, balanced there for a while with his chest inside the dark car and his legs dangling outside.

"Boy, come in or get out," a voice from the shadowy interior said. "Don't just hang there."

The big green touring car came rather rapidly over the top of the hill. Then its rear two wheels locked and it went into a skid as George Summers applied the brakes, the sudden stop necessitated by the fact that the road they'd been following abruptly ended, cut off by a barbed-wire fence backed by a low stone wall.

"Damn!" Bob Canfield exclaimed. "What the hell happened to the road? Look at that! It just disappeared!"

Bob was riding in the front passenger seat beside George, and like George, he was wearing goggles. Billy Canfield was seated on one of the two rear-facing jumpseats, though he was on his knees facing forward, as he had been for most of the trip. Pearl Summers had taken advantage of having the entire back seat to herself and stretched out, falling asleep, though the sudden stop woke her.

"What is it?" she asked. "Are we there?" She sat up and began rubbing her eyes.

The engine popped and sputtered in protest as George throttled it back. Bob stood up, raised his goggles, then looked forward over the windshield and said again, "Damn!"

"Is something wrong?" Pearl asked.

"Pearl, you've been asleep for more than two hours," Billy scolded, turning back toward her. "How can you sleep through all the excitement? You're missing all the fun."

Pearl looked over the automobile's hood. On the far side of the fence-and-wall barricade, the muddy ground of a large pasture had been chewed up by the hooves of a medium-sized herd of cattle that were placidly standing and watching the new arrivals. To the right was a steeply rising hill and to the left a swiftly flowing stream. Between the stream and the car orange and black monarch butterflies fluttered through a stand of even brighter orange daylilies, while all around them grasshoppers worked the dusty weeds. One jumped into the car and landed on Pearl. Picking it off and tossing it back, she remarked dryly, "Yes, I can see some of the fun I've been missing."

"Billy, don't you be worrying about what Pearl is missing," Bob said. "Just hand me the map. I know we didn't take a wrong turn anywhere."

"It's not a real map," Billy reminded him, pulling the folded-over paper from the pouch on the back of the seat and handing it up to his older brother.

"Well, it's as much a map as I could come up with," Bob replied. "You may as well turn off the motor, George. We might be here a while."

The ignition died with a final wheeze and bang as Bob stepped down from the car. He spread the map open on the left front fender, and when a breeze threatened to blow the map away, Bob picked up a couple of egg-sized rocks and held the paper down with them.

"George, why don't you have a look at this map with me, and let's see what we can figure out," Bob suggested. When George climbed out from behind the wheel and walked over to examine the map, Bob pointed to their route with his finger. "Now, according to the map, the road should continue right through this farm, but as it's plain to see, it doesn't."

"Are we lost?" Pearl asked anxiously. She, too, had stepped out of the car and was alternately picking off the grasshoppers and smoothing the wrinkles from her dress.

"No, I wouldn't say we're lost," Bob said. He smiled at her. "When you're lost, you don't know where you are. I know exactly where we are."

"Where are we?" Pearl asked.

"Why, we're right here," Bob replied, holding his arm up and waving it around. The others laughed. Bob looked back at the map. "What I *would* like to know, though, is where's the road? According to the railroad people who made up the map, this road should continue, uninterrupted, all the way to Perryville."

"Mr. Bob, would you be wantin' me to see if I can find a farmhouse somewhere close by and ask for some directions?" George asked.

"No, you'd better stay here with the machine. I'll go see what I can find out. Why don't you look after the car? Maybe we ought to put some more water in the fuel tank or something."

"Ha!" Billy laughed. "That shows how much you know. You don't put water in the fuel tank, Bob; you put gasoline in the fuel tank. I'm sure glad *you* aren't driving."

"Well, I know you put water somewhere," Bob replied, winking at George to show that he'd been teasing Billy.

"You put it in the radiator, don't you, George?" Billy said.

"That's right," George agreed, chuckling. He took a bucket from the back of the car and handed it to Billy. "But Mr. Bob is right about maybe we need some. You want to walk down to that creek and get it? And while you're gettin' the water, I'll check on the oil and gasoline."

"George, if we need some gasoline, may I put it in?" Billy asked.

"I reckon you can, if you want to. But I purely hope we don't need any. We only got ten extra gallons of gas and five extra quarts of oil, and I don't know where we might get some more before we get to where we're goin'."

"Are we in danger of running out?" Bob asked.

"I don't rightly know, Mr. Bob," George admitted. "This automobile can make twenty miles to the gallon of gasoline and forty miles to the quart of oil. As the crow flies, I make it to be a hundred and fifty miles from

Sikeston to St. Louis. That means with what we've already got in the tank, we ought to have plenty of fuel. But maybe you've taken notice of the fact that we ain't exactly goin' to St. Louis the way a crow flies."

Bob laughed. "Yes, now that you mention it, I guess I did notice," he said. He took off his duster and goggles and laid them on the front seat of the car. "I'd better get going. I won't be finding anyone just standing around here."

"Bobby, would you like—" Pearl began before looking at the ground in embarrassment. She felt her father's eyes boring into her. "I mean Mr. Canfield," Pearl corrected, "would you like me to spread out our lunch? It's about time to eat."

"Sure," Bob said, smiling easily. "If you can find us a nice shade tree with no ants."

"I'll go find us a place, Pearl, soon as I put water in the radiator," Billy offered, heading toward the stream.

"Thank you, Billy," she called after him.

"And I'll be back as quickly as I can," Bob said, starting down the road. "I saw a house off to the left not too far back."

George raised the louvered side panel of the car's hood and began checking the engine. Several minutes had passed when he called over to his daughter, who was getting a red-and-white checkered tablecloth out of a wicker basket.

"Pearl?"

"Yes, Papa?" Pearl asked, looking up.

"You goin' to have to watch things like that when you're in St. Louis, girl."

"Things like what, Papa?"

He nodded toward Bob Canfield, now well out of earshot. "Things like callin' Mr. Bob, Bobby."

She sighed. "We grew up together, Papa. I always called him Bobby."

"And now you're callin' Billy, Billy. That's all right, because he's just a child. But Mr. Bob is a full-grown man now."

"And I'm a full-grown woman."

George looked at his daughter. "You may be a full-grown woman, darlin', but you're still colored. You say things like this around the wrong white man, he's goin' to be thinkin' you're nothin' but an uppity nigger. You'll get fired quicker than spit dryin' on a hot stove."

"I'm sorry, Papa. It just slipped out."

"Hand me that box of wrenches," George said, and when Pearl brought the box over to him, he selected a tool, then began tightening nuts and bolts on the engine. "It don't matter much with Mr. Bob, or with any of the Canfields for that matter," George said as he worked at tightening down the valve cover. "They're good white folk who treat the coloreds decent. But you don't know nothin' about this man you'll be workin' for in St. Louis, so you got to be extra careful, you hear me, girl?"

"I hear you, Papa," Pearl said.

"Ouch!" The wrench had slipped off a nut, and George had slammed his hand hard against the engine block. He pulled his handout and looked at the blood on the skinned knuckles.

"Here," Pearl said. "I'll walk down to the creek and wet a cloth so I can clean that off for you."

"No need for you to bother yourself with it. It ain't nothin'," George said.

"Papa, you don't want to get dirt and grease in the cut," Pearl said. "The wound will get infected."

"Infected? What's that mean? I never heard that word before."

Pearl laughed. "Unfortunately, until recently a lot of *doctors* had never heard the word, either," she said. "People used to get sick and die and doctors didn't know why. Then they found out about infection, which is something that happens when a wound gets dirty."

She started down toward the stream when her father's voice called after her, scoffing, "Girl, if you think I'm goin' to die from a little old cut on the knuckles, you've been readin' too much."

Pearl had only gone several yards when she met

Billy coming back from the stream, and as he was already carrying a pail of water, she dipped her cloth into it, explaining why, and then walked back with him toward the car.

Billy came around to the side of the Packard and asked, "Are you okay, George?"

"I'm fine," George answered. "I scraped my knuckles, and this girl is just carryin' on about it, that's all."

"Yeah," Billy said, pouring the water into the radiator. "Women are like that—always wanting to tend to you and do for you and such things. I've noticed that."

Pearl chuckled. "You've noticed that, have you, Billy, in all your vast experience with women?"

"Yep," Billy said, unaware he was being teased. "George, do we need any gas?"

"No, it's fine."

"Shoot. I wanted to put some in. Well, in that case, I'm going to go look for a place where we can eat," the boy announced, and he put the bucket down and hurried off again.

Pearl continued to clean her father's wound, and as she worked on it, she could feel her father studying her closely. She looked up at him. "Papa?"

George put his other hand on her cheek. "Pearl," he said in a soft voice, "I don't know how the Lord came to bless me with such a beautiful child. You're the most beautiful thing I've ever seen. And the smartest, too. Your mama and me, we haven't always understood you, but we always loved you."

"I know you have, Papa," Pearl said, putting her hand on top of her father's. "And I've always felt very special because of it."

"I got to tell you, though, that I was mighty surprised that your mama agreed to let you go to St. Louis to take that job. I was sure she'd be comin' up with all sorts of reasons to keep you home with us. But she was the one who figured it'd be good for you to go."

Pearl said nothing, but she kissed her father's hand.

"You sure now, girl, this is somethin' you're wantin'

to do?" George went on. "You truly do want to go to St. Louis to live?"

"Yes, Papa." She smiled at him. "I truly do want to go to St. Louis to live. And it doesn't mean I don't love you and Mama or that I'm tired of living with you. It's just that, well, *St. Louis*, Papa! Think of all the wonderful things there are in a city like that. Even for a colored girl."

George sighed. "And I can't think of nothin' more wonderful than what we've got back home," he said. "Well, I guess that's the difference 'tween us. There's nothin' in the city that would interest me—and there's nothin' in the swamp that can hold you."

"Of course there is, Papa. You and Mama could hold me."

"Girl, we would never do that. Why, that wouldn't be no more right than a mama robin tryin' to hold her baby birds in the nest. That's God's way of things, Pearl. When it's time for little ones to leave, there's nobody who's got the right to stop them from goin'."

"Hey! I found the perfect spot for our picnic!" Billy suddenly and loudly called, and Pearl and George turned to watch him race through the meadow. "Come on," he said, panting, when he had reached them. "I'm starving."

The boy had found a nice, level, shaded place alongside the stream. By the time Pearl had the lunch spread out for them, Bob had returned.

"This is where we're supposed to be, all right," Bob explained. He pointed to the stream. "You see that cypress up there? Well, just on the other side of it is where we an ford the stream. Then we have to follow alongside the fence until we get to a red barn that's about a half-mile farther. We can't see it from here because it's just over that rise."

"Then what?" Billy asked, shoving a spoonful of baked beans into his mouth. The barbecue sauce Pearl's mother had used on the beans was running down Billy's chin, and Pearl automatically reached over with her napkin to wipe his face.

"Then we open the door and go right through the barn," Bob said, "literally. This farm belongs to a Mr. Abernathy. He allows the county to run a road across his land, but he charges a toll to people who use it. It's going to cost us a nickel to get across. Seems Abernathy has a brother on the country road commission, and they arranged to route the road through here and through the barn." Bob laughed. "The fella who told me about it said he thinks it's awful, but I got the feeling he wouldn't think it quite so awful if the road had gone through *his* farm and *he* could have charged us a nickel."

A short while later, with the lunch eaten and the picnic basket put away, the travelers restarted the Packard and continued their trip. When they reached Mr. Abernathy's barn door, George squeezed the bulb on the horn, and a moment later a tall, thin man with white hair and a long white beard opened the door of the barn and waved them in. When they were inside, he signaled for them to stop, then closed the door behind them.

He walked over to the car and peered at Bob. "It'll be costin' you a five-cent piece to come through here."

"Yes, sir, Mr. Abernathy, so we've been informed," Bob said, handing the coin over.

Abernathy walked over to a table and dropped the nickel into an empty cigar box that he now used for this purpose. He scribbled something on a piece of paper, then brought the paper back and handed it to Bob.

"Give this to my boy when you go out the far side of the pasture," he said. "It's my marker, showin' that you paid. That way he won't try and charge you again."

"All right, thank you."

"Don't recollect that I ever seen you folks before," Abernathy said, stroking his beard and looking at them curiously. "You from these parts? Cape Girardeau, maybe?"

"A little farther south. Sikeston."

"That's a fact? That's a pretty far piece to be comin' in an automobile, ain't it? Most folks from down that way comes by train when they come this far."

"I suppose that's true," Bob agreed.

"We're goin' to St. Louis to see the World's Fair," Billy called as Abernathy walked to the far wall of the barn and opened the door out.

"I've heard it's really somethin'," the farmer called back. "I ain't had time for it myself. Got a good-sized herd needs tendin'. By the way, don't hit none of them. If they come too close, blow that horn at them. That generally scares 'em away."

"Thanks," Bob said. "Okay, George, let's go." George opened the throttle, and, with the engine popping loudly, they exited the barn and began bouncing out across Mr. Abernathy's open pasture.

The cows caused no trouble, but an hour and a half later they encountered a mud puddle in the middle of the road that was wheel-hub deep. The car had no sooner stalled in the middle of the quagmire when a farmer showed up with a team of mules. After some negotiation the farmer agreed to pull the car free for a quarter.

"Boy," Billy said after they were under way again. "We were sure lucky that farmer came along with that team when he did."

Bob laughed. "That wasn't luck."

"What do you mean it wasn't luck?"

"You figure it out."

"George, what does he mean it wasn't luck?"

George chuckled. "What he means, boy, is that that farmer probably put that hole there and keeps it full of water. He probably tends to that old hole like it was a garden or somethin'."

"Oh," Billy said. "Oh!" he then repeated, George's meaning apparently dawning on him. "He does that on purpose! He wants autos to get stuck so folks'll give him money for him to pull them out."

"You got it, Billy," Bob said.

"Well, that's . . . that's not fair," Billy complained.

Bob turned around and looked at his little brother.

"Well, as Loomis Booker, a friend of mine at college, once told me, life isn't fair," he said, then turned back.

"What does that mean?"

"Someday you'll find out, Billy," Pearl said gently. "And when you do, it'll be one of the most important lessons you'll ever learn."

CHAPTER SEVEN

It was late afternoon, and J. P. Winthrop was busy at work in his office at the Morgan Trust Company, inventorying the financier's pre-Columbian artifacts, when a young messenger appeared at his door.

"Are you Mr. J. P. Winthrop?" the boy, who was about thirteen, asked.

"Yes."

"Then this is for you, sir."

Accepting the envelope, J.P. handed the boy back a dime. The young messenger touched his hat brim in salute and withdrew as J.P. began reading:

J.P.,
    Please come to 417 Central Park West, apartment 5G, as soon as you receive this note. It is a delicate matter of some urgency.

Lucinda

J.P. tapped the note with his fingernail as he contemplated its meaning. Lucinda didn't say she was in any particular difficulty, only that it was something urgent. He wondered what it could be.

He turned to his assistant, a slight-looking man of thirty, who was busy making entries in a ledger. "Mr. Forbes, I must go out."

"Very good, sir," Forbes replied. "And should anyone inquire, will you be returning today?"

J.P. shook his head as he folded the note and put it in his pocket. "I don't know. Probably not. If there are any more messages for me, just leave them on the blotter on my desk."

"Certainly, Mr. Winthrop. Good evening to you, then, sir."

J.P. hurried out into the street and hailed a cab, continuing to wonder about the nature of Lucinda's summons. They had been seeing each other practically every day since meeting at Mrs. Astor's party; some days their meeting was a chance encounter, but more often they met by design for dinner or a show or a ride through the park. Occasionally they'd even managed to find a few minutes alone in a semisecluded spot and exchanged desperate kisses that left their nerves raw and jangling but which they'd come to need, despite the frustrations engendered.

The cam seemed to creep, and J.P. leaned forward on the seat, silently urging the horse to go faster. The traffic was so heavy that it almost would have been quicker for him to get out and walk.

The cab neared its destination, and J.P. paid the driver beforehand, hopping out of the carriage the moment it stopped in front of the building. He trotted up the foot-polished marble steps to the front door, which was promptly opened by a doorman, then took the elevator to the fifth floor and, stepping from the elevator almost before the doors were fully open, hurried down the wide, floral-carpeted corridor to apartment 5G. When he knocked on the door, it opened almost immediately, and Lucinda grabbed his arm to pull him inside.

"Come in, quickly," she said. She looked up and down the hall, then closed the door.

"I came as fast as I could," he said, glancing quickly around the candle-lit room. "What is it? What's wrong? And who were you looking for? Is someone lurking in the hall?"

"I don't know," Lucinda replied, answering his last question. "Did anyone see you?"

"No. That is, yes, of course. The doorman and the elevator operator."

She smiled, clearly relieved. "They won't say anything. This apartment is kept for a friend of mine by her lover, who's a married man of some prominence, so the elevator operator and the doorman have learned the value of discretion."

"Lucinda, why are you concerned about discretion? What is this all about? I believe your note did say it was a matter of some urgency."

Lucinda stepped closer to him. "It *is* urgent. To me." She put her arms around his neck, then pressed against him, kissing him with open lips and darting tongue. She ground her body against his, then, with her arms still around his neck, leaned her head back and looked intently into his dark eyes. "My," she said, pushing her pelvis against his, "it's obvious that you're beginning to rise to the sense of urgency as well."

"Lucinda!" J.P. gasped. He tried to pull away from her. "What are you doing? We mustn't—"

"We mustn't what," she interrupted. "J.P., do you mean to tell me that after all the trouble I went to, arranging this apartment for our assignation, that you aren't interested?"

"Of course I'm interested. But I'm also concerned about compromising you. I wouldn't want to do anything that would harm your reputation."

She laughed. "My gallant, gallant darling. You don't realize it, but soon I'll be like Caesar's wife. My reputation will never be questioned because it cannot be questioned. Do you understand?"

He shook his head. "No, I don't."

"Of course you don't, my darling. But you will soon. Mama has seen to that." She pronounced *mama* in the French fashion. "But, of course, if you wish to leave . . ."

"No! No, I don't wish to leave."

Audibly sucking in a breath through pursed lips, she gazed at him through hooded eyes that were smoky with desire. "That's good, J.P. I'm glad you want to stay. Now, if you will just relax and do what I say, I'll show you sensuality beyond your most vivid dreams. You have dreamed of me, haven't you?"

"Yes," J.P. answered hoarsely. He had suddenly discovered that his throat was dry, and his tongue seemed almost too thick for him to speak. Only thirty minutes ago he had been minutely examining gold Incan treasures. And now he was in a private apartment, alone with the most desirable creature he had ever known. He couldn't believe this was happening to him.

"We will begin with a bath," Lucinda told him as she walked over to a sideboard.

"A bath?"

"Yes, a bath." She poured a snifter of brandy, then handed it to him. "Even as long ago as the eighteenth century, the courtesans of the French court understood the sensual aspects of a warm bath," she explained. "Now, I have already lit the water heater. If you would, please, go into the bedroom"—she pointed down the hallway to a door on the left—"you'll find a robe on the bed. Put it on, and when I call you—but, please, not until I call—you may join me in the bathroom."

"All right," J.P. agreed, his excitement rising. Taking the brandy, he went into the bedroom, which was also dimly lit by candles. As he began undressing he heard the splash of water being drawn for the bath, and when he turned around, he saw steam wafting from under the connecting bathroom door. Hurriedly he put on the maroon silk robe she had selected for him, and then he sat on the edge of the bed, sipping the brandy and staring at the closed door, waiting expectantly for her summons. After what seemed an eternity the water stopped.

"J.P., would you come in now, please?" Lucinda called softly.

Standing immediately, he went into the bathroom, also lighted only by candles, and found her sitting in the tub beneath a mound of soap bubbles. Her breasts were adorned, but not entirely covered, by the suds. One of her nipples peaked through, and it was maddening to his senses.

"Come in with me," she invited.

Dropping his robe, J.P. climbed into the tub and sat down in the hot water, then reached for her.

"No," Lucinda admonished, drawing back from his reach. Then in a gentler voice she suggested, "Please, J.P. Don't be impatient. Enjoy your bath. Wait for it. It will be far more pleasurable that way, I promise you."

As they bathed, J.P. noticed that he was gradually seeing more and more of Lucinda's body. At first he thought it an accidental result of bathing; then he realized it was a studied movement. Each moment after tantalizing moment she was exposing more of herself to his view, until finally almost every delightful curve was visible. But only briefly, because as soon as she had completely removed the suds and was completely exposed, she stepped out of the tub and wrapped herself in a large towel. For an instant—just a suggestion, really—she displayed herself totally nude to him; and then, once again, she protected her body from his lustful gaze.

"Would you anoint me?" she asked, holding up a flask of amber-colored oil, and the light shining through it made it appear as if it were liquid fire.

"Yes." J.P. took the bottle, half expecting it to be hot from its brilliance, and followed Lucinda into the bedroom. With her back still to him she removed the towel, then lay across the bed on her stomach.

J.P. lay beside her and poured some of the oil onto her beautiful, smooth skin. He began rubbing, and the sensuousness of the act coursed through his fingers and all through his body.

Lucinda rolled onto her back and looked up at him. Her eyes were wide and glowed with an inner light, showing a depth of feeling that J.P. knew couldn't be put into words. Her tongue darted across her lips, leaving them soft and shiny.

"Now," she whispered urgently, arching her back up and putting her arms around his neck, pulling him toward her. "Come to me now."

On a freight train rolling through Wyoming, Eric McKenzie sat listening to the man who had advised him to "come in or get out" of the open boxcar. Eric's newfound companion was a big man, in his thirties Eric figured, dressed in a collarless shirt and the remnants of what had once been a blue pinstriped suit. The man had quickly guessed that Eric was very new at this game so, without even being asked, he began providing the youth with some needed instruction.

"The first think you have to know is my name," he told Eric, who had introduced himself. "I am Benjamin Ely, and you will call me Mr. Ely. Not Benjamin and not Ely, but Mr. Ely. I, in turn, will call you Mr. Twainbough."

"You don't have to call me Mr. Twainbough. I'll call you Mr. Ely if that's what you want, but you can call me Eric." Having just coined the name Twainbough, Eric still wasn't that comfortable with it.

"I will call you Mr. Twainbough," Mr. Ely insisted. "We may be bums, but we are still citizens of this great country, and we have a citizen's rights. The colonel led a group of brave men in Cuba to assert the rights of free Americans, and though I have surrendered just about everything else, I do not intend to surrender my right to be addressed as mister."

"The colonel? Who's the colonel?"

"Who is the colonel?" Mr. Ely said. "My God, Mr. Twainbough, don't you know who the colonel is? Why, Teddy Roosevelt of the Rough Riders."

"The President? Are you talking about the President of the United States?"

"That I am, Mr. Twainbough, that I am. Mind you,

there were probably other political, geographic, and economic reasons for the war with Spain, but I emerged from that conflict with my own set of standards. I will be addressed as mister, and I will extend that same courtesy to everyone I speak to. Will you have trouble with that, Mr. Twainbough?"

"No, sir, Mr. Ely," Eric answered, slightly amused by the formality of Ely's speech. "I won't have any trouble with that at all. Did you fight in the war with President Roosevelt? The colonel, I mean?"

Benjamin Ely stared at Eric, and a steel curtain seemed to descend over his eyes. The sudden change in expression surprised Eric, and for a long moment he wasn't even sure that Ely had heard the question. Then the stony stare passed, the eyes brightened again, and Ely smiled. "I think we're going to get along just fine, you and I," Ely declared. "Now, pay attention when I speak, Mr. Twainbough, because you have a lot to learn."

"Yes, sir," Eric promised.

The youth listened, learning such things as what kind of trains to hop and when to hop them and even a new language. "Bumming a ride" or "grabbing iron" was the act of hopping a train. A "jungle" was a hobo camp, and "mulligan" was the hobo stew, generally cooking in the camp. Mulligan consisted of "hoppins," which were vegetables, and "gumps," which were chickens, usually stolen.

He also learned about a danger he had never considered before.

"There are men whose orientation toward sexual commerce is misdirected," Ely explained. "I have heard them referred to as puffs, faggots, or dandies. They are debauchers, men who prefer young boys to women. Beware of them."

Eric laughed. "I should be afraid of sissies?" He didn't know much about such men, though he'd heard Jake and Marcus mention them a few times, generally in connection with some joke, but he had it somewhere in his mind that such people were more like women than men, and he certainly didn't think he had any reason to ever fear a woman.

"You have the wrong impression, sir," Mr. Ely said. "I am not talking about your delicate, civilized dandies who have high intelligence, good manners, and sensitive souls. I am talking about men who have been without women for so long that they have changed over. They even have a saying. 'Better to hear a fat boy fart than a pretty girl sing.' And they are just as mean and just as tough as any other man. Mr. Twainbough, you, especially, should be on guard against these people, for you are young and unscarred, and that is the kind they like most."

He gave Eric many more useful hints, but where he was most helpful was during the train stops when the brakemen moved up and down the cars, searching for riders. The brakemen went about emptying cars of unauthorized riders in a brutal but most efficient manner. Every time they found a hobo, they'd drive him off the train by the simple expedient of smashing him over the head and shoulders with their saps—leather tubes filled with lead pellets.

"If you don't want your head busted by the sap, you have to learn to stay ahead of them," Ely explained. "And never underestimate them. You see, they have been at this game as long as any 'bo on the high iron, and they know every place a man can hide. They check everything—the rods, the bumpers, every car that has the door open though it be the tiniest crack, and I've even seen them look in the possum belly."

"What's the possum belly?"

"That's the toolbox underneath the crummy . . . the caboose."

"If they check the whole train, how can you ever hope to hide from them?" Eric asked.

"Simple." Ely smiled. "You don't stay on. You hop off the train every time it stops, and you hide in the weeds along the tracks until the train starts out again. Even then, you have to wait until it has picked up a good rate of speed before you jump back on. But always be sure to grab the ladder at the front of the car; that way if you miss you will get thrown against the side of the car, not between them."

"There's a lot to learn," Eric said.

Ely leaned back against the wall of the car, folded his arms across his chest, and closed his eyes. "Only if you want to stay alive," he said. Within seconds, it seemed, he was asleep.

Eric stayed where he was for several minutes, listening to the rhythmic clack of wheels over joints and feeling the gentle sway of the car. Then he got up and walked over to the open door and looked out over the wide, empty spaces of Wyoming. At least he assumed he was still in Wyoming . . . though he realized they might have passed into South Dakota by now.

The sun was nearly down, and riding big and low and red on the western horizon, it painted the closer buttes and plains vermilion, orange, and brown. In the distance deepening shadows spread darker hues of blue and purple on the mountains. Gazing at the scene, Eric thought how he had always enjoyed the light effects brought on by the rising or setting sun.

He also thought of Jake and Marcus—and Mr. Ebersole and his other friends back at the Flying E. He wondered if they knew about the attempted train robbery by now and of Jake and Marcus being killed. If they did know, what did they think of him?

Mr. Ebersole had trusted them to watch out for each other, and he had failed that trust. He knew the rancher would be forgiving . . . but he couldn't forgive himself, and he couldn't face his boss.

The youth felt tears come to his eyes again, and he wiped them away, then looked back around to see if his companion had noticed. He would have to watch that; he couldn't be crying like a baby every time he thought of Jake and Marcus, or of Mr. Ebersole. That part of his life was behind him. Eric McKenzie had no future; Eric Twainbough had no past.

Twice before midnight the train stopped, and both times Eric and Ely got off, getting back on only when it started again. Each time the train stopped, Eric saw several hoboes thrown from the train. One of the brakemen, Eric noticed, seemed much more brutal than the others. Though all of them used their saps, this particular crewman beat the tramps with such enthusiasm that it was obvious he enjoyed it. Ely identified him as Abner Slocum.

"Mr. Slocum seems to have a particular calling for his trade," Ely explained. "He can move up and down a train like a cat; he can see in the dark. The hottest sun, the stormiest night, even the snow and ice of winter mean nothing to him. And when he finds some poor 'bo, he takes particular pleasure in inflicting pain—and especially in killing. If you'll notice Mr. Slocum's sap, he has fourteen loops of red cord tied around the handle. People say that he has one cord for every 'bo he's killed."

It grew very cold during the night, but despite the cold, Eric managed to fall asleep from pure exhaustion. Then, during the night, he felt someone touching him, and, because he had been dreaming of Abner Slocum, he awoke with a start. He had his pistol out and the hammer thumbed back in an instant, shoving the barrel of the gun into the chest of the man hovering over him.

"Take it easy, Mr. Twainbough, take it easy! It's me, Mr. Ely!" Ely shouted, jerking away from him.

It was dark in the car, but a bar of moonlight slashed in through the partially open door, and in that soft, silver light Eric could see the fright in Ely's face.

"What . . . what are you doing?" Eric asked.

"You were shivering. I was covering you with paper, that's all."

"Paper?"

"Left over from the previous shipment in this car. Whenever you can, you should always pick a car that has a lot of paper on the floor. It makes a good blanket at night, when you need one."

"Oh. Uh, thank you." Eric eased the hammer down on his pistol and put it away, saying, "I'm sorry about pulling a gun on you. I didn't know what was going on."

Ely grinned. "Did you think I was Mr. Slocum, or perhaps one of those men I told you about? The ones who like boys?"

"Maybe a little of each," Eric admitted sheepishly.

"Mr. Twainbough, if you would take some advice, get rid of the gun."

"Get rid of the gun? No, I couldn't do that. I might need it. Why would you even say such a thing?"

"There are only two things can happen to you if you continue to carry that gun," Ely answered. "Somebody, maybe someone like Mr. Slocum, will get hold of it and use it on you—not a very pleasant prospect, as I'm sure you will agree. Or, you will use it on someone. Do you want to kill someone?"

"No."

"If you keep that gun long enough, you'll have to," Ely cautioned.

"I'll be careful," Eric promised.

He lay down on his elbows and pulled some of the papers over him, finding that they did work as a blanket. But he was also aware of a blast of cold air coming in through the open door of the car. "Why don't we just shut the door?" he asked. "That'd make it a lot warmer in here. And you said yourself, the brakemen never check a closed door."

"An excellent idea," the older man said, his tone sarcastic. "And then when they finally open the doors in Cleveland or some such place two weeks from now and find us both dead from thirst and starvation, they can say, 'At least they were warm, and the brakemen never caught them.'"

Ely went on to explain that when riding the cars, one should always spike the door so that it stayed open. A closed door couldn't be opened from inside, and if an empty car was being returned to the pool of cars, it might be weeks, even months, before anyone bothered to check inside.

Nodding, Eric lay back down, and because he had been awake the entire night before, and because he was drained physically and emotionally, he slept more soundly in that drafty, rattling old boxcar than he had his last night in the bunkhouse. He didn't wake up the next morning until Ely shook him awake.

"It's time to get off."

"Get off? Where?"

"Here."

"But the train is still going."

"It won't get any slower until it stops, and then it will be too late."

"Okay, if you say so," Eric agreed.

Ely stepped over to the open door and looked out at the passing telegraph poles. From Eric's perspective, inside the car, it appeared as if the poles were marching by the train, rather than the train rolling by the poles.

"Are you ready, Mr. Twainbough?" Ely asked.

Eric stood in the door beside him. "I'm ready, Mr. Ely"—he looked down at the ground—"although it looks like we're still going pretty fast."

"Remember, hit the ground upright, ready to run as fast as the train is going. Otherwise you'll fall, and I've known a few unfortunate souls who even rolled under the train."

"I'll be ready to run," Eric promised.

A moment or two passed; Ely called, "Now!" and launched himself through the open door. Eric jumped right behind him, which meant he was forward of Ely when the two men landed.

Despite Ely's warning to be standing and ready to run when he hit, Eric wasn't able to maintain his balance, and he pitched forward. In his mind's eye he saw himself being crushed beneath the wheels, and he panicked. Even as he rolled painfully over the stones, he hurled himself to the right, away from the train, bouncing and tumbling down the ballast-covered embankment. It made his fall even more painful, but it guaranteed that he was in no danger of rolling under the train. He wound up flat on his back in the bottom of a gully parallel to the track, staring up at the blue-white sky.

"Mr. Twainbough? Are you all right?" Ely asked,

coming easily down the embankment and standing over Eric's prostrate form. Even as Eric bounced and tumbled down the embankment, he had managed to catch sight of the older man trotting nimbly by, having kept his footing after the leap.

"I'm okay," Eric replied. Sore and aching, he stood up and began brushing off his clothes. He was sure he would have some bruises, but he didn't think he had any broken bones, and there were no bad cuts that he could see. Overhead, the long freight continued to rattle by, car by car, until finally Eric saw the short, red caboose at the end of the train. A brakeman was standing on the back platform of the caboose, and when he looked down toward the gully and caught sight of Eric and Ely, he gave a casual, almost friendly wave.

Eric gasped. It was Slocum, the brutal brakeman who had so enjoyed beating the hoboes last night! Eric wondered if Slocum knew they had been on his train, and he mentioned it to Ely.

The hobo laughed a short, bitter laugh. "Oh, yes, he knows, all right. Don't you worry about that, my friend. He knows. And he got a good look at both of us—so he'll recognize us the next time. You see, what Mr. Slocum is doing is telling us that while we put one over on him this time, the next time we had better watch out. I'd say he has marked us for his special effort."

"Mr. Slocum frightens me," Eric admitted.

Ely chuckled. "Does he, now? Good. He should frighten you; you may live longer that way. Now, are you sure you're all right? No damage from the fall?"

"Yes, I'm sure."

"Then we'd better be going." Ely smiled, then stuck his hand in his pocket. He pulled out a potato and handed it to Eric. "Here."

"What is it?"

"A potato."

"I can see *that*. I mean what's it for?"

"We're going to get breakfast down here. But we can't go into the jungle empty-handed. We'll have to have something for the mulligan."

"Hoppins?" Eric asked, smiling.

"You're learning, Mr. Twainbough, you're learning," Ely said. "Mr. Beans Farley tends the mulligan in this camp, and he's one of the best. Wait until you taste it. It's generally quite good."

Eric suddenly realized that he was very hungry and wasn't even sure how long it had been since he last ate. He thought of the big meal he and Jake and Marcus had bought in Newcastle . . . the meal he hadn't been able to eat because he was about to have a woman for the first time and was too nervous to eat. He wondered now just how long ago that had been. Not more than a few days, surely, yet it seemed like weeks, months—like something that had happened in another lifetime.

"Ah, this is what I was looking for," Ely abruptly said. "Do you see that?" He pointed to a broken tree limb that someone had stuck into the ground near a bush. An empty tin can was inverted over the top of the stick. "That's the mark of a hobo jungle. The path should be just over here. And, indeed, there it is," he said, gesturing.

The path led down from the bottom of the railroad embankment to the bank of a small river. Before Eric saw the camp, he could smell it—or at least the smoke of a campfire. Ely led the way through a small clump of trees, and when they stepped in the clearing on the other side, Eric saw ten or twelve men sitting around the jungle. It was, he decided, not all that unlike a cowboy's camp during roundup, though perhaps with less bantering. At the campfire a man was tending to a large kettle, stirring its contents with a tree limb that was about twice the thickness of a man's thumb and which had been stripped clean of bark.

When Ely and Eric walked up to the fire, Eric got a good whiff of the savory aroma. It smelled so good and he was so hungry that his stomach growled. He looked around in embarrassment, hoping no one else had heard. If they had, they were paying no attention.

"Hello, Mr. Ely. Haven't seen you in a few months."

The speaker was a medium-sized, blond-haired man whom Eric guessed to be around forty.

"Hello, Mr. Farley. I guess it has been a while, hasn't it? I've been moving around quite a bit. By the way, this is my friend, Mr. Twainbough. Mr. Twainbough, this is Mr. Farley."

"I'm Beans to everyone but Mr. Ely," Beans said, smiling. "You got any hoppins?"

"Potatoes," Ely replied. He held his out and so did Eric.

"Put 'em over there in that tote," Beans instructed. "I'll peel 'em and put 'em in later. You got a kit?"

Ely reached down into his jacket pocket and pulled out a spoon and a collapsible tin cup. "I do," he said. "But I don't think Mr. Twainbough does."

"It's all right. The boy can use one of them cans over there," the cook said, pointing. Following Beans's finger, Eric saw several tin cans sitting on a flat piece of lumber. "Mr. Twainbough, you be sure and clean it and put it back when you get finished," Beans went on. "There'll be others comin' through here who'll be needin' a kit."

"Yes, sir." Eric walked over to look at the tin cans, examining them carefully to find the one with the least amount of rust.

"Hey! Hey, look at that! That boy's carryin' a hogleg!" one of the men in the camp suddenly noticed.

"Beans, you know the rules," one of the other men complained to the cook. "Can't nobody with a gun get into one of these camps. You're the head of this camp; you're gonna have to run him out."

Beans looked up from stirring the mulligan and stared down at Eric's thigh. He then looked sharply at Benjamin Ely. "I didn't notice your friend's pistol before," Beans said. "Goober's right." He pointed to Eric. "What'd you bring him in here like that for? You know there can't nobody come into a jungle with a gun. A knife's okay, but no gun."

"Listen, don't worry about it," Ely said. "He's just a boy. Besides, he's wearing the gun out in the open so everyone can see it; he isn't trying to conceal it or anything. He'll get rid of it as soon as he can sell it. Isn't that right, Mr. Twainbough?"

"Yes," Eric replied. "Yes, that's right."

"Why don't he just toss it away somewhere?" one of the hobos suggested.

"Are you crazy?" Ely asked. "He could get as much as ten dollars for that. Ten dollars could feed a whole camp for a couple of weeks. He'd be a fool just to toss it."

"You'll be responsible for him then, Mr. Ely?"

"No. I am responsible for no man except myself, and no one is responsible for me." Ely looked at Eric. "But I will say that I have been with this young man long enough to form an opinion, and my opinion is that even though he is armed, he represents no danger to any of us."

"That's right," Eric said quickly. "I'm just passing through. I'm not going to do anything to hurt anyone."

"All right. I guess it'll be okay this one time," Beans said. "Bring your can over here, boy, and get some of this stew." He pointed to the pistol. "But you better watch out with that thing. There ain't one jungle in ten that'll let you come in when you're carryin' like that."

"Thanks," Eric said, nodding. "I'll remember that."

The stew was delicious. Eric didn't know if it was because he hadn't eaten anything in so long, or if it really was that good. When he began scraping the bottom of the can, he heard Ely laugh.

"It's been a while since you have eaten, hasn't it, Mr. Twainbough?"

Eric was embarrassed by the fact that his hunger was so obvious, and he cleared his throat self-consciously. "Yes, sir," he answered.

"Go get some more if you want," Ely said. "Nobody here will mind."

Hesitantly, Eric walked over to the pot and held his can out. Beans poured in another serving without question, and Eric returned to where he'd been sitting and ate the second helping, enjoying it as much as he had the first.

There was coffee, too, and a few of the men even

had tobacco, and they rolled cigarettes, passing them around. A few of the ones Ely identified as alkies passed a bottle back and forth. The men talked, sharing information as to where jobs could be found. One man told of a company paying a penny a box to build shipping crates in Denver. "A good man can put together fifteen or twenty an hour," he said. Another reported that a construction firm in Omaha was paying to make bricks, while a third spoke of cotton chopping going on way down south.

"You don't never want to do that kind of work," one of the other men cautioned.

"Why not?"

"Too many niggers choppin' cotton."

"Bullshit," one of the others scoffed. "You don't want to do it 'cause it's hard work."

"That ain't it. It ain't all that hard."

"If you think choppin' cotton ain't hard, then you ain't never chopped cotton. It *is* hard work, but the pay's pretty good. Three dollars a day. And the niggers don't bother you none if you don't bother them. Fact is, everybody's more or less the same out there under that sun."

"What kind of work you been doin', boy?"

Eric, who had been sitting with his knees drawn up under his chin and his arms wrapped around his legs, was surprised to be spoken to. He had not been participating in the conversation, only listening quietly.

"The last thing I did was punch cattle," Eric replied.

"You mean to tell us you was a cowboy?"

"Yes."

"Now, that'd be the thing. Just ridin' around on a horse all the time, eatin' three squares a day, and sleepin' in a nice, clean bunkhouse at night. Soft, easy livin', I'd say."

"It's a good life," Eric agreed.

"Then why'd you leave, if you had it made like that?"

"Mr. Goober," Ely said pointedly, "the boy's new to the life, and he doesn't know all the rules. He doesn't know, for example, that he need not answer prying questions of someone so rude that he won't mind his own business."

"I don't mean to be rude. I was just tryin' to be friendly, is all," Goober mumbled.

"I have never told anyone why I am here, and I would not take it as a friendly gesture were you to ask." Ely took in the other men with a wave of his hand. "You think the rest of the gentlemen gathered here would take it as being a friendly gesture, if you started asking them why they left their former professions and took up the life? In fact, would you care to share with us what brought *you* onto the rails?"

"No. No, I wouldn't," Goober admitted. He looked over at Eric. "Sorry, kid," he said. "Mr. Ely's right, I had no business tryin' to pry into your affairs like that. No offense meant."

"That's okay," Eric said. "No offense meant and none taken."

CHAPTER
EIGHT

When it grew dark at the end of the first day of their great auto trip to St. Louis, Bob Canfield and George Summers hooked a large tarpaulin to the side of the Packard, tied the other two corners to a couple of nearby saplings, then spread four bedrolls on the ground beneath. The travelers felt fortunate to have the canopy when a light rain came up just after midnight, but while the canvas kept them from getting wet, it didn't slow the attack of mosquitoes that immediately followed the shower, and the foursome slept fitfully, if they slept at all.

The next morning, itching from dozens of mosquito bites, aching from a night on the hard, damp ground, and with eyelids heavy from too little sleep, the travelers resumed their journey, back in the auto and on their way before sunup. They revived quickly when, shortly after six A.M., they reached their destination.

Wide awake now as they drove through the paved

streets of St. Louis, they began to get excited at what lay before them. Bob was surprised to see that Skinker Road was already beginning to fill with autos for the parade, though it wasn't due to start for at least four more hours.

They turned off Skinker onto the street where the Batemans lived. An affluent residential area, Forsythe Street was quiet at this time of morning. Uncollected morning newspapers lay on front walks that bisected well-manicured lawns, and here and there wisps of smoke curled from the kitchen chimneys, evidence of breakfasts being prepared for the neighborhood's earlier risers.

"There it is, George," Bob said, pointing to the Bateman house. "Turn in at that drive."

"My, what a beautiful house!" Pearl Summers exclaimed. "You never told me how beautiful it would be. Why, this is like a palace!"

"It *is* very nice," Bob agreed. "Actually, it belongs to the college, but because Professor Bateman is the college president— No, I'll correct myself. He's the university chancellor now. At any rate, he and his family get to live here because he's in charge."

"Bob, did you see how clean all those other autos were?" Billy piped up. "Look at ours. We can't be in the parade with this one. It's all covered with dirt and mud."

"We've come a long way through some hard country," Bob said. "You didn't expect it to still be shining, did you? But don't worry. If we all pitch in to clean it, we'll have this thing shining again in no time."

"Honk the horn, George! Let them know we're here!" Billy said excitedly.

With a laugh, George reached over and squeezed the bulb just as they turned into the drive. Almost immediately, Connie stepped through the front door and out onto the porch.

She smiled and waved at the intrepid travelers, who quickly bustled out of the Packard. "My, I just can't believe that you actually drove that automobile all the way up here," she said.

"I can believe it, ma'am," Pearl quipped, putting

her hand on her backside. "I can still feel every bump and every pothole of every road we traveled over."

Connie laughed. "You must be Pearl."

"Yes, ma'am. Pearl Summers, here to work for your father, if he'll have me."

"Oh, I think that'll be no problem. Bob has spoken very highly of you," Connie assured her.

"What about me? Has he said anything about me?" Billy asked. "I'm his brother, Billy."

"Oh, I know who you are, Billy. You're the most handsome of the Canfield men. Bob didn't say much about you because I think he was a little afraid that once I met you, I might prefer you to him," Connie teased.

"He doesn't think that. Bob, you don't think that, do you?"

"I don't know," Bob said as he began unloading the car. "Connie's right, you are better looking than I am."

"I suppose I am," Billy agreed. "But you sure don't have to worry about me taking your girl away from you. I don't even like girls. Especially somebody as old as Connie."

"As old as I am? I'll show you who's old!" Connie grabbed Billy and began kissing him on the forehead and cheeks.

"Hey, stop that! Quit it!" Billy squealed in protest, finally managing to struggle free. "I told you, I don't like girls. Anyway, we have to get the auto cleaned up for the parade."

Bob laughed. "I'm afraid he has you there, Connie. It's a terrible mess. We're going to need a water hose, some soap, and cleaning rags."

"And some help," Billy added.

"Some help? I don't know. Aren't you afraid I'm too old to help?"

"Well, you aren't *that* old," Billy said, retracting slightly. "I mean, you aren't as old as my mom or anything."

"Well, all right. Since you admit that I'm not as old as Methuselah, I'll get those cleaning things and then lend a hand." She looked down at her dress. "Just give me a moment to change clothes."

Connie fulfilled her promise, and ten minutes later, the car was covered with soap, while George, Bob, Billy, and Connie scrubbed it, splashed each other, and screamed in delight. While the others were busy, Professor Bateman took the opportunity to show Pearl around and interview her for employment.

Gesturing at the servant's quarters, he explained, "This was meant for two people, a man and his wife. However, I do not lead an extravagant life; therefore a colored woman who can cook and keep house is sufficient for my needs. Mr. Booker does all the heavy work. He's the handyman for the col— I mean the university." He smiled. "I'm still adjusting to the change myself."

The servant's quarters the professor was referring to was the small house behind the main house. Built as a miniature of the larger dwelling, the servant's house was constructed in the same style and in the same color brick, with even a scaled-down version of the columned porch that marched across the front of the main house. Like its counterpart, the servant's quarters also had dormer windows on the roof, though these were much smaller and served no function other than decorative. The little house consisted of only four rooms: bedroom, sitting room, small kitchen, and attached dining room. But—wonder of wonders to Pearl—it also had a full bathroom, with running water, an absolute marvel as far as she was concerned.

"What do you say, Miss Summers? Would you like to work for me?"

"Oh, yes!" Pearl said enthusiastically.

Professor Bateman smiled broadly and rubbed his hands together. "Wonderful! Well, then I suppose there is nothing more for me to say except you're hired. As you have your Sundays free, you can begin working Monday morning. My daughter and I take our breakfast at seven o'clock."

"Yes, sir. Thank you, sir. And I promise you, Professor Bateman, you won't be sorry you hired me."

"Well, you come highly recommended by Mr. Canfield, so I have no doubt that you will do an excellent job." He turned and looked out the window. "Well, I see that the Packard is sparkling, the cleaning equipment has been put away, and the cleaners have changed into dry clothes. It appears that they are about ready to line up for the big parade, so I suppose I had better be going." He smiled conspiratorially. "If you noticed, I managed to keep both of us busy just long enough to avoid having to help wash the automobile. Don't you think that clever of me?"

Pearl laughed. "Yes, sir, most clever," she replied. She already liked this man. But then, if Bob liked him, she should have known he would be a good man.

The professor opened the door, saying, "Even though I was of absolutely no help in getting the vehicle prepared for the parade, I have been invited along as a participant, and I must admit there is still enough of the youth in me to find that prospect rather exciting. So, if you have no more questions, Miss Summers?"

"No, sir. Everything is just fine," Pearl answered.

"Good, good. Then I'll be going. Oh, if you like, while we are gone, you may have a look around the house and acquaint yourself with the surroundings."

"Yes, sir, I will. Thank you. And have a nice time at the parade and fair."

As soon as Pearl heard the Packard leave, she hurried into the bathroom of her new house and examined the small, claw-footed porcelain tub. Two water spigots were over the tub; the pipe for one of them ran from a small coal-fired water tank, and the other pipe ran directly from the city water supply. By merely turning the handles, Pearl could produce a torrent of water.

Because it was warm enough that she felt no need for hot water, she didn't even bother to light the water heater. Instead, she turned on the cold water spigot and watched in awe as the tub filled. She had never seen such a wonderful thing before. She had always thought that the Canfields lived very elegantly, but not even they had running water.

A bar of soap was in the soap dish, and when Pearl picked it up, she gasped. Her name was on the soap! As she looked closer, though, she saw that the name wasn't Pearl, but Pear. It wasn't a homemade soap, but a commercial brand. Holding the bar, she found it smooth and beautifully shaped by a mold, and its cleansing agents had been combined with a perfume to give the bar a very pleasant scent. Pearl held it under her nose for a moment, enjoying its floral fragrance as the water continued to cascade into the tub.

When the tub was filled, she took off her clothes and climbed in, finding the effect of the water and the porcelain as cool and refreshing as if she had wrapped her body in silk. It was the most delectable sensation she had ever experienced, and she lay her head back against the edge of the tub, closed her eyes, and relaxed, as the rigors of the long auto trip fell away.

Leaving the Bateman house, Bob had directed George over to Lindell Boulevard to pick up David Gelbman and Terry Perkins, who had gone to David's by trolley earlier. The two extra passengers brought the total to seven, but with Billy sitting in the back seat between Bob and Connie, David and Terry in the jump seats, and Professor Bateman in the front seat alongside George, the Packard was big enough to handle them all.

The occasion of the great parade this morning had drawn thousands and thousands of spectators to the fairgrounds. Even those people who had seen so much of the fair that they had grown somewhat jaded by it found their interest rekindled by the prospect of such a magnificent show as the one planned for this morning.

The number of autos on Skinker Road earlier had increased many times over. Now they were parked on both sides of Skinker as well as up and down all the cross streets, and, like the Packard, they had all been cleaned, polished, and buffed to a high sheen, their yellows, greens, blues, whites, and blacks glistening and shining under the bright sun.

Here and there mechanics leaned over open hoods with an array of tools spread alongside them as they made last-minute adjustments, working under the curious gazes of men and boys who'd gathered around to get a closer look at the machines. The mechanics worked diligently to ensure that the vehicles wouldn't prove an embarrassment by an untimely breakdown during the parade. As one of the auto owners remarked to a fellow owner, if there was one thing he didn't want to hear this morning, it was the taunt, "Get a horse!"

The air was rent with the sounds of hundreds of engines being tested, horns being honked, and the calls and shouts of the drivers and mechanics speaking to each other in what to the spectators was a mysterious language all its own.

"Try leaning the fuel."

"Adjust the choke."

"Advance the spark."

Adding to the cacophony were the sounds of the "Pike," as the midway was called. At the "Gallery of Beasts," a lion roared, and in response a woman screamed, then laughed nervously.

An exciting mélange of smells wafted by on the warm morning breeze, adding their own subliminal inducements to the sights and sounds already assailing the senses: tangy popcorn, the sweet fragrance of pulled taffy, the aroma of frankfurters roasting over open fires, essence of gasoline, and the exotic odor of wild animals. All along the parade route and onto the Pike throngs of people waited patiently for the spectacle to begin. Newsboys and food and beer vendors took advantage of the gathering, hurrying up and down the streets to work the crowd.

Leaving George with the Packard, the others piled out of the automobile and found places on the sidewalk to view the parade. Billy spied a food vendor and bought a hot dog, ate it quickly, then immediately began looking for another hot-dog vendor. Connie was particularly fond of the iced tea, a concoction not heard of before an enterprising restaurant began selling it at the St. Louis

Fair. Its invigorating briskness caught on immediately, and it rapidly became one of the most popular drinks on the Pike.

"Wait until you try the ice cream cone," David told Billy. "They're wonderful."

"What's an ice cream cone?"

David chuckled. "Like all truly great inventions, it's the result of necessity. It seems that one of the ice cream vendors on the fairgrounds ran out of paper plates, but another vendor nearby was selling waffles. The ice cream vendor bought several of the waffles, fashioned them into cones, and put a scoop of ice cream in them. You eat not only the ice cream, but the waffle as well, and there's nothing to throw away."

"That sounds good," Billy said. "Can I have one, Bob?"

Laughing, Bob replied, "Certainly—if you think you'll have any room left in your stomach by the time we get there."

Terry bought a copy of *The Chronicle* from one of the newsboys and handed it to Professor Bateman, folding it in such a way as to display the story he had written about the imminent auto parade. "Perhaps you might want to read this, sir," he said.

WORLD'S FAIR PARADE TO FEATURE TEN THOUSAND AUTOMOBILISTS IN 2,500 MACHINES
by Terry Perkins

At least 10,000 automobilists, riding in 2,500 automobiles worth an estimated $5,000,000, will congregate Saturday morning in St. Louis to partake in the World's Fair Parade, marking history's greatest assemblage of motorcars. Every style of automobile will be present, from touring cars of the $8,500 pattern to runabouts costing $650. The spectacle of thousands of begoggled drivers and passengers in auto costumes is certain to be observed by tens of thousands of fairgoers and reported in prominent newspapers the world over, which will benefit automobiling far more than could be gained in any other way and will dramatically educate the public as to the value of this invention.

The parade will in no way be a race, and indeed fast traveling will not be tolerated; however, an automobile race will be run on one of the local tracks after the parade. In this race will be such swift machines as the "Grey Wolf," driven by Henry Schmidt, which made a 5-mile course in but 4 minutes and 21.6 seconds, and the Winton machine, driven by Barney Oldfield, which has made the mile in 43 seconds. William K. Vanderbilt, driving a Mercedes, made a mile in 39 seconds, but his record was on the straightaway. There is no doubt that from among these three autos will be selected the fastest machine in America.

"Well," the professor said as he finished the story and handed back the newspaper. "I'm impressed. We are going to be a part of history."

"Listen!" Billy said, swallowing a bite from his second hot dog. "What's that sound?"

The trumpeting noise sounded again.

David smiled. "Billy, my boy, get ready. The parade is about to begin. That sound you hear is an elephant."

"I've never seen an elephant," Billy said excitedly.

"Well, that's about to be amended," David remarked.

The autos actually formed the last unit of the parade, enabling the drivers and their passengers to watch the first part of the parade, which was led off by an elephant, followed by camels and donkeys, and then a smartly uniformed brigade of fire fighters pulling a glistening and steaming brass fire wagon.

After the fire fighting brigade came a company of British soldiers, followed by a company of Boer warriors. They gave daily shows on the fairgrounds, duplicating the climactic battle of the war they'd fought against each other but two years earlier. Now they were marching in concert.

The soldiers were followed by a float depicting the

great Galveston flood. Papier-mâché water lapped at a cardboard house, while perched on the roof was a tragic-looking young mother, clutching a baby to her bosom. O SAVE MY CHILD! read a sign on both sides of the float, and three handsome rescue workers, sweating in yellow slickers and rain hats on this hot and sunny day, perpetually reached toward her in vain as the float made its procession down Skinker.

The Galveston flood float was followed closely by a model of a gunboat. The *Columbia* was supposed to be belching smoke from its guns and stacks, but the emission was so puny that as the gunboat drew even with him, David cupped his hands and shouted, "Will the cigarette smoker inside please produce himself?"

Those nearby laughed at David's call and repeated it so that it was passed all along the parade route in match time with the progression of the ship.

Lucille Mulhall, a "cowgirl" dressed in a split buckskin skirt, matching vest, and flat-crowned Stetson, was next, riding a prancing white horse and waving and smiling prettily at the crowd. "Oh!" Terry exclaimed, suddenly clasping his hands over his heart and melodramatically staggering backward. "Did you not see that?"

"See what?" Billy asked.

"Cupid's arrow," Terry replied. "It hit me right here! I fear he has struck me a fatal blow."

Connie laughed. "I'm sure you'll recover—but if you don't, I shall come to your funeral and weep bitter tears."

"Good. I shall hold you to your promise," Terry quipped. Sighing, he added, "Alas, for me the parade is over. I have seen the lovely Miss Mulhall; there is nothing left to see."

"Yes there is. Here come the Eskimos!" Billy pointed out.

"Look at the poor beggars," David muttered, "sweating in their sealskins."

After the Eskimos came Indians, adorned with paint and feathers and riding in coaches and on scrawny ponies. Their squaws marched on foot, leading ponies that dragged travois holding sleeping papooses. The Indians were followed by representatives of all sorts of nationalities: Parisian beauties with bare shoulders, cossack soldiers in turbans and heavy felt overcoats, geisha girls in elaborate makeup, ancient Romans with golden helmets, Irish lasses carrying green flags, Spanish bullfighters waving scarlet capes, and dancing Turkish swordsmen.

When screeching clarinets, thumping drums, and clinking brass castanets ended the first part of the parade, a man riding a horse came through shouting instructions through his megaphone: "Ladies and Gentlemen! Would those of you who are automobilists kindly garb yourselves and line your machines up for the parade?"

"We'd better go back to the auto," Bob suggested. "George will be waiting for us."

Reaching the Packard, they found that George had already moved the motorcar into the column and was sitting behind the steering wheel, glancing around apprehensively. He looked relieved when he saw the little party approaching, and he smiled when Billy broke into a run in order to beat the others.

As before, Professor Bateman was seated beside George, while Terry and David occupied the two jump seats. This time, however, instead of sharing the back seat with Bob and Connie, Billy hopped into the front and sat between George and the professor.

"Gentlemen, you may proceed!" the parade director, who was mounted on horseback, called. With a racing of the engines and a grinding of gears, the automobiles began their procession.

Standing up on the front seat, Billy looked excitedly forward. As far as he could see, there was a steady string of automobiles—big ones, small ones, and all sizes in between. Turning, Billy saw the same sight behind—a seemingly unending queue of brightly colored motorcars.

When the column of autos first began moving, it was an exciting adventure, and Billy waved to the crowds on both sides of the road as they drove along the parade route. After a while, however, the excitement began to wear off under the oppressive, stifling blue-white exhaust fumes from the hundreds of automobile engines, which was exacerbated by the snail's pace at which they were required to crawl. Everyone in the Packard found the pace frustrating, but Billy especially grew impatient. He would alternately stand with his hands on top of the windshield, staring anxiously ahead, or plop back between George and the professor with his arms folded in disgust across his chest.

"Why is everyone going so slow?" he asked. "What's the good of having an automobile if everyone goes so slow? Heck, we could walk faster than this!"

"There are just too many autos crowding the street," Professor Bateman said. "Perhaps it would have been better had fewer participated. We could then have proceeded at a brisker pace."

The slowness started taking its toll, and as engines began overheating or some other mechanical malfunction afflicted the motorcars, the drivers would steer the vehicles out of the traffic stream and park them alongside the road. By the time the parade was half over, the Packard had passed scores of autos felled by such a fate. In every case the disabled autos were marked by open hoods, steaming engine compartments, and disgruntled and somewhat embarrassed drivers and passengers, still dressed in their automobiling garb. And at every incapacitated car crowds of curious spectators gathered, like flies drawn to carrion.

When the travelers finally reached the fairgrounds entrance, a policeman stood waving a flag, indicating that the automobile parade was over, and the drivers could either continue on into the parking lot, or they could move off on their own. Bob selected a third alternative: to leave the machine alongside the road and proceed into the fairgrounds on foot.

After George found a place to park, Professor Bateman excused himself from the others and headed for his office in Spengeman Hall, which, far from standing empty during the summer months, was being used as administrative offices for both the fair and for the Olympic Games in progress in conjunction with the fair. Jefferson University was being paid handsomely for the privilege.

Momentarily watching her father urgently striding across Skinker Road, Connie was amused by his expressed, though polite, distaste at having "all those strangers roaming through the corridors," as he had put it. Then she caught up with Bob, Billy, David, and Terry. At Terry's insistence, they entered the fair through the principal gateway, because it gave them, in his words, "the main picture." From here they had an unobstructed view of the Hall of Festivals—the symbol of the fair, the central jewel of the entire architectural effort.

The building itself sported a dome larger than that of St. Peter's in Rome, and from a concealed source on the north side of the Hall gushed a flow of water fifty feet wide. The stream splashed down ninety-five feet through a series of cascades and bottomed out as the Grand Basin, which then split in three. On these waterways glided graceful gondolas, carrying hundreds of visitors to lagoons in various parts of the fairgrounds. Punctuating the system of lagoons, and placed for dramatic effect, were a series of gushing fountains.

As the quintet of fairgoers moved down the Pike, taking in all the sights and sounds, Connie found that she was most fascinated with the latest examples of twentieth-century living, such as a demonstration of "housecleaning done by pneumatic process without removing the carpets." This device, the fair guide explained, created a vacuum that literally sucked the dust and dirt from the carpet.

Bob wanted to see Mechanical and Transportation Halls, and everyone agreed to go with him but Billy, who had something else in mind. From the moment the group had first stepped onto the midway, Billy had but one desire: to ride the giant observation wheel. He asked Bob to let him ride while the others visited Mechanical Hall.

"There's a lot to see in Mechanical Hall," Bob advised his brother. "We may be in there for a long time."

"Stay as long as you want," Billy said. "I'll just keep riding till you're finished."

"Billy, I've had friends who told me that they became dizzy while riding the Ferris wheel," Connie cautioned. "When you're on top, you're two hundred and fifty feet high. Are you sure you want to ride it?"

"Yes!" Billy answered emphatically. "And I won't get dizzy. I wish it would break down with me on top!"

"Don't say that when you get on," Terry warned, laughing. "For if it does break down and your fellow riders know you made such a wish, I fear they might want to toss you off."

After seeing Billy safely onto the Ferris wheel, the group visited Mechanical Hall, where they saw dozens of examples of labor-saving devices, all noisily whooshing or whirring or clanking. From there they proceeded to Transportation Hall, which boasted a network of railroad tracks carrying an array of full-scale models of the earliest engines to the latest in powerful locomotives and luxurious passenger cars. There was even a refrigerated freight car in which, a sign proudly proclaimed, "perishable products may be sent without risk of spoilage."

Leaving Transportation Hall, they went to check on Billy. They called up to him, and, spotting them, he waved and smiled broadly. Bob shouted up, "Do you want to ride longer?" and Billy nodded his head in an enthusiastic yes.

David suggested that they next visit the Magic Whirlpool. "I read an article about it," he explained. "The water comes from the Mississippi River, and the effect of a giant whirlpool is created by using centrifugal pumps that draw forty-nine thousand gallons of water a minute. Spectators get into a boat and are swirled about, then carried down one of the canals through a display of fountains, grottoes, and flower gardens."

"Oh, that sounds lovely," Connie said. "Let's do it, Bob."

"I warn you, though, you can't do it without getting a little wet," David added.

"On a day like today, that could only be an advantage," Terry quipped, laughing.

"Forty-nine thousand gallons of water a minute, you say?" Bob mused. "Can you imagine that? I'd love to get a look at the pumps that can do such a thing."

Connie laughed. "You want to look at the pumps? They have grottoes and fountains and flower gardens, and all you can think of is the pumps?"

Bob smiled. "It isn't that I don't appreciate the more romantic elements. But think of it: If they can move that much water, then they could certainly drain our swamps."

Because of the snoring, wheezing, and consumptive coughs of a dozen or more hoboes, the former Eric McKenzie, now Eric Twainbough, did not sleep as well in the camp as he had on the train. He was awake before sunrise, and, unable to go back to sleep, he sat on a large exposed tree root and watched the sun come up.

It was barely light when Beans emerged from the tar-paper-and-cardboard shack that he called home. The old man, who was clearly used to being the first one awake and having the early morning all to himself, started his day unaware of Eric's quiet observation. He urinated, blew his nose onto the ground, and hacked and wheezed for a while. Then he went back into his shack, to reemerge with a brown shaving mug and brush. Pouring a little water onto a sliver of soap in the mug, he worked up a lather and shaved, using a broken piece of glass for a razor. After he'd finished his ablutions, he walked over to the burlap sack, the "tote" where Eric and Benjamin Ely had put their potatoes the night before. Taking out several vegetables, Beans sat on a chair made from a packing crate and began paring and quartering potatoes, onions, carrots, turnips, and cabbages, dropping the prepared vegetables into a bucket as he worked.

"Boy," Beans said quietly after a while, "you goin' to just sit over there and stare at me all day, or'd you like to take that bucket down to the creek and get some water?"

"Oh," Eric said, startled by the comment. He hadn't been aware that Beans even knew he was there. "Yes. Yes, I'll get the water."

"Good. That'll be helpful."

Picking his way through the sleeping camp down to the bank of the stream, Eric scooped up a bucket of water, then brought it back.

"Go ahead and pour it into the mulligan," Beans instructed from his perch on the packing crate. "And if you'd like, you can give it a stir or two," he added.

Nodding, Eric poured the water in, then stirred the contents of the kettle with the peeled tree limb. As he stirred, he looked over toward Beans's shack, commenting, "You've made a nice house there. It's the nicest one in the camp."

"Yeah, well, I've hung around long enough to get it just the way I like it," the hobo remarked. "You see, I'm what they call a jungle buzzard. I don't ride the trains no more. I'm too old and too crippled. Most hoboes don't like jungle buzzards, 'cause they generally just lie around and mooch off the others. They tolerate me, though, 'cause I tend to the mulligan and I'm the mailman."

"The mailman?"

"Yeah. If one hobo wants to leave a message for another, he tells me. Eventually they all come through here, and when they do, I pass the messages on. So"—he glanced back at his shack—"I've managed to put up a pretty nice house for myself. I guess it'll last till the law comes and knocks everything down. Then I suppose I'll have to move on."

"The law will come knocking everything down? Why would they do that?"

"The law don't like havin' a hobo jungle near any of their towns," Beans explained. "They say it's 'cause we come into town and steal, but the real reason is that it makes 'em look bad." He chuckled. "Of course, we do cop a few chickens and some vegetables every now and again, but just between you and me, I always thought mulligan tasted a lot better when the gump and hoppins is stolen. Don't you agree?"

"I don't know," Eric said. "To tell the truth, last night was the first time I ever tasted mulligan." He smiled. "And it was so good, I don't see how it could be any better."

Beans laughed. "You were hungry, boy, and, like Mr. Ely says, hunger's the best spice."

Eric grinned. "Yes, that sounds like something Mr. Ely would say."

"You just met up with him, have you?"

"A couple of days ago. How long have you known him?"

"A long time."

"He seems different from everyone else," Eric remarked. "The way he talks . . . the way he calls everybody mister and wants to be called mister."

"Nothin' wrong with a man wantin' a little respect," Beans said.

"No, I guess not."

"You got to understand. Mr. Ely is a educated man."

"Then why is he—" Eric abruptly stopped. "I'm sorry. I have no right to ask questions, do I?"

"Nope. But that's all right, boy, 'cause you're learnin'. You're learnin'."

"How long do you think it'll be before the others start to get up?" Eric asked.

"Maybe an hour," Beans replied. "But if you're wantin' to eat now, why, you just go ahead." He laughed. "We sure as hell don't stand on no ceremony around here."

"No, it's not that," Eric said. "I thought I'd go down to the creek and take a bath."

"You're wantin' to take a bath, huh? Got the fixin's for a bath and shave?"

"No. I, uh, don't shave yet," Eric admitted. "I saw you were shaving with a piece of glass, though. I've never seen that done before."

Beans chuckled. "You haven't, huh? Break the glass just right, and it'll give you as fine a shave as any razor you're ever likely to strop," he bragged. "Well, since you don't shave, it won't be hard to get you took care of. All you'll be needin' is some soap, and if you'll go up to the first bend, why, I reckon you'll more'n likely find a bar of soap in the crotch of the tree. Just put it back when you're finished so the next man'll have some."

"Okay. Thanks."

Eric walked down toward the water, finding the soap just where Beans had said it would be, then took off his clothes and hung them in a tree. He hid the pistol under a rock. Since the others knew he had it, he was afraid one of them might decide to sneak up and steal it while he was bathing. He didn't intend to make it easy for them. Then he waded out into the water and began to work up a lather, though that didn't happen easily because the water was hard. It was also so cold that it took his breath away.

As he began bathing, he recalled the Saturday-night baths all the cowboys used to take back at the Flying E. It wasn't because the cowboys were a fastidious lot that they took such regular baths; it was Ebersole's rule. He was convinced that bathing once a week would prevent sickness, and he enforced his idea on the men who worked for him. Amid a great deal of horseplay and carrying on, the men would fill a watering trough behind the bunkhouse and take turns. All of them used the same water, so that by the time the last got into the trough, the water was so dirty that it was debatable whether washing was an improvement over his original condition.

"Well now, ain't that about the prettiest little ass I ever did see?" a hoarse-sounding voice suddenly asked.

Startled, Eric looked toward the bank. The man who had spoken to him had a flattened nose and a welt of flesh—a grotesque-looking scar that flashed like a purple lightning bolt—from the bottom of his right eye to the corner of his mouth. If this man had been in camp last night, Eric hadn't seen him.

"When did you get here, sweet thing?" the man asked.

Eric didn't answer.

"My, my, not talkin', are you? Does the cat have your tongue?" the man asked. He grabbed himself. "Well, never mind, I have somethin' for you."

Eric felt his stomach rise to his throat. This was one of the men Benjamin Ely had warned him about, and, as Ely had cautioned, this man certainly was no sissy and more like a woman than a man. This person was as frightening as anyone Eric had ever seen. The youth glanced at the rock he had hidden his pistol under—but he wouldn't get to the gun before the man got to him. Eric stood absolutely motionless.

"Are you comin' out of the water, you pretty little boy? Or am I goin' to have to come in after you?"

Eric knew he had to do something . . . at least say something. And he had to get control of himself somehow.

"Mister, there's a good mulligan in the camp," he finally said, forcing himself to speak. "Why don't you go on over and get some?"

The big man laughed—if the evil-sounding grunts that came from his mouth could be called laughter. "Well, so the sweet thing can talk. A good mulligan you say? Uh, uh. I'm not interested in food right now. But you know that, don't you? You know what I want." He patted a flat-topped rock. "Why don't you come on over here and belly down on this rock? You be nice to me and make me feel real good, and I'll treat you proper. I'm that ready for a pretty boy's ass that it'll be over in no time."

Eric didn't move.

"Come on, boy. The longer you wait, the harder it's goin' to be on you." Suddenly he laughed, a wheezing, rasping laugh that sprayed spittle from his lips. "That was a joke, boy, d'ya get it? The longer you wait, the harder it's goin' to be on you? Except it can't get no harder than it already is, and I'm gettin' tired of waitin'. Now, are you comin' over here like a good sweet thing?"

"No," Eric said resolutely, shaking his head.

"Well, then we'll have it your way." The big man started into the water when, behind him, Eric suddenly saw Benjamin Ely emerge from the trees.

"So, Mr. Twainbough, this is where you got to," Ely said in a well-modulated, almost conversational tone. "If you'd like to come out of the water and get dressed now, I thought we might have breakfast together."

"Mr. Ely, am I glad to see you," Eric said. He started toward his clothes.

"Hold it, boy!" the big man said, pointing his hand at Eric. "Me and you ain't finished with our business."

"I don't think Mr. Twainbough is interested in doing any business with you," Ely said.

The big man, who was knee-deep in the water now, turned and glared at Ely. Going back out of the water, he demanded, "Who the hell asked you to butt into this?" His voice was loud and even raspier sounding now than it had been when he was talking just to Eric. "Listen, you son of a bitch, I don't like someone stickin' their nose into my affair. I reckon I'm just goin' to have to teach you a lesson."

"If you think there is anything you can teach me, you buggering bastard, you are certainly welcome to try," Ely said. In contrast to the loud gruffness of the big man's voice, Ely's tone was quiet, cold, and calculating. It was also the first time Eric had ever heard him address anyone by anything other than mister.

One of the other hoboes had heard the loud exchange of words, and when he was close enough to the creek to see what was going on, he called back to the others in camp, "Hey! It's a fight! Everybody come! A fight's goin' on down here!"

Within moments a half-dozen hoboes, including Beans, had come down to the creek bank. Taking advantage of the situation, Eric dressed quickly. He started to strap on his pistol but changed his mind, fearing that if he did, this could well be one of those times Ely had warned him about—when he'd be forced into a position to either kill or be killed. And there was no doubt in his mind: If he had to kill this big man to keep him away, he'd do it.

As the other hoboes gathered alongside the stream, Eric entertained the hope that they might break up the fight, but he soon saw that they had no such intention. In fact, just the opposite appeared to be the case, for they began shouting at the two men, urging them on, anxious for a fight to provide them with some excitement. The one consolation was that everyone seemed to be for Ely. However, Eric worried that should it actually come to a fight, his friend, though powerfully built, was much smaller than the would-be rapist and thus seemed to be at a disadvantage.

"Come on, Mr. Ely, tear Dogmeat to pieces," someone called, and when another referred to the big man in the same way, Eric asked Beans if Dogmeat was the scar-faced man's name.

"That's what every one calls him," Beans replied. "I don't know what his real name is. But the son of a bitch has tried on more than one occasion to put dog meat into the mulligan. That's how he came to be called that."

The man in question sneered at Benjamin Ely. "Are you goin' to fight me for your little sweetheart, you son of a bitch? Or are you just goin' to stand there and beat your meat?" Dogmeat asked, then laughed out loud at his own joke.

"You seem to be the one who is doing all the talking," Ely responded.

"Then let's get to it," Dogmeat growled, swinging wildly in a punch that Ely was able to avoid.

A hush fell over the hoboes as they watched the two combatants. Ely and Dogmeat circled about, their fists doubled in front of them, each trying to test the mettle of the other.

Eric noticed that Ely was holding his fists in the fashion of a real boxer, whereas Dogmeat was letting his hands dangle much lower, raising them only when necessary. Dogmeat swung again, as wildly as before,

and Ely countered with a swift left jab that caught
Dogmeat square in the face. Despite the power of the
blow, the bigger man just laughed it off.

Surprisingly, Eric was able to observe the fight with
an almost detached interest, curious how Ely would
handle his foe. The youth knew it would have to be a
mustering of quickness and agility against brute
strength, and he hoped to learn by watching.

After easily evading another of Dogmeat's clublike
swings, Ely counterpunched with a second quick jab.
Again it caught his opponent flush on the jaw, and again
Dogmeat laughed it off. As the fight went on, it was
apparent that Ely could hit Dogmeat almost at will, but
since he was bobbing and weaving, he couldn't set
himself for a telling blow, and so his scores didn't faze
Dogmeat at all.

Ely hit Dogmeat in the stomach several times,
obviously hoping to find a soft spot, but none was there.
Giving that up, he started throwing punches toward
Dogmeat's head, but they were just as ineffectual until a
quick opening allowed him to slam a left square into
Dogmeat's face. Eric saw Dogmeat's already-flat nose go
even flatter under Ely's fist. From that Eric knew it had
been broken, the latest in what appeared to be a long
line of breaks. The nose started bleeding profusely, and
the blood ran across the big man's teeth. It was a
gruesome sight, but Dogmeat continued to grin wick-
edly, seemingly unperturbed by his injury.

Ely kept trying to hit the nose again, but Dogmeat
started protecting it, which indicated to Eric that the
nose was undoubtedly hurting. Dogmeat nonetheless
continued to throw great swinging blows toward Ely,
who managed to slip by any real impact, catching them
on his forearms and shoulders. Eric feared that if just
one of them connected with his friend's head, Ely would
be finished.

A moment later Ely managed to get another sharp,
bruising jab through to Dogmeat's nose, and for the first
time Dogmeat let out a bellow of pain. But it was clear
that the triumph would be momentary, for the thunder-

ous punches that had repeatedly assailed Ely's shoulders and forearms were beginning to tell as he moved more slowly. Then Dogmeat managed to land a straight, short right, and Ely fell to his hands and knees.

With a yell of victory, Dogmeat rushed over to him and tried to kick him, but at the last second Ely rolled to one side. He hopped up again before Dogmeat could recover for a second kick and, while the big man was still off balance, sent a brutal punch straight into Dogmeat's groin.

When Dogmeat instinctively dropped both hands to his groin, Ely slugged him in the Adam's apple. Dogmeat clutched his neck with both hands and sagged, gagging, to his knees. Ely hit him one final time, right on the point of the chin, and Dogmeat fell facedown, unconscious.

The onlookers were at first stunned; then they cheered. "Did you kill him?" Beans finally asked.

Ely looked closely at his fallen adversary. "No, I don't think so."

"You better. You better kill him now. If you don't, when he comes to, he's going' to kill you."

"Yeah, why don't you step on the son of a bitch's neck and break it?" one of the others asked. "It'd save us all a lot of grief if he was dead. Don't nobody like the bastard, and you'd be doin' everyone a favor."

"No," Ely responded. "I've no intention of killing him. I'll be gone when he comes to." He looked over at Eric. "Mr. Twainbough, you are your own man, of course, but you are quite welcome to come with me. Dogmeat will be coming for you as well, and the only way you are going to be able to stop him is to kill him. You know that, don't you?"

"Yes," Eric mumbled.

"Then, what will it be?"

"I'll come with you."

CHAPTER NINE

Pearl Summers was washing Professor Bateman's breakfast dishes when someone knocked on the kitchen door. Puzzled as to who would come around to the back of the house, she wiped her hands on her apron and went to see who it could be. When she opened the door she caught her breath. Standing there on the back porch was a tall, broad-shouldered colored man who was, without a doubt, the most handsome man she had ever seen.

"Good afternoon," the man said, his liquid-brown eyes looking into hers. His voice was deep and resonating. "I take it you're Miss Summers. I'm Loomis Booker. Professor Bateman said you needed an icebox moved."

"What?" Pearl asked, staring at him as if mesmerized.

"An icebox?" Loomis queried. He raised his hand in front of Pearl's eyes and waved his fingers. "Hello? Are you there?"

"My God! You are beautiful!" Pearl exclaimed.

"What?" Loomis replied, clearly shocked by her response and looking not at all sure that he'd heard what he thought he had.

"I said you are the most beautiful man I have ever seen," Pearl repeated.

Loomis laughed. "Miss Summers . . ."

"Pearl."

"Pearl, I've never heard a man described as beautiful. Handsome—though I would not be so immodest as to make such a claim for myself—but never beautiful."

Pearl shook her head as if shaking herself awake, then put her hand to her hair and smoothed it back. She laughed nervously. "I'm sorry," she said. "I guess you think I'm some dumb little swamp girl. Imagine me coming up here to the big city and making a fool of myself like this." She stepped back from the door. "Won't you come in?"

"You have an icebox you want moved?" Loomis asked again.

"Yes, it's over here," Pearl replied. "I've already emptied it and cleaned it out."

"Where would you like it moved?" the handyman asked, stepping farther into the kitchen.

"Over there, against the back wall, close to the sink."

Loomis looked at where the icebox was now and where Pearl wanted him to put it, on the opposite side of the kitchen. He shook his head. "Are you sure you want to do that? Mrs. Jackson thought it was more convenient near the pantry."

"This is *my* kitchen," Pearl stated firmly.

"I beg your pardon?"

"Professor Bateman has hired me as his cook and cleaning lady. The icebox is near the pantry because Mrs. Jackson had it put there. But it's my kitchen now, and I want it by the sink. She had her way of doing things, I have mine."

Loomis laughed. "Okay, if that's what you want."

He walked over to the pantry and picked up the refrigerator. The muscles in his arms and neck bulged and, as Pearl watched, she felt herself growing warm inside.

He moved the box across the room, then set it down. "Right here?"

"Maybe a little more to the left." She smiled to herself, enjoying again the flexing of his muscles as he moved the appliance.

"How is that?"

"Fine, thank you. Would you like a glass of lemonade, Loomis Booker?"

Loomis smiled. "Lemonade would be nice," he said.

Pearl walked over to the sink and chipped off a piece of ice from a block in a pan, under a cloth. As she put the chipped ice in a glass, she pointed to the heavy block, and Loomis picked it up and put it in the chest of the icebox. Nodding her thanks, she emptied the pan of melted water, then set it back beneath the refrigerator. After that, she poured already-made lemonade into the glass.

Handing it to the handyman, she said, "So you are Loomis Booker. Bob has told me about you."

He nodded, neither questioning who Bob was nor commenting about her having used his first name.

"He says you're one of the smartest men he's ever met," she went on.

Loomis took a swallow of his drink and studied her over the glass for a moment.

"He says you're an educated man, too, with enough schooling for two or three degrees."

He still didn't answer her, and, growing flustered, Pearl demanded, "Why don't you answer me, Loomis Booker? When I talk, why don't you talk back?"

"What will you be doing Sunday afternoon?" he asked.

"Sunday? Why, I don't know. Sunday's my day off," she said. "I suppose I'll just rest."

"No, you won't."

"I won't?"

"I will stop by for you, Sunday," he stated. "Pack a picnic lunch for us."

"All right," Pearl agreed.

Loomis finished the lemonade and put the glass down on the table. "Anything else you need moved?"

"No."

"Then I'll see you Sunday." He started out the kitchen door, then turned and looked back with a smile. "Pearl, the next time we meet, how about you keeping quiet so that I can tell you how beautiful *you* are?"

On the other side of St. Louis, in the office of *The Chronicle*, Terry Perkins tapped lightly on Thomas Petzold's office door.

"Come in."

"You wanted to see me, Mr. Petzold?"

"Yes, Terry, sit down," the publisher answered.

Puzzled by the unexpected summons, Terry took the chair offered him and reviewed in his mind all the stories he had written over the last few weeks. Had he done something wrong? Written something that caused the paper trouble?

"Terry, have you heard of the Wright brothers?"

"The Wright brothers? No, I don't think so. What baseball club do they play for?" He smiled. "Is that what this is about? You want me to do a story about two brothers playing on the same team?"

Petzold chuckled. "No, this isn't a story about baseball," he said. "Though I suppose it is a sporting story. *The New York Times* carried their report of the Wright brothers on the sports page."

"What exactly was the report?"

"They are bicycle mechanics from Dayton," Petzold said. "And apparently they have flown, and are flying regularly, on some man's farm just outside that city."

"We should get them to come to St. Louis," Terry proposed. "The fair officials have promised free hydrogen to any aeronaut who'll bring his airship or balloon here."

Shaking his head, the publisher said, "Apparently it's neither device. It's some sort of machine that mysteriously defies gravity. Listen to this." Petzold picked a letter up from his desk, adjusted his pince-nez on his nose, then began:

Your readers will no doubt be interested to hear of the scientific experiments of Messrs. Orville and Wilbur Wright. These two fine young gentlemen from Dayton, Ohio, have plucked the secret of flight from the very ages and have mimicked, in every detail, the majestic soaring of birds!

They were first successful in North Carolina in December of last year and have flown their machine many times since then. It is not a balloon or an airship, as it depends on no lifting gas except the very air upon which it floats. I have seen them make many flights from a pasture of Mr. Huffman, a farmer near here.

Petzold put the letter down and peered up at Terry. "I want you to go to Dayton," he said.

"Do you think there's anything to it?"

"I don't know," Petzold admitted. "This letter was written by someone who seems quite reputable. It may be a hoax, but . . ."

"But you believe it," Terry said. It was a statement, not a question.

"Yes, I think I do. I know, it seems impossible, but when you stop to think about it, look at the amazing scientific advances in just the past few years. No one who has visited the fair could have any doubt of man's eventual victory over all the mysteries of science. Motion pictures, wireless telegraphy, machines that talk, automobiles . . . Why, if our grandfathers could return to see the wonders of the twentieth century, they would think themselves in a world of magic."

Terry stood up. "Mr. Petzold, I'll go to Dayton. And if the brothers Wright are flying, I'll come back with a story—and with proof."

Terry Perkins had gotten the Wright brothers' address, 7 Hawthorn Street, from the Dayton, Ohio, city directory. Making his way on foot from the train station, when he reached the house, he stood looking at it from the sidewalk, trying to summon the courage to go up and knock on the door. There was nothing prepossessing about the house: It was a white-frame, two-story dwelling with a porch that stretched all the way across the front and around one side, and though it was fairly large, it wasn't particularly elegant. An iron fence circled the modest yard, and a two-wheel bicycle leaned against the fence.

As Terry stood in front of the house contemplating his next move, a young, very attractive woman came walking down the street toward him. She turned through the gate and started up the walk toward the house.

"Excuse me, miss?" Terry called. "Is this the home of Wilbur and Orville Wright?"

"Yes, it is," she answered, turning around and smiling brightly. "I'm Katherine Wright, their sister. Are you from the government?"

"The government? Uh, no," Terry said. "Why would I be?"

"It's just that the boys got their patent a few weeks ago, and we thought that perhaps—" She stopped abruptly in midsentence as if she might be giving out more information than should be given. "Never mind," she said. She peered closely at him. "Who are you?"

"My name is Terry Perkins. I'm a reporter from St. Louis."

"You're from a St. Louis newspaper?"

"Yes, ma'am. And not just any St. Louis newspaper, the *best* St. Louis newspaper. *The Chronicle.*"

"Why are you here, Mr. Perkins?"

"Well, I'm here to investigate a story I heard about your brothers. I was told they've invented some sort of flying machine."

"You have been told correctly, Mr. Perkins. They *have* invented a flying machine."

"Are they here? Might I meet them? Talk to them?"

"I don't know," Katherine replied. "I'm afraid the newspapers have not been treating my brothers very kindly. Many of them have published articles ridiculing them, without even bothering to check whether or not the claim is true. Needless to say, my brothers have become a bit wary."

"Please don't take this the wrong way, Miss Wright, but I can understand the newspapers' skepticism. The idea of man flying without the aid of a lifting gas—flying like a bird on wings—is almost impossible to accept. That's why I'm here. I came to investigate, see for myself if it's true."

"Of course it's true," Katherine said. "In fact, they'll be flying today. If you've really come to investigate as you say, perhaps you would like to see them."

"I would very much like to see them."

"All right. You'll find them out at Huffman's pasture. That's a farm about eight miles east of town."

"About eight miles, you say. Is there a sign there, or something? How will I know if I'm at the right place?"

Katherine smiled. "Why, I should think it would be very easy to recognize, Mr. Perkins," she said. "I'm quite certain it will be the only pasture with someone flying over it."

Terry laughed. "Yes," he said. "Yes, I guess you're right. And, now, if I could just trouble you for one more piece of information. Could you recommend a stable where I might rent a horse and buggy?"

"That won't be necessary. That is, if you can ride a bicycle. Can you ride a bicycle, Mr. Perkins?"

"Yes, of course."

Katherine pointed to the two-wheeler. "Then why don't you take that one? It's one that my brothers built, and I'm sure you'll find it quite easy to operate."

"Thank you," Terry replied, walking over to the bicycle. "That's very kind of you."

"No, Mr. Perkins, it is very kind of *you*," Katherine

remarked. "Of all the reporters who have written about my brothers, you are the first to come to see for yourself whether or not the story is true. I appreciate that, and I'm sure my brothers will."

Following Katherine's directions to the Huffman farm, Terry rode for about a half hour. He didn't see a pasture with someone flying over it, but he did find a field in which a handful of people were clustered around a strange kitelike contraption. It had to be a flying machine, Terry decided. There was nothing else it could be. He rode the bicycle toward it, then laid the two-wheeler carefully on its side in the grass.

As Terry examined the object of everyone's attention, he started searching his mind for some way he could describe it to his readers. It was made up largely of two pairs of wings, each pair consisting of one wing above the other, made of sailcloth over a wooden framework. The smaller pair was positioned at the front end of the machine, while the much larger set was in the back. Another pair of appendages was at the rear, and these fabric-covered vertical struts appeared to act in concert as a rudder.

Two men in business suits, complete with starched collars and cuffs, were puttering about on the craft and at the same time giving orders to the others, telling them where to place certain ropes, when a particular action was supposed to take place, and so forth. When Terry heard one of the men in a suit addressed as Mr. Wright, he was disappointed. It was obvious they didn't intend to fly today after all—not dressed as they were.

"You," one of the brothers said to Terry. The speaker was clean-shaven with a long narrow face and a receding hairline. "You look to be in pretty good athletic condition. Would you like to be of some help?"

"Yes, sure," Terry replied. "What would you like me to do?"

"My brother, Orville, is about to launch," Wilbur Wright said. He pointed to a wooden tower behind the machine that Terry guessed to be some twenty-four feet high and recently built. "We're going to use a weight-

and-pulley system from the tower to effect the launch," the inventor continued. "That means it'll start out pretty fast, so we'll need someone in good-enough physical condition to keep up with the flyer as it starts down the track. The craft must be supported until it's ready to support itself. Shortly after that, of course, it will rise from the ground."

"I take it you're Wilbur Wright."

"Yes, I am."

"Mr. Wright, I'm Terry Perkins. I'm a reporter with—"

"Oh, I see that my brother is about to launch, Mr. Perkins," Wilbur said, cutting Terry off. "If you would, take your position alongside the other wing. Just run along it as the craft gains momentum. Don't touch it, unless it's about to fall off the track. In fact, you probably won't have to touch it at all. This is merely a safety precaution."

"Yes, sir," Terry said. "Is he going to fly like that?" He pointed to Orville.

"Like what?"

"In a business suit."

"Yes, of course he is. What would you expect him to wear?" Wilbur asked, as if puzzled by the observation.

"I don't know," Terry replied. "I suppose I thought there would be some special costume for such a thing."

"Just what sort of costume could there be, Mr. Perkins?"

"Well, I've seen pictures of flyers before, and they always had on some special costume."

"Have you ever seen a picture of my brother or myself?" Wilbur asked.

"No, I don't think I have."

"Then you have never seen a picture of a flyer, for no one else in the entire world has ever flown—*really* flown, in terms of controlled flight—except us. And as we're the only two human beings who have ever done this, whatever we choose to wear is correct, simply because we choose to wear it."

Terry chuckled. "I suppose you have a point there."

The novice reporter looked over at Orville, whom he knew from his research to be four years younger than Wilbur. Orville had a full mustache and considerably more hair, but the two brothers were almost the same size, and other than the difference in hair, they were remarkably similar in appearance. Orville climbed onto the machine and lay belly down on the lower rear wing. Reaching forward, he grabbed a couple of levers, moved his hips until they were positioned in a cradlelike device, then put his feet securely on the footrests at the back of the wing.

"Start the engine," he ordered, and two of the men who had been helping stepped up to the propellers, counted to three, then gave the propellers a jerk. The engine roared into life, and the two whirling blades became a blur. The craft started vibrating, and the guy wires between the upper and lower wings began to hum as the craft strained against its restraint, as if anxious to leap forward.

"Mr. Perkins, are you ready?" Wilbur shouted from the other side of the flyer, where he would handle the same chore he'd assigned Terry.

"I'm ready, Mr. Wright," Terry called back. The sound of the roaring engine, and a sound that was new to him—the whirring buzz of the spinning propellers—excited him much more than he would have believed.

"Drop the weight!" Wilbur commanded, and one of the helpers pushed a lever that allowed a massive lead weight to drop from the top of the tower. The weight was connected by a system of cables and pulleys to the front of the craft. Under the impetus provided by the dropping weight and the thrust of the propellers, the craft began to move swiftly down the track, quickly pulling away from Terry, even though he was running at his best.

The craft reached the end of the track, then nosed up, up into the air, twenty, thirty, forty feet and higher. It moved majestically toward the end of the pasture, then turned completely around and started coming back toward them.

The noise from the engine and propeller, a painful roar a moment ago when Terry was right next to it, was now a subdued echo from above, and as the craft passed overhead, he could see Orville lying on the bottom wing, manipulating levers and moving his hips to maintain the craft's delicate balance. The flying machine itself was poised on the wind, moving about as gracefully as a wheeling hawk. Terry felt an unbelievable excitement: He was actually watching a man fly! Not held aloft by the lifting power of gas, but flying—actually flying, like the birds. This was, he knew, the realization of man's fondest dream since the beginning of time.

The machine landed, setting down on its skids as gently as a feather, and the engine was shut off. Terry looked over at Wilbur, expecting him to run excitedly to his brother. Instead, he walked calmly as if what they had just witnessed was the most common of occurrences. Terry hurried over to see what momentous things they might be saying to each other, thinking they should be yelling and shouting and slapping each other on the back. But they were merely talking quietly of technical things that totally escaped Terry's understanding.

"I'm having difficulty maintaining stability of the longitudinal axis," Orville said.

"Perhaps we need to adjust the tension—" Wilbur started.

"—in the warping wire," Orville finished.

"What about pitch?" one of the other men asked.

"No problem. We—" Orville began.

"—cleared that up," Wilbur concluded.

As Terry watched the brothers make adjustments on the machine and issue orders to the others, he learned that they frequently completed sentences for each other. He understood then why the Wright brothers had been successful in an enterprise that had brought failure to so many others. When he mentioned to Wilbur a few minutes later how each brother seemed to know what the other was thinking, the inventor chuckled.

"From the time we were little children," Wilbur said, "my brother Orville and I have played together, worked together, and, in fact, thought together. In all our joint projects it's impossible to say which of us contributed what, or to determine which of us is the scientist and which the skilled mechanic. Our minds work as one."

The brothers made three more flights that day, all as exciting to Terry as the first had been. After each one the brothers exchanged positions so that they both made two ascents. When the flying was concluded, they moved the craft, which Terry learned they were calling the "Flyer II," into a shed located on the pasture, built for just that purpose.

Exiting the shed, Orville Wright came over and shook the young reporter's hand. "Mr. Perkins, welcome to Dayton." Terry realized that that was the first time he had been officially greeted, yet throughout the long day he had felt welcome—indeed, almost a part of the group. "My brother and I want to thank you. You provided some valuable assistance today."

"Won't you come home and take supper with us, Mr. Perkins?" Wilbur invited.

"Why, yes," Terry answered, grinning. "Yes, I would be very honored."

Following the brothers back on his borrowed bicycle while they rode their own, Terry's mind was whirling with questions that he had for the Wrights. He had to bottle his fervor when they reached the brothers' home and they excused themselves to wash up. Finally, during supper, he got the answers he had been hungering for as he listened to the brothers describe their many experiments and tell of the letters they had exchanged with the other "experts" in the aviation field.

"We learned early on," Wilbur said toward the end of the meal, "that there was no flying art, only a flying problem."

"Our first experiments were flawed," Orville explained, "because we were relying too much on the findings of Otto Lilienthal, who, you may know, was renowned for his experiments with gliders before his tragic death in 1896, when one of his craft got out of control."

"We experimented on our own, using a wind tunnel we built, to determine new values of lift and camber," Wilbur added.

"That wind tunnel is out back, in the shop, if you would care to see it," Orville offered.

"I'd love to," Terry replied.

"Well, if you're finished eating, why don't we go?" Wilbur suggested.

Dabbing at his mouth with a napkin, Terry thanked Katherine and the Wrights' mother for the excellent meal, then followed the two brothers into the back.

"When we returned to Dayton in 1901, after several weeks of experimentation at Kitty Hawk," Wilbur began, "we appraised what we had done—"

"—and read everything that had been printed, plus the letters of Octave Chanute," Orville continued.

"And came to the rather startling realization that we were closer to conquering the secret of powered flight than anyone else in the world," Wilbur concluded.

"Ah, here we are," Orville said, opening the door. He turned the gas valve, and the lamps lit up brightly, affording Terry a view of the workshop. There were lathes, band saws, and drill presses, all operated by a series of pulleys and belts that turned by an overhead shaft driven by a gasoline engine the brothers had built themselves. A series of curved wooden pieces, one of which was clamped in a vise while the rest were stacked on one of the work tables, were called ribs, and Wilbur explained that they formed the skeleton of the wing. In the middle of the room was a large wooden box mounted on a stand. One end of the box was ducted and had a fan attached, and the top had a small window so that one could look inside.

"That is our wind tunnel," Wilbur said.

"Before we built it, we used to mount air foils on our bicycle and ride as fast as we could to test the effect of the wind," Orville put in.

"The tunnel proved to be much more efficient," Wilbur added.

"So here," Terry said quietly, almost reverently, "in this room, was unlocked the secret that has challenged man since Icarus."

"We studied him, too," Wilbur said with a chuckle.

"Really? And what did you learn?" Terry asked.

"We learned that he was as wrong as Lilienthal," Orville answered, "and he met the same fate."

J. P. Winthrop examined the card in his hand, making certain that the room number was correct. He was on the second floor of the Plaza Hotel on New York's Central Park South, standing just outside the "Balcony Suite," so named because this suite of four rooms opened onto a balcony over the hotel's entrance that overlooked the park. He adjusted his collar and cuffs, then rapped sharply on the ornately carved door in front of him. A moment later the door was opened by a young woman who, though wearing the black-and-white dress of a hotel maid, was obviously assigned to the full-time duty of attending to the occupant of this suite.

"Sir?" she asked.

"Would this be the suite of Lord Alexander Percival Chetwynd-Dunleigh?"

"Aye, sir, t'would be," the maid replied in a thick Irish brogue. "And could I be tellin' his lordship who is callin'?"

"I am J. P. Winthrop, representing J. P. Morgan on a business matter."

"Won't you come in, sir? Sit you down, and I'll summon his lordship."

"Thank you."

J.P. crossed the thick deep-blue carpet to one of the overstuffed gold-brocade chairs sitting on either side of the matching sofa. Looking around the sitting room with an appraiser's eye, J.P. knew that when the hotel had been completed some fifteen years ago at a cost of three million dollars, it claimed to be "the model hotel of the world." He also knew that the Waldorf-Astoria had already overshadowed it, and the owner was planning to tear this building down and put up an even larger, more splendid hotel.

J.P. looked down at the card in his hand. He was here to meet Lord Chetwynd-Dunleigh for the purpose of appraising a painting that the Englishman wished to sell to Morgan. Before arriving, J.P. had done some research, locating the information he sought on the Earl of Dunleigh in a small book entitled *English Peerage, 1904*:

> Dunleigh Hall, the home of the Earl of Dunleigh, is a fine old Jacobean pile started in 1604 and completed with the addition of the newest wing in 1824. It is located one hundred thirty miles from London and is said to be the exact geographical center of England. The earldom was created June 10, 1444; the family name, Chetwynd-Dunleigh, was hyphenated at the creation of the earldom by royal recognition of the legitimate claim of Arthur Chetwynd to be the bastard son of Henry Alton Dunleigh. The Dunleigh name is mentioned in the Domesday Book, the list of England's landowners in 1086.
>
> The current Earl of Dunleigh, Sir Alexander Percival Chetwynd-Dunleigh, is an accomplished polo player, yachtsman, and fencing master, having represented the United Kingdom in the International Games (the modern Olympics) held in Paris in 1900.

"Ah, Mr. Winthrop. Thank you so much for coming."

J.P. rose to greet Dunleigh, who was slightly shorter than he with a narrow, aristocratic face, a prominent nose, and piercing blue eyes. His hands were as small and delicate as a woman's, and the nails were exquisitely manicured.

"Good morning, Lord Chetwynd-Dunleigh."

Dunleigh laughed and waved his hand. "Heavens, dear fellow, don't get all caught up in the lordship and

hyphenated nonsense. I much prefer to be called Alex.
And do you go by your initials?"

"Yes."

"I've noticed that about Americans. I suppose if one
would make judicious use of the alphabet, one wouldn't
need names at all." Dunleigh laughed at his own joke,
and J.P., though he didn't find it nearly as funny,
laughed as well.

"Lord—" J.P. started, then, when Dunleigh held up
his hand, corrected himself. "Sir Alex," he went on, "I
understand you have a painting you wish to sell."

"Yes, a family portrait really, one of those dreary
things that march up the wall alongside the staircase at
Dunleigh Hall. It isn't my personal favorite, and I
wouldn't mind parting with it, if the inducement is right.
Mr. Morgan, I have been told, is engaged in a one-man
campaign to collect everything in the world."

"You've brought the painting with you, correct?"

"Yes. I commissioned a special case to be built for it,
and I assure you, it suffered no damage in transit. Would
you like to see it?"

"Yes, if you don't mind."

"Come this way. I have it hanging in the dining
room."

Though Dunleigh hadn't identified the artist, J. P.
recognized him the moment his eyes lighted on the
painting, and he thought it appropriate that it was
hanging in the dining room, for his eyes virtually feasted
on the work. The subject of the painting was heroically
mounted on a white horse, distortedly elongated by the
angle of the viewer and illuminated by vivid colors and
dramatic lighting effects. This painting was obviously an
El Greco, although J.P. was puzzled. El Greco was one
of J.P.'s favorite painters, and he thought he knew every
work the sixteenth- and early-seventeenth-century artist
had done. But he had never even heard of this piece. He
stepped closer to the canvas and studied the detail.
There was no mistaking the style.

"Do you recognize the artist?" Dunleigh asked.

"The artist, yes. But I must confess, I have never heard of this particular picture."

"There is no reason you should have, dear boy," Dunleigh said. "This painting has been in our family's private collection since the artist painted it in 1610. It has never been exhibited."

"How much are you asking for it?"

"Twenty-five hundred dollars," Dunleigh said.

J.P. looked around sharply. "Twenty-five hundred?"

"Is that too much?"

"No, it isn't too much," J.P. replied. He looked at the painting again. He was prepared to tell Morgan that the painting was worth ten times Dunleigh's asking price; the question in his mind now was, should he tell Dunleigh?

"Tell me, Sir Alex. Why do you wish to sell it? It is, truly, a magnificent work."

Dunleigh laughed self-consciously, then looked around to make certain that the maid wasn't within earshot. "I, uh, need the money to pay the hotel bill." When J.P. looked at him in surprise, Dunleigh laughed again. "I see you find it strange that one with my *pedigree*, shall we say, is experiencing financial difficulty."

J.P. thought it not strange at all. His own position was virtually the same—the Winthrop name worth far more than his actual worth. "No," he said, "I can understand temporary reversals."

Dunleigh laughed. "Heavens, dear boy, this isn't a temporary reversal. This is a state of absolute deprivation. Desperate measures are called for if the Chetwynd-Dunleigh estate is to survive."

"Surely you don't intend to sell off all your art? If so, where would you go from there?"

"No, I have an even more desperate measure than that in mind, I'm afraid," Dunleigh said. "I have sold myself."

"Sold yourself?"

"I am to be married, dear boy. That is the reason for

my voyage to New York—the reason I must maintain appearances by staying in this overpriced and underclassed hovel. It is also the reason I am in need of immediate funds. Once I am married, all my troubles will be over. The father of my intended will, at the conclusion of the ceremony, endow me with one million dollars, while I will make a countess of his daughter."

"It appears as if it were more a business arrangement than an affair of love," J.P. remarked.

Dunleigh's ringing laughter sounded like shattering crystal. Although elegant, like some delicately blown goblet, it was a bit too brittle, as if somehow flawed during creation.

"Love? Love, my dear boy? How quaint. As if such a thing really mattered," the earl scoffed.

"Are you saying it *doesn't*?" J.P. thought of his own feelings for Lucinda. "I would think love is the most important consideration."

"I suppose such a thing may matter among the plebeians," Dunleigh said. "But in my class, marriages have been arranged for centuries . . . a political union between warring factions, a religious union to satisfy the church, even an incestuous marriage in order to keep the bloodlines pure. Why is an economic union any more sordid than they?"

"I didn't say it was sordid," J.P. reminded him.

"You didn't?"

"No."

"My, I wonder where that word came from?" Dunleigh looked at the painting for a long moment—more, J. P. believed, to avoid looking at him than to study the canvas. "How say you, J.P.? Will you advise your employer to buy my little oil?"

"Yes. I will."

"Ah, good, good. By the way, there will be a dinner party tomorrow night at the Waldorf-Astoria, hosted by the father of my bride-to-be." Dunleigh took a calling card from his jacket, then wrote "admit bearer" on the back and handed the card to J.P. "I would like very much for you to come. If Mr. Morgan has agreed to the sale, you may inform me then."

"Very well, Sir Alex," J.P. said, tucking the card into his pocket. "I'll see you then."

J.P. left the Plaza and took a cab to his namesake's house. When he arrived, the young curator was shown by the butler into the library, where J. Pierpont Morgan was sitting in front of the huge, cold fireplace, puffing on a big cigar. Kneeling angels on the marble mantel seemed to be paying homage to the financier, who was busy playing solitaire on a custom-made cherrywood card table. Morgan was going through the deck, laying red cards on black and gradually bringing the cards into submission. J.P. knew that the game was therapy for Morgan, who often retired to play it when he was contemplating some of his thorniest problems.

"Did you see the painting?" Morgan asked, not taking his gaze from the cards but occasionally thoughtfully tapping those remaining in his hand on the sterling-silver card box perched beside him.

"Yes, I saw it."

"And how much is he asking for it?"

"Twenty-five hundred dollars."

"Is it worth the price?"

"It's worth ten times that," J.P. replied. Morgan looked up in surprise, and, answering the older man's question before it was asked, J.P. explained, "It's an El Greco. Not one that is known, but it is El Greco, nonetheless."

"You are sure of it? It isn't a fake?"

"I'm sure of it."

Morgan stood up and walked over to an end table, where he ground his cigar out in an ashtray. He looked back at his employee. "Why is he asking so little for a painting worth so much?"

"There are a couple of reasons," J.P. answered. "For one thing, I don't believe he really knows the value of the work. In fact, El Greco has been little known until recently, though some collectors are beginning to recognize his real significance. The Chicago Art Museum,

for example, has just offered forty thousand dollars for El
Greco's 'The Assumption.'"

"And the other reason?"

"A rather distasteful one, I think," J.P. said. "It
seems his lordship is about to marry an American
girl . . . not for love, mind you, but for money. She
will get a title, the earl will get one million dollars. Until
that time he needs money to pay the hotel bill and living
expenses, and he's willing to sell the El Greco to do
that."

Morgan chuckled. "I take it you don't approve of his
nuptial arrangements?"

"I think they are crass."

"Who's the American girl who will soon be elevated?"

"I don't know. Sir Alex invited me to a reception
tomorrow night, where the announcement will be made.
You know, now that I think about it, there's something
rather odd about this."

"What?"

"Sir Alex gave me the invitation in the form of his
personal calling card. But why didn't I receive a formal
invitation? Lord knows, I've been invited to every other
soiree in the last two months."

Morgan smiled. "Maybe you're losing your charm,"
he quipped. "Now, about the painting. If it really is
worth much more than twenty-five hundred dollars, I
certainly don't want to be accused of 'stealing' it. On the
other hand, a man who is about to get one million dollars
just for marrying some girl doesn't deserve to have the
ante raised. Do you have any suggestions?"

"Yes, one," J.P. replied. "Suppose the New York
Museum buys it for twenty-five hundred dollars . . .
and then you buy it from the museum for twenty-five
thousand? That way you can't be accused of 'stealing' the
painting, and if Sir Alex learns the true value of the
painting, he can be placated by being told that his letting
the museum have it at such a bargain price was actually
an eleemosynary gesture on his part."

Morgan laughed. "By Jove, J.P., I believe you have

it," he said. "The museum will then be the beneficiary, not his lordship. Very well. Make all the arrangements, will you?"

"Yes, of course."

The young man started to leave, but Morgan called out to him. "By the way, your grandmother Winthrop came to speak to me, urging me to give you a more responsible position."

J.P. felt his cheeks redden. "I'm sorry, sir. I'm terribly embarrassed by that. I had no idea she would do such a thing. I hope you don't think—"

Morgan cut him off with a chuckle and a wave of his hand. "Don't be embarrassed," he said. "Your grandmother and I think alike on a lot of things, not the least of which is your value to me. I think you are doing excellent work, but I want you happy. If you would rather be somewhere else . . ."

"No!" J.P. assured him. "This is where I want to be. I love what I'm doing."

Morgan walked over and put his hand on J.P.'s shoulder. "I can tell that you do, son. It shows in your work. You just keep on with it; I'll placate your grandmother. After all, we are family."

"Yes, sir," J.P. said, grinning.

Before J.P. left the Morgan house, he used the telephone in the front hall to call Lucinda to tell her about the reception that would announce the engagement of Sir Alex and his bride-to-be and invite her to go with him, if she hadn't already received an invitation. Also, since he knew that she generally had her ear to the ground, she might very well know what young woman had compromised herself by such an arrangement.

A servant answered the telephone on the second ring, saying, "Delacroix residence."

"Hello, Miss Delacroix, please. This is J. P. Winthrop."

"One moment, sir," the tinny voice responded.

A moment later Lucinda's mother came on the phone. "Mr. Winthrop? This is Maggie Delacroix. May I help you?"

"Oh, hello, Mrs. Delacroix. I wonder if I may speak with Lucinda."

"I'm sorry, that wouldn't be convenient right now," she answered. Her voice, while not cold, was flat and expressionless.

"Oh, well, do you know when it might be convenient? I could call back later."

"That would not be a good idea."

"I don't understand."

"Mr. Winthrop, please don't call here anymore."

"What? Why? What's wrong?"

J.P. heard a click from the other end. "Hello? Hello, Mrs. Delacroix, are you there?"

"This is central," a new voice said. "Your party has disconnected. Shall I ring again?"

"No, operator, thank you," J.P. mumbled. He slowly replaced the receiver, then looked at the instrument as if it had personally affronted him. Why would Mrs. Delacroix act so strangely toward him? Why wouldn't she let him talk to her daughter?

Suddenly J.P. gasped. *My God! She knows about us!* he decided. *She knows that I have compromised Lucinda! She has branded Lucinda a wanton woman and me a despoiler!*

CHAPTER

TEN

Eric Twainbough sat in the open doorway of a Burlington and Missouri River freight car, riding south through northwestern Nebraska and looking out over the prairie and the stream of water running parallel with the track. It was about nine o'clock at night, but the sky was clear, the moon was full, and visibility was excellent. Benjamin Ely had told him earlier that the river was called Snake Creek; under the bright moon the creek looked like a flowing stream of molten silver, and the gently rolling hills were delineated in shades of gray and black under the great, glowing pearl in the sky.

A lone farmhouse stood out in the distance, its windows glowing a soft gold from the kerosene lamps inside. Eric thought of the family in that house, imagining that the mother would be sitting by one lamp, sewing or perhaps piecing a quilt, and the father by another, reading. Between the mother and father a young boy would be sitting on the floor, playing with a handful of carved wooden toys. Somewhere, in the deepest recesses of his mind, Eric could remember such a scene from his own childhood.

"I've been over this route before," Ely said, joining Eric in the doorway, his legs dangling over the edge. "No towns, crossings, or water stops for nearly fifty miles. You just keep an eye outside because the next thing you know, we're going to be running forty miles an hour or better. They really pour on the coal through here."

"I thought it felt like we were beginning to go faster," Eric said, nodding.

"Are you hungry?"

Eric answered with a little laugh. "Well, I guess I am. But there's nothing I can do about it."

Ely smiled broadly. "Sure, there is. That is, if you like beans." He held up a can of baked beans.

"Where did you get that?" Eric asked in surprise.

"You remember when we were lying low under the warehouse loading dock back in Edgemont, waiting to catch a train south?"

"Yes."

"You may also recall that I slipped out to have a look around. Well, I found a broken crate, so I confiscated a couple of cans. I have some hot peppers, too, if you would like one cut up."

"Sure," Eric said.

The hobo cut open the can of beans and poured half of the contents into his collapsible cup, then gave the can to Eric. Next, he cut up a hot pepper, keeping half for himself and giving half to his companion. "They had some tinned beef, too," he said as he handed it over. "But I wouldn't touch that with a ten-foot pole."

"You don't like beef?" Eric asked in surprise. He had no fork or spoon, so he ate the beans by slowly pouring them directly into his mouth.

"Sure, I love beef," Ely answered. "My mother used to make a roast beef that was . . ." The sentence trailed off, and the hobo stared off into space for a long, silent period, looking as if he were fighting back memories he had inadvertently dredged up. "But I won't eat tinned beef," he said a bit gruffly.

"Why not?"

"You may not realize it, Mr. Twainbough, but during the war with Spain we had but a few hundred soldiers killed by enemy action. However, we had nearly one thousand killed by beef that had gone bad in the tin." Again he got a faraway look in his eyes. "They were dropping like flies," he said. "We had no idea what was wrong. We never thought . . . never dreamed . . . that our own people would sell us bad—but, never mind. That's all past now."

They ate in silence for awhile; then Eric announced, "I'm going to St. Louis."

"St. Louis? It's a good town."

"Have you ever been there?"

"Oh, sure, lots of times. I'll just bet you didn't know, Mr. Twainbough, that St. Louis happens to have more paved streets and more streetcars than any other city in America."

"No, I didn't know that. The truth is, I don't know anything about St. Louis."

"Beer, shoes, and caskets," Ely said.

"What?"

"That's what St. Louis is famous for. Beer, shoes, and caskets."

"I didn't know that, either."

Ely picked up a piece of paper from the floor of the car and wiped his cup very thoroughly, then collapsed it and put it back in his pocket. With a wry smile he looked at Eric. "Tell me, Mr. Twainbough. Since you know nothing about St. Louis, just why are you so anxious to get there?"

"I'm going to see the wonders," Eric said. "The World's Fair is in St. Louis. I read about it in a newspaper. That's how come we started on this journey in the first place."

"We?"

"Yes, Jake and Marcus and—" Eric stopped, surprised that he had said so much. "I mean, well, they're a couple of friends who started out with me."

"What happened to them?"

The youth looked down at his lap. "They aren't with me anymore."

"You don't have to tell me anything if you don't want to, Mr. Twainbough," Ely said softly. "I certainly will not pry. On the other hand, if you feel a need to tell, I'm a good listener, and I know how to keep my mouth shut. Some people like to get things off their chest every now and then. In fact, you know what they say: Confession is good for the soul."

"I've never heard that," Eric said.

"Then you aren't Catholic, are you?"

"No," Eric said. "At least, I don't think I am. I guess I've never really thought about it. I mean, I guess I believe in God and Jesus and all that, but I've never been to any kind of a church. Mr. Ebersole has an Anglican Book of Common Prayer and a wonderful Bible with lots of colored pictures. I've read it. It's very interesting, and there are some really good stories in the Bible . . . Noah, Joshua, Jonah and the whale, Cain and Abel, and how Jesus was nailed to the cross and everything."

"You must read a lot for someone of your tender years," Ely remarked.

"I guess I do. I know I really like to read. Someday I would like—" He stopped in midsentence and laughed. "I mean, I used to think I'd like to be a writer."

"That's an admirable ambition. What made you change your mind?"

"This."

"This?"

"Look at me, Mr. Ely," Eric said. "I'm a bum. I'm hopping rides on freight trains, I'm eating stolen food, a few days ago I was nearly raped by a crazed man. Who am I to say I'd like to be a writer?"

"Who would have a better right than you to say it?" Ely asked.

"Someone who's been educated in a fine school,

someone who's done wonderful things . . . someone like you."

"Like me?"

"You were educated in a fine school."

"How do you know?"

"I can tell," Eric said. "You don't talk the way anyone else I've ever known talks, except maybe Mr. Ebersole. And of course, he was English, so that explains why he talked funny."

Benjamin Ely laughed. "And you think I talk funny?"

"Well, no. I mean, not with an accent like Mr. Ebersole. But the way you say things . . . the words you use."

"You are an astute lad, Mr. Twainbough."

Eric laughed. "See? That's what I mean. Saying things like 'astute lad.' Nobody else I've ever known talks like that. You *are* educated, aren't you?"

"You are right, Mr. Twainbough, I was educated in a fine school," Ely admitted. "To my thinking, it is the finest school in the world. I graduated from the United States Military Academy at West Point."

"I know about West Point," Eric said. "The men who graduate from there become officers in the army."

"That's right."

"You were an officer in the Army?"

"I was a captain."

"A captain? Wow! That's a very high rank, isn't it?"

Ely chuckled. "Well, it's not all that high. But it's high enough."

"Why did you " Eric smiled sheepishly. "I'm sorry. I have no right to ask the question I was about to ask."

"Why did I leave the Army?"

Eric nodded.

Ely looked intensely at Eric. "Mr. Twainbough, do you remember when I told you that if you didn't get rid of that gun you carry, you might have to use it?"

"Yes."

"That wasn't an idle observation; I was speaking

from experience. You see, I, too, used to carry a pistol. And I had to use it to kill a soldier."

"But you were a soldier," Eric said. "Soldiers use their guns to kill enemy soldiers."

"This soldier wasn't an enemy," Ely said quietly. "He was one of my own men."

Eric was shocked by the revelation, but he said nothing, assuming that if the hobo wanted him to know more, he would tell more.

"It happened in Cuba, at La Guardia ridge, which means 'The Guardian,'" Ely went on. "That was a good name for it, because it commanded the main road. The battle of La Guardia ridge wasn't much of a battle, really. It's hard to even find mention of it in the stories of the war in Cuba. But the Spanish were there, and they fought back. They had artillery, seventy-five-millimeter guns, dug in on top of the ridge. As we started up the hill they opened fire."

Ely abruptly quit talking, as if composing his thoughts, and the two men just sat in the open door of the freight car, looking out over the fields that rolled by. Then the older man took a deep breath and went on with his story.

"We continued up the hill. Our own artillery was firing from the valley behind us, the Spanish were firing from in front. Gatling guns were rattling away all around us, and the hillside was alive with shot and shell and smoke and cordite that burned our eyes and choked our lungs. Despite all that, my men, roaring defiance, went up that hill. They were the most magnificent bastards you would ever want to see. No military unit in the history of our nation was ever more heroic or determined. And we took that hill, Mr. Twainbough. When the smoke had cleared away after the last shot was fired, we were standing on the crest of the hill with the Stars and Stripes waving from the flagpole and the Spanish ensign nothing but a souvenir for our battalion. It was the proudest moment of my life." He paused, then said softly, "Little did I know that less than two minutes later I would experience the lowest point of my life."

"What happened?"

"My first sergeant, a very fine man named Danny Webb, went over to examine one of the field guns the Spanish had left behind. None of us realized that the Spanish had planted a bomb in the barrel of the gun and, as Sergeant Webb was looking at it, the bomb went off. The result was terrible to behold. Sergeant Webb's legs went one way, his arms another, and his body, open and bleeding, another still. I rushed to him. He was screaming in pain, but there was nothing I could do. His intestines were lying in the dirt, and I could see his lungs. By all rights he should have been dead or at least insensible to pain, but he wasn't. He was still alive, and in agony with every breath. I knew he would die within seconds, and as I knelt beside him, I prayed that God would take him at once."

Ely grew quiet and pinched the bridge of his nose. Eric thought he might be crying, and, embarrassed, he looked toward the moon, giving the man a moment to compose himself.

"He didn't die," Ely continued. "He hung on in that half-alive, half-dead state, pleading with me to shoot him. 'For the love of God, if you have an ounce of humanity in you, Captain, shoot me,' he begged.

"'Hang on,' I replied. 'The doctor is coming. He'll be here in a minute.'

"'Kill me, kill me!' he shouted. 'Kill me! If you love God, if you love your mother, kill me!'

"I looked into his eyes and saw that his plea was genuine. Then I pulled out my pistol and put the barrel between his eyes. 'Yes, yes,' he said, nodding his head. And then, 'God bless you, Captain. God bless you.'"

Ely was silent for almost a full minute after that, and the two drifters just sat there, listening to the measured click-clack of steel wheels rolling over joints. Far ahead the train engineer blew the whistle. Eric had never heard it sound more sorrowful, almost like a cry in the night. When Eric looked over at his companion, he could see the big man's shoulders shaking as silent sobs racked his body, and tear tracks on his face gleamed softly in the moonlight.

"Afterward," Ely said, when he had finally composed himself, "I was court-martialed. I had no right, the Army said, to end Sergeant Webb's pain. What no one realized was I didn't end his pain . . . I merely transferred it, for now I feel it here"—he put his hand over his heart—"and I have felt it with every heartbeat since the moment I pulled that trigger, six years ago."

"I'm . . . I'm so sorry," Eric murmured.

Ely looked over at Eric and twisted his face into what he might have believed was a grin. "So you see, Mr. Twainbough, whatever it is you are running from, it can't be worse than the burden I've been carrying all this time, now, can it?"

Eric thought of watching Jake and Marcus die. It had been a terrible experience, but at least he hadn't been the one who killed them.

"No, Mr. Ely," he said quietly. "My burden isn't as heavy as yours."

Ely stood up then and stretched. "What do you say we try and grab us a little shut-eye? We'll be reaching the Union Pacific tracks along about two in the morning, and if you're wanting to go on to St. Louis, you'll need to catch a train going east."

"Okay," Eric agreed, getting up and walking with Ely toward the front of the car. As they began piling the paper up for their bed, Eric suddenly realized that the older man's offer to hear Eric's story was in reality a plea to let him tell his own. In fact, even as they shoved the paper into position, Ely's mood had lightened so much that he began singing. He sang, "Meet me in St. Louie, Louie, meet me at the fair. . . ."

"What's that?" Eric asked. "Did you just make that song up?"

"Make it up? Oh, my, no, Mr. Twainbough. That's a song that was composed for the fair. I suspect you'll be hearing it more than once, when you get there."

"It's a good song," Eric said, and he repeated it, "Meet me in St. Louie, Louie, meet me at the fair—"

Suddenly a shadow blotted out the moonlight, and, startled, Eric and Ely looked around at the open doorway. A large, hulking shape was swinging in from the top of the doorframe, having dropped down from the roof of the car.

"Well, now, what do we have here?" the hulk asked. "I do believe you two bastards are the bums who got away from me last week, aren't you?"

"Mr. Slocum!" Ely exclaimed. "What are *you* doing on this line?"

"Didn't you know, bum? I don't work for any one line. No, sir. I'm so good, I hire out my services to whoever needs me. I'm what you might call a troubleshooter. Now, you two bums, get off the train."

"The train is going too fast right now," Ely said in a reasoning voice. "If we tried to jump, we'd be killed."

Slocum chuckled. "Yeah, that's likely so. But you ain't got no choice."

"When the train slows, we'll get off," Ely countered.

Slocum laughed again, this time a low, evil chortle. "All right," he said, "have it your way. You can stay on the train and let me work you over real good and slow with my sap, then jump off when the train slows . . . if you still can. Or, you can jump now and take your chances."

Suddenly Ely scooped up a length of two-by-four that was lying on the floor of the car, then held it at the ready. "We'll get off when the train slows," he said fiercely. "And if you come toward us with that sap of yours, I'll knock your brains out."

"You bums, you never learn, do you?" Slocum retorted easily. He reached into his back pocket, and Eric thought he was going for his sap. To his surprise, when Slocum's hand came around front, he wasn't holding a sap, he was holding a pistol. "Good-bye, bum," Slocum said.

A sudden, brilliant flash of orange light lit up the inside of the car. The sound of the shot was deafening.

The impact of the bullet knocked Benjamin Ely against the back wall of the car, and he slid down to the floor, leaving a swath of blood on the wall behind him that looked black in the dim light.

"Mr. Ely!" Eric screamed.

"You're next, kid," Slocum said, and his gun flashed and roared a second time.

Eric dropped to the floor and rolled to his right just as Slocum fired, avoiding the bullet. He wound up on his stomach with his gun in his hand, aiming it directly at Slocum's head.

"Where are you, you son of a bitch?" Slocum shouted. When he located Eric he smiled and pointed his gun at him again. "Ah, there you are."

Incredibly, Slocum didn't even seem to notice the gun in Eric's hand, perhaps because he didn't expect to see one.

"No!" Eric shouted, as he saw Slocum thumb back the hammer.

"When you get to hell, kid, tell your friend and all those other bums I've sent there that Slocum says hello."

Eric fired, and in the light of the moon he saw a dark spray of blood explode from the top of Slocum's head. Slocum dropped his gun and went down. Slowly, Eric rose to his hands and knees and looked over at him. The railroad man was lying on his back, his arms and legs splayed, his head tilted back, and his mouth and eyes open. There was a small, inoffensive-looking black hole right between his eyes and a much larger black hole at the top of his head toward the rear. Blood, bone, and brain matter seeped from that hole.

"Is the . . . son of a bitch dead?" Ely asked from the dark behind Eric.

"Yes," Eric answered, surprised to hear the hobo's voice. He left Slocum and hurried over to his friend. "I . . . I thought *you* were."

"I am," Ely whispered. He coughed, and blood came out of his mouth.

"No," Eric said urgently. "We'll get you to a doctor. I've got twenty-five dollars. When we reach the next town I'll get you a doctor."

"Save your money, Mr. Twainbough." Ely tried to

laugh, but it turned into another blood-spewing cough. "You'll need that money to see those wonders you were talking about at the World's Fair."

"No, I—"

"Hush. There's not time for all that now. You have to promise me something. Will you promise me?"

"Yes, anything," Eric said softly.

"When we get to the next stop, I want you to get off the train and leave me here. Dead or alive, I want you to leave me."

"I can't do that."

"You *will* do it, Mr. Twainbough, and that's an order," Ely said sharply. "And another thing. You'll leave that pistol with me."

"No! Mr. Ely, I'm not going to let you shoot yourself."

The hobo shook his head and spoke, more gently this time. "I'm not going to shoot myself. I'm about to put Sergeant Webb's pain down, do you hear me? I'm about to put it down forever, but I have no intention of transferring it to you. That's not why I want you to leave me your pistol."

"Then, why?"

"I'll be dead by the time the authorities look inside this car. They'll see me lying over here with a bullet wound in my chest and a gun in my hand. They'll see Slocum over there with a bullet in his head and a gun in his hand, and they'll figure we shot each other. No one will ever bother to come looking for you."

"Mr. Ely, I can't do that," Eric protested. "I can't have them blaming you for this."

"Eric," Ely said, and it was the first time he had ever addressed the youth informally, "I had one friend to whom I could give only death. Please, let me give you life."

"All right, Mr. Ely," Eric said quietly. "All right, if that's what you want."

"That's a good lad."

Eric walked over to the door and stood there for a long moment. The train was going around a curve, and from this angle he could see the engine, the white tendrils of steam escaping from its cylinders as the mighty drive wheels pounded against the track. Finally, when the entire train was around the curve, Eric turned back toward Benjamin Ely.

"Mr. Ely, how long do you think it'll be till we reach the next stop?"

When he didn't answer, Eric moved closer to him. "Mr. Ely? Mr. Ely!"

Quickly, Eric knelt beside him. He put his hand in front of Ely's nose and, feeling no breath, tried to find a pulse. There was none.

He lowered his head and cried.

The very rich were arriving at the Waldorf-Astoria like so many brilliant kites on the wind, displaying their status with pomp and circumstance. The occasion was the reception given in honor of Sir Alexander Percival Chetwynd-Dunleigh, and the sudden influx of liveried carriages and chauffered automobiles, complete with footmen, created enough of a traffic jam to demand the services of extra policemen. Scores of spectators massed on the sidewalks to get a glimpse of the wealthy men and women descending from their carriages and autos, displaying the trappings of their special breed—striking formal attire, elaborate coiffures, sumptuous ball gowns, and magnificent jewels.

Alighting from his own carriage, J. P. Winthrop thought it appropriate that the gathering of these golden ones was held at the Waldorf-Astoria, considered, unquestionably, the finest hotel in the world. J.P. thought it a fitting parting gesture by William Waldorf Astor, when he had grown tired of New York a decade earlier and decided to move to England, that, before leaving, he tore down the house his father had left him on Fifth Avenue and built the huge Waldorf Hotel, replete with bas-reliefs, turrets, and finials.

Chuckling to himself, J.P. recalled that William's Aunt Caroline, *the* Mrs. Astor, had certainly deemed it vastly other than fitting. But though incensed that William would build such a vulgar and commercial edifice right next to her house, the grande dame of New York society had no recourse and continued to live in her four-story mansion, which, dwarfed as it was by the massive hotel, looked like a tiny cabin clinging to the side of a giant cliff. Finally, however, Mrs. Astor could take it no more, and she abandoned her house and moved to her château at Sixty-fifth and Fifth. Her son John, angry with his cousin for building the hotel, had considered razing his mother's house and putting in a stable to ruin the hotel's business. However, because profit was even more palatable than revenge, he had decided instead to build his own hotel right next door to the Waldorf, naming it the Astoria.

But even before the new hotel was completed, the two hotels had been joined into one operation—although the cousins also agreed that the connection between the two buildings could be sealed off if need be, providing for a separation should the alliance prove to be unworkable. With a thousand bedrooms, many public rooms, plus a ballroom that could hold fifteen hundred guests in radiant splendor, the Waldorf-Astoria was the largest and most expensive hotel in the world and became *the* place of the very rich, where in order to dine in the most exclusive of the restaurants, even on an ordinary night, guests were required to wear evening clothes. The atmosphere was wealthy, the air was scented with the most expensive perfumes, and on any given night, the halls and rooms would be rife with jewels, furs, and silks.

The maître d' at the Waldorf Astoria, a man named Oscar, was a legend in his profession, a practiced snob keenly aware of social gradations and a man who could be counted on to guard against any unwanted guests at the more discriminating affairs. Money and power alone did not guarantee entry, for Oscar had once barred the very wealthy and very powerful August Belmont from attending a party to which he had not been invited. Belmont let it be known that he had better be invited to the very next party or he would ruin half the members of society. Angry at the threatened blackmail, the social set wondered what to do. Oscar offered a suggestion.

Belmont was then invited to a party at the Waldorf, and on the given night Oscar was in his usual place just outside the ballroom to welcome, with just the proper deference, August Belmont and his wife. Not one other guest arrived.

J.P. was recalling the tale with amusement as he walked under a seemingly endless string of chandeliers dotting Peacock Alley, the corridor that connected—or separated, depending on the point of view—the two hotels. Near the reception room the chandeliers, as well as the mirrors and marble pillars, were garlanded with roses. At the end of the corridor, standing sentry at the entrance to the large public room where the reception was being held, stood Oscar.

J.P. presented Sir Alex's card to Oscar, who promptly examined the gold-leafed, red-leather book that sat on the highly polished desk. Looking up, he handed the card back to the new arrival and said, "I'm sorry, Mr. Winthrop. I'm afraid I don't see your name on the guest list."

"I didn't actually receive an invitation," J.P. explained. "But as you can see, this is the personal card of the Earl of Dunleigh, granting me entrance."

"Yes, sir, the card is most impressive," Oscar said. "However, while the Earl of Dunleigh is the guest of honor, he is not the host. Therefore, I'm afraid that card will not grant you entrance. Only your name in this book will do that."

By now other guests were starting to bunch up behind J.P., who was himself feeling embarrassed. A definite tinge of red began to flame in his cheeks, in sharp contrast to his black suit of tails and crisp white shirt, and he wished he could leave without anyone noticing he was here. He turned to go.

"J.P., old man! How are you doing?" Stuart Parks, one of the new arrivals, greeted him. The same age as J.P., Stuart was a teammate on the New York Athletic Club polo team. "Wait until I get my hat and gloves properly deposited, and we can go in together. You'll notice I'm wearing my Harvard pin. That should provide some class to an occasion that is seriously in need of same, don't you think?" Stuart quipped.

"I'm afraid I won't be going in with you," J.P. said.

"Oh? And why not?"

"There's been some mix-up in the invitation."

Frowning, Stuart turned to the maître d'. "Come, what is this, Oscar?" he questioned. "I know Mr. Winthrop went to some new college out West somewhere, but that's certainly no reason to keep him out, is it? Just be a good fellow and let down your Teutonic barriers, won't you?"

"I'm sorry, Mr. Parks, but my instructions are quite specific," Oscar replied. "No one is to be admitted if their name is not in this book."

"Don't worry about it, Oscar. I'll leave," J.P. said. "I certainly don't wish to cause any trouble."

"Sorry, old boy," Stuart said as he started inside. "I don't know what the mix-up could have been." Smiling broadly, he added, "You may rest assured, however, that I will register my protest with the host as soon as I get inside."

"No, don't bother," J.P. replied, but Stuart was already disappearing into the swirl of color and gaiety.

With a sigh J.P. started back down the corridor.

"J.P.! J.P., wait!" a woman's voice called.

Turning, J.P. saw Lucinda running after him, holding up the skirt of her voluminous dress. As she ran, her high-heel-shod feet and silk-stockinged ankles flashed from underneath the weighted hem of the gown.

"Lucinda," J.P. said. "Hello. I telephoned your house. I was going to ask you to come with me." He held Sir Alex's card out with a little laugh. "But I suppose it's best I didn't get to talk to you. I was just turned away, and it would have been even more embarrassing had you been with me."

"J.P., let's go someplace where we can talk," Lucinda said, putting her hand on his arm and leading him down the corridor.

"Okay, sure." J.P. grinned lasciviously. "what about the apartment of your friend? You know, where we—"

"This will be fine," Lucinda said, pointing at a sofa between two potted palms up against the honey-colored marble wall.

J.P. waited until Lucinda was seated, then sat beside her. Lucinda reached out and took his hands in hers.

"Dear J.P.," she murmured, "please, don't hate me." To J.P.'s surprise, Lucinda's eyes brimmed with tears.

"Hate you? Don't be silly. Why should I hate you?" he asked.

"Because of what happened the other day."

"Lucinda," he whispered. He lifted her hands to his lips to kiss them, but she drew them away.

"No," she said quietly.

"Lucinda, I'll admit that I may have acted rather like a fool, but you can charge that off to ecstatic surprise. If you think that I hold you in any less—"

"No," she cut in, shaking her head. Now the tears were flowing in earnest. "You don't understand. Please, J.P., don't say anything. Don't say another word until I've explained."

"All right," he responded, puzzled by her odd behavior.

"When you telephoned me, I tried to answer. Indeed, I was in the very act of reaching for the telephone when Mother took it from me. She has forbidden me to ever talk to you or see you again. Except for this meeting, tonight. When we heard you were trying to get into the reception, I told her that if she didn't let me speak with you, explain things to you, I would cause such a scene she would never be able to live it down."

So far, Lucinda's explanation was raising more questions than it was answering, but J.P. had promised to let her speak uninterrupted, so he said nothing.

"You weren't left out by mistake. Your name wasn't

in the invitation book because when my parents made up the guest list, they specifically excluded you."

"Your parents?"

"Yes. J.P., when I sent the note to you asking you to meet me the other day, the day of our . . . the day we met in that apartment . . . my mother had just informed me of an arrangement she had made on my behalf."

"What sort of an arrangement?" Though J.P. still wasn't sure where she was going, the tone of it was beginning to disturb him.

"An arrangement with the Earl of Dunleigh," Lucinda said. "J.P., I am to marry him."

"*You?* You are the American girl he is to marry?"

Lucinda nodded.

"But this is insane! Lucinda, you can't be serious! You can't do this! He doesn't love you, I know he doesn't, for I've spoken to him. Of course, I had no idea you were the girl he was planning to marry, but I knew that he didn't love her. And I also know that you don't love him."

"No, I don't love him," Lucinda said quietly.

"Then you can't marry him! You mustn't!"

"I must and I will."

J.P. felt a hollowness in the pit of his stomach and a lightness in his arms and legs. He also felt as if he had just had the breath knocked out of him, and he sat there for a long minute, wondering when he would breathe again—or even *if* he *would* breathe again. Finally he choked out, "For God's sake, Lucinda, will you at least tell me why?"

"You of all people should know why. If I don't do this, I'll be disinherited, provided with a pension as long as I remain single, but cut off without a cent if I marry anyone but the earl. Don't you understand, J.P.? If I married you, I wouldn't have a cent of my inheritance."

"But you don't need—"

"Stop it!" Lucinda snapped. "We've known each other all our lives. I've watched your mother struggle to make ends meet on the pittance your grandmother has provided. I've heard the talk, the pity of the others. Your father married your mother for love, and what did it get him? Nothing. I can't go through life like that . . . I *won't* go through life like that. I love you, J.P., and I will never love another. But I am a weak woman. I cannot—and I will not—give up what is rightfully mine."

"And the time we spent together in the apartment?" he asked, feeling sickened. "What of that?"

"I make no apologies for that," she replied. "I am going to marry Sir Alex and move to England. There I shall be a countess and do whatever in God's name it is that countesses do. But I couldn't do that if I didn't have a small part of you tucked away in a secret compartment in the innermost chambers of my heart. Please, my darling, forgive me. And know that for the rest of my life I will love you."

"That's little comfort," J.P. replied quietly, bitterly.

"I'm afraid, dear boy, that you will have to take what comfort you can from it," a man's voice suddenly said, and, startled, J.P. looked around to see Sir Alex standing just on the other side of the potted palm.

J.P. stood quickly. "How long have you been there?" he asked, feeling humiliated.

"Oh, quite long enough to hear the whole, touching story. I am touched, you know. I mean, really, I am not a man without a heart. And you are right—I don't love Lucinda, and it is obvious that she doesn't love me. But we are both willing to marry for money, and I think that gives us enough in common to build a relationship. Certainly a relationship that would withstand the test of our circumstances." He offered his arm to Lucinda. "Dear, if you'll come now. I do believe your father is about to make the happy announcement."

"Very well," Lucinda said, standing and taking his arm.

"Oh, and dear boy," Sir Alex said to J.P. "I must apologize about the calling card in lieu of an invitation. It was really quite poor form, I know, but it would have been enough had you not enjoyed your peculiar relationship with the bride-to-be. I, of course, knew nothing about it at the time, or I never would have subjected any of us to the embarrassment. I do hope you will forgive me."

"Yes, of course," J.P. mumbled.

Lucinda looked at J.P., and he saw a curtain descend over her eyes. The tears, hurt, and pain were gone, and, in a strange way, he believed Lucinda was as well. "Good-bye," she said flatly.

"Good-bye," J.P. responded. He turned and walked away.

As he hurried away down Peacock Alley, he heard Sir Alex say almost conversationally, "Quite a nice chap, that. I can see why you were so taken with him. Oh, and did I tell you? He arranged the sale of a painting for me, to the New York Museum."

J.P. quickened his stride.

CHAPTER ELEVEN

The bell clanged and coupling pins rattled as the long, slow freight eased its way into St. Louis. On the outskirts of the city young boys, drawn by the seductive lure of the engine's whistle, hurried to the track to wave at the engineer and count aloud car by car as the train passed.

Inside the twenty-third car, another boy, not too many years older than the local youths, lay sleeping. Physically and emotionally drained by the ordeal of the last few weeks, Eric—who by now had come to think of himself as Twainbough, not McKenzie—didn't realize that his long journey was nearly completed. He didn't feel the train slow; neither did he notice the difference in the sounds the wheels were making on the tracks. And when a brakeman dropped down into the open car to check for illegal riders, Eric continued to sleep the sleep of the exhausted, unaware that he was in any danger.

"Off! Get off of my train, you goddamn bum!" the man shouted at the top of his voice, and Eric awoke to see an angry, sneering face looming over him. The brakeman, a very big, very powerful man, grabbed Eric by the shirt and jerked him to his feet.

"What the hell are you doing on my train, you son of a bitch?" the trainman shouted. His spittle sprayed Eric in the face. "I'm goin' to bust your head open like a ripe watermelon."

"No, wait, wait!" Eric begged. "You don't have to do that! I'll get off!" He tried to push the brakeman away.

"You're goddamn right you're goin' to get off," the brakeman replied. "And I'm goin' to help you." He raised his sap, then brought it down hard.

Eric instinctively jerked his head to one side in an attempt to avoid it, and the blackjack missed his head and hit him on the shoulder instead. For a split second Eric felt nothing; then he experienced a searing jolt of pain so intense it left him nauseated. His left arm went numb, and when the brakeman brought his sap down the second time, Eric found that he was unable to move or do anything to avoid it. This time the sap caught him just above the left ear. He saw a flash of red, then fell to the floor of the car. After that it was almost as if he were in two places at once. A part of him could feel the pain and the nausea, but another part of him was detached. It was as if he were watching almost disinterestedly the brakeman lifting a body—his body—from the floor and tossing it through the door. At the same time he was aware of tumbling through space, then falling into a thicket of briars and brambles that tore and cut at his flesh. But painful though the thorns were, they probably saved his life, for they broke the impact of his fall from the train.

At the point on the KATY line where Eric was thrown from the train, the track bed ran along the crest of a long, narrow ridge that was level with the tops of the poplars growing in a dense stand down in the gully. Eric tumbled and rolled all the way to the bottom of the gully, where he lay unable to move while the train rattled by overhead. His clothes were ripped to shreds, his body was covered with cuts and bruises, and his arm was still paralyzed from the blow he had received on his shoulder. Stunned, having no idea where he was, he finally stood up, thinking that he'd better reboard the train. If he hurried, he told himself, he might be able to catch one of the last cars.

Eric tried to climb the hill toward the rumbling train, but he got no more than two or three steps when he was overcome with nausea and dizziness. His eyelids fluttered, his knees weakened, and he grabbed for a tree limb to keep himself from falling.

After that, everything went black.

Loomis Booker and Pearl Summers strolled through the campus grounds to a wooded area that ran alongside the railroad tracks. They entered the woods, walking until they reached a small clearing. There, a fallen log made a wonderful bench, and they had come here many times, picnicking on occasion. Protected by the trees, they felt as if they were absolutely alone in the world.

When they reached the fallen tree trunk, the place they called "their spot," Pearl sat down.

"We can dance the hootchie-kootchie," Loomis sang.

"And I'll be your tootsie-wootsie," Pearl answered, laughing.

"And *will* you be my tootsie-wootsie?" Loomis asked.

Pearl pulled a long stem of grass from the ground. She cleaned it off, then stuck the end of it in her mouth and smiled coquettishly up at Loomis.

"Well, I don't know," she said. "No one has ever told me what a tootsie-wootsie is. How can I be your tootsie-wootsie if I don't know what it is?"

"I don't know what the other folks think it is," Loomis said, standing over Pearl. "I know what I think it is." He reached down to touch her, to let his fingers rest on her high cheekbone, and he stared at her with such intensity that his eyes were windows to his soul.

Pearl looked into his eyes for a long moment. Then,

nervously, she got up and moved to the other end of the log, where she stood looking away from him.

"Don't you want to know what I think it is?" Loomis asked. When Pearl didn't answer, Loomis went on. "I think it means you're my woman. Are you my woman, Pearl?"

"No," Pearl answered. She said the single word so quietly that Loomis could barely hear her.

"What?" Loomis asked, puzzled by her reply.

Pearl turned toward him, and Loomis was surprised to see that her face was streaked with tears.

"I can't be your woman, Loomis."

"Why not? My God, Pearl, are you married?"

"No," Pearl replied, shaking her head.

"Then I don't understand. Why can't you be my woman?"

"Because . . ." Pearl took a deep breath. "You're a good man, Loomis. You deserve a good woman and I"—she paused, then took another deep breath and plunged on—"I haven't been a good woman. There was another man. I thought I loved him . . . I thought he loved me. I let that man lie with me, Loomis."

"I see," Loomis said quietly.

"No, I don't think you do. At least, you don't see it all. There's something else about that man."

"He was white?" Loomis asked.

Pearl gasped. "Yes! How did you know?"

"I didn't know. I just guessed, by the way you're acting." A disturbing thought passed through Loomis's mind, one that he wanted to put to rest right away. Hating himself for what he was thinking, he asked, "Does Bob Canfield know about you and this man?"

"No," Pearl said quickly. "I would die of embarrassment if he knew about it."

Then it wasn't Bob Canfield, Loomis thought. He was ashamed of how relieved he felt.

"It was to keep Bob and the other Canfields from knowing that I came to St. Louis," Pearl went on. "When Mama found out about it, she was afraid there would be big trouble. She thought it would be better if I would just leave."

"And make a new life for yourself somewhere else?" Loomis asked.

"Yes," Pearl said, practically swallowing the word. "That was Mama's idea."

"Then why don't you?"

Pearl looked at Loomis. She was obviously confused by his statement. "Why don't I what?"

"Your mama wanted you to come here to make a new life for yourself," Loomis stated. "So why don't you?"

"I did. I have," Pearl answered. "I'm working for Professor Bateman, I'm seeing new things, I'm—"

"—still dragging your old life around with you," Loomis interrupted.

"I don't know what you are talking about."

"Pearl, I just asked you to be my woman," Loomis said. "You told me you couldn't do it. It looks to me like you don't want to make a new life for yourself."

"Oh, I do! I really do," Pearl insisted. "But I have to tell the truth about myself, don't I?"

"All right," Loomis said. "You've told me the truth. Now, give me the true answer to this question. You said you thought you loved this man. Do you still think that?"

"No!" Pearl said quickly. "The real truth is, I don't think I ever did. I mean, I didn't have any idea what love really was. Not until now, not until . . ." Pearl stopped.

"Not until you fell in love with me?" Loomis asked.

Pearl nodded, but she said nothing.

Loomis went to her quickly and wrapped his arms around her, pulling her to him. "Pearl, I don't care why you came to St. Louis. I only care that you *did* come and that I had the great good luck to meet you. Something has happened to me since you came. I never thought I'd find a woman to love—in fact, I never thought I would even want to. I was prepared to live the life of the academic, to content myself with study for the rest of my life."

Pearl stepped back to look at him. "Loomis, I

wouldn't want to take you away from your studies," she said fervently. "I know what that means to you."

"You won't take me away from my books, Pearl. You can share them with me."

"Me? You would let me study with you?"

"Yes, of course I would," Loomis replied. "Don't you know that one of the things I find most attractive about you is your hunger for knowledge? You are not only a beautiful woman, Pearl Summers. You are a kindred soul."

"A kindred soul," Pearl repeated. She smiled. "I like that. That's very poetic, isn't it? Someone should use that in a poem sometime."

Loomis laughed. "I'm sure it has been used, a dozen times or more. But it doesn't alter things, Pearl. We are kindred souls, you and I. And now that we've found each other, we can't let ourselves separate. I love you, Pearl."

Pearl shivered.

"Is there something wrong?"

"No," Pearl said. "It's just that . . . I've never heard those words spoken before. I had no idea what a thrill it would be to hear them for the first time. And I love you, Loomis Booker!"

"Excuse me," a young male voice suddenly interjected. "Could one of you please tell me where I am?"

At the unexpected sound of another voice, Pearl screamed and jumped toward Loomis. Loomis put his arms around her.

"Who the hell are you?" Loomis asked in a gruff voice. The intruder had suddenly appeared as if materializing in thin air.

"My name is Eric. Eric Twainbough." He put his hand to his head, just above his ear, and when he brought it down, there was blood on his fingers.

"Loomis, he's hurt," Pearl pointed out.

"How did you get here, Eric? Were you thrown from a train?" Loomis asked.

"Yes," Eric replied sheepishly. "How'd you know?"

"It's happened before," Loomis replied. "Though they generally aren't as young as you. And I don't believe

I've seen anyone else as badly hurt. You're in terrible shape."

Eric looked at Loomis and Pearl for a long moment, then blinked several times as if he were just noticing something.

"Why, you're . . . you're colored, aren't you?" he said. "I've never seen any colored people before." Eric's eyes suddenly rolled up into the back of his head, and he collapsed.

"Loomis!" Pearl cried. "What is it? What's wrong with him?"

Quickly, Loomis knelt beside Eric and put his hand on the artery on Eric's neck; then he felt the side of his head.

"There's a lot of swelling around this head wound," he said. "If I had to guess, I'd say he's suffered a skull fracture, and there's been enough bleeding to cause pressure against his brain."

"Is he going to die?"

"He could." Loomis put his arms under the boy and scooped him up.

"What are you going to do?"

"I'm going to take him to my apartment," Loomis replied. "Then I'm going to clean him up; and put him in bed. That's about all you can do for a skull fracture."

"But . . . should you do it?"

"Pearl, we can't just leave him lying here," Loomis rejoined. "Look at him. He's just a boy." Loomis shook his head. "Only a boy, but God knows what all he's been through."

"Maybe you should inform someone—the police or someone."

"And have the boy wind up in jail? No, he's been through enough already. I'll look after him."

Suddenly and inexplicably, Pearl smiled broadly.

"What are you smiling at?" Loomis asked, puzzled by her reaction.

"I haven't made a mistake this time, Loomis Booker. You are a good, good man, and I love you, love you, love you."

• • •

When the gasoline engines on the pumps started, their
bellow sent the beavers scurrying and set into flight a
large flock of cranes. Unmuffled and unbridled, the
engines were not only loud but also poured out great
blue clouds of noxious exhaust smoke to drift across the
water. After a few moments of popping and growling the
pumps finally primed themselves, then kicked in. Gushing streams of water spilled into St. John's Bayou from
the mouths of several long pipes.

"Wow! Look at the water spewing out of there!" Bob
Canfield exclaimed. "I'll bet Old Faithful geyser doesn't
make any prettier a splash than that."

On the side of the pumps not connected to the
gurgling pipes were hoses sucking up water from the
sloughs and pools of low-lying Canfield land. Bob had
bought ten such pumps in St. Louis, and now he was
putting them to work, and not since the clash and clang
of saws and axes and the roar of a half-dozen sawmills
working at full capacity had the swamp echoed with such
industry. Working collectively, the ear-shattering pumps
sucked up water at the rate of better than ten thousand
gallons per hour.

"I have to hand it to you, son," Jack Canfield said,
beaming broadly. "I didn't think that crazy idea of yours
would work, but damned if I don't believe we're going to
have every acre drained in no time at all."

"It'll take us fifteen days," Bob stated.

"You're pretty sure of yourself, aren't you? What
makes you say fifteen days?"

Bob smiled. "Pop, you did send me off to school to
get an education, didn't you?" he teased. "I'm just
putting that education to work. It's a simple mathemat-
ical problem—how many acres we have under standing
water, how deep the water is, and how fast the pumps
will work. When you put in all the parts of the equation,
it comes out to fifteen days. After that we can start
clearing away the stumps. This time next year when we
look out across this land we'll see wheat, oats, barley,

rye, corn, and just about any row crop you can think of."

Jack stroked his chin as he watched the water gush from the pipes. "You really think we'll be able to grow all that after we get it drained?"

"Yes, I do, Pop. I believe this land will turn out to be the finest farmland this side of the Nile River valley," Bob replied. "All one hundred and fifty thousand acres that you and Grandpa bought up."

"Yes, well, that's just what I told your grandpa," Jack said. "You can't tell it now, I said, but one of these days, all this land that's under water and trees and infested with mosquitoes and cottonmouths is going to be the land of milk and honey, the Promised Land. And when that happens, folks are goin' to be talkin' about how clever old Green and Jack Canfield were."

"You told Grandpa that, did you, Pop?" Bob teased.

Jack laughed. "Well, maybe I didn't tell him that exactly, but if this works out all right, a hundred years from now our descendants actually might get it in their heads that your grandpa and I were pretty smart fellows."

"And why shouldn't they?" Bob asked. "If you and Grandpa hadn't bought the land, we certainly couldn't be draining it now, could we?"

"No, I reckon not." Jack chuckled. "Wouldn't that be somethin', though, if this really did turn out to be the land of milk and honey? That would sure make the rest of the state sit up and take notice of us, wouldn't it? I mean, everybody in Missouri figures that those of us who live down here are some sort of a strange, amphibious breed. In fact, Milo Gresham told me that when he was up to Jefferson City, arguin' a case one day, the clerk of the Missouri Supreme Court asked him if all the people down here had webbed feet, and he wanted to know why it is that we aren't bothered by mosquito bites like ordinary folk."

"What did Mr. Gresham tell him?" Bob asked, grinning.

Jack laughed again. "He said we're no different from anyone else, except that the women down here wean their babies on alligator's milk. And the hell of it is, that clerk was too damned dumb to know that alligators don't even have teats."

Bob laughed at his father's story, then, out of the corner of his eye, saw his brother coming out of the house. "There's Billy," he said. "Maybe he'd like to see this."

"Wait a minute," Jack said abruptly, staring intently at the hose. "Bob, what's happening to the water? It's stopped."

"Oh, don't worry about it. It'll come back," Bob said. "It's just cavitating."

"It's what?"

"Cavitating. That means that the pump is pumping, but there's nothing to pump. You see, sometimes the hoses suck up a little air and when they do, the pump stops for a moment. But it's easy enough to take care of." He walked over to the pipe, which was just trickling water, and shook it. A second later the water began to gush out as thick as it had before. "See?" he said. "All you have to do is shake the air bubble out of it."

"Where'd Billy go?" Jack asked, turning toward the house. "I thought you said you saw him."

"I did see him."

"Well, where'd he go? I thought he'd be runnin' over here to see what was goin' on."

Bob laughed. "You forget, Pop, that boy went to the World's Fair and saw all the wonders of the world. Now, after all that, do you really think he's going to be interested in watching water pouring out of a few pipes?"

"I guess not," Jack said, laughing. "He was some taken with that fair, all right. And the way he keeps talkin' about that machine he rode on—what was it called again?"

"A Ferris wheel," Bob answered.

"Yes, a Ferris wheel. To hear that boy talk, there's nothin' in this world that can compare with having a ride on that Ferris wheel, short of flyin' itself."

"Who knows? Maybe he's building himself one of those contraptions out in the machine shed, right now," Bob suggested. "I know he's got something out there.

He's gone into that shed and holed up in there every day since we got back."

"Yes, I've noticed that myself. But, whatever it is, it's keepin' him out of trouble," Jack said. Then he pointed. "Oh, oh, Bob. Look at that pipe down there. It fell off the stand, and it's puttin' the water back in the field."

"I'd better go reposition it," Bob said.

Inside the machine shed Billy looked through a crack between the boards at his father and brother. They seemed awfully excited about draining off the water from the land, though for the life of him, Billy didn't understand what all the fuss was about. If it were up to him, he would just as soon leave the water right where it was. There were several sloughs he knew where the fishing was really good, and he could also gig for frogs just about anytime he wanted. He couldn't help but wonder what would happen to the fish and the frogs if the water dried up.

But right now he had more important things on his mind. He reached under the workbench to the very back, to a board that couldn't be seen unless someone bent over specifically to look under the table. This was a secret place, and what he had hidden here was a secret from everyone. Feeling around until his hand came in contact with it, he pulled it out. He looked at his burlap-wrapped prized possession and breathed a sigh of relief that no one had discovered it and that it was still here. He was never sure from one day to the next if it would be.

Billy recalled purchasing this wonderful device. He had gone to the World's Fair with Bob and Connie every day for a week, and on the last day Bob agreed to let Billy wander up and down the Pike alone. There had been dozens of booths along the midway, selling everything from food and souvenirs to the latest in wondrous appliances. The product that had caught Billy's attention most was something called the Strenva Vacuum Organ

Developer—a rather strange-looking device, consisting of an elongated glass tube that was open at one end and had a pump handle at the other. Though he hadn't known exactly what it was for, Billy had the feeling that there was something forbidden and exciting about it. He had picked it up for a closer examination, and the vendor walked over.

"Son, I'd be willing to bet that this device is exactly what you need," the man had said.

"What is it?" Billy had asked. "And how do you know I need it?"

"Are you a country boy, or a city boy?"

"I guess I'm a country boy."

The vendor had smiled. "You didn't have to tell me. I knew you were . . . a big, healthy-looking boy like you. You see, I was a country boy myself, so I can always pick one out. But now, tell me, son, do you ever go swimming bare with the other fellows?"

"Sure," Billy had said. "Everybody does."

"Is it embarrassing sometimes?"

"What do you mean?"

"Well, are any of the other boys older than you?"

"All of them are."

"Uh-huh. And you're embarrassed when all of you take off your clothes, aren't you?" the vendor had continued. He had looked around then, checking whether anyone was close enough to overhear their private conversation. "The other boys tease you, right? They tease you because your organ is so small."

"My organ?"

"Your pecker," the vendor had explained. "It's very small, isn't it? And you're embarrassed by it."

Bill had gasped, then blushed fiercely. "How do you know how big it is?" he asked. "And how did you know the other boys teased me?"

"You don't think you're the only one that's ever happened to, do you?" the vendor had asked kindly.

"I don't know. I know I would never tease anyone who was smaller than I am. That is, if I ever *see* anyone who's smaller than I am," Billy had added.

The vendor had smiled again and pointed to the device in Billy's hand. "Son, you buy the Strenva Vacuum Organ Developer, take it home, and use it every day—every day, now, without fail—and I guarantee you . . . everyone you see will be smaller than you."

"Really?"

"Guarantee," the vendor had sworn, raising his right hand. "My friends and I invented this machine just to keep fine young boys like you from ever having to be embarrassed again."

Billy had bought the Strenva Vacuum Organ Developer and managed to keep it hidden from everyone else until they got back home from St. Louis. It was his secret, and it would remain his secret until it had done its work. After using it for a few weeks, Billy planned to suggest to Bob that they go swimming, and as he stripped down he would display himself proudly, but not too obviously.

"Billy," Bob would say. "When did you get so large?"

"Oh, it's nothing," Billy would answer as if he were barely aware of what Bob was talking about. "I'm just growing up, I guess."

Billy had been using the organ developer every day since they came back, just as the vendor told him, but so far he hadn't noticed any dramatic changes. He took out the printed directions and read them again to make certain he wasn't doing anything wrong.

The Strenva Vacuum Organ Developer is a local treatment applied directly to the weak and disordered part. It gives strength and development wherever applied. Old men with lost or failing manhood, or the young or middle-aged who are reaping the results of youthful errors, excess, or overwork, are quickly restored to health and strength. You will see and feel its benefit from the first day. The blood is the life, the fertilizer, of the human body. This instrument forces blood into circulation where most needed, giving strength and development to weak and lifeless parts.

"You will see and feel its benefit from the very first day," the instructions promised. Well, maybe so, Billy thought, but so far he hadn't noticed anything. However, he wasn't ready to give up just yet. Looking again through the crack between the boards to make sure that neither Bob nor his father would suddenly come in on him, Billy unbuttoned his fly, then pulled out his penis and stuck it in the end of the vacuum tube, then began pumping. He could feel a pressure on his penis and it began to swell.

Now! he thought. If it would stay this big all the time, he could really believe this thing was working. But the problem was, as soon as he took the vacuum tube away, his penis went back down again.

Why wouldn't it stay this way? If it would just stay like this, he could go down to the St. John's Overflow, right now, and go swimming naked with the other boys. No one would dare tease him about being so small. Of course, even like this, he wasn't as big as Roy Beck or Ernest Dean Fawcett. They were sixteen, and they already had hair around their peckers. But if his would just stay this way, wouldn't he be able to show them something?

Billy decided that maybe he wasn't pumping it up hard enough, so he pumped it more, making the vacuum stronger and pulling his penis even farther into the tube. It got big—bigger than he had ever seen it before—and the pressure was greater than it had ever been, almost on the verge of pain. And it was turning blue.

"Wait a minute! I don't want a blue pecker," Billy said aloud. He tried to turn the little valve that would let air back in, but it wouldn't move.

"Ahh!" Billy yelped. "Help!" he shouted. "Somebody help me!"

The door suddenly opened, and George Summers stood in the doorway. Peering inside the shadowy shed, his hand shading his eyes from the bright sunlight behind him, George asked, "Billy, are you in here? I heard you cryin' for help, but I can't see nothing' just yet."

"George, I'm over here, I'm over here!" Billy answered, his voice full of pain and anguish. "Hurry! It hurts, it hurts!"

"I'm comin', Billy," George said, moving quickly toward the sound of the voice. Reaching Billy standing in the corner of the shed, he asked, "What's wrong?"

"George!" Billy said in a frightened voice. "I'm going to have a big blue pecker for the rest of my life. And it hurts real bad!" Billy turned toward George, and George, seeing what Billy had done, was so shocked that he stopped in his tracks.

"Boy, what you got your pecker stuck in that jar for?"

The thunder boomed sharply at first, then continued to roar, finally slacking off to a distant, protracted rumble, like the roll of timpani. Bob Canfield walked to the kitchen door and pulled the curtains open to look outside. The sky was gray and dismal, so heavy with rain that the clouds practically touched the ground. The water fell in torrents, just as it had been falling for six days—six days without letup.

Bob saw a rabbit bound across the back yard, then find temporary refuge under a wagon. The rabbit, bedraggled and miserable looking, stared out from under the wagon through large, soulful eyes. His dangling ears were long, dripping wicks, and his coat was soaked. The rabbit shivered, and even in a kitchen still warmed by the dying fire of the supper meal, Bob could feel for him.

The rain drummed against the screen wire of the back porch and poured out in rivulets from the grooves of the corrugated tin roof. The storm was a symphony of sound, from the bass notes of the distant thunder to the flutelike trills of the drops falling on the windowsill.

From Bob's vantage point he could see the fields

where they had been working the last three months. The fields had been cleared, first of water and then of the remaining tree stumps. But the work of three months had been turned around in as many days. St. John's Bayou, into which all the swamp water had been pumped, was now a solid stream of water, stretching nearly two miles from bank to bank. In three days, nature had reclaimed its own, and Bob's great experiment was a failure.

Jack Canfield came into the kitchen and looked at his son staring through the door at the swampland that was his heritage. "Coffee?" Jack offered, picking up the blue pot from the stove.

"Thanks," Bob replied.

Jack poured two cups, then came over and handed one of them to his son. "Don't feel bad," he said. "You gave it a good try."

Bob took a long swallow and stared out at the water before he answered. "I'm not giving up," he finally said.

"What do you mean?"

"I mean I'm going to pump the fields out again."

"Comes the next good rain, they'll flood again," Jack warned him.

"Then I'll pump them out again, and again, and again, just as long as the pumps hold up," Bob stated.

"Son, you're talking like a damn fool," Jack said.

"Pop, I know what we have here," Bob countered. "I know the potential of this land. All we have to do is get at it."

"That's quite an order," Jack reminded him.

"We can do it, I know we can. All I have to do is find a way."

"There is no way," Jack said. "God made this land swamp, and that's the way it's going to be from now till the end of time."

"Pop, before it was swamp, it was ocean," Bob said.

"Ocean? The hell you say."

"No, Pop, I'm serious. All the geologists and archaeologists agree. The Gulf of Mexico came right up to here.

But it's not ocean now, and it doesn't have to be swamp forever."

Jack ran his hand through his hair, then chuckled. "All right," he said. "I reckon you wouldn't be a Canfield if you weren't stubborn. We'll do it your way."

"Thanks, Pop," Bob said. "First thing tomorrow, we'll take a boat out and recover all the pumps. They're going to have to be put back in shape before we try this again. And then"—he grinned—"well, we'll just have to do it again. Only next time it's going to work."

CHAPTER TWELVE

March, 1907

The small town of Sikeston, Missouri, was bustling with activity. At the Sikeston Mercantile Company, whose sign proudly proclaimed SUPPLIES FOR ALL MANKIND, dozens of people in heavy mackinaws and thick woolen scarves moved in and out of the double doors, bound on their errands of commerce and enterprise. Across from the mercantile was Railroad Park, and on the far side of the park was Iron Mountain Depot, where an engine pulling a seven-car string of "varnish" sat facing west, heading toward Poplar Bluff, fifty miles away. There, a turntable would rotate the train so that late in the afternoon it would pass through Sikeston again on its eastern transit.

Though the cold, muddy streets of the town were still filled with horses and buggies, there were nearly as many automobiles as there were wagons. A sign in front of one of the business establishments advised that the proprietor not only sold automobiles—FEATURING THE MITCHELL LITTLE SIX, THE FINEST AUTOMOBILE MANUFACTURED, a banner declared—he would also provide an automobile and driver on a rental basis at the rate of fifteen dollars for four passengers for a twelve-hour day.

The Fidelity Bank of Sikeston sat on the triangular corner opposite the Sikeston Mercantile Company. The bank was housed in a redbrick building, and above the corner entry door, just below the roof of the building, was a large clock with Roman numerals on the face. It had been imported from Germany and was the bank's pride and joy. According to this clock, it was now ten minutes to two.

Inside the bank two stoves popped and snapped as the fires burned. The bank reeked of coal smoke, an odor that would linger long into summer, held inside the building by the heavy green curtains that hung at the windows and door. Two tellers' cages sat along the back wall, and both cages were busy. A sign between the tellers read: TODAY IS TUESDAY, MARCH 12, 1907.

The tellers were both men in their late forties who were attired similarly in suits, snow-white shirts with starched collars, green-shaded visors, and spectacles. They kept wet sponges in small bowls beside them so they could dampen their fingers as they counted out money. When they spoke, they did so quietly, aware of their positions of great responsibility.

On the highly polished oak floor of the bank sat two equally polished brass spittoons. Hanging against the west wall of the bank was a large, oval-framed photograph suspended from the picture-hanging rail by two long piano wires. The bald-headed man in the photograph was looking toward the camera through the large, vacant eyes of one who seemed to realize that he would be staring out at nothing for eternity. A small brass plaque beneath the photo said simply: BERNARD C. MC-MULLEN, 1827-1899.

At his desk on the side of the bank opposite the photograph, Bernard's grandson, Boyd McMullen, pulled a cigar from his humidor. He held a match to the end of it, puffed several times until his head was enveloped in a huge cloud of blue smoke, then pulled the cigar away.

Sitting across the desk from him was Bob Canfield.

"Oh, I'm sorry, Bob. Would you like a cigar?" Boyd asked, holding out the humidor.

"No, thank you," Bob answered.

"It's a very good cigar," Boyd insisted, examining the tip of it. "It comes from Havana, you know." He chuckled. "It's been nearly ten years since we took Cuba, and for my money the war was well worth it to give us an unlimited supply of Havana cigars."

"Boyd, what about the loan?" Bob asked, his voice impatient.

"Ah, yes, the loan." Boyd flicked an ash off the end of the cigar and looked at a map that was spread out on his desk. When the front door of the bank opened as a new customer came in, a gust of wind fluttered the map, and Boyd placed an ashtray over the corner of it to hold it still. "This is all your land, here?"

"Yes, the area that's crosshatched."

"And how much of it's tillable?"

"Potentially? I'd say just about all of it."

Boyd held out his hand and smiled condescendingly. "Come now, Bob. I didn't say 'potentially.' I want to know how much of it is tillable now."

"Last year we had ninety-six thousand acres under cultivation."

"And when we had late rains, you lost everything, I believe," Boyd said. His words and his tone were more factual than challenging.

"Yes," Bob admitted. "Well, we made the crop, we just couldn't get it out. We couldn't get into the fields for the harvest."

Bob spread his hands. "How many years have you been tryin', Bob? As I recall, you first pumped out your fields back in 1904, didn't you? It was right after you came back from the World's Fair, all gimcrack full of new ideas. Gasoline-powered pumps, you said. They were goin' to be the salvation of swampeast Missouri. They'd drain the fields, and where we'd been seein' stagnant water and naked tree stumps, we'd begin to see rows of corn, wheat, barley, and oats." Boyd chuckled. "Yes, sir, you painted quite the rosy picture. But you were flooded out almost before you got started that year. Then, in 1905, even though you drained the fields three times, you weren't able to get a crop in at all. And last year you couldn't get the crop out because of the rains. In the meantime, you've duped a lot of poor fellows around here into believin' in you, and in your idea."

"I didn't dupe anyone, Boyd," Bob snapped. "I haven't asked anyone for any money for anything. If they tried to drain their fields, then it was because they thought the idea had merit—not because I talked them into it. I've had enough trouble with my own fields."

"Yes, I daresay you have, haven't you?" Boyd said. "But you're wrong when you say you haven't asked anyone for any money. You borrowed from this bank last year and the year before that. And now you're in here again, hat in hand, tryin' to borrow more."

"Hat in hand?" Bob repeated angrily, rising from his chair so quickly that it fell over with a crash, and a few of the bank's customers looked over to see what was going on. Bob leaned over the desk and stared down at Boyd. "I'm not exactly standing on the street corner like some beggar, Boyd McMullen. After all, this is a bank. And I believe that lending money is what banks do. My family has borrowed money from this bank—and has been one of its largest depositors, I might add—for over forty years. Now, that certainly should give me the right to discuss a business transaction with you, wouldn't you think?"

"Bob, Bob, take it easy," Boyd murmured. He got up and walked around to pick up and reset Bob's chair. "It wasn't my intention to make you angry. Sit down, for heaven's sake, and let's discuss this like businessmen— and like the two old friends that we are."

Bob sat back down, and Boyd returned to his side of the desk.

"We may have drifted apart some when you went to Jefferson College and I went to Cape Normal," Boyd went on, sitting back down in his own chair, "but we did attend high school together, remember? Or have you forgotten who your classmates were?"

Bob laughed. "Sikeston High? It'd be sort of hard to forget my classmates, wouldn't it? There were only nine of us."

"Five girls and four boys," Boyd confirmed. He sighed, then leaned forward and looked at the map. "All right, Bob, tell me what you want the money for. Just what do you have in mind?"

Eased by Boyd's placating manner, Bob began explaining his proposition, referring to the map. "Well, first, I want to dredge out Little River, then enlarge the two bayous, St. John's and Wolfhole," he said, pointing to the streams. "I want to make them deeper and wider."

"Why on earth would you want to do that? They're the biggest problem we have down here. They flood over at the slightest rain, and during heavy rains they sometimes stretch two miles across. And you want to make them bigger?"

"Yes," Bob said. "Don't you understand? The reason they flood now is because there isn't enough channel to handle the water flow. If the channels were made deeper and wider, the bayous wouldn't come over their banks." He pointed to a series of lines on the map. "Now, look, here's how it'll work. I've already surveyed the land, and I know where the low spot is in every field. At each low spot I'll dig a trench, and three trenches will lead into a network of somewhat larger ditches that will, in turn, lead to a system of still larger canals. Those canals will empty into the two bayous, the bayous will empty into Little River, and Little River, of course, drains into the Mississippi."

"But look at the map, Bob," Boyd said. "It's literally covered with ditches and canals. It looks like a bunch of blood vessels or somethin'."

Bob smiled. "Yes, that's it, exactly. And just as capillaries, veins, and arteries move blood efficiently through the human body, these ditches will move the water out of the fields and into the bayous."

"But aren't you pumpin' into those two bayous now?"

"Yes, I am."

"Then why's it necessary for you to dig all these ditches? It seems to me like the pumps could move the water easier, faster, and certainly cheaper."

"I thought about that," Bob said. "I thought that perhaps I could just enlarge the channels of the bayous so they'd be able to handle more water. But that won't work, Boyd. At peak flood conditions, even with deepened channels the bayous can't drain all the water quickly enough. And because we're right over the Mississippi River aquifer, our water table is just too high to allow the rains to seep down through the ground. That leaves the water with no place to go but back up into the fields. However, a network of drainage ditches would act as sort of a holding tank. The fields themselves would stay high and dry, and the crops would be saved."

"You make it sound so simple," Boyd said.

"It *is* simple," Bob insisted. "It's also very expensive, but it's simple."

"And it's your belief that the entire floodplain of southeast Missouri can be drained this way? Turn all our swamps into tillable land?"

"Well, yes, in a manner of speaking. But to do the entire bootheel would take the coordinated efforts of all ten counties, plus all the landowners, and perhaps even the U.S. Corps of Engineers. But right now I'm not concerned with the entire district. I'm only concerned with Canfield land."

"All right, then, how many miles of canal would you have to dig, just to drain Canfield land?"

"Perhaps a hundred miles," Bob replied.

Boyd laughed incredulously. "A hundred miles? Are you serious?"

"Give or take a mile or two," Bob said. "Why? Is there something significant about that number?"

"You might say that," Boyd replied. "It just so

happens that I was readin' an article the other day about the Panama Canal. Interesting project, that. Do you realize that before the United States even started on that canal, the French lost thousands of men and spent over one and a half billion francs? And still they failed? They were tryin' to excavate a canal only fifty miles long—half the distance you want to excavate."

"Then no doubt you'll be pleased to hear that the project I have in mind will cost considerably less than one and a half billion francs," Bob said. "Instead, no more than five dollars an acre."

Boyd, who had been studying the map, looked up sharply. "Five dollars an acre? Do you know the current market value of undrained land?"

"I'm not certain," Bob admitted. "But I'm sure it's less than five dollars an acre."

"It's a dollar and a quarter an acre. A dollar and a quarter," Boyd repeated, making certain that his point hit home. He smiled. "I don't know what kind of economics they taught you in that fancy St. Louis college of yours, but up at Cape Normal we learned that it'd be foolish to spend five dollars an acre on land that's only worth a fourth of that."

"Boyd, if that land were drained, it would be worth seventy-five dollars an acre, and you know it," Bob argued.

"Land that stays drained is worth seventy-five dollars an acre," Boyd reminded him. "Land that gets drained and then floods again, like your land, is worth a dollar and a quarter."

"I thought that was the whole point of this conversation," Bob said, his frustration rising. "I've already proven I could drain the land, and I've already proven how fertile the land really is. Our wheat would have made twenty-five to thirty bushels an acre last year, if we could've gotten it in. All I have to do now is keep the land drained, and this canal-and-ditch system will do it."

"Just how many acres are you plannin' to drain?"

"One hundred and fifty thousand," Bob said easily.

"That means you are asking for . . ." Boyd started to calculate the amount, but Bob answered for him.

"Seven hundred and fifty thousand dollars."

Boyd gave a low whistle. "Bob, you don't seriously expect this bank to lend you three quarters of a million dollars on your land, do you? Why, the bank's stockholders would lynch me."

"Don't give me that, Boyd," Bob countered. "The stockholders of this bank are all McMullens. Look, everybody knows that John Sikes founded this town, but your grandpa's bank and my grandpa's lumber are what saved it. There wouldn't even *be* a Sikeston if the McMullens and Canfields hadn't worked together in the past, and I see no reason why that cooperation shouldn't continue."

"Bob, I'd like to help you, I really would. The friendship of our two families means somethin' to me. But a bank has to run on sound business principles, not on friendship."

"This *is* a sound business principle," Bob protested. "If this area is going to survive, then reclaiming the swampland is the only way we're going to do it. We were once the premier hardwood-timber-producing area in the entire nation, but no more. The timber's gone. Without the lumber resources my family's land is worth less than two hundred thousand dollars, and everyone else is in the same boat. And I remind you, Boyd, if everyone goes broke, no one's going to have any money to put in the banks. There are three banks in town, and the three of you are going to be fighting like cats and dogs over what little money is left."

"I realize that the timber industry is gone," Boyd said. "But you're askin' to borrow three times what your land is worth."

"If that land were drained, it would be worth over eleven million dollars."

"Oh, I admit, on paper it all sounds quite plausible," Boyd agreed. "However, there's many a slip 'twixt the cup and the lip." Boyd drummed his fingers on the table. Outside, a car backfired as it drove down the street. Over on the Iron Mountain line, the train whistled, then puffed loudly as it started to pull out of town. Overhead the great German clock sent two loud chimes reverberating up and down the town's streets. "How's Pearl?" Boyd asked, breaking the silence.

"Pearl?"

"The colored girl that used to live on your place."

"I know who you mean. She's fine," Bob said, clearly surprised by Boyd's inquiry. "She got married a couple of years ago."

"Well, I hope she got herself a good man."

"She did," Bob said. "His name is Loomis Booker, and he's as good a man as you'll find anywhere. But what does this have to do with what we're talking about? Why are you asking about Pearl?"

Boyd laughed. "No particular reason. The girl used to work for me, don't you remember?"

"Yes, I do. I'm just a bit surprised that you remember her, that's all."

Boyd looked quickly around, then leaned across the desk and spoke in a conspiratorial voice. "Somebody like Pearl's not all that easy to forget. But then, I reckon you know what I mean, don't you?" He snickered.

"No," Bob said, stiffening. "I'm not sure that I know what you mean."

"Oh, come on now, Bob. A pretty little high-yellow like that? Don't tell me you didn't 'change your luck?'"

"Change my luck?"

Boyd grinned. "Yeah, you know what they say. Screw a colored girl and you change you luck."

Bob stood up. "I don't much care for the way this conversation is going," he snapped. "Pearl is a fine young woman. And she is my friend."

"She's a colored girl, Bob."

"She is my friend," Bob said again, pointedly.

"All right, all right, you don't have to get testy," Boyd replied, calming him down. "Maybe I just had the wrong idea about things, is all."

"Yes. Maybe you did."

"Now, about the loan," Boyd said. He stroked his

chin. "I'll tell you what I'll do. Let me take it to the Board of Directors and see what they say. I don't have much hope for you, but I'll do what I can."

"Thanks," Bob said. He reached for his map.

"No, leave that. I may want to show it to the board."

"Your board doesn't need to know the specifics, just the general idea," Bob said. "I paid for this survey. If anybody else wants one, they'll have to pay to have one made, just as I did."

Rolling up the map, Bob nodded curtly at Boyd, then strode out of the bank. George Summers was waiting for him, sitting in the front seat of the Canfields' new car that was parked at the curb—a 1907 wine-colored Great Arrow.

"I'm sorry if I took so long, George. Did you get too cold?"

"You don't have to worry about old George, Mr. Bob. I had the lap robe to keep me warm."

Bob climbed into the front seat as George stepped out to crank the car. The engine caught on the first turn and George stowed the crank, then climbed in behind the wheel, smiling broadly. "This new engine runs so quiet, I don't always know when I got it cranked," he said. "I'm afraid one of these days I'm liable to stick the crank back in while the engine's runnin', and when I do that, it's gonna break my arm or somethin'."

"It's a smooth-running motorcar all right," Bob said. Then he asked, "Is Pop still at Dr. Lennox's?"

"Yep."

"Let's go get him and go home."

Nodding, George pulled out and drove to King Street, where Dr. Lennox lived in a big, two-story brick home, the downstairs of which served as his office. George parked the car out front while Bob went in to get his father. When he stepped through the front door, the middle-aged physician was standing at the front of the stairs, his hand resting on the newel post and his face grim.

"Hello, Bob," he said. "Your father is still inside, getting dressed." He pointed toward the waiting room.

"Why don't you have a seat over there by the fireplace? I'd like to talk to you for a moment, if you don't mind."

On the other side of the long room—originally the parlor—were two chairs facing the fire, and at Dr. Lennox's invitation, Bob sat in one of them. The doctor sat in the other, then came right to the point.

"Your father is dying, Bob."

"What?" Bob gasped. The news came like a bolt out of the blue. "From what? Dyspepsia? All he had was a little stomach upset."

"I wish that were true," Dr. Lennox said grimly. "Unfortunately, it is much more serious than that. What he had wasn't indigestion. It was angina pectoris—paroxysms of the heart."

Shaken, Bob gestured toward the examining room. "How is he?"

"He's free of pain right now, and he generally will be, between the attacks. But there will be more, and they'll get worse and worse, until one day he'll have an attack from which he won't recover."

"No, I won't accept that. What can I do? Where can I take him to be cured? St. Louis? Chicago? New York? I'll take him wherever I have to."

Dr. Lennox shook his head slowly. "There's nowhere you can take him, because there's no cure," he said. "You can sometimes delay death by being very careful, by doing nothing that will agitate the mind or body. By taking it easy, in other words. But you are only delaying the inevitable."

Bob leaned his head back against the chair and closed his eyes. His throat felt as if he had swallowed a baseball, and his eyes burned as he fought hard to keep tears from forming. He took several deep breaths. "How long?" he finally asked.

"There's no way of telling. It could happen tonight, next month, next year. The only thing I'm certain of is that it will happen."

"Have you told him?"

"I didn't have to tell him. He already knew."

Bob stared at the physician. "How?"

"I don't know how," Dr. Lennox replied. "Sometimes God just gives a person an awareness of when his time is near."

"How is he taking it?"

"You tell me, Dr. Lennox said. "He knew he was dying before he came here."

"I had no idea. He didn't say anything to me."

"I know. He wanted me to tell you," Dr. Lennox said. "He figured it would go down easier, coming from me. Then he figured that the two of you could break the news to your mother and your brother."

Bob heard his father clomping along the hall. "Well, Bob, there you are," Jack said, stepping into the room. "Did you get your business all taken care of at the bank?"

"Yes, Pop, all taken care of," Bob said, standing and wiping his eyes quickly so that his father wouldn't see the tears that had formed.

"Don't tell me the son of a bitch is actually going to lend you the money?"

'Lend you the money,' not 'lend us,' Bob noted to himself. It was subtle, but it was telling. "McMullen didn't decide," he answered. "He's going to take it before the board."

Jack took his jacket down from the coat tree and put it on. "I'll tell you what he's takin' to the board, son. He's takin' your idea. You mark my words: If the board likes it, the only way you're ever goin' to know about it is when the McMullens start buyin' up land and drainin' it. You're goin' to have to find that money somewhere else."

"Yeah, I figured that," Bob muttered.

"You aren't givin' up, are you?"

"No, sir."

Jack smiled. "Good. Don't worry about those pissant McMullens. You'll find the money somewhere. Now, come on, let's get on home. Doc Lennox may have told you I don't really have all that much time to waste."

"Pearl! Pearl, I fixed it! Come look at it now!" Eric Twainbough called. He had spent the better part of the last half hour repairing a leaky water faucet. Now he turned it on and off several times, proudly showing Pearl Booker that the leak had stopped.

"Oh, you did a good job, Eric," Pearl answered, wiping her hands on her apron as she stood at the kitchen sink in Professor Bateman's house. "But don't forget, now. You and Loomis and I have to meet with the school principal at Millard Fillmore High School at three o'clock this afternoon."

"I haven't forgotten," Eric said. "I'll be done in plenty of time to get cleaned up for that." He began picking up the tools and dirty rags, while Pearl returned to her work in the kitchen.

It had been over two years since Loomis and Pearl found Eric more dead than alive near the tracks, and during that time, Eric had lived on the campus of Jefferson University. While he mended, he and Loomis had gotten very close, trading confidences. Loomis had said that he sensed a kindred spirit in Eric similar to what he had felt in Pearl, and he told the youth about his past, about fleeing Virginia in the middle of the night after fearing he had killed one of the youths who had tried to kill him. Emboldened by Loomis's trust in him, Eric had confessed about the aborted train robbery by his former saddlemates and about the killing of the brutal trainman in self-defense. To Eric's immense relief, he received compassion and understanding from Loomis, rather than censure and disgust. After that the bond between them had steadily strengthened, to the point where each began to think of the other as the brother he had never had. When Loomis and Pearl were married, Loomis had moved in with Pearl, in the cottage behind the chancellor's house, while Eric took Loomis's old apartment.

Though Eric had proved himself to be an excellent worker who did many jobs around the university, he wasn't carried on the school's payroll because the school's budget didn't allow for an assistant handyman. So Loomis had assumed financial responsibility for Eric, feeding him at his own table as well as providing him with a place to live. For his part Eric had become an extremely valuable assistant to Loomis, taking on fully half of the older man's work load. Because of Eric's help, Loomis was able to find more time for his studies, and he was now recognized not only by the students, but by the professors as well, as the most learned man on the Jefferson University campus.

But Loomis was a teacher as well as a learner, and Eric was his beneficiary. When Eric had told him that he hoped someday to be a writer, Loomis constructed a curriculum for him that included grammar, literature, philosophy, history, and Latin.

"Why Latin?" Eric had complained.

"Because if you're serious about writing, then words are going to be the tools of your trade. A craftsman would never use the wrong tool, would he?"

"I wouldn't think so," Eric had agreed.

"No, of course he wouldn't," Loomis had said. "And neither should you. Nearly half the words in the English language come from Latin. By studying Latin you'll be exposed to the building blocks of language and thus be aware of the most subtle tone and the most delicate tint of the meaning of words. You won't use one word when you mean another."

Eric had proved to be a very good student, and when the youth was old enough, Loomis had decided he should enroll in the university.

"Why? Aren't you teaching me everything I need to know?" Eric had asked.

"Perhaps I am," Loomis had replied. "But I see no reason for you to be denied credit for your education. There are no barriers to stop *you* from getting a degree, and I think you should get one."

"I don't need one."

"Then I would hope that you would do it simply because I asked it of you," Loomis had remarked.

Knowing it was important to Loomis, Eric had attempted to enroll at Jefferson. But he soon discovered that it couldn't be done easily. Though his personal tutoring from Loomis had made him more than qualified academically, he wasn't technically qualified to enter Jefferson because he didn't have a diploma from an accredited high school.

In fact, in Eric's entire lifetime he had spent less than three months inside a school building. What education he had received had come first from his mother, then from Rodney Ebersole, and finally from Loomis. He was afraid he'd have to go to school for twelve years in order to meet the qualification requirements for university admission.

"And that means I'd be thirty years old before I graduated from high school," he had moaned.

"Let me talk to the professor," Loomis had suggested.

Loomis did talk to William Bateman and learned that Eric wouldn't have to take twelve years of schooling to get a diploma. All that was necessary was for him to pass a battery of tests, which would allow him to enter high school in the senior class, and that way he'd only have to go one year. The school board did ask, however, that Eric and his parents present themselves for an interview with the principal this spring so that he could discuss what would be expected of them for next fall's class. As Loomis and Pearl were the closest thing Eric had to parents, he asked them to go with him.

The meeting was held in the principal's office. James Marshall, the principal, was a bald-headed, hawk-nosed man with wire-rim glasses. He was reading the application form when Eric, Loomis, and Pearl arrived.

"Mr. Marshall, I'm Eric Twainbough," the youth announced.

Marshall looked up and, seeing Loomis and Pearl, cleared his throat. "Mr. Twainbough, if you would, please, have these people wait in the outer hallway, then ask your parents to come in."

"My parents are deceased," Eric said.

"Ah, I'm sorry. Well then, you brought a guardian who can speak for you?"

"Yes, sir. These are my guardians, Mr. and Mrs. Booker," Eric said, indicating Loomis and Pearl.

"These people? But they're *colored,* Mr. Twain-bough."

Eric smiled, then looked at Loomis. "I told you that the first time I ever saw you," he quipped. "Didn't I say you were colored?"

Loomis returned the smile and held up both his hands. "All right, all right, so you've finally found someone to agree with you. What can I say? I admit it, I am colored."

Marshall's expression as he watched the exchange between the two suggested that they had gone mad. "See here," he said. "Do you think this is some sort of joke?" He took off his glasses and began polishing them vigorously, as if in that way he could show his displeasure at their levity. "Getting an education is a serious undertaking."

"Yes, sir, I know it is," Eric said. "That's why I'm here. I tried to enroll in the university but they wouldn't even consider me until I had a high school diploma."

"And that is as it should be," Marshall stated. He put his glasses back on, fitting the earpieces laboriously, almost ritualistically, onto each ear, one at a time. "Actually, what you should be worrying about, Mr. Twainbough," he went on, "is not whether you are qualified for college, but whether you can qualify for our secondary school. I think you will find our standards are quite high."

"And I think that you will find, Mr. Marshall, that Eric is quite a remarkable young man, with an educational background more than adequate to meet your standards," Loomis said.

"And just how did he come by this educational background?" the principal asked.

Loomis smiled proudly. "Why, I taught him," he said.

"I see. And how did you come by *your* background, if I may ask?"

"You might say I am a self-taught man," Loomis replied.

"Yes, well, Mr. Booker, honorable though that may be, the fact remains that neither you nor your *pupil*"—he came down sarcastically on the word—"has what you could call an accredited educational background. Add to that the fact that he has no legal guardian—"

"I told you, the Bookers are my guardians," Eric interrupted.

"Have the Bookers been appointed as your legal guardians by the court?"

"No, sir, not yet," Eric admitted. "But we'll get a court appointment."

Marshall sighed. "They cannot be your guardians, Mr. Twainbough. They are *colored*."

"You keep saying that."

"Well, that fact hasn't changed, Mr. Twainbough. They were colored when you came in here, and they are colored now."

"Mr. Marshall, if I may point out, Missouri law does not prohibit a Negro from being a guardian," Loomis interjected.

"Of other Negroes, Mr. Booker, of other Negroes," Marshall answered as if long-suffering. "That law was certainly not written in such a way as to allow they races to be mixed."

Loomis smiled. "Well, now, that's where you're mistaken. I have looked this up, you see, and I can cite at least ten precedents where a white man has been appointed the guardian of a Negro. And there are a hundred cases where white men have acknowledged that they are the fathers of Negro children."

"Perhaps so, but that is a white man over a colored, not a colored man over a white," Marshall said.

"Why do I even have to have a guardian?" Eric asked.

"Because you need the guiding hand of mature judgment," Marshall said. "Mature *white* judgment," he added pointedly.

"Mr. Marshall, when I was twelve years old, my mother and father died in a blizzard in Montana. I buried both of them and was on my own until three years ago. Since that time I've been working for, and learning from, Loomis and Pearl Booker. They are the closest thing I have to a family. Now, I don't figure I even need guardians, but if the law says I have to have them to get into school, then Loomis and Pearl are the ones that I want."

"That's quite impossible," Marshall said flatly.

"Suppose we let the court decide that?" Loomis suggested.

Marshall smiled broadly, then took off his glasses and began polishing them again. This time he polished with an air not of agitation, but of triumph. "Yes, why *don't* we let the courts decide?" he agreed. "You see, in the cases concerning guardianship of a student or potential student, the court will ask for my recommendation . . . and my recommendation has never been overturned."

"And you will recommend no?" Eric asked.

"Most emphatically," Marshall said.

"Come on, Loomis, Pearl, we're just wasting our time here," Eric said in disappointment.

"Mr. Twainbough, you should have known better than to have even tried such a harebrained scheme," Marshall said. He looked at Pearl, who thus far had been absolutely silent. "And as for you, Miss . . ."

"It's Mrs.," Pearl corrected. "Mrs. Loomis Booker." Pearl smiled, then affected a very broad dialect. "'Course, now, my man and me, we jus' jump over a broom handle; we didn't have no preacher speak no words over us or nothin'. But I still likes to call myself Mrs."

Eric smiled at Pearl's tweaking of the stuffy principal. In fact Loomis and Pearl had been married by an associate state supreme court judge, a friend of Professor Bateman's, and the civil ceremony had been conducted in the living room of the professor's home with a number of the university's academicians in attendance—far removed from "jumping over a broom handle."

"Yes. Well, Mrs. Booker, you yourself are not much older than this boy. Surely you can see the impropriety of being appointed his guardian, even if you were of the same race, and even if you were legally married. Didn't your mother ever tell you about such things? I don't know about colored people, but among my people a young woman's mother would have instructed her in such matters."

Pearl's mischievous smile grew broader, and Loomis, knowing her all too well, knew that she was about to come out with something outlandish. "Pearl!" he cautioned. "Don't do it!"

His warning was too late.

"Mr. Marshall," Pearl said sweetly, "the only thing my mama ever told me was, 'Don't fart in a white man's bed.'"

The principal gasped and turned purple with anger, Eric hooted with laughter, and though Loomis tried to act angry, he couldn't keep the smile off his own face. "Come on," he said. "I expect we had best get out of here while we still can."

As was his custom, Thomas Petzold was perusing the dozen newspapers that he received every day. He was a subscriber, by mail, to newspapers from Boston, New York, Washington, Norfolk, Montgomery, New Orleans, Memphis, Chicago, Denver, Houston, San Francisco, and Seattle. What held his attention today was a small article buried in the inside pages of the *New Orleans Picayune*:

RIGHT-TO-LOOT LETTER
FOUND ON BODY OF NICARAGUAN SOLDIER

A letter brought to this office by a person who has recently returned from Honduras shows the evil extent to which President Zelaya is conducting war. Not only do gunboats from Nicaragua patrol the coastline of Honduras, threatening the coastal towns and settlements, but the Nicaraguan Army has shown its savagery in recent fighting. The letter alluded to is one that was found on the body of a Nicaraguan soldier. In that letter, President Zelaya invites his soldiers to "loot the first city, town, or village in Honduras that falls under your control. In so doing you will strike terror to the hearts of our enemies, and you will help establish Nicaragua as the dominant power in Latin America."

Although the United States has vital interests in Honduras, the Nicaraguan government has not promised that those interests will be safeguarded. A representative of the United Fruit Company, which built most of the railroads and modern facilities in Honduras, has called upon President Roosevelt to give assurances to the American banana-plantation owners that their lives and their property will be protected.

At an editorial meeting later that day, Petzold asked his international editor, Charles Linton, how he was interpreting the news coming from Latin America.

"Do you mean the Panama Canal?" Linton replied.

"No. I mean the business around Honduras and Nicaragua."

Linton shook his head. "I'm not aware of anything going on there," he said.

"You know nothing about the war going on between those two countries?"

"Oh, well, yes, sir, I knew there had been some fighting. But there's always fighting going on down there. We have baseball, they have war."

Everyone around the meeting table laughed except Petzold, and when the others looked at his serious visage, their laughter died in their throats. The publisher slid the New Orleans paper across the table toward Linton. It was folded in such a way as to show the story, and the article itself was outlined in black ink.

"I want you to read this story," Petzold ordered. "Then I want you to send some wires. Contact our people in Washington. Find out just how seriously the United States is treating this issue."

"Yes, sir," Linton replied.

"Tomorrow," Petzold went on, "I want you to be the most informed man in American on this subject. If the President of the United States contacted you and said,

'Charlie, what should we do?' I want you to be able to tell him."

"Yes, sir," Linton said again.

"Gentlemen," Petzold continued, "I know you may think that I am placing an undue emphasis on this, but I assure you I am not. Anything that happens down there will be of vital interest to us from now on. And it has nothing to do with whether or not there will be enough bananas to make a nice pudding. It is because of the Panama Canal. I suspect that before long, as far as the United States is concerned, Latin America will be the most important place on the globe."

"Mr. Petzold?" Terry held up his hand for attention.

"Yes, Mr. Perkins?"

"I've been doing some preliminary work on the Panama Canal. You may remember I'm going down there next month."

"Yes."

"Well, I found out that the cruiser *Olympia* will be sailing for Panama from Norfolk next week, and it's supposed to visit Honduras. I didn't know why then, but now I'm sure it has something to do with this."

"I'm sure it does, too."

"Perhaps, since I'm going to Panama anyway, we could just move my trip up a few days?" Terry suggested. "If you could get me accredited by the Navy Department, I could go down aboard the *Olympia*."

"Yes, yes, that's an excellent idea," Petzold said, smiling broadly. He looked back at Linton. "Mr. Linton, while you are making yourself expert in this matter, see to it that Mr. Perkins has the authorization he needs to go along with that battleship."

"Cruiser, sir," Terry corrected.

"Young man, I am your employer," Petzold said. "If I say it is a battleship, it is a battleship."

"Yes, sir, it's a battleship. It's the biggest battleship I ever saw. Bigger than the *Dreadnought*. Bigger than the *Lusitania*. Bigger than—"

"Enough, enough," Petzold said, laughing, and the others, who had been trying to hold their own laughter back, were relieved to let it out. "But Terry . . ." It was rare when he called one of his employees by their first name, though he seemed to feel a special affinity with Terry and had from the time the young reporter came to work for him.

"Yes, sir?"

"I want you to be very careful. I have a feeling about this. I don't know why—there is no rallying cry, such as 'Remember the Maine'—but I can't help but feel that shots are going to be fired. And when they are fired, I don't want you in front of the bullets."

"I'll be careful, Mr. Petzold," Terry promised.

"Good, good. Now, let's move on to the next item of business."

"The Harry K. Thaw case is still big," someone reminded him. "Our readers are following it very carefully."

"What is the latest on it?" Petzold asked.

"Sanity hearing."

"He's guilty," someone stated.

"He's crazy," another added.

"He's still guilty."

"That's never been the question. He shot Stanford White in front of dozens of witnesses. A man would have to be insane to do that."

"He'll get the death penalty."

"No, he won't. He's rich. He won't even go to jail."

"He won't go to jail, but not because he's rich. He won't go to jail because he's crazy."

"All right, we'll keep it big," Petzold interjected, finalizing the matter. "Let's go three columns, front page. And somebody do a sidebar on Miss Evelyn Nesbitt."

"You mean Evelyn Thaw. She's his wife now, don't forget."

"And with a picture," the publisher added. "You can never go wrong putting a pretty woman's picture on the front page."

"Even if she has led a debauched life?"

"*Especially* if she has led a debauched life."

The meeting broke up with the laughter that greeted that remark. As everyone was leaving the meeting room, Linton called Terry over.

"You really want to go down to Honduras on a gunboat?"

"Sure."

"You're crazy, kid. I could've gotten you first-class passage on a luxury steamboat. You would've been traveling like a wealthy man. Now you'll be going down there like some common sailor."

"It'll be an adventure," Terry said.

Linton sighed. "Okay, it's your funeral. Listen, a few of us are going over to O'Grady's for some beer. You want to go?"

"Thanks, but no. A friend of mine is leaving for Europe tomorrow, and he's invited me to dinner at his house tonight."

"Europe, huh? Where's he going?"

"Vienna."

Linton smiled. "Now, *that's* a smart man. They say Vienna is beautiful. He'll be living it up over there, while you're sweating and steaming in a hammock strung between two cannons down in the bilge or something."

Terry laughed. "I don't think you can put cannons in the bilge," he said.

"Yeah, well, whatever, I'm glad it's you and not me. I'll get you accredited as soon as I can."

"Thanks," Terry said. "Have a beer for me tonight, will you? And tell all the fellows hello."

"I'll tell you what. The first beer that passes through my kidneys will be for you," Linton promised.

Terry laughed again, then walked over to his desk and telephoned David Gelbman's house, asking for David when the maid answered. A moment later, his friend's voice came over the receiver.

"Hello?"

"David, it's me, Terry. Did you hear from Bob?"

"Yes. He arrived this morning. He and Connie will be at dinner tonight."

"Good," Terry said. "I was hoping he could come."

"What about J.P.? You're going to meet him at Union Station, aren't you?"

"Yes. I'll be waiting for him when his train arrives at four-oh-four."

"Wonderful," David said. "It's going to be great to see everyone again. I know it's not something one would like to think about, but, Terry, have you considered that this might be the last time the quad quad is ever all together?"

"Jesus, David, you really know how to put a damper on a party."

David laughed. "Okay, no more maudlin sentiments, I promise. Only wine, women, and song."

"Right. I'll see you at six."

CHAPTER

THIRTEEN

"Wait until you hear this one," Connie Bateman said. She held up the shiny black disc, displaying it to Bob Canfield, and it gleamed in the early afternoon sun that streamed through the parlor window. Placing the record on the gramophone, she wound the side crank, then set the needle and turned it on. From the ornately decorated bell came the sound of an orchestra and a woman singing:

> Shine on, shine on harvest moon
> Up in the sky.
> I ain't had no lovin' since
> January, February, June, or July.

"Isn't it wonderful?" Connie asked, singing along with the music.

"Are you trying to tell me you 'ain't had no lovin' since January, February, June, or July'?" Bob quipped.

"Are you trying to tell me you *have*?" Connie rejoined. "If so, Mr. Canfield, we have some serious matters to discuss."

"Maybe we have some serious matters to discuss anyway," Bob suggested.

Connie, who was leafing through a stack of records to select the next song, looked up at Bob. "Like what?" she asked, a little apprehensively.

"Like marriage."

"Marriage?" Connie's voice was quiet and skeptical.

"I want us to get married, Connie. And I'd like for us to get married right away."

Connie gasped once, then smiled broadly. "Bob, are you serious?"

"Of course I'm serious. I've always planned to marry you; you know that."

"Well, yes, I had hoped you harbored such intentions. In fact, I thought we might get married on my graduation. But when that came and passed and still there was no proposal, I wasn't sure that you hadn't had a change of heart."

"I wanted to marry you then, Connie, I really did. But I had the rather noble idea that I shouldn't marry you until I had converted the Canfield swamp into the Canfield farm," Bob explained. "I wanted to be able to give you anything you might ever want."

"Silly boy," Connie said. "Don't you know that the only thing I really want is love?"

"The only thing you really want is love? Am I actually hearing this? Aren't those words a little sentimental to be coming from the lips of a suffragette?" Bob teased.

"I stand corrected," Connie said, holding up her forefinger. "The only *things* I really want are love and the recognition that women should have equal rights with men."

"And the vote?"

"Yes, of course the vote. I definitely want the vote," Connie affirmed. She put the records down and walked over to Bob. Putting her arms loosely on his neck, she looked into his eyes. "But mostly I want your love," she said.

"I do love you, Connie," Bob replied. "And, if I have never formally done so before this moment, I am asking you now to marry me. Will you marry me, Constance Bateman?"

"Oh, yes, Bob. Yes, I will marry you," Connie answered. She leaned her body against his. "But isn't there something you're supposed to do right now? Some sort of traditional ritual you're leaving out?"

"You mean . . . you want me to get down on my knees?"

Connie laughed. "No, that isn't necessary. But when a man asks a woman to marry him and she answers yes, don't they usually seal the agreement with a kiss?"

"Now that you mention it, I believe they do," Bob answered. He bent his head, closing the small distance between them. The kiss started gently. Then it grew in intensity, becoming so hungry and urgent that they might well have been alone in the wilderness rather in the parlor of her father's house. At any moment someone could walk in, yet they were oblivious of that possibility, and the kiss went on and on, growing more forceful and passionate, allowed by Connie to run its course. Finally Bob found the strength that Connie didn't have, and their lips separated.

"Well now, I must say, I like that tradition," he said.

"That was quite a kiss," Connie agreed. She smiled up at him, her eyes bright. "But now, tell me, my gallant, shining knight, what made you decide you wanted to get married right away? Have you given up on your dream of draining the swamp?"

"No," Bob said. "And it's more than a dream—it's a vow. I *am* going to drain that land, Connie. If I have to buy a shovel and dig the ditches myself, I promise you, I am going to drain that swamp."

"Then you'd better buy two shovels," Connie suggested.

"Two?"

"Yes. I believe in equality for women. And that

means in the workplace and on the home front as well as in the voting booth. If you are out there digging ditches, my darling husband-to-be, then I'm going to be right alongside you, ankle-deep in the dirt."

Bob laughed. "It'll be more like butt-deep in the mire," he warned.

"Oh, my, sir! How scandalously you do talk!"

The record stopped playing, and the scratching sound of the needle going around and around came loudly through the trumpet. Connie walked over and lifted the needle arm, stopped the turntable, and removed the record. She started looking through the stack for another song to play.

Bob watched her in silence for a moment, then said quietly, "Pop is dying, Connie."

Her eyes wide, Connie looked up and in a small, pained voice asked, "What? How? Why? What's wrong?"

"It's a disease of his heart," Bob answered. "Angina pectoris, the doctor said. He's already had two or three seizures of the disease. They call them heart attacks."

For a long moment Connie remained fixed to the spot. Out in the hallway the pendulum of the grandfather clock measured time, as it had for over fifty years. However, its tick-tock seemed exceptionally loud and intrusive at the moment. Connie's eyes filled with tears. "Oh, Bob, that poor dear. Is he . . . is he in pain?"

"No. Whenever he has one of those heart attacks, he suffers, but in between those spells, there's no pain."

"How long before . . ." Connie couldn't finish the sentence.

"I don't know. Dr. Lennox couldn't tell me," Bob answered. He took a deep breath, as if about to make a confession. "Connie, maybe I should tell you why I'm so anxious to get married right away. You see, I want Pop to live long enough to see his oldest son starting a family. If you think that's presumptuous of me, I understand. I mean, here we aren't even married yet, and I'm already planning a family."

"I don't think it's presumptuous at all," Connie

responded. "I think it's prudent. And of course we'll have a family."

"Maybe we won't have a child in time for him to see his grandson, but . . ."

Connie, smiling through tears, walked quickly over to Bob. She put her arms around him again. "If we don't have a child right away, Bob Canfield, I promise you that it won't be for lack of trying," she said. Then her smiled turned mischievous. "Though who said anything about it being a grandson? You mustn't overlook the possibility that you may be presenting him with a granddaughter, instead."

"What? You mean we might have a girl?" Bob said in mock horror.

Connie laughed. "Why, yes. I hope that's no big surprise to you. Half the children born are girls, you know."

"I never thought of that," Bob said, as if the idea were completely foreign.

"Would you be terribly disappointed?"

"What? No! Are you kidding? If we have a daughter, I know she'll be just like you. How could I possibly be disappointed?"

"Oh, Bob, may we tell the quad quad tonight, at David's dinner party?"

"That we're going to have a daughter? Or just that you're going to have a baby?" he asked, grinning broadly.

"Bob! Don't be telling people I'm going to have a baby!"

"Aren't you?"

"Well, yes, I certainly hope so. But you mustn't go around telling people that now. They'll get the wrong idea. They'll think I *have* to get married."

"You do have to get married," Bob said. "You don't think I'm going to let you out of it now, do you?"

"Yes, but that isn't the same thing, and you know it. Why, I'd be scandalized."

"Not down in the swamp. Nobody in the swamp

ever worries about such a thing," Bob continued to
tease. "Barefoot and pregnant is a way of life."

"Bob, be serious. Besides, I thought you said you
were draining the swamp. You drain the swamp, I'll
introduce some culture to the area."

"All right, it's a deal. And if you insist, I won't tell
anyone that you're having a baby—yet."

"Bob, you are impossible," Connie said, laughing.
"Oh, but we will tell people we're getting married," she
added. "I don't want to keep *that* a secret."

An autocar turned into the driveway just then, and
they glanced out the window to see Loomis Booker
driving the Bateman auto.

"What's Mr. Booker doing in your car?" Bob asked.

"He took Father down to the bank. They called him
this morning and asked him to come by." Connie smiled,
assessing her fiancé. "You always call Loomis 'Mr.
Booker,' don't you?"

"Of course I do. That's his name."

"To everyone else he's Loomis."

"Not to me."

"He's always been very special to you."

"Yes, he has. And so has Pearl."

"Oh, I love Pearl, too. She is such a dear," Connie
said. She laughed. "But she certainly isn't what you'd call
a meek person, is she? It's too bad she's a colored
woman. She has just the kind of spirit we're looking for
in the suffrage movement."

"You aren't trying to secure the vote just for white
women, are you?"

"No. No, of course not. But it wouldn't do to have
Pearl be too active in the movement. I mean, seeing her
might cause some others to . . ." Connie let her voice
trail off.

"I know what you mean. It isn't fair, but you're
right." He pointed through the window at Loomis.
"There's something else that isn't fair. There's Mr.
Booker, driving your father around, tending the school
furnaces, and cleaning out the septic tanks, and yet he is
measurably the most intelligent man I have ever met."

"Oh, Bob, let's tell him about us," Connie enthused. "Let's let him be the first to know."

"Okay," Bob agreed. "Let's do it."

They hurried into the kitchen and opened the back door, anticipating Loomis's arrival. When the handyman climbed the back stairs and found them waiting for him, he looked expectantly from face to face.

"Is something wrong?" he asked, concern in his voice.

"On the contrary!" Bob fairly shouted. "Something is very right. Connie and I are going to be married. And we wanted you to be the first to know."

"That's wonderful!" Loomis exclaimed. "And I am the first to know, you say?"

"The absolute first."

Loomis stuck his hand out. "Then that means I also have the honor of being the first to congratulate you. When is the happy event?"

"When?" Bob asked. He and Connie looked at each other, then laughed. "Why, I don't know," Bob admitted. "I guess we haven't gotten that far yet. All I can say is soon. As soon as we can."

"Loomis, where's my father?" Connie asked. "I want to tell him."

"He asked to be let off at his office." Loomis shook his head. "You know, I'm a little worried about him."

"Worried? Why?"

"I don't know. He didn't say anything when he came out of the meeting at the bank, but I got the distinct impression that it wasn't a very pleasant occasion. He was quiet for the whole drive, and then when we reached the campus, he asked me to let him off at Spengeman Hall. He said he'd walk home later."

"We could go over there now, if you'd like," Bob said to Connie.

"Okay," Connie agreed. "I'd like you to meet Eric, anyway. He lives in Loomis's old apartment over there."

"Eric's not there now," Loomis said. "He went downtown with your father and me."

"And he stayed downtown?" Connie asked. "Why would he do that?"

"Have you ever heard of the Buffalo Bill Wild West Show?" Loomis asked.

"Yes, I have."

"Well, it's in St. Louis, and Eric has gone to see it." Loomis chuckled. "As you know, Eric used to be a cowboy himself, and he said he was very curious to see just why people would pay to go see them."

It was, without doubt, the biggest tent Eric had ever seen. He was inside, standing on the ground between two sets of bleachers and watching as a "runaway" stagecoach careened around the sawdust-packed arena, chased by several riders on horseback. A young woman passenger in the coach had her head and shoulders sticking out the window, and her long, blond hair was flying in the wind and the sawdust churned up by the drumming hooves and spinning wheels. It was a very dramatic picture, intensified by the young woman's screams.

"Help!" she shouted. "Somebody help!"

The driver was on the seat of the coach, but the reins had fallen, and he was sitting empty-handed, unable to do anything. For a moment Eric, like everyone else in the audience, really believed the coach was in trouble. Then he saw something practically no one else in the audience would notice: A second set of lines ran from the six-horse team and passed inside the coach through a narrow slit cut across the front of the vehicle. The real driver, Eric realized, was squatting down inside, handling those reins. Though it looked as though the team was a runaway, it was actually well under control.

As the audience continued to scream and shout, unaware that the girl was in no real danger, Eric smiled. He could see why the Wild West show was so popular.

A white horse dashed out of the pack of those chasing the stage, and the rider, dressed in a dazzling

white outfit complete with silver spangles, drew even
with the team that was pulling the coach. To gasps of
amazement from the crowd the rider leapt from his
mount onto one of the team's trailing horses. He swiftly
moved from that horse to the one ahead and then to one
of the lead horses, where he brought the stagecoach to a
stop. Then he jumped down, ran back to open the door,
and, hat in hand, made a sweeping bow as the lady he
had just "rescued" stepped out of the coach onto the
ground.

The blond placed her right hand over her heart and
held her left arm out toward the crowd. "My hero!" she
proclaimed.

The band, which had been providing background
music to the whole event, played a crescendo chord, and
the crowd, realizing now that the event was all a part of
the show though still not aware of how it was done,
cheered lustily.

The other riders rode by then, tipping their hats
first to the young woman and the man in white who had
rescued her, then toward the crowd. The crowd applauded, and the man in white helped the lady back into
the stagecoach. Then he remounted and rode alongside
the coach as it exited the arena while another act entered
from the opposite side of the tent.

Eric had never seen anything quite like the performance the Wild West Show was putting on. There were
shooting exhibitions, trick riding, roping, stagecoach
holdups, an Indian war, buffalo hunts, and gunfights.
Though none of it related in any way to anything Eric
had ever experienced as a real cowboy, he was nevertheless quite impressed and watched the show with a
great deal of interest and genuine admiration for the
riding, roping, and shooting skills of the men and women
performing.

Then toward the end of the show, during an act that
was billed as "The Great Cattle Drive," something
unexpected happened. A long-horned steer suddenly
broke away from the rest of the herd and started running
toward the stands. For an instant Eric thought this was

all part of the stunt; then he saw the reaction and the expressions of the drovers and realized that this was no act. This steer really was out of control!

The crowd screamed as the huge animal—its horns spread nearly eight feet from tip to tip, its eyes blood-red, and mucus streaming from its nostrils—rumbled toward them. None of the cowboys who were a part of the act were in position to do anything to stop it; in fact, all they could do was call out a warning.

"You people, watch out!" a cowboy shouted.

Standing very near Eric was a riderless horse with a lariat hanging from the saddle. Without pausing to think of the consequence of his act, Eric ran to the horse, leapt into the saddle, and spurred the animal on. The horse was well trained and was more responsive to Eric's commands than any horse he had ever ridden. Within seconds Eric, who was much closer than any of the show cowboys, was within a few feet of the runaway steer.

Taking the rope in his hands, the youth formed a loop. He had done some roping while working on the ranch, though he had never been as good at it as Jake, and as he twirled the rope over his head, he thought of his old friend, realizing that this was the first time he had done so in several months. He remembered Jake's instructions, how to widen the loop and, more impor-tantly, how to keep it open when he threw it. He could almost hear Jake's words, as if his friend were there, riding alongside him.

The steer left the sawdust arena and started up a small wooden ramp toward some temporary bleachers that had been erected—"ten-centers" they were called, because they were the cheapest, most crowded, and most uncomfortable seats in the house. The steer's hooves drummed on the wood like a roll of thunder, and he tossed his head from side to side.

The crowd panicked and raced to get out of the way. A little girl fell down, then screamed in fear, and her father started back for her. They were directly in the path of the steer's lumbering charge, and people shrieked in horror.

Eric threw the loop, and it dropped around most of the animal's head and one horn. Quickly, he wrapped his end of the rope around the pommel, and the horse dug in its haunches. With the rope taut, Eric jerked it back, pulling the steer's head abruptly to one side, and the runaway animal fell to his knees and rolled over. When the steer stood back up a second later, all the run and fight was gone from him, and he turned back toward the arena and began walking docilely toward the cattle pen on the far side. A couple of cowboys from the act were there by then, and they took charge of him.

The crowd, thinking by now that the entire episode may have been a part of the act, cheered lustily. Eric, red-faced and embarrassed by the applause, returned the horse to where he had found it, then tried to sneak away. He hadn't gone far before two men caught up with him.

"Mr. Cody wants to see you," one of them said.

"Is he angry with me? I'm sorry," Eric said. "I know I shouldn't have done anything, I just—"

"Are you teasin' us, kid? You're a genuine hero," the other man said. "Mr. Cody wants to thank you personally, that's all."

Eric was led outside the main tent to a smaller tent, then ushered inside it. There, standing in front of a full-length mirror, stood Buffalo Bill. He was dressed in a fringed suit of light buckskin and a crimson shirt that was highly visible under his open coat. A broad-brimmed sombrero hung from a hat rack that had been made from a set of antlers. Buffalo Bill was staring into the mirror as he applied some sort of darkener to his mustache and spade beard.

Eric had, of course, heard of Buffalo Bill. One time one of the cowboys back on the Flying E Ranch had brought in a bunch of Ned Buntline dime novels about the celebrated scout, and Eric had read the books aloud to Jake and Marcus. Though some of the more outlandish stunts had been scoffed at and laughed over, they truly enjoyed the stories, and Eric remembered how Marcus had once put his horse's reins in his mouth, then galloped across the prairie, firing a pistol from each hand, "just to see if it could be done."

Now Eric was standing no more than three feet away from the man he had read about. Buffalo Bill was older than Eric had imagined, though, despite his age, he was still tall and straight and handsome.

"How long till the next show?" Buffalo Bill asked of the two men who had delivered Eric to his tent.

"About an hour, Mr. Cody."

"Good. Good. Leave us now," he instructed.

Eric, misunderstanding, turned to leave, but one of the two men who brought him shook his head and, with a gesture of his hand, told him to stay.

Eric stood after the men were gone, just watching as Buffalo Bill continued to preen himself for his entry into the arena. Muffled by distance, the band music was almost inaudible, but other than that, here, inside Buffalo Bill's personal dressing tent, there was silence for a good two minutes. Eric wondered if he was expected to initiate the conversation. But no, he reasoned, he didn't ask to come here, he was sent for. He decided to be quiet and see what Buffalo Bill wanted with him.

"How old are you, boy?" the great showman finally asked, not taking his eyes from the mirror while he brushed lint from his buckskin jacket.

"Nearly eighteen."

"Where did you learn to ride and rope like that?"

"I always could ride as well as the next fella," Eric said. "No better than, but as well as. The truth is, though, I'm not much of a roper."

Buffalo Bill glanced at Eric's image in the mirror. "That's not what I heard. I heard you threw a loop nearly thirty feet and brought that steer down just in the nick of time."

"I was lucky."

"You're being modest."

"No, sir, I mean, I hope I'm a modest enough person, but I'm telling the truth about roping. Nearly everyone else on the ranch was a better roper than I was.

I generally had to ride right up to an animal and drop the loop right down on him. I really was just lucky today."

Buffalo Bill finally finished his preparations, and he turned to face Eric. Eric thought he had never seen eyes as strikingly intense as Buffalo Bill's, and he wondered if any of what he'd read about the man had any element of truth. From the showman's appearance, Eric was almost ready to concede that there was.

"You're a cowboy? Isn't that rather difficult, here in St. Louis?"

"Yes, sir, I reckon it would be," Eric replied, smiling. "I was in Wyoming when I cowboyed."

"Why'd you give it up? I would think that that'd be an exciting life for a young man."

"It was all right, I guess," Eric said, forcing the painful memories of the abrupt end to his former life from his mind. "But it always seemed like it was too cold in the winter and too hot in the summer. The days were long and the nights too short. The food got pretty boring, there wasn't much to do, and I have to believe that cows are the dumbest creatures God ever put on earth."

Buffalo Bill slapped his knee gleefully, then threw his head back and laughed out loud. "Yes, sir," he said. "Yes, sir, you *have* been a cowboy. You'd be surprised at the number of young men I've had come to see me who claimed to be a cowboy, but really weren't. I could tell in a moment if they were lying or not, and you, young man, are not lying. Was there anything you liked about being a cowboy?"

"Yes, sir," Eric answered. "I liked the fellas I worked with, and I liked the man I worked for. And there were other things I liked about it, too. I like riding nighthawk when the stars are so big and bright you feel like you can just reach up and grab a handful of them. And I liked the early morning, when the light was soft and the air was cool, and you could smell smoke and coffee and bacon from the cookie's breakfast fire and hear the men stirring in their bedrolls, knowing that they had to get up and go to work, but you were off till noon."

Buffalo Bill's eyes clouded over, and he looked

away, as if unable to meet Eric's gaze. He stared at one of his show posters, gaudy in bright reds, yellows, and blues. For a moment, Eric could almost believe that Cody wasn't here, in a tent in St. Louis, but was somewhere back in time, before the life of grease paint and sawdust and band music and barkers selling popcorn and taffy and Wild West Show souvenirs.

"Damn, boy, you should be a writer," Buffalo Bill said.

Eric smiled. "I'd like to be, someday."

"How'd you wind up in St. Louis? Your parents move here?"

"No, sir. My folks are dead. They died in Montana when I was twelve. I've been mostly on my own since then, and I came to St. Louis back in oh-four to see the World's Fair."

Buffalo Bill chuckled. "The World's Fair, huh? Did you see it?"

"Yes, sir. It was really something. I guess I'll remember it for the rest of my life."

"It was some show," Buffalo Bill agreed. "Bigger than mine—but, then, mine gets to travel around."

"Yes, sir."

"What's your name, son?"

"Eric Twainbough."

Buffalo Bill put his hand on Eric's shoulder. "How'd you like to work for me, Eric? How would you like to come travel with my show?"

Eric smiled broadly. "Yes, sir, I'd like doing that. I'd like doing that a lot. I figured maybe you use real cowboys to handle your stock."

Buffalo Bill smiled. "You'd be doing that, all right," he confirmed. "Most of the fellas do. But you'd be performing, too."

"But what would I do, Mr. Cody? I've never seen such marvelous riding and roping and shooting skills. I couldn't do anything like that."

"You were the star of the show today, Eric," Buffalo Bill said. "Believe me, when the folks go home to tell their family and friends what they saw, they're going to be talking most about the young man who leapt onto a horse and roped that steer to save that child and her father."

"But I told you, that was luck."

"Yes, sir, I suppose it was. After all, luck does come in handy—but you can't count on it all the time. That's why in show business, you build in a few safeguards."

Eric smiled. "You mean like the extra set of lines on the runaway stage.

Buffalo Bill chuckled. "You saw that, did you?"

"Yes, sir."

"You're a pretty observant lad. You'd be amazed at how few people do notice it. But, yes, that's the kind of thing I'm talking about. Now, how about it, Eric? Would you like to come work in Buffalo Bill's Wild West Show? From here we're going to Chicago for two weeks, then two weeks in Detroit, two in Cleveland, three weeks in Baltimore, three weeks in Philadelphia, and after that we'll spend the rest of the summer in New York City at Madison Square Garden."

"New York?" Eric asked, his eyes lighting up.

"Ah, you have an interest in New York, do you?"

"Yes, sir. That's where all the books are published."

"I do believe you're right. And any self-respecting writer would have to visit that city before embarking upon his writing career, don't you agree? Besides, think of the new experiences you'll gain if you come with us . . . great new experiences that can be incorporated into your writing. So, what do you say, lad? Would you like to become one of Buffalo Bill's Wild West Show star performers?"

"Yes, sir! I think I would like that a lot."

"Then go home and gather up whatever you want to take with you, and come on back here. We'll be leaving St. Louis tomorrow morning." He smiled slyly. "St. Louis is my wife's hometown, you know. I can never get out of it fast enough to suit me. Oh, and here," Buffalo Bill added, taking a card from his pocket. "This is a gate pass. It'll let you enter through the employees' entrance. Don't lose it."

"No, sir, I won't," Eric said, taking the pass. "And I'll get back as quickly as I can."

"Don't forget to tell all your friends good-bye. It's likely to be quite a while before you return to St. Louis."

"I will, sir," Eric promised.

Professor William Bateman stood at the window of his third-floor Spengeman Hall office, staring out at the statue of Henry Spengeman. Several seniors were ensconced in their sanctum sanctorum inside Statue Circle, while here and there other students strolled across the quad, women as well as men. The routine appearance of the scene gave nothing to indicate that it might all come to an end.

But Professor Bateman had just learned something that none of the students and few of the staff knew: No longer was there a Jefferson University trust fund. The school's business administrator had, over a period of years and without consultation, made a series of unwise investments, covering up those losses with false entries in the books. Fearing discovery when he had learned about an imminent audit, he embezzled the remaining money and left the country. As a result of his mismanagement and embezzlement, the school had lost almost two million dollars over the last three years—and that meant there was very little chance the school would be able to open its doors again next fall. In fact the school was now so close to bankruptcy, it might well have to close its doors even before graduation this spring.

With characteristic determination Professor Bateman had decided to tackle the problem, one situation at a time. Somewhere, somehow, he would find enough money to keep the doors open until graduation this year. After that he would begin looking for a source of money to open the doors next year. He couldn't face the possibility of failure. He refused to consider it, even though he needed at least a million and a half to pay off back debts and cover operating expenses for the entire school year.

It would be nice if he could just find a benefactor, someone who would endow the school with a great deal of money. Such men existed, he knew, and schools like Vanderbilt, Stanford, and Cornell were evidence of that.

The professor's one source of comfort was the fact that his school was not the only private institution having a difficult time making ends meet. He recalled an article he had read only last week in *Colliers Magazine*, in which the difficulties being faced even by well-endowed universities were discussed. The article cited how for the first time in its history, except for war interruptions, Harvard's registration was diminishing, owing to a decrease in students from western states, since the growth and efficacy of universities in those states now ensured quality education nearer home. Jefferson's problem was even more acute, because in addition to competition for students from state universities in Missouri and Illinois, it had to compete with Missouri's regional teachers' colleges, which now offered full degrees for only twenty dollars per year, while Jefferson's tuition was two hundred and fifty dollars.

Nevertheless, Professor Bateman had had reason to be encouraged. Last year's enrollment, while still below the peak it had enjoyed in 1902, was actually up slightly from the year before. The erosion had stopped, and changing it from a college to a university and opening its doors to women had started to pay off. The professor had begun entertaining the hope that things were turning around.

Then came the summons from the bank and the terrible news that the Jefferson University account was gone. And, since the embezzling business administrator had not been an employee of the bank, but rather of the university, the bank was not responsible for the loss. Professor Bateman was going to have to face the Board of Directors and tell them the news, and it wasn't a job he was looking forward to.

"Daddy?"

The professor turned at the sound of his daughter's

voice. Connie and Bob Canfield were standing in the doorway.

"Well, hello there," he greeted, gesturing for them to enter. "I was wondering what you two were doing this afternoon."

"Daddy, we have some wonderful news for you," Connie said.

Professor Bateman smiled. "Good. That's just what I need. Some wonderful news."

"Actually we never were really the quad quad anyway," Terry Perkins declared, leaning back in his chair. He was seated on one side of the Gelbman dining table at the conclusion of the friends' farewell dinner, during which many stories had been swapped—and many fond memories recalled. "We were more accurately the quad *quint*," he amended, gallantly saluting Connie Bateman.

The others laughed at his quip, and J. P. Winthrop asked, "When is the wedding?"

"In three days," Bob Canfield answered. "Though I don't suppose you can call it a wedding in the traditional sense. I mean, there won't be a church and a crowd of people and all that."

"We're getting married in the parlor of my father's house," Connie explained.

"The ceremony's just as valid as if it were performed in a church," J.P. said.

"Or a synagogue," David Gelbman added.

"What a wonderful thing for us to celebrate, just before David and I leave," Terry said. Referring to his newspaper assignment on board a U.S. Navy warship during a military expedition to Latin American, he explained, "I know it isn't a grand and glorious war like the Spanish-American conflict, or even a big war like the Russians and Japanese fought. But it's the only war we've got, and if I'm going to be a true journalist, I feel that I should see it firsthand."

"Make sure you wear a lifesaving jacket at all times,"

Connie said. "If they shoot a cannonball at you and sink the ship, it might come in handy."

"As long as you don't try and catch the cannonball," J.P. added.

When the laughter ebbed, Connie smiled at David and said, "Bob tells me you're going to Vienna. I envy you. I hear it's a wonderfully romantic city."

"Well, I don't know how romantic *I* will find it," David said, shaking his head. "Leo Blumberg, the husband of my father's cousin, died three months ago. He owned a store there, and Cousin Sarah is unable to run it. She wrote my father, asking for his advice—"

"—and the advice I gave her was, 'Sarah, sell the store,'" David's father finished. "'Sell the store, sell your house, sell all your things and come to America. America is the promised land.'" He shrugged. "But she is too proud to accept any financial help from me or my offer for her and the children to live with us—she feels that she would be putting a burden on us—so she did not wish to leave Vienna."

"I think she may be right, Mr. Gelbman," J.P. said. "Oh, if she accepted your help and came to St. Louis, perhaps it would work out all right. But I wouldn't advise any Jewish person to go to New York, not unless they have a lot of money."

"I went to New York with very little in my pockets," Chaim remarked, "and I did not find it such a bad place."

"You haven't seen it lately," J.P. said. "There's been a good deal of unrest in Europe—many countries have passed laws against your people—so the Jews are leaving their homelands in enormous numbers to come here. On some days Ellis Island processes as many as fifteen thousand immigrants, and most of them are Jewish."

"And they all stay in New York?" David asked.

"Most of them have no choice. By the time they arrive in America, their money is gone. They've paid for taxes and bribes to officials in Europe, land transportation and then steamer passage, plus the cost of feeding their family for up to three months—all this with no income. And, I'm ashamed to say, the bribes and extortion don't quit when they reach America. So most of the immigrants can afford to go only as far as their nearest relative—and that means the Lower East Side, which by now has become the most densely populated area in the city. With more than seven hundred people per acre, it's said that it's more densely populated than even the worst sections of Bombay. In the tenement buildings children, parents, and grandparents are crowded together in a two-room apartment—three rooms if they're lucky—with water available only from a community faucet outside."

"That sounds horrible," Connie said with a shiver.

"It *is* horrible, believe me. And the streets are just as crowded as the tenements, especially the market areas. There's a place on Hester Street, near Ludlow, that's called the 'pig market.'"

"The *pig* market? For *Jews*?" Golda Gelbman asked, her eyes wide. "Is this true?"

J.P. laughed. "That's their sense of humor at work," he explained. "They couldn't name it after what *is* sold there, since practically anything can be bought from the peddlers' pushcarts—a quart of peaches for a penny, used eyeglasses for thirty-five cents, and old carts for fifty cents—so they've named it for the one thing that is *not* sold from the pushcarts. Pigs."

"You have seen all this?" Chaim asked.

"Yes," J.P. replied. "Many times."

"Why would someone like you be in a place like that?"

"I did some volunteer work for the Baron de Hirsch commission, and they run a settlement house downtown."

Clearly saddened by the description painted, Chaim put his hand on J.P.'s shoulder. "You are a good and decent young man to concern yourself with the troubles of others," he said. "I had no idea things were so bad."

"Then you agree, Papa," David spoke up, "that Cousin Sarah is right not to come to America?"

"I agree," Chaim said. "She will have a much better

life in Vienna. Stay there and help her, David. Stay in Vienna and work for Sarah for as long as it takes to make the store a viable business again."

"You may have quite a job cut out for you," Bob suggested.

"Yes, but I'll also have the adventure I've been looking for," David replied, smiling broadly.

"Do you realize," Connie asked, "that after today, the paths you've all chosen will be leading you, literally, in different directions?"

"It is our sacred mission," J.P. proclaimed in a pompous tone. "For behold, we must take the quad quad to the four corners of the world and spread ourselves among the masses."

"Lord help the masses," Terry groaned, and they all laughed.

David poured four glasses of wine. "Connie, you will forgive us," he said. "And you too, Papa, Mama, for this is a toast that I think should be drunk only by the quad quad." He handed a glass to each of the other three, then raised his own. "A toast," he said, "to scholarship and to the paths that lie before us. We must each go our own way, but wherever we go, and whatever we do, we will always—like a ship finding a safe harbor by the lamp of a friendly lighthouse—be able to take our own bearings on the bright and shining beacon of our friendship."

"Here, here," Terry responded.

"To the quad quad," Bob said, raising his glass to the others.

"L'Chaim," J.P. added. The four of them managed, awkwardly, to loop their arms together, then, with their arms intertwined, to drink the wine. There was absolute silence until the last drop was drunk, and then Terry laughed.

"I didn't think we were going to be able to do it," he said.

"My boy," J.P. said, "for the quad quad, nothing is impossible."

CHAPTER FOURTEEN

U.S. MARINES DEFEND AMERICAN INTERESTS IN HONDURAS
By Terry Perkins
Special to *The St. Louis Chronicle*

March 21, 1907, aboard the U.S.S. *Olympia*, off the northern coast of Honduras—The first impression one gets is of brilliant color. Flashes of red and yellow signal flags wave from the halyards, gleaming brass fittings catch the eye from everywhere on the spruced-up ships, dazzling white uniforms dot the decks, and, of course, there is the blue of the water and the sky.

The blue-gray surface of the water is streaked with paler foamy wakes from the small boats that move back and forth between the ships on one errand or another. From the bridges of these ships the captains exchange their messages, either by flashing Morse code or by signalmen who wigwag their colorful flags in semaphore, the language understood only by them that is then translated by them for the captains they serve.

I have been given quarters on board the *U.S.S. Olympia*, a heavy battle cruiser that fairly bristles with guns. This ship, readers may recall, was Admiral George Dewey's flagship during the recent war with Spain, and I have stood on deck in the exact spot the Hero of Manila stood when he issued his famous order: "You may fire when you are ready, Gridley." Once again she is serving as the flagship of an American fleet, albeit one of but three ships.

The advance landing party has already gone ashore, and signals are being flashed from there as well, relaying instructions to the marines on board the three vessels of this flotilla. The marines are preparing to go ashore or, as they prefer to say, "on the beach," as if embarking on some holiday.

But though there is, indeed, a holidaylike atmosphere to the proceedings, the officers in command are well aware that this is not a pleasure jaunt. They have instructed their men to be most vigilant during this trying time, for while a full-scale attack by the Nicaraguans is not likely, there may well be sharpshooters hidden ashore, anxious to take advantage of their concealment to shoot down the unwary members of this expeditionary force.

This will be the first time since the Boxer Rebellion in China that an American force has landed on foreign soil for military purposes. U.S. authorities are quick to point out, however, that this is not an invasion; it is merely a display of our intention to safeguard American lives and American-owned banana plantations from the Nicaraguan forces invading Honduras.

When Terry had finished his story, he got up from the desk where he had been working in the *Olympia*'s wardroom and walked over to the porthole, poking his head out and looking out at the other two vessels also riding at anchor in the deep water just off the northern coast of Honduras. Terry was amused to note that though a military landing on foreign soil was about to take place, the routine of daily naval life went on. Illustrative of this was the fact that, just below his porthole, three sailors were holystoning the ship's drab gray deck, while another three chipped away at the painted bulkhead. A thousand yards across the sparkling blue water lay the sandy beach and verdant jungle of the Honduran northern coast.

The story Terry had just written was his first report since coming aboard, and he knew that by the miracle of wireless, cable, and telegraph, his story would be in *The Chronicle*'s composing room tonight. When the sun came up tomorrow morning, the newsboys of St. Louis would have his article on the streets. It gave Terry a feeling of satisfaction that he would have been hard-pressed to describe as he thought of people like Professor Bateman, Chaim Gelbman, and a quarter of a million other St. Louisians reading his words at their breakfast tables.

"Mr. Perkins, would you care for a cup of coffee?" a voice asked, interrupting Terry's thoughts.

"Yes, thank you, Major Tobias. I would like a cup."

Major John Tobias was standing at a silver-plated coffee urn. This urn, like the very long mahogany buffet it sat on, the dining table, the china closets, the red-leather sofas and chairs, and the glossy hardwood floor, seemed out of place on a ship of war. Such appointments would have been acceptable in the dining room of a fine private club, which, Terry had learned since coming aboard the *Olympia* in Norfolk, the wardroom of a U.S. Navy ship was very much like. It served the captain and his officers as a dining hall and recreation room as well as a place for conducting meetings.

The wall behind the buffet was hung with paintings of ships famous in American history: the *Mayflower;* the *Bon Homme Richard;* the *Constitution;* warships from the Revolutionary War and the War of 1812; the *Savannah,* America's first steam-powered, oceangoing ship; the *Flying Cloud,* Donald McKay's beautiful clipper ship; and even the *Olympia* herself.

The marine poured a cup of coffee for Terry, then brought it over to him. "Would you like to go onto the beach with us?" Major Tobias asked as he handed the cup over.

"Very much. Do you think anyone would object?"

"No, I don't think so. Our shore party has reported no Nicaraguan soldiers. It should be a very simple operation." Major Tobias chuckled. "Not much for you to write about, I'm afraid."

"I'd rather have nothing to write about than to write about American soldiers being killed," Terry remarked.

"Well, yes, there is that to consider."

Their conversation was interrupted then by the blare of a bugle. Raising his eyebrows, the major got up and walked over to the porthole. "I'll be damned," he said.

"What is it? What is that bugle call? I've heard the calls for reveille, assembly, mess call, retreat, and taps, but I've never heard that one," Terry remarked.

"That's battle stations," Major Tobias said.

"Battle stations? For what purpose? To land the marines?"

"No, it wouldn't be necessary to go to battle stations to land troops," Tobias explained. "There were reports of Nicaraguan gunboats sighted in these waters, but surely they wouldn't be so foolish as to challenge the United States Navy."

Tobias stepped out onto the deck with Terry close behind. Some sailors came hurrying by, awkwardly putting on their life jackets while on the run. The men who'd been working the deck and bulkhead detail were gone now, their paint buckets, holystones, and chippers the only evidence of their former presence.

"Sailor! What is it? What's going on?" Major Tobias shouted at one of the hustling sailors.

"Nicaraguan gunboats, sir!" the sailor replied excitedly, shouting back over his shoulder. "The lookout spotted them. Excuse me, sir. I must get to my gun station."

"Yes, of course." Tobias turned toward Terry with a smile on his face. "Well, it appears I was wrong. The Nicaraguans *were* that foolish. Mr. Perkins, perhaps you'll see some action after all. But if you'll excuse me, I must get to my men now."

"Yes, of course," Terry replied. As the officer hurried away, Terry stepped to the railing, where he could get a better view of what was going on yet still be out of everyone's way. The entire ship was galvanized into activity, and Terry could feel his pulse racing as he watched sailors roll back canvas covers, exposing the big guns, then ready them for action by removing the tampons from the ends of the barrels.

A young ensign suddenly approached. "Mr. Perkins, Captain Fulman's compliments, sir, and he asks if you would care to join him on the bridge."

"Yes, I certainly would. What's the best way to get there without getting in anyone's way?"

"Follow me, sir," the ensign offered, turning on his heel.

They quickly reached the bridge, which, like the rest of the ship, was a flurry of activity as officers and enlisted men prepared for battle.

"Signal rocket aloft, sir," one of the sailors reported.

"One of ours?" Captain Fulman asked.

"No, sir."

"Where away?"

"Three points off our starboard bow."

Captain Fulman raised his binoculars and stared toward the distant line of ships. Terry looked in the same direction, but the vessels were too far away for him to make out anything. Then someone handed him a pair of binoculars.

"Try these," the sailor said.

"Thanks," Terry responded. He raised the glasses and looked through them. Suddenly he saw several winks of light, like sparks on a loose electrical connection. He was about to ask what it was, when Captain Fulman said in a low voice, "They have opened fire on us."

"My God, they've opened fire?" Terry gasped.

"Do you wish a course change, sir?" the officer of the deck asked.

"No, Mr. Quinn. They have no chance of hitting us."

A line of geysers erupted in the water nearly a thousand yards away.

"You're right, sir. They're way off," Quinn remarked.

"What's the matter with your gunners over there?" Fulman asked, as if speaking to the Nicaraguan ship's captain. "Can't they do any better job than that in estimating range? They need to elevate their guns about another ten degrees."

"Either that or add an additional charge," Quinn noted.

"They need to take a few lessons from our gunners," one of the sailors said, and the others voiced their agreement.

Terry wondered if everyone on the bridge had lost their minds. The Nicaraguans were trying to sink this ship! They were firing heavy guns with hostile intent, and yet Fulman and Quinn and the other sailors on the bridge were talking about it as if it were just another routine event.

"Mr. Crane, to the foremast please, with the stadimeter."

"Aye, aye, sir," an officer answered. This was the same ensign who had brought Terry to the bridge, and he took an instrument from a felt-lined box, then stepped outside and started climbing the mast.

"What is that device he has?" Terry asked.

"An instrument that can gauge the distance to the target," the captain answered.

At that precise moment a shell, fired by one of the Nicaraguan gunboats, landed so close to the *Olympia* that its explosion threw a sheet of water all the way up to the bridge platform and through the open windows, drenching everyone, Terry included, in salt water.

"Gunnery Officer," Fulman called. "Inform the guns that we will engage."

"Aye, aye, sir," the officer addressed replied. He

spoke into a speaking tube. "Gun captains, we will engage, we will engage," he ordered.

Terry heard a cheer from the sailors, and he moved over to the window where he could see and hear the nearest gun crew. There was a lot of shouting back and forth among the men.

"Set fuse, point detonating!" he heard one gun captain yell.

"Fuse, point detonating, set!" came back the response.

"Load one round, explosive shell!"

Two men picked up a black cone and carried it to the rear of the gun. They set it on a track, and then a third man pushed the shell into the gun with a long rod.

"Shell loaded!"

"Load charge, two bags!"

Two linen bags of gunpowder were placed in behind the shell.

"Belay that last order. Charge, three!"

An additional linen bag was put behind the other two, and then the breechblock was closed and screwed down.

"Charge loaded!"

"Range, three-five-double-zero yards!"

Two men began turning a crank, and the gun barrel was slowly elevated. The gun captain who had been shouting the orders looked through an aiming device, then stepped back.

"Number one turret, ready for firing!" he shouted. The other turrets were also calling in their own readiness so that within a moment every gun on the ship was ready to fire.

"Mr. Perkins, I would recommend that you cover your ears," Captain Fulman suggested calmly. Then to Quinn, "You may pass the word to fire at discretion, Mr. Quinn."

Quinn nodded to the gunnery officer, and the command was passed to fire.

Terry had never heard a noise as loud as the sound of all the guns erupting at the same time. Huge billows of smoke poured out from the ends of the barrels, and for a second it was as if a cloud had come down to cover the ship. Then, as the smoke cleared away, he saw a series of explosions as the shells fell on their target. The other American ships fired soon afterward, and even from a distance their noise was deafening. Smoke and fire erupted from those shells that had scored hits on the Nicaraguan ships, and the men cheered their success.

"Mr. Perkins, away from the glass, please," Captain Fulman abruptly called.

Terry stepped away from the window, and moments later another volley of shells from the Nicaraguan fleet arrived. One burst about a hundred feet above them, and shrapnel rained down onto the ship. The window where Terry had been standing but seconds earlier was shattered, spraying out great shards of glass. One piece hit the helmsman, but outside of inflicting a rather clean cut to his arm, it did no more damage.

The *Olympia* returned fire, and every time she fired a salvo, the ship shook so hard that Terry had to hold on to something to keep his balance. The noise of the firing was so loud that it was painful to his ears, and when a sympathetic sailor handed him a couple of wads of cotton, he thankfully stuffed them in his ears.

The American fleet sailed back and forth in front of the Nicaraguan ships, firing often and accurately. Terry had a ringside seat to the action, which the young reporter thought looked like some carefully rehearsed show rather than a real battle. The ships moved in a stately fashion, firing regularly and ceasing their fire only when the smoke became so thick that their targets were obscured. Terry discovered that he could actually see the shells in their flight, and he followed the black projectiles as they arced out toward the Nicaraguan ships, many of them crashing into the vessels and then exploding in a flash of fire. After several minutes all four of the Nicaraguan gunboats were burning fiercely.

Terry looked down at the American sailors on the deck. He was surprised to see how calm and orderly they were, handling the guns and ammunition with a mechanical precision that belied the fact they were in a life-and-death struggle.

"Captain, the engineering officer reports the temperature in the engine room is over one hundred thirty degrees," one of the officers said. "Some of the men are passing out."

"Very well. Tell the engineering officer to start a shuttle," Captain Fulman responded. "Have him send one third of his men up to the deck for ten minutes, then switch them around."

"Aye, aye, sir."

One hundred and thirty degrees! Terry thought about those men in the engine room, having to spend this battle battened down without ventilation, baking in the heat of the furnaces and engine boilers, debilitated from the physical exertion of shoveling coal. He hurried to the opposite side of the bridge and saw ten of them tumble out onto the deck. Naked except for shoes and drawers, they were covered in sweat and soot. They lay near exhaustion, breathing hard, and showing no concern or interest whatever in the battle still raging.

As the fight continued Terry was able to discern Captain Fulman's plan: The American ships would steam by the Nicaraguan fleet at a steady speed of six knots; then, at the end of the line, the ships would bear around, returning to the fray at the starting point. The *Olympia* was leading the oval formation, and each time it returned to the beginning, they were a little closer to the Nicaraguan ships. Finally they were so close Terry could see the Nicaraguan sailors quite clearly with his naked eye. It was obvious that they were suffering far more than the Americans, for every Nicaraguan ship had been severely damaged. Many of their guns were out of operation and the gunners, now without jobs, stood at the railing, watching the battle. Naked to the waist and black with the residue of spent powder, many of them had their heads wrapped in water-soaked towels, and their bodies glistened with sweat.

For the American gun crews there was no respite at all, and the men continued to load shell after shell and charge after charge, each weighing upwards of two hundred pounds, into the huge guns. And, as if the heat of the battle and their exhaustion wasn't enough, the sun was so hot it was melting the pitch on the decks.

An hour and a half after the battle had started, the Nicaraguan gunboats, badly wounded, broke off the engagement and began limping away.

"Shall we follow them, Captain?" Quinn asked.

Fulman rubbed his chin and watched as the ships retired; then he shook his head. "No," he replied. "We've inflicted a terrible defeat upon them. Our countries are not technically at war, so to proceed further would take this beyond self-defense and into an act of savagery. Secure from battle stations and prepare to disembark troops."

"Aye, aye, sir," Quinn replied.

It was another hour before the landing operation got under way. Major Tobias, the commanding officer of the marines who would go ashore, invited Terry to the deck to watch as the landing operation began. Transportation was provided from ship to shore by small steam launches, each pulling a boat loaded with men. When the launches got the boats close to shore, the men would cut themselves loose, paddle through the surf to the beach, then unload, while two men stayed in the boats to return back through the surf to rejoin the launches. The launches would then pull the empty boats back to the ships for another load. Terry watched more than two hundred men be put ashore in this way.

On the third such trip the young reporter was informed that he could now go ashore. He anxiously scrambled down the net and took his seat in the small rocking boat, and from this perspective the side of the *Olympia* loomed above him like a steel cliff, and he studied the ship from an angle he had never before seen. Her sides were white, and her hull curved in at the waterline and then bowed out as it worked its way up. Four rows of portholes, all open, dotted the hull, and a number of heads protruded from the portholes as the sailors, their own tasks completed, watched the proceedings with great interest.

About forty feet behind the gently bouncing boats a bilge pipe on the ship began emptying water into the sea. When one of the marines saw what Terry was looking at, he grinned and asked, "Looks a bit like a whale takin' a piss, don't it, sir?"

Terry laughed. That was exactly what it looked like, but of course—and unfortunately—he couldn't use that analogy in any of his stories.

On the deck, high above, the head and shoulders of one of the officers leaned over the rail. He raised a megaphone to his mouth and called down to the steam-launch captain. "Away the boat!" A moment later, the *Olympia* began pulling away—then Terry realized that it was merely an illusion. The ship stayed still; it was they who were moving.

By the time Terry reached shore, a beach headquarters had already been established. There, Major Tobias was standing and watching the landing of a boatload of horses, which were proving to be more difficult to get ashore than the men. Loaded onto large lighters, the animals had then been pulled as close in to shore by the steam launches as they could get. Then they were shoved off into the sea, where they were caught by men in small boats, led to the breakers by their halter shanks, then turned loose to be washed ashore.

Terry felt sorry for the poor beasts, who of course had no idea why they were being subjected to such treatment. After the horses swam ashore, they were taken to a picket line, where they stood quietly, a picture of dejection and weariness.

"Major, look at that group!" one of the men shouted. "They're swimming the wrong way! They're going out to sea!"

Terry looked at the group of horses the man had indicated and saw that at least a dozen of them had become disoriented by the breakers and were swimming away. He knew it wouldn't take long for them to tire and drown.

"Bugler! Sound 'to the post'!" Major Tobias called.

The bugler ran down to the edge of the water and played the bugle call that Terry recognized as the one that called horses to the starting gate in a horse race. It was also, he was told, the call the military used to assemble mounted troops into their proper formations. Well trained to respond to all bugle calls, the horses wheeled around, as if in formation, and began swimming to shore. Terry laughed appreciatively and, with the other men, applauded Major Tobias for his quick, life-saving thinking.

Whipping out his notebook, Terry jotted down a few pertinent sentences and phrases. These would jog his memory when he sat down and wrote his next article, which would be at the end of the day—whenever that might finally come. The young reporter mentally shook his head. He was exhausted—and all he did was observe; he wondered how these fighting men bore up . . . and he decided that that would be the theme of his next story.

Though the wedding of Connie Bateman and Bob Canfield had been decided very hurriedly, Professor William T. Bateman enjoyed a position of sufficient prominence in St. Louis to get things done quickly. Connie was an Episcopalian, Bob was not, yet Connie's father had arranged for them to be married according to the rites of the Episcopal Church, even managing to convince the local bishop to suspend the prerequisite counseling. He had also managed to get the publishing of the banns of marriage suspended, and, to top it all off, the bishop of the diocese of Missouri would be personally performing the ceremony. The wedding would take place in the Bateman parlor, which, when its usual furniture was removed and rows of folding chairs were put in, would make an adequate temporary chapel.

Terry Perkins and David Gelbman had already

embarked on their world travels, but Bob had prevailed upon J. P. Winthrop to delay his return to New York long enough to act as his best man. The two young men were waiting in the Bateman library for their cue, and the groom opened the door a crack to peer at the waiting guests, seated and talking quietly among themselves. The room positively reeked from the sweet scent of flowers and greenery, and if Bob had been told that every greenhouse in St. Louis was emptied for the occasion, he would have believed it.

"I didn't think there'd be so many people," he said softly. "I thought this was going to be a small, quiet wedding. Where the hell did they all come from?"

"You and Connie have many friends in St. Louis," J.P. said.

"Yeah, but there are a hundred and fifty to two hundred people out there. I may know ten of them."

"Well, then, *Connie* has a great many friends in St. Louis," J.P. quipped. "And, don't forget, the professor is a prominent man."

"I don't know. . . ." Bob groaned. "All these people . . . and a bishop, for crying out loud. We can't get married by a justice of the peace or a simple clergyman. Oh, no. We have to get married by a bishop, no less. I thought you had to be married in a cathedral or a church to have an Episcopal wedding." He moved away from the door, and J.P. walked over to eye those gathered.

"The rubrics of the Book of Common Prayer say that the marriage ceremony may be performed in the body of the church or in some proper house," J.P. said. "Being not only an Episcopalian but a vestryman as well, I know about such things, and— Oh, oh, there's the signal. It's time for us to get out there." He turned to his friend. "What's the matter, Bob? You look a little nervous." He chuckled. "Come on, lad, buck up."

"Buck up? That sounds like something Teddy Roosevelt would say. Next you'll be telling me that getting married like this is my patriotic duty."

J.P. laughed. "Are you coming, or am I going to

have to drag you? That would be quite a picture, don't you think?"

"Hold your horses, I'm coming," Bob grumbled.

Bob and J.P. walked from the library to the front of the parlor, where Bob took his place by the bishop. Then he turned to wait for Connie to proceed down the aisle. His eyes roamed the faces of those assembled; everyone was smiling at him. In the back of the room stood Loomis and Pearl, ostensibly present as servants to tend to the guests, though in Bob's eyes fully as much guests as anyone here. Loomis smiled and nodded at him, and Pearl, after cautiously looking around, gave him a little wave.

The pianist began playing the *Wedding March*, and Bob felt his heart start to pound. Connie appeared at the rear of the parlor, framed by the double doorway that led into the dining room, wearing a dazzling white bridal gown and carrying a bouquet of yellow roses. Bob took a short, quick breath, thinking he had never seen anyone more beautiful. It took but moments for Connie to walk up the aisle on her father's arm, then take her position to her groom's left as the two of them faced the bishop.

"Dearly beloved," the bishop began, "we are gathered together here in the sight of God and in the face of this company to join together this man and this woman in holy matrimony."

The bishop continued reading the marriage rites for a few minutes longer, finally coming to the part where he asked Bob if he would love, comfort, honor, and keep Connie in sickness and in health, forsaking all others.

"I will," Bob answered.

The bishop then turned to Connie. "Wilt thou have this man to thy wedded husband, to live together after God's ordinance in the holy estate of matrimony? Wilt thou obey him, and serve him, love, honor, and keep him in sickness and in health, and, forsaking all others, keep thee only unto him so long as ye both shall live?"

"I will . . ." Connie answered, but even as the bishop was asking, "Who giveth this woman," Connie unexpectedly amplified her answer. "I will serve him, love, honor, and keep him in sickness and in health, and, forsaking all others, keep only unto him so long as we both shall live."

For a moment Bob didn't know why she had repeated the words, and it was also clear that the bishop hadn't understood either. Then Bob realized that she had purposely omitted the word *obey*. He looked at her and saw the sly smile on her face, then was unable to hold back the laugh that bubbled forth. The bishop, Professor Bateman, and J.P., still not understanding what had just happened, looked at them in surprise. Recovering quickly, the bishop went on with the service as Connie squeezed Bob's hand.

As Bob thought about it, he realized that if Connie hadn't made that slight alteration of the ceremony, he would have been disappointed. He was still smiling about it when, a few moments later, he heard the bishop pronounce them man and wife. The couple joyfully kissed; then, to the polite applause of their guests, they strolled back down the aisle, arm in arm, into the living room, where buffet tables groaning with food, all prepared by Pearl, had been set up.

After mingling with their guests for several hours, the couple left the reception, and Loomis, using the professor's car, drove the newlyweds down to the river. There they boarded the *Delta Mist*, a passenger-carrying riverboat, and managed to get settled in just in time for the boat's six-fifteen departure.

The sun was already very low on the western horizon when the riverboat pulled away from its mooring at Laclede Landing and turned south. With the five-mile-per-hour current pushing it along, the boat slipped downriver at a fairly brisk clip, and the city of St. Louis fell rapidly behind. A long wake rolled out from the low, rounded bow, while the river frothed and boiled from the churning, splashing paddle at the stern.

The *Delta Mist* was one of the more elegant packet boats still in service on the river, for boats like it were rapidly becoming a rare breed. Six trains a day ran from St. Louis to New Orleans, and the fastest one made the run in less than twenty-four hours. By contrast, only three passenger boats per week left St. Louis for points south, and it took them five days to reach New Orleans and eight to return. First-class passage on a riverboat was also much more expensive. But neither time nor cost was a factor for Bob. He chose the boat because the three nights and two days that they would be on the river would give him and Connie some time alone.

"Oh, Bob, I think it was a wonderful idea to take this instead of the train," Connie said as she put her small suitcase down on the bed. "I had no idea how luxurious such travel could be. Would you look at this stateroom? Why, it even has its own bathroom! This is as elegant as the finest hotel in St. Louis."

"And many times more expensive," Bob said with a grin. "But then it should be. I'll have you know, Mrs. Canfield, that you are staying in the Royal Suite."

"Mrs. Canfield," Connie murmured, her eyes shining brightly. "Doesn't that sound wonderful?"

"Perhaps I should say the *disobedient* Mrs. Canfield," Bob quipped.

Connie laughed. "You aren't angry?"

"Did I look angry?"

"No. But the bishop looked surprised."

"Surprised? I think shocked would more appropriately describe it," Bob corrected.

"If he had realized what I was doing, he may have even stopped the wedding. He's really quite strict."

Suddenly musical tones were heard coming from the corridor.

"What are those chimes?" Connie asked.

"I don't know," Bob said. Stepping to the door, he opened it and looked outside. A black steward, resplendent in a gold-braided red jacket and white trousers, was walking down the rose-colored carpeted corridor carrying what appeared to be a small xylophone. As he walked he struck the notes A, G, C, and E.

"Steward? What is that you're announcing?" Bob asked.

"Dinner is now being served in the dining salon, sir," the middle-aged man replied.

"Oh, I see. Thank you." Bob closed the door and looked at Connie. "Do you want to eat?" Bob asked. "Or . . . ?" He let the word hang.

"Or?"

"Or, uh . . ." Bob made a gesture toward the bed.

"Oh," Connie said; then, when she realized what he had meant, she said again, louder this time, "Oh!" She looked at the bed and then back at Bob. "Let's eat!" she said quickly. "I mean, don't you think we should?"

Bob chuckled. "Connie, don't tell me that the woman who was brazen enough to change the wording of a two-thousand-year-old wedding ceremony has a case of postwedding nerves?"

"I am a little nervous," Connie admitted. "Aren't you?"

"Me, nervous? No," Bob said.

"Not even the tiniest bit?"

"Well, maybe a little," Bob confessed. "Come on, you're right. We should eat." He smiled broadly. "If for no other reason than to make sure we can keep our strength up during the night ahead of us."

"Bob!" Connie gasped. "Don't let anyone hear you say such a thing." Her admonishment, however, was tempered by laughter.

Grabbing her shawl, Connie draped it over her arm and stepped out of their stateroom. Bob took her other arm and led her to the dining salon, where they stood but a moment before the mâitre d' escorted them to their table.

The floor in the dining salon was covered with a light-blue, flower-bedecked carpet that, a small note on the menu pointed out, was all of one piece and woven in Belgium especially for the *Delta Mist*. The walls and ceilings of the salon were decorated with intricate white-and-gold molding and hung with ornate crystal chandeliers. The silver service was beautifully engraved, the linen monogrammed, and every piece of china decorated with a picture of the riverboat.

A wine steward brought the couple of bottle of wine, and after Bob gave it a ritual taste and nodded his approval, the steward poured two glasses, then left the bottle in a silver bucket of ice. The newlyweds toasted each other and had taken just a few sips of the wine when the first course of their meal—terrapin soup—was served. The soup was followed in regular intervals by their entreé of duck with applesauce, boiled potatoes, and asparagus, and this was topped off by a dessert of Neapolitan ice cream. Bob and Connie talked of inconsequential things during the lengthy meal, carefully avoiding anything that might increase the nervousness that both of them were feeling.

"Would you like to take a turn about the deck before we go back to the stateroom?" Bob asked when they had finished.

"Yes, I would," Connie said. She reached across the table and put her hand on his. "I think of all the walks we used to take in Forrest Park and of the way I practically threw myself at you. And now I'm being such a nervous Nellie. You must think me deranged."

Bob smiled at her. "No, I don't. I'm told that a little nervousness on your wedding night is perfectly natural. But millions of others have made it through their first night, and I suspect we will, too."

They left the dining room and strolled out onto the deck. Night had fallen, and as they looked over toward the Missouri side, they could see the riverbank sliding by in the dark, great gray masses of trees and hills. The river itself was pitch-black, though an occasional ripple of water flared white in the moonlight. There were no other passengers on deck, but somewhere out near the railing a deckhand took a puff on his cigarette, and a spark from the glowing tip was whipped away by the breeze. They walked as far forward on the Texas Deck as they could go, finding a bench that overlooked the bow. They sat there and looked ahead into the night, at the river as it unfolded before them. They could hear the muted whisper of the river and feel the throbbing of the engines somewhere in the bowels of the boat.

"Bow watch, standing by to sound, Cap'n," a voice suddenly called in the velvet blanket of darkness.

Following the direction of the voice, Bob nudged Connie and pointed at a man stepping up to the railing at the very end of the bow, carrying a weighted line.

"On the bow!" came a shout—presumed to be the captain—from the bridge. The voice was augmented by a megaphone so that Bob and Connie could hear it quite clearly.

"By the bow!" the answer came from below.

"Sound the bow!" the captain ordered through the megaphone.

The deckhand dropped the weighted line overboard, then turned and answered, "By the mark . . . ten!"

Bob stood up and called down to the deckhand. "I thought the river was clear. Why are you sounding?"

"There was a big storm here last week, sir," the deckhand called back. "The sandbars have shifted." He turned his attention back to the line. "By the mark . . . seven!" he shouted, having sounded a second time.

"How much will we draw?" Bob asked.

"A little over five feet," the crewman answered. "Any less than six and it could be dangerous. He tossed the line in again. "By the mark . . . six!" he called up to the captain.

"Oh, Bob," Connie said, putting her hand on Bob's arm. "Did you hear what he said?"

"By the mark . . . five and a half!"

"Bob, it's under six!"

From the stern of the boat, the slapping, splashing sound of the paddlewheel suddenly stopped, but the boat continued to drift forward, its momentum and the current enough to carry it on.

"By the mark . . . five and a quarter!"

"Let's hope it gets no less," Bob said.

"By the mark . . . twain!" the deckhand suddenly called. "Mark twain, Cap'n! We're clear of the bar!"

The paddlewheel started splashing again soon after

that, and the boat resumed its normal speed. The deckhand drew in his line and weight, waved up to Bob and Connie, and wished them good night.

"Well," Bob said, smiling at Connie. "How was that for a little excitement?"

Connie studied his face wordlessly for a long moment. Then, gripping his arm with both hands, she asked quietly, "Can we go to our room now?"

"Sure," Bob replied. He kissed her then, first on the lips, then on the eyelids. He could feel her trembling.

"You're shaking."

"I'm sorry," she said.

"Don't be."

"I have an idea," Connie said. "Would you mind if I took a hot bath? I've always found a hot bath relaxing." Connie smiled, and her teeth shone softly in the moonlight.

"Sure, if you'd like," he said, putting his arm around her shoulder.

They slowly walked back to their stateroom and stepped inside. The wall lamps had been turned down very low, giving the room a darkly mysterious air, and neither Bob nor Connie adjusted them. She went directly into the bathroom to take her bath, while he walked across the room. He removed his jacket and draped it over a chair, then lowered his braces and took off his starched shirt, leaving only his undershirt. He turned and stepped to the open window. Music was wafting softly from somewhere, and he decided it was coming from the grand salon. As he stood listening to the music and watching the moonlight play over the river, he thought of Connie and of the future he hoped to give her. She was a city girl, and he realized that she might have some difficulty adjusting to life on a farm outside a small town. A farm, he thought and smirked. It would only be a farm if he could get it drained and planted and *harvested*. So far he hadn't been able to do that.

Bob wasn't sure how long he had been standing at the window when the door to the bathroom opened and then closed behind him.

"Bob?"

He turned toward the sound of Connie's voice, and at the sight of her standing there he took a deep, gasping breath. *My God!* Was she nude? At first he couldn't be certain because she was standing beyond the light of the low-burning wall lamps. Then she stepped farther into the room, and he saw that it was true. Her body was highlighted and made all the more mysterious and intriguing by the subtle shadows and lighting.

Bob moved to her and rested his hands lightly on her bare shoulders. Her skin was soft and smelled of lilac soap. He kissed her again as he had kissed her on the deck, as he had kissed her many times over the last few years—but this time, as in no other, the body that was pressed against his was naked.

He ran his hands over her back and felt her nipples rise against him. She drew in a sharp breath—not of protest, but of pleasure. Gently, he led her to the bed and pulled down the coverlet, then took off his remaining clothes and crawled in beside her.

"Bob, I love you," Connie said. And when she reached for him and pulled him toward her, he knew that her nervousness was gone, replaced by a hunger as intense as his own. Connie's arms and legs were smooth and soft under his hard, muscled limbs, and he delighted in getting to know her beautiful body as well as he had come to know her wonderful mind. Then came the moment of truth, and Bob abandoned all thought save his quest for the ultimate sensation, the lightning strike of pleasure that drove him on.

Later, as they lay naked side by side, the bed musky with their lovemaking, Bob's arm lay across Connie's stomach, his hand resting possessively just above, but not quite touching, her pubic mound. Over their quiet breathing came the strains of the band from the grand salon, playing "A Londonderry Aire."

Connie shifted slightly, pressing herself more tightly against him, then put her hand on his torso, mirroring where his was on her. After a moment he realized that his interest was being rekindled, and Connie apparently realized it as well, for she chuckled softly.

"What are you laughing at, Mrs. Canfield?" Bob asked, his voice husky.

"I am laughing at the power I have over certain parts of your anatomy," Connie replied. "Do you see how I can make things happen?"

"All right," Bob said. "You've got things started; now what are you going to do about it?"

Connie turned on her side and looked into Bob's face with eyes that, even in this dim light, found some way to glow. "Why, Mr. Canfield, I'm going to do anything you want me to do."

CHAPTER FIFTEEN

David Gelbman's first step in Vienna was nearly his last.

"Look out, *mein Herr!*"

At the shouted warning David jumped out of the way of the heavy, steel-wheeled baggage cart that was careening down the long ramp between the trains after getting away from the baggage handler who had been pulling it. The cart rattled across the brick pavement, spilling suitcases and scattering the detraining passengers before it crashed into the side of the train David had just left. There it dumped the remainder of its luggage both onto the platform and down on the track.

The baggage handler, a white-haired old man, hurried along after the cart, trying to pick up the pieces of luggage that had fallen off. But the task was too much for him, and as he picked up a new piece he'd drop one of those already retrieved. The chief handler, his face red with anger and embarrassment, came running from the opposite end of the train, screaming at the hapless employee. One of the passengers, seeing his luggage among the pieces scattered on the track, shouted his own invectives, adding verbal abuse to the old man's problems.

Feeling sorry for the man, David began picking up a few of the bags himself. "It would be more productive to pick up suitcases than to yell at him, don't you think?" he told the chief handler.

"Who are you to interfere?"

"Just a concerned citizen."

"A citizen? But you are not even Austrian."

"No, I am American. But this is the country of my father."

"And what is your name?"

"Gelbman. David Gelbman."

"*Herr* Gelbman, your father should have instructed you in proper manners," the chief handler said coldly.

"*Manners?*" David exploded. "Are you trying to tell me that *I* need instruction in manners? Your behavior is in question here, not mine."

"I am the chief handler; you are but a passenger, *Herr* Gelbman. This does not concern you."

David looked at his fellow passenger for support, but saw contempt instead. Turning to the old man, David read a pleading look in his eyes that suggested David was making matters worse by being his champion.

The young man looked back at the chief handler. "I want your assurance that you will—" David began, but the chief handler interrupted him.

"I could call the police, sir."

David sighed. "No, that won't be necessary." He glanced at the old man again, wanting to say something encouraging, but by now the old man had crawled under the train after a few more bags. Shaking his head slowly, David started walking toward the depot.

"Who does he think he is, this American?" David heard the passenger ask.

"Did you hear his name? He is the son of a Jew," the chief handler replied. "A Jew who went to America and became rich, no doubt. Now the Jew's son comes back to tell us how to run our country."

David's cheeks flamed in anger, and he almost turned back. Then he realized that he was not in St. Louis, he was in Vienna. He didn't know what rights he had here . . . if any. The best course would be to say nothing.

Other than that incident, David was amazed by the similarities between the Westbahnhof in Vienna and Union Station in St. Louis. Like Union Station, the Westbahnhof had several tracks under a great, covered shed, and—also like Union Station—the train shed smelled of coal smoke, steam, and teeming humanity. Even the aroma of bratwurst and kraut wafting from the many restaurants was like the smells back in St. Louis, where a high proportion of Germans and Austrians had made their impact. This shed, like its American counterpart, was a symphony of sound: steel rolling on steel, clanging bells, chugging pistons, rattling cars, shouted orders, and the cacophony of hundreds of individual conversations.

When David reached the main lobby a thin, sallow-faced young man with an unruly shock of dark brown hair and piercing blue eyes approached him. "Would you like me to collect your bags, sir?"

"Yes, thank you," David replied. He pulled a piece of paper from his pocket. "I'll be going to twenty-one thirty-seven Lerchenfelderstrasse," he said, showing the address to the young man. "Is it far?"

"Yes, far enough that you shall require a taxi," the youth answered. "After I collect your luggage, I will get one for you. You are English?"

"No, American." David gave the youth his claim ticket, and the young man hurried back to the baggage room. Several minutes later he returned, carrying David's two leather suitcases.

"So, you have come to see the sights of Vienna?" the boy said, resuming the conversation. "In that case, you must not miss the wonderful art at the Court Museum."

"Do you like art?"

"Yes," the youth replied. "I am an artist," he added proudly. "This job is merely to supplement my income while I study at the academy."

"Then, upon your recommendation, I shan't miss the Court Museum."

"Or any of the other buildings on Ring Boulevard," the youth added. "Especially don't miss the Court Opera. They are performing Wagner this season."

"I intend to see them all," David promised. "I'll be staying in your native city for a while."

The youth smiled and brushed the shock of hair away from his eyes. "Oh, Vienna isn't my native city. I came here from Linz, though I was born in Branau, a little village on the river that separates Austria from Bavaria. Ah, there is a horse-taxi for you. The driver wearing the bowler hat is called a *faiker*. You can always tell the taxi drivers by the bowler hats, for they never take them off, even when they are eating their meals."

"Thank you," David said. He tipped the young man, and then, because it seemed to him that the youth had gone out of his way to be pleasant—especially compared to the chief handler back in the train shed— David doubled what his tip would have been.

The young man laughed and handed a few of the coins back. "You don't understand our money, do you? This is too much."

"Oh, I understand it. I meant it to be that much. You've been of more service than just carrying my bags. You've provided me with some good information as well."

"Thank you," the young man said. He held up his finger. "One moment. I will instruct the taxi driver how to take you. That way you will not be cheated."

"That's most kind of you."

The young man waved one of the taxis over, and when it drew to a stop in front of them, he loaded the bags. Then he began talking to the driver. As David watched, a strange transformation came over the youth. Whereas with David he had been polite almost to the point of servility, with the driver he was authoritative, almost domineering. Gesturing with his right hand, his finger sometimes pointed in a specific direction, other times it pointed at the driver, and still other times it jabbed into the air. His eyes already piercing, seemed hypnotic, and though the driver was much older and in a much more important position than that of a mere youth who made his money by carrying bags, he sat quietly, listening and nodding as if he were a servant receiving orders.

"There," the youth said, smiling triumphantly at David and again brushing the hair from his eyes, "the *faiker* has been given his instructions. You have my guarantee: You will not be cheated."

"Thank you," David said, climbing into the cab. As the driver pulled the carriage out into the traffic, David turned to look back at the young man, but he was already heading toward another arriving tourist.

David had eaten on the train shortly before arriving in Vienna, but when he reached the Blumberg house, he found that his cousin Sarah had prepared an enormous dinner in his honor. There was nothing to do except smile bravely, express his gratitude, and sit down to the unending spread of soup, dumplings, potatoes, cabbage, sauerbraten, bread, preserves, and pudding.

"I have heard much of the American cousin who is coming to save us all," the young woman beside him said. Though she called David *cousin*, he wasn't really, for Anna Rosenstein was Sarah's niece by marriage. She was tall and dark, full-bosomed and small-waisted, and her long, slender legs managed to express their sensuality even through the long skirt she wore. A strikingly beautiful young woman of twenty-one, she had a delicate nose, fine lips, and amber eyes. Anna—the daughter of Sarah's husband's sister—had been a member of the Blumberg household since her own parents died when she was four. As Sarah also had four children and her husband's two aged parents living with her, Anna was a welcome addition because she was a great help around the house.

"I will, of course, do what I can," David responded sincerely.

"Then tell me, my American cousin, what miracle will you be able to perform that will rescue Blumberg's Store from bankruptcy and ruin?"

It wasn't until that moment that David noticed the sarcasm in Anna's voice. The sharpness of it surprised him, and he looked up from his plate with a confused expression on his face. "I'll help in any way I can. I have no intention of performing miracles."

"Anna!" Sarah admonished. "David is our guest!"

"I withdraw my words, Cousin David, if you find them offensive," Anna said. She sipped her wine, studying him over the rim of the glass.

"I am not offended," David replied. "Just confused. Why are you being so disagreeable?"

Anna put the glass down and smiled, though the smile itself was mocking. "Oh, am I being disagreeable? I don't intend to be."

"Tell me, Cousin David," Miriam, the oldest of Sarah's four children—a lovely, dark-haired, dark-eyed fourteen-year-old—interjected, "in America, are the streets paved with gold?"

"No, of course not," David answered with a little laugh. "Why would you think that?"

"One does hear such things, you know," Miriam replied solemnly. "Is that not true, Anna?"

"Yes," Anna agreed. "And many of our people, believing this, have gone to America. When they go, they never come back. You are unusual in that you *have* come back."

"Not really. That is, I haven't come back. I was born in America. But if the prejudice I heard expressed at the depot this afternoon is any indication of Austrian intolerance, I can see why Jews who have left here wouldn't want to come back."

"What happened?" Sarah asked. After David had relayed the story, she shook her head and made a tsking sound. "I agree, that would certainly be an unpleasant welcome."

"In America, have you never heard an anti-Semitic word?" Anna asked.

"Well, I won't say there's no prejudice, but I will say that, by and large, we Americans are very tolerant of Jews."

"*You* Americans are tolerant of *Jews?*" Anna said, her eyebrows raising sharply. "You say that as if you are not a Jew."

"Well, of course I'm a Jew. But I consider myself an American first. And it isn't as if I am a practicing Jew. I mean, I do attend *shul* occasionally, even if I don't follow all the rituals with literal exactness."

"One cannot deny their Jewishness any more than one can deny their sex," Anna said. "You do not need to follow all the rituals of the male to be a male. You are what you are. That you would deny being a Jew—"

"Now, just a minute, I'm not denying anything," David snapped. "I'm just trying to tell you that things are different in America. My father is a very successful man there, a much-respected man. I attended a very fine university, and I have made many friends who accept me for *who* I am, not for *what* I am."

"They do not know what you are," Anna countered, "because *you* do not know what you are."

"That isn't true. We don't hide our heritage . . . indeed, we're proud of it. But we are, for the most part, assimilated into the American culture. It's so with everyone—Poles, Italians, Irish, Germans—and that's why America has been called the melting pot."

"All the more reason why our people should not go there," Anna said. "Jews have wandered the world and been oppressed for seventeen centuries, but we have always managed to hang on to our identity. Now there is a place that, you say, does not oppress the Jews. But I say the oppression in America is the most insidious kind. It exacts a terrible place for allowing your father to be a successful man and you to attend a fine university and have many friends. It exacts the price of genocide. They would kill the entire Jewish people by assimilating them."

"And is it better in Austria?" David asked. "Vienna is known as the city of artists and intellectuals—people like Mahler, Kraus, Altenberg, Schnitzler, Hofmannsthal, Wittgenstein, Schoenberg, and perhaps the most famous of all, Sigmund Freud. All of these men are Jewish, and yet the world does not think of them as Jews—the world thinks of them as Austrian."

"That is why we must have our own homeland," Anna said. "So that our people will be *our* people: *Jews.*"

David put his fork down and looked at her with a quizzical smile on his face. "Why, you're a Zionist, aren't you? I didn't realize that. I've read about such people, but until now I'd never met one."

"And so, when you return to your assimilated American friends—the ones who don't follow all the rituals with literal exactness, and who attend *shul* occasionally— you will tell them you have met a Zionist. How will you describe me? Have I horns and a tail?"

"No, Anna. I will describe the first Zionist I ever met as a beautiful young woman who is also very intelligent and high-spirited."

David's unexpected compliment clearly disarmed Anna, and she flushed in embarrassment and stared at her plate for a long moment, unable to respond. Finally, Sarah spoke for her.

"Anna, aren't you going to mention the opera to Cousin David?"

"Oh, yes," Anna said.

The tone of her voice was completely changed now . . . not challenging, but almost acquiescent. David smiled. It was clear that Anna was a person who drew her strength from confrontation and intensity. When someone said something nice to her she was put on the defensive. "Cousin David, I have tickets to the opera tonight, if you would care to attend."

"Yes, thank you," David said. "I'd like that very much."

"I would like to go to the opera too," Simon said. Simon was nine, the second oldest. After him came Yuri, who was seven, and Margot, who was three.

"You can't go, Simon," Miriam said.

"Why not?"

"Because such a thing is for a man and woman together," Miriam said. "They will wish to share each other's company and not want a little boy along to bother them."

"So who do you think you are?" Simon asked. "The matchmaker?"

"Simon!" Sarah scolded, but the laughter of everyone else around the table eased the sting of her raised voice.

The opera house was presenting Wagner's "Das Rheingold," part of *Der Ring des Nibelungen*. During an intermission, David and Anna were walking around the sumptuous foyer, looking up at what was known as the Imperial Stairway, when David saw the young man who had helped him at the station. He smiled at him.

"Well, hello again," David said. "I see you don't just speak of the opera, you come as well."

"Yes," the youth said. "Thanks to your generosity. And are you enjoying it?"

"Very much," David said.

"Wagner is the greatest musical artist of all time," the young man said. "His music has power and majesty, fire and blood."

"It's a bit jingoistic though, don't you think?" Anna asked. "As well as anti-Semitic?"

The young man looked at Anna for a long moment. "You are a Jew?"

"Yes."

"If you find Wagner's music offensive, you should not have come." He turned to David. "How do you like the building?"

"The building? You mean, this building?"

"Yes. Have you observed the harmonious proportions of the sculptural and painted decorations? Did you know that these murals were the last work of Schubert's friend Moritz von Schwindt? I must confess that I have nearly as great a love for the buildings of Ring Boulevard as for the art they contain, be it the museum and its paintings or the opera and its music."

"Yes," David agreed, "the building is quite beautiful."

"Though I am sure your Jewish lady friend might find this, too, a bit overpowering," the youth challenged. Inside the auditorium they could hear the orchestra beginning to tune up for the next part of the performance.

"I am also Jewish," David said, his tone sharper.

"But you are an American, and not a part of the European Jewish problem."

"We must go," Anna told David. "They are getting ready to begin."

"I, too, must leave if I am to be seated in time. I have the most inexpensive seats in the house, as I am sure you can understand. The acoustics are quite good, but they are some distance away." Nodding curtly, the youth turned on his heel and left.

"Who was that irritating young man?" Anna asked as they returned to their own seats.

"As a matter of fact I never learned his name," David replied. "He carried my bags at the station. I had no idea he was so anti-Semitic. Actually, he was most helpful to me today."

"There is something about him that is somehow frightening. Did you see his eyes when I called Wagner jingoistic? I felt as if I were looking into an abyss." She shivered. "I could almost feel him stepping on my grave."

David laughed. "Really, Anna, you are giving him far too much thought," he said. "He's just one more starving young artist. He'll probably try his hand at it for a while, grow tired of starving, then find some more conventional means of employment. You'll never see or hear from him again, so don't let him bother you."

"Would you like another biscuit?" Connie Canfield asked, holding out a plate piled with them.

"Oh, no, I don't think so," Bob Canfield answered, putting down his fork. He leaned back in his chair and patted his stomach. "At the rate you're feeding me now, I'll swell up before you do."

"Bob!" Connie gasped. "How can you say such a thing?"

"Well, isn't that what we want you to do?" Bob quipped. "I mean, I'm trying my damnedest."

"Well, if it's that odious a task to you, Mr. Canfield, just don't bother coming to my side of the bed tonight."

"Hold on, now. I didn't say it was an odious task. I just said I was trying hard, that's all."

Getting up from the kitchen table, Bob walked over to the stove and picked up the coffeepot, pouring himself another cup. They were eating in the kitchen because this house, not too far from the Canfield family home, had no dining room. Newly married, they wanted a place of their own and so had set up housekeeping in one of the now-empty dwellings that—before the forests were all timbered out—had belonged to the lumber mills' section foremen. It was a temporary arrangement until a much nicer house was completed up on the ridge. Construction had already started on their real home, and for several days now green wagons bearing the legend MARTIN BROS. CONSTRUCTION COMPANY, SIKESTON, MO. in yellow lettering on the side had rolled steadily back and forth along the road, bringing building materials out to the site.

"Mr. Martin said the windows for our new house were in," Connie said. "They're going to install them today. I thought I'd go over and take a look at them."

"Would you like me to drive you over?"

"No, Billy said he'd come pick me up."

Bob chuckled. "I figured he would. Any excuse for him to drive. I've never known anyone who liked motorcars as much as he does." Bob pulled out his watch and glanced at it. "Oh, I guess I'd better get going," he said. "I have a crew working in the sycamore section today, and I want to get over there in time to make sure they know exactly what I want."

"Don't get bitten by a water moccasin," Connie warned. "George told me there are a lot of them out there."

"That's just George," Bob said, smiling. "He's so scared of snakes that he sees one behind every mud clod."

Bob drained the last of his coffee, kissed Connie on the cheek, then walked out front to crank up his Model T Ford. Not nearly as handsome or as comfortable as the Great Arrow, the seven-foot-tall, flat-nosed, ugly box on wheels had already made itself as indispensable to Bob as a wagon and a good team of mules. The Model T had just been introduced this year, and it was a phenomenal success, meant as it was to dispel the idea that automobiling was the exclusive right of the rich and to provide the opportunity of motoring to the common man. It also turned out to be ideal for farmers. It not only handled the muddy, rocky roads with ease, it could also pump water, plow fields, run saw blades, and even generate electricity.

With the spark and gas levers set to "ten till three," Bob twisted the crank a couple of times; then, when the engine started wheezing and popping, he ran around, climbed in, and started out across field and dale, for the section where a new drainage ditch was being dug. But as he approached his destination, he saw his men standing around idle. However, another group of men were busy—stringing a barbed-wire fence right across the middle of the field.

With the low-speed pedal pushed to the floor, Bob gave the auto all the gas it would take, and he bounced and lurched crazily across the top of the furrows until he came to a stop at the edge of the fence. He shut down the car, and as it died with a final gasping wheeze, he climbed out and started toward his men. L. E. Parker, the foreman of his group of workers, met him halfway.

"Mr. Canfield, I was just about to send for you," he said. "But one of the boys seen the dust boilin' up, so we figured it might be you comin' out to see how we was gettin' along. Which, as you can see," he added, pointing to the fence, "ain't none too good. How come they put a fence right across the middle of your field like that? Why don't you get the law out here on 'em?"

Bob let out a sigh. "Technically, it isn't across the middle of my field."

"What? Why, I thought this whole field was your'n. I mean, we put it all in oats last year, didn't we?"

"We did put it in oats last year, but half of the field belongs to Mr. Dumey," Bob explained. "I've been renting it from him. I never got around to buying it." He started toward the fence. "Guess I'd better find out what's going on."

The men who had been digging the ditches for Bob, a nearly fifty-fifty mixture of black and white, stood leaning on their shovels, watching, unsure of what to expect and unsure of what was expected of them.

Smiling at the workers, Bob nodded and spoke to a couple. "Troy, how's that big boy of yours?"

"He doin' fine, Mr. Bob. He doin' just fine," replied a big, powerful black man whose muscled arms and shoulders gleamed in the early morning sun.

"Good, good. Abner, how's your pa?"

A thin and pale white man with stringy, wheat-straw hair, Abner looked as if an hour of hard work would kill him. But he was the wiry kind who could match Troy shovel for shovel for an entire day, as Bob had seen time and time again. "Pa's a mite better, Mr. Canfield. I thank you for askin'," he answered.

"Well, fellas, let's see what all this is about, shall we?" Bob said, rubbing his hands together. Looking across to the other side of the fence, he recognized the foreman of the group and asked, "Jim, what're you doing putting this fence up? You know I've been renting this land from Mr. Dumey."

"Yes, sir, I know that, Mr. Canfield," the man replied. "But this here land don't belong to Mr. Dumey no more."

"It doesn't? Who does it belong to?"

"McMullen," Jim said, "Boyd McMullen."

Bob felt his stomach clench. "I see. And what is he going to do with it?"

"Well, sir, I don't know the answer to that. All I know is, he hired me and my men to get this fence up to stop you from crossin' over with your ditch. Then he wants us to build a dike right here where this fence is."

"A dike? You mean a dam?" Bob asked.

"Yes, sir, you might call it that. Though I reckon it's more like a levee. The way I understand it is he wants to keep all your water over on your own land. He doesn't want a ditch runnin' through here, collectin' all your water."

"Collecting it? It won't collect it, Jim," Bob said. "It'll let it flow right straight on through to the Little River."

"No, sir, not through here it won't," Jim said. "Not through the next field I'm gonna be workin' in, neither."

"Where are you going next? Can you tell me that?"

"McMullen bought the Grant land, too," Jim said. "We'll be goin' over there soon as we're finished here."

"The Grant land? That'll cut me off from Wolfhole Creek. Damnit, Jim, you're hemming me in."

"Sorry about that, Mr. Canfield," Jim said. "But he's got the title to the land and he wants the work done. If he don't hire me, he'll hire someone else, and I figure I gotta pay my men."

"I know, I know," Bob muttered. He stroked his chin and looked around at his own men. "I don't hold it against you, Jim," he said.

"I'm obliged for that," Jim answered.

"And I'm obliged to you for sharing the information. Well, I'll see you around." Bob started back toward the auto. "L.E.," he called.

"I heard what he said," the foreman remarked, joining his boss as Bob spread open a map on the hood of his car. "If you ask me, I'd like to break Boyd McMullen's neck."

"Much as I agree with you, that wouldn't do us any good," Bob said. He studied the map. "Look, they've got us cut off from Little River up here, and Wolfhole down here. If they cut us off from St. John's too, I don't know where we'll go with our water."

"Who owns this land right here?" L.E. asked, pointing to the map.

"Petersen," Bob replied. "And since his daughter is going to marry Boyd McMullen, that eliminates it."

L.E. laughed and pointed to another spot on the map. "At lease you don't have to worry none about that piece right there," he said. "I own it, and you can rent it, buy it, or anything you want."

"Thanks, L.E. Hmm, look here," Bob said, pointing to a long, crescent-shaped piece of land. "If I could get my hands on this piece, I'd have access to all three outlets: Little River, Wolfhole, and St. John's. Mc-Mullen could buy everything else in the bootheel, and I wouldn't give a damn."

"Who owns that land?"

"I'm not really sure, but I think Pop told me once that it belongs to somebody up in St. Louis. I'll be eating supper with Pop tonight, so I'll ask him about it."

Bob lay his fork down on his plate. It was empty again, after being filled a third time. "Mom, if there's anyone in the world who makes better chicken and dumplings than you, I'd sure like to know who it is." Bob looked over at Connie and smiled broadly. "In fact, if I could find such a woman, I think I'd divorce Connie and marry her."

"Bob!" Connie said.

"That's okay, Connie," Billy put in. "If Bob divorces you, I'll take you."

"Now there's a fate worse than death," Bob retorted. "But of course you could avoid all that just by learning to make dumplings like Mom's."

Connie grimaced and looked at her mother-in-law. "I've tried to make them, Mother Canfield, but I've never been able to get them to come out like yours."

"Heavens, child, you should have seen some of *my* efforts in the beginnin'," Margaret Canfield said, grinning. "Jack's mama's dumplin's came out right, time after time, but mine were awful." She laughed. "Once I made four batches, trying to make them come out right. The first batch all stuck together in one big ball, the second batch just fell apart, the third was hard as rocks. Well, as I kept makin' them and they'd turn out bad, I'd hide the bowl in the cupboard. Finally, on the fourth batch, they turned out all right. Not good, mind you, not like Mother Canfield's, but you could at least eat them. I served them for supper, but you know, I forgot all about those other three bowls until a couple of days later when Mother Canfield came over to the house. She was helping me with dishes when she discovered all those bowls of dumplin's and started pullin' them down. I was so mortified that I just broke down and cried."

Everyone laughed at Margaret's story, and Connie leaned over to kiss her on the cheek. "Thanks for telling me that," she said. "And for reminding me that there was a Mother Canfield for you just as there is for me."

Margaret laughed again as she stood up to get dessert, which was a peach cobbler. "Dear, when your children are grown and married, *you* will be the Mother Canfield—and so on, on down the line. I never quite felt that I could please my mother-in-law, you'll no doubt feel that you can't please me, and your daughter-in-law will have the same problem. That's just the way of things."

After dessert Bob and his father went into the parlor. There, Bob spread open the map and pointed out the piece of land he needed to buy in order to ensure access to all the major streams. "What do you know about this land?" Bob asked.

"That's six hundred and forty acres, and it belongs to the Puritex Corporation," Jack Canfield answered.

"Puritex? You mean the feed company? What would they be doing owning land down here?"

Jack explained, "Buying the land was Elmer Nelson's idea. He owns Puritex. He developed a feed for horses that was better than corn and cheaper than oats. Actually, it's a mixture of the two, formed into those little pellets. Pure textured pellets, Elmer called them, and from that came the name Puritex."

"How come you know so much about the company, Pop?"

"Elmer and I almost went into business together."

"I didn't know that."

Jack chuckled. "No reason you should. You were only eight or nine at the time."

"Well, what happened?"

"I met Elmer when he came down here and bought up some land and hired me to timber it out for him. I think he had it in mind to branch out into the lumber business . . . but he finally decided that there was no future in it. He realized that the land couldn't be reforested, and he'd be left holdin' a lot of worthless acreage—like this section of land."

"Yes, only now we know it isn't worthless," Bob said. "McMullen has proved that for us. You were right, Pop. He's doing exactly what you thought he'd do— buying up as much land as he can get his hands on. Only he's also trying to cut us off from the spillways."

Jack shook his head. "It's just like the old days out West, when the big cattle ranchers got control of the water to squeeze out the smaller ranchers. Only this time it's just the opposite: We have water we need to get rid of."

"Maybe, but we aren't exactly what you'd call the smaller ranchers. We're going to beat Boyd, Pop. I could always whip his ass when we were kids, and I can whip him now. And I'm going to start by buying up this land from Puritex."

"Okay. We'll go up to St. Louis and talk to Elmer tomorrow."

"We? Pop, I don't know. Remember what Dr. Lennox said. You aren't supposed to—"

"Goddamnit, Bob, I'm not dead yet," Jack snapped.

Bob looked down at the floor, stung by his father's sharp retort. Jack put his hand on Bob's shoulder. "I'm sorry, son," he said, softening. "I didn't mean to bark at you like that. It's just that . . . well, I feel so useless right now. Time was I could get out in the flatboats and lumber with the best men I had. Now I sit or lay around the house all day long, drinkin' coffee, readin', listenin' to that damned Victrola, and I feel as worthless as tits on a boar hog. I know I can't be out there helpin' you dig the ditches, but I have to have *somethin'* to make me feel worthwhile. Now, I know Elmer Nelson, and I've been knowin' him for many years. If we're goin' to buy that section of land from him, it might help to have me along."

"All right, Pop," Bob said. "I'll get tickets for us first thing tomorrow morning. We'll leave on the afternoon train."

"I can't," Elmer Nelson told them, leaning over the huge table in the middle of the Puritex boardroom. "I wish I could, but I can't." Nelson was short, overweight, and nearly bald—though he attempted to conceal that by parting his hair down by his right ear and combing the strands over. When he had ushered Bob and Jack Canfield into the boardroom and sat down, he opened his jacket, exposing his green suspenders, and unbuttoned the top of his trousers, sighing with relief.

"Has McMullen already made you an offer?" Bob asked.

"McMullen? No. No one's made me an offer. Let's see, he's a banker down there, isn't he?"

"Yes."

"No, as I said, no one's made me an offer for that land. As far as I know, it's as useless now as it was when we took the last stick of timber from it. Though obviously something has changed, or you wouldn't be trying to buy it."

"The land itself is still relatively valueless," Bob explained. He spread his map open on the table in front of Nelson and pointed to the network of drainage ditches and canals—those he had already built, and those he would need to build. He jabbed his finger on the Puritex section. "However, as you can see, your land occupies a key position in the overall scheme of things. If Mc-Mullen gets control of it, I'm bottled up."

"All you need is permission to cross the land, right?" Nelson asked.

"Yes."

"Well, there's no problem with that. I'll grant you permission for, say, one dollar per year."

"I appreciate your offer, Mr. Nelson," Bob said. "But I'm afraid of it. If somehow McMullen were to get hold of the land, then I'd be in the same position I'm in now."

Nelson laughed softly. "You needn't worry about that, my boy,"he said. "McMullen won't be able to buy the land any more than you can. Unless he's willing to buy the entire corporation."

"Buy the entire corporation? What do you mean?" Jack asked. "Elmer, is the corporation for sale?"

"In a manner of speaking, I suppose it is," Nelson said. "Though, for the life of me, I can't think of who would want it." He uttered a short, bitter laugh. "I remember when I went into this business back in 1883. I was looking for something that would weather all the ups and downs of the economy, something that would always be needed. Well, horses always have to eat, I thought. And I was right. Horses *will* always have to eat. What I didn't realize was that there won't always be a need for horses. Last year our business was down to only thirty-seven percent of what it was in 1900. And 1907 is going to be worse. You want to know why you can't buy that land from me? Because this entire corporation is about to go into receivership. The land, for what it's worth, is considered an asset, and we've already reached the point where I've been cautioned, by court order, not to start stripping the company of its assets. That's why I said the land can't be bought, by you or by the McMullens, unless you're willing to buy the entire corporation."

"How much would it take to buy the corporation?" Jack asked.

Bob looked at his father, surprised by his question. "Pop, what are you doing?" he asked.

"Look," Jack replied, "we have to have that land, right?"

"Yes. But we don't need a company that makes horse food."

"If it's the only way we can get the land, then we need the company," Jack said. He looked back at Nelson. "How much?" he asked again.

"Jack, I'll be honest with you," Nelson said. "The biggest part of buying the company now would be in satisfying the creditors. I'd like ten thousand dollars above that. I believe that with ten thousand dollars, I could go to some place like Florida and live modestly for the rest of my life."

"What do you think, Bob?" Jack asked.

"I don't know," Bob said. "I'm using every cent I can raise now to drain the land, because each acre I drain increases the overall loan value of the property. But, like you say, if we can't get control of this piece of land, we're fighting a losing battle anyway."

"It's your decision to make, son," Jack said. "The future belongs to you and Connie and Billy, not to me. But I'll back you to the last cent I have."

"Would it be difficult for you to get together a list of your debts?" Bob asked Nelson.

Nelson shook his head. "Unfortunately, that's not hard at all," he replied. "That list has been my constant companion for the last two or three years. I'll bring it right in to you."

When Nelson stepped out of the boardroom, Bob got up from the table and walked over to the window, then opened it and looked down. The boardroom was on the seventh floor of the big redbrick building. Just below the line of windows delineating this floor he could see the top of the large black band with its white-painted legend, THE PURITEX FEED CORPORATION, ST. LOUIS, MO., that ran the length of the building. He could also smell the cooking process that turned corn and oats into "Puritex Pellets."

Bob noticed that as the factory was operating at only one-third its normal capacity, only one of its three chimneys was smoking. In the factory yard below he saw two wagons and teams and an equal number of motor trucks backed up to a loading platform that could accommodate three times that many vehicles. Railroad tracks crisscrossed the yard, though for the moment no trains were on any of them. Nearly a dozen boxcars sat empty, and on one flatcar a large piece of machinery of some sort—whether it had been removed or remained uninstalled Bob couldn't tell—sat rusting in the sun.

The seventh-floor vantage point gave Bob a good view of St. Louis, and in contrast to the almost moribund condition of the Puritex Company the rest of the city was alive with activity. Automobiles and wagons clogged the streets, trains chugged on the tracks, and factories belched forth smoke, spreading a large brown cloud to cover the entire region. This noxious haze that irritated the eyes and burned the noses and throats of all the citizens of St. Louis was, according to an article in that morning's *Chronicle*, ". . . the healthy sign of progress. Weep not from the smoke that covers St. Louis," the article added. "Rather, weep for those cities that lack the smoke, for it bespeaks a place going nowhere."

"Here's the list." Elmer Nelson's statement broke into Bob's reverie, and Bob turned from the window as the entrepreneur laid a folder on the conference table.

Bob quickly crossed the room to peruse it, and after a moment he remarked, "The major creditors seem to be your employees."

"Yes. They haven't missed a payroll yet, but, in an attempt to keep the company going, they formed an employee investors' group to loan the company a great deal of money."

"I can understand that," Bob said, nodding. "They have their jobs at stake."

A man appeared in the doorway for Nelson, telling him of some business within the plant. Nelson excused himself, leaving Bob and his father alone again.

"What does it look like to you?" Jack asked.

Bob smiled. "You know, Pop, in one of my classes at Jefferson, the professor talked about a new concept called creative financing. Perhaps if we could put a little of that concept to work here, we might be able to arrange something. But if we do, it's going to mean we have to keep the company going."

"Would that be so bad?"

"I don't know how we could run the company *and* the farm."

"What about this employee investment program?" Jack suggested. "Someone had to come up with that idea, and someone has to be the president of that group. How about letting *him* run the company?"

"Good idea. When Mr. Nelson comes back, I'll have that man sent for," Bob said. "I might as well make the pitch to both of them at the same time."

When Nelson returned some ten minutes later, the Canfields explained their plan, and the entrepreneur immediately sent for Mike Thomas. Mike was a muscular man of five ten who wore a neatly trimmed mustache, and Bob recognized him immediately, for he had been a star football player for St. Louis University. To Bob's surprise, Mike recognized him as well.

"You were a runner for Jefferson University, cross-country and track," Mike said, shaking Bob's hand. "I remember you. You were pretty good."

"Thanks," Bob said. He smiled. "I'm flattered that you know me. Runners never got as much written about them as baseball and football players."

"At least running is something you can continue after school. My football days are long over. So, Bob, are you going to buy Puritex?"

"I hope so," Bob said. "But I'm going to need help from you and Mr. Nelson."

"What sort of help?" Mike asked.

Lacing his fingers together, Bob rested his elbows on the table as he leaned forward. "Mike, your main concern, and the concern of the other employees, is to keep the company operating, is it not?"

"Of course."

"And your concern, Mr. Nelson, is to be able to get out from under the burden of debt and live comfortably, with no more worries. Right?"

"Correct."

"So, gentlemen, here is my proposal. Mr. Nelson, I'll pay you ten thousand dollars . . . on paper. But what I want from you is an immediate reinvestment of that ten thousand dollars back into the company. In return, the company will pay you a monthly stipend, sufficient for your needs, without encroaching on the stock your ten thousand dollars has purchased."

"And the employees?" Mike asked. "What do you want from them?"

"I want the employees to renegotiate the loan."

"For stock?"

"No," Bob said. "I'm afraid that would dilute the stock too much. The only thing I can promise is that I won't liquidate the company."

"Come on, Bob, you wouldn't liquidate the company anyway," Mike said. "There's not enough value in the physical equipment to make up for what you're investing in, in the first place."

"Mike, we aren't playing a poker game here," Bob said. "So please believe me when I say that I'm not bluffing to strengthen my position. Quite simply, the only thing I really want from this company is a piece of land it owns down in the bootheel of this state. I could—and would—sell this entire operation brick by brick and lose money, yet still come out ahead. But for the sake of the employees, I'll keep this company going, if they're willing to renegotiate the loan."

"With Mr. Nelson gone, who are you going to get to run the company?" Mike asked.

Bob smiled. "Why, you, of course. With five percent of the stock and an option to increase your holdings up to twenty percent. Whether the company survives beyond that and whether your five percent ever grows depends on you and the other employees. So if you have any good ideas about running this company, now's the time to share them."

"Mike, you do have an idea, remember?" Nelson said. "Tell them your idea about toasted corn chips."

"Toasted corn chips?" Bob said. "What's that?"

"A breakfast cereal," Mike explained. "People food," he added. "Maybe we're about to run out of horses, but we aren't about to run out of people, and *they* still have to eat."

Jack Canfield laughed. "I know what you're talking about. You're talking about that dry stuff like the Kellogg company's cornflakes and that rolled wheat of Nabisco's, aren't you?"

"Yes, I am."

"But who really eats that stuff?" Jack wanted to know. "People need to start off the day right, with eggs, sausage, and biscuits and gravy. Maybe a mess of potatoes on the side."

"That may be your idea of breakfast, Mr. Canfield," Mike said. "But last year Americans spent more than one hundred million dollars on cornflakes and shredded wheat."

"The hell you say!" Bob exclaimed, his interest perking up. "*One hundred million dollars?*"

"Yes, sir."

"What would it take for us to convert a part of the plant over to manufacturing these toasted corn chips?"

Mike smiled broadly. "Nothing," he said. "That's the beauty of it. The process we use now to make Puritex Feed Pellets could be used to make the chips. The ingredients, corn and oats, would also be the same. We'd have to refine our cooking process a little so that the end product comes out as flakes and not as pellets, but that's all there is to it."

"I think it's a wonderful idea," Nelson put in.

"Excuse me for asking this, Mr. Nelson. But if you like the idea so much, why haven't you tried it before now?"

"I don't know," Nelson replied with a sigh. "Mike's been trying to get me to do it for the last eighteen months. But I'm too old and too tired to go into something new. You have to understand, producing the new product isn't going to be the most difficult part of the task. What's going to be hard will be selling it to the public. They're used to thinking of Puritex as horse feed. Without a great deal of money spent in advertising, I'm afraid a significant number of them are going to believe that you're just serving them a horse of a different color, if you will."

"In other words, they're going to believe we're trying to tell them that horse feed is all right for people."

"Yes."

"Mike, you sure we can produce a product that people will like?"

"If they'll eat Kellogg's Corn Flakes, they'll eat our toasted corn chips," Mike said.

"Uh, uh," Bob said, shaking his head and smiling broadly. "They'll eat our Corn Toasties."

"Corn Toasties?" Mike replied. Now he smiled broadly. "Yes," he agreed, "yes, that does sound better."

"What do you say, gentlemen?" Bob asked. "Do we have a deal?"

"We do," Nelson said.

"Mike?"

"I'll have to speak to the employees." He smiled. "But I'll tell you this. I'll be speaking to them as your advocate."

"In that case, I consider it done," Bob replied. He looked at his father. "Well, Pop, what do you think? We're now St. Louis businessmen."

"That's fine," Jack replied, chuckling. "As long as I don't have to move to St. Louis."

CHAPTER SIXTEEN

DISPATCHES FROM THE PANAMA CANAL
By Terry Perkins
Special to *The St. Louis Chronicle*
May 15, 1907—

It is an intimidating land, a land of jungle as wild and wet and untamed as the day Balboa first discovered it. It is also a land of disease-bearing mosquitoes, broken dreams, and shattered reputations.

The work is unbelievably difficult. It begins with native laborers using machetes to clear away the jungle. First the trees are hacked down to knee level; then the machete wielders are followed by other natives who burn the vegetation and dig up or blast away the stumps. Monkeys swinging from those trees left undisturbed watch the activity and chatter loudly in protest.

The scarred land over which the fifty-mile-long ditch (called a cut) is progressing is as ugly as it is intimidating. Stubble is everywhere, and it is pockmarked by literally hundreds of black ash heaps where

foliage has been burned. Snaking out across this denuded land are several miles of railroad tracks, including
the main line and a spidery network of spur tracks.
Gargantuan steam shovels, mounted on flat railcars,
chew up the mountains in bites as big as houses. Out in
the channel dredges suck up the mud in one place and
spit it out in another. Dynamite blasts go off every few
minutes, sending enormous geysers of rock and water
high into the sky. When the echo of the blast dies away,
the air is rent by the babel of forty-five languages and
dialects.

Whistles blow at five o'clock in the afternoon,
signaling the end of the workday for most of the men.
The great shovels cease their relentless digging, equipment trains lay up for the night, and the men who have
been working since seven a.m. start for their homes in
the villages or gather in groups to wait for the labor
trains to take them back to the camps.

But the work doesn't cease entirely, for what is the
end of the day for some is the beginning for others.
Repair trains go out to the sites, carrying skilled mechanics who labor to put right those pieces of equipment
that broke down during the day. Coal trains rumble
about to refill the coal bins of the steam shovels. Whole
armies of track-repair squads scurry around to attend to
their duties.

During the long nights, lanterns, locomotive lights,
and even electric lights gleam in the dark. Then, an hour
or so before morning, a heavy mist settles in the cut. The
opposite bank is visible, but there is a white river of fog
in the trench that is so dense, it looks like water. Even
during that time of decreased visibility, the work must
go on. So the trains move slowly along the hidden tracks,
lanterns are held close to the work, and the toil continues.

By the time the morning sun disperses the fog, the
night crews have already climbed into bed for a much-
needed rest, the day crews have arrived, and the cycle
begins anew.

Digging a canal across the isthmus is the greatest
engineering feat ever undertaken by man, and a task
many say is impossible. Yet the gallant men working

here are daily proving the critics wrong. The jungle is being whipped, the land is being parted, and someday, in the not-too-distant future, the waters of the two greatest seas of the world will be joined. On that happy day the souls of thirty-five thousand workers—many already in their graves—will join and give a resounding cheer to the American genius and determination that will have brought this ancient dream to reality.

Terry read over his copy. Though he had been here for nearly a week now, this was his first article, and he wanted it to be a good one. He was inspired to this ambition by the long cable of congratulations he had received from Thomas Petzold, praising him for his story of the sea battle and the landing of American troops in Honduras:

Your vivid writing style has allowed every reader of our paper to experience with you the exciting events of our country's military adventures in Central America. It was one of the finest stories it has ever been my privilege to publish, and you have set a standard of excellence to which all future *Chronicle* reporters will aspire.

Terry treasured that message, and he intended to have it framed and hung on his wall when he returned to St. Louis. He realized, however, that it was as much a challenge as it was a congratulations. While not specifically saying so, Petzold had let Terry know that from now on anything less than excellent would be considered substandard work. Terry had no intention of letting his boss down.

"Mr. Perkins?"

Terry turned around from his desk and saw Major David Gaillard standing just outside the screen door. The forty-eight-year-old West Point graduate was not only second-in-command, Gaillard was also in charge of the Central Division of the Panama Canal excavation. His was the largest part of the job, consisting of the 31.7 miles of valley and low-lying hills between Gatun Dam on the Atlantic side and Pedro Miguel Lock overlooking the Pacific. Already more than fifty million tons of dirt had been excavated from the Central Division, and the best estimate was that at least that much more would have to be dug up and hauled away. "To put that in perspective for you, Mr. Perkins," Gaillard had explained during his preliminary briefing, "if the dirt we've removed were loaded onto one train, that train would stretch all the way across the Atlantic Ocean."

"I'm about to go to dinner," Gaillard now offered, "and I wonder if you'd care to join me."

"Why, yes, thank you," Terry responded. He stood up and reached for his jacket.

"You won't need that. We don't stand on ceremony here. The important thing is to be comfortable."

"Comfortable?" Terry asked with a little laugh. "In this heat? I'm afraid you've set yourself an impossible task."

Gaillard laughed with him. "Haven't you heard? We specialize in the impossible. But, we do like to be as comfortable as possible under the circumstances. By the way, Colonel Goethals has returned from his inspection trip, and he's most anxious to meet you. We've been invited to dine with him."

"That's great," Terry said. Goethals had actually returned earlier in the afternoon, for Terry had seen him from afar. This evening would be the first opportunity to meet the man, and the young reporter was pleased at the prospect.

Before coming down here to do the story, Terry had done research on Colonel George Washington Goethals. Goethals had succeeded to the post of chief engineer of the Panama Canal project after John F. Stevens resigned. It was a difficult assignment, not only because of the work involved, but because Stevens was regarded by the entire country as a hero. His name was as inexorably linked with the canal as, a few years earlier, Admiral Dewey's had been to Manila Bay. Stevens was the single person most responsible for reorganizing the divisions of labor and instilling in everyone—workers on the site and

Americans at home—a sense that the project would be successful. Stevens had also defended the decision to build the canal by using a system of locks and dams rather than the sea-level route followed by the French. Terry now knew that this decision, more than any other, was responsible for having advanced the project this far.

It had been a difficult battle to get the lock-and-dam system accepted. The congressional committee on construction had voted to build a sea-level canal and threatened to withhold funds if their wishes weren't followed. Stevens took the fight directly to President Roosevelt, convincing him that his way was the only chance of success.

"And what about Gatun Dam?" one of the opposing congressmen had asked him. The congressman had been invited to the meeting by the President to defend the committee's decision.

"What about Gatun Dam?" Stevens had replied.

"If you build the canal the way you suggest, the entire project depends on that one dam. Don't you think you should at least make it stronger?"

Stevens was a man who spoke bluntly. "The dam is strong enough," he had answered. "It's like killing a duck. A dead duck cannot be made to be more dead."

Laughing richly, President Roosevelt had polished his glasses, perched them back on his nose, then looked directly at Stevens. "Build it however you think it should be built, Mr. Stevens. You fight the jungle and the mud slides and the mosquitoes down in Panama. I promise to protect your backside from Congress."

Congress withdrew its objections, and work progressed nicely. Then, for reasons he did not disclose, Stevens suddenly and unexpectedly resigned. Following Stevens's resignation, and acting on the advice of the chief of the Army Corps of Engineers, President Roosevelt and Secretary Taft appointed Colonel George Washington Goethals. Except within Army circles, where he was recognized as an excellent engineer and a highly efficient administrator, Goethals was totally un-known.

Even though he had been appointed, when Goe-thals arrived at the Panama Canal Zone he didn't know if he would have a job or not. He had learned that a petition, signed by over ten thousand men and including every American in the Canal Zone, had been sent to Stevens, begging him to withdraw his resignation. But Stevens didn't change his mind, and within three weeks after Goethals arrived, power had been transferred so smoothly that the work suffered no ill effects whatever.

Terry had seen Goethals earlier this afternoon wan-dering about the work sites, clad in a spotless white suit and smoking a cigarette, and the young reporter was looking forward to having dinner with him. He and Gaillard were almost to the mess hall when Terry heard a series of shouts from far out on the work site. Each shout was repeated by someone nearer to him until finally he was able to understand the words.

"Fire in the hole!" they were shouting. By now Terry knew that that meant another dynamite blast was about to be set off. He looked around, trying to locate the point where the blast would occur.

"It'll be over there," Gaillard said, pointing. He had no sooner pointed than a geyser of dirt erupted from the ground, followed by a plume of smoke. A couple of seconds later the sound reached them. The heavy boom of the explosion shook his stomach, and in the mess hall behind them could be heard the dishes rattling on the tables. Gaillard laughed and said, "That'll shake them up inside."

The mess hall was light and airy, constructed for comfort. The walls, which were really only half walls, were made of clapboards, and between them and the roof was nothing but screen wire. The openness of the building allowed for ample ventilation, while the screens kept out the mosquitoes. This particular mess hall was for the officers and supervisors of the project, though there was another one, similarly constructed if some-what larger, for the laborers.

Gaillard introduced Terry to Colonel Goethals as well as to the others who were sharing Goethals's table.

"Are you comfortable, Mr. Perkins?" Colonel Goethals asked. "Settled in all right?"

"Fine, except for the mosquitoes," Terry replied. "They're almost unbearable at night."

"Are you not using the mosquito netting around your bed?"

"I don't have mosquito netting."

"Cameron?" Goethals asked, raising his eyebrows at a captain who was sharing their table.

"I'm sorry, Colonel. We didn't have any when he arrived. A new shipment came in today, however, so I'll have someone take some over and put it over his bed."

"Well, that should help you sleep better," Goethals said, smiling.

"Thank you," Terry replied.

"Let's see, you were on board the *Olympia* when the American fleet was attacked by the Nicaraguans, weren't you?" Goethals asked. He took a fresh cigarette from a gold cigarette case and lit it from the still-burning butt of the one he had been smoking. "You wrote a story about it, didn't you?"

"Yes, sir," Terry answered. He knew that his story had been picked up by the wire services and reprinted in the English-language newspaper that served the men down here.

"It was a very exciting story, Mr. Perkins. You made me feel as if I were right there with you."

"Thank you, sir. I hope I can do the same for the Panama Canal project."

"I'm sure you'll do a fine job."

"I'd like to ask you a question, Mr. Perkins, if you don't mind," Captain Cameron put in. Like Goethals and Gaillard, Cameron was an engineering officer. He was responsible for rations and billeting, and Terry had met him the day he arrived when he drew his equipment.

"Certainly, Captain Cameron," Terry answered. "What is it?"

"What happened after the American troops landed

in Nicaragua? Why didn't you say anything about them in your story?"

"There was nothing to say," Terry replied, shrugging. "A few skirmishes took place between the Hondurans and the Nicaraguans, but no fighting whatever by the Americans."

"That's too bad. I'd like to teach those Nicaraguans that the United States gives the orders."

"The Nicaraguans are a proud people," Terry said. "I'm not sure they'd be willing to take any orders from the United States."

"They would *have* to take orders, if those orders were issued from the mouth of a cannon," Cameron remarked.

"Isn't that a little drastic?" Terry asked, surprised by Cameron's comment.

Major Gaillard chuckled. "You'll have to excuse Captain Cameron," he said. "I'm afraid he is a very bellicose young man."

"I wouldn't call it bellicose," Cameron complained.

"You wouldn't? Well, what would you call it?"

"Patriotic. In fact, you know what I think we should do?" Captain Cameron asked rhetorically as he spooned sugar into his coffee. "I think we should serve notice, right now, that we are the masters of this part of the world. In my opinion the President is making a big mistake if he doesn't send the Army down to take Mexico."

"Mexico?" one of the other men around the table said. "Wait a minute! I thought we were talking about Honduras."

"Yes, that, too. Honduras, Nicaragua, and every other place between Texas and the northern coast of South America. We should take over their little countries."

"Well, hell, why stop there, Captain?" Gaillard mocked. "Why not go on down and take all of South America as well?"

"No, sir, I'm serious," Cameron went on. "If Teddy Roosevelt doesn't take whatever military action is necessary to defend this canal, he'll be the most despised man in American history."

"And that's your justification for invading half the Western Hemisphere? To protect the canal?" Terry asked.

"Yes. I mean, here we are, digging this canal, correcting a mistake God made—"

"Wait a minute, Captain," Goethals interrupted him, "let me get this straight. You mean Roosevelt isn't the only one making mistakes? God has made them too?"

The others roared with laughter, and Cameron flushed.

"Laugh if you want to, sir," he said. "But I believe history will prove me right. If we don't take care of all these countries now, we'll still be dealing with them a hundred years from now."

An exceptionally loud rumble sounded then. At first Terry thought it was another dynamite explosion, and he wondered who was still working with that stuff, now that it was dark. But when a second booming rumble came, even louder than the first, Terry realized he was listening to thunder—but thunder the likes of which he had never heard. It would break sharply at first, then fade off into a sustained rumble, and then build up again for one last boom before it died.

Major Gaillard got up from the dinner table and walked over to look outside. "Gentlemen," he said. "You had better hold on to your hats tonight. Unless I miss my guess, this is going to be one jim-dandy of a storm."

Terry was awakened during the night by loud crashing and smashing sounds coming from outside his quarters. Startled, he sat up in bed, then found that the wind was whistling through his small cabin with such ferocity that the structure was in danger of blowing down around him.

Terry pushed his newly issued mosquito net aside, got out of bed, and walked over to the door. With some difficulty he managed to get it pushed open against the wind, then stepped outside. It was raining fiercely, the wind driving the water with such force that the streaks of rain were horizontal, and the drops were needle sharp as they hit his skin. Lightning was practically continuous so that everything was displayed in harsh, colorless white and featureless black. The on-off, on-off, on-off lightning flashes illuminated a large piece of corrugated tin—a roof, Terry realized—rolling across the ground, and the stroboscopic effect marked the progress of the piece of tin in jerky, stop-action sequences.

The trees were bent sharply by the howling gale, their limbs waving about furiously as if pleading desperately for help. As Terry watched, one large tree was uprooted, and it fell with a thundering crash. It was then that the young reporter realized that it was the crash of a falling tree that had awakened him, for already several of them were lying around. Seeing the situation, he felt lucky that no tree had fallen across his cabin to crush him in his bed.

A terrible wrenching sound caught his ears, and he saw the roof of the officers' mess hall ripped away. This slab of corrugated tin scurried and flapped across the ground to join the roof that had danced away earlier. Suddenly Terry's own roof was whipped off, and one wall of his cabin fell in. He instinctively let out a quick yelp of alarm and hopped out of the way of the crashing timber just in time.

"Mister . . . Perkins! Are . . . you . . . okay?" Gaillard shouted against the roar of the wind.

Terry could barely hear Gaillard, even though his cabin was right next door. He cupped his hand around his mouth and shouted back, "I'm . . . all . . . right!"

Gaillard fought his way through the wind-whipped debris to reach Terry at the remains of his cabin.

"Does it always rain like this?" Terry asked.

"No," Gaillard answered. "In fact, I don't think I've ever seen a storm this severe."

"How encouraging," Terry quipped.

"Come on, Mr. Perkins. We have to get out of

here," Gaillard ordered. "If one or two of the lesser dams break now, a million cubic yards of water is going to come crashing through here, and we'll be thirty feet under!"

Terry went back into what was left of his cabin and put on his rain slicker and hat. For a moment he thought about trying to pack a bag, but another loud crash convinced him otherwise.

"Come on, we've no time to waste!" Gaillard shouted at him.

Terry hurried out of the cabin and followed Gaillard and the others who were also evacuating the campsite up a path that led to the highest ground around. The hill itself wasn't really all that high, but because the valley had been chewed away by the giant earth-moving machines, it had been deepened to the point that any hill, no matter how small, provided some degree of safety.

As they slipped and slid their way up the path, Terry recognized having come up this same hill the day he arrived, wanting to get a better, overall view of the work going on around him. Then it had taken him about ten minutes to climb; tonight, against the fearsome wind, the torrential downpour, and the river of mud, it took the climbers over a half hour. When his group finally reached the top, Terry found Colonel Goethals and hundreds of other people already there. Surrounding hilltops were similarly populated, and Terry estimated that better than three thousand personnel were clustered in the area. They were all miserably wet, but no shelter was available. And even if there had been, Goethals would not have let them go inside, for fear the storm might collapse the buildings around them. Terry noticed that, even in this downpour, Goethals had somehow managed to light his ever-present cigarette and stood cupping his hand over the end of the cigarette, protecting the red spark from the rain.

"I'm glad to see you made it up here, Mr. Perkins," Goethals said. "I'd hate to lose you so soon after your arrival."

Despite his misery, Terry chuckled. "I'd hate to be lost," he said.

"Shit," one of the men near Terry grumbled. "I've seen drowned rats that weren't as wet as I am. I should've stayed in my cabin. I'd be a lot drier."

Gaillard glanced at him. "Then you'd be just like those rats—drowned."

"You think Gatun might let go?" Terry asked Goethals.

"No," the colonel said with conviction. "The dam will stand, have no fear of that."

"How can you be so certain?

"Because I know what went into building it. We built it stronger even than the hills that anchor each end of the dam's legs."

"I hope you're right," Terry said.

Goethals laughed. "Oh, you're doing more than hoping I'm right," he said.

Terry shook his head. "I don't understand."

"You're betting your life that I'm right. If Gatun Dam bursts on us tonight, you and I and everyone on this hill will be swept away. So, Mr. Perkins, you're betting your life on the strength and integrity of that dam."

The storm broke just before dawn, and the rising sun showed the destruction it had wrought. Looking down into the valley, Terry saw that the water was up to the roofs of the buildings—those buildings that still had roofs. Steam shovels and locomotives were inundated, some had been turned over, and great sections of the spillway trestles had been carried away. The Panama Railroad, which was separate from the canal, was under eight feet of water, and there were places, Terry later found out, where the water was forty-two feet deep. One hundred square miles were flooded by the storm, and Terry learned the truth of how much danger he had been in the night before when he heard that eighty men had drowned.

"Would you like to come along with us, Mr. Perkins?" Major Gaillard asked Terry. The expression on his face was grim.

"Where are you going?"

"Colonel Goethals has secured a tugboat for us. We're going to take a look at the damage."

"Yes, thank you," Terry said. "I'd like that. I'd like very much to go."

As the small tugboat cut its way through the flooded valley, Terry sat on a box near the railing, viewing the destruction. The engineers studied everything very closely, and each time they saw something new, they'd point to it with groans and curses.

At one point Major Gaillard threw up his hands, uttering a strangled, choking sound that was almost a sob. He walked over to sit on the deck in front of the wheelhouse, then pulled his legs up in front of him, wrapped his arms around them, and lay his forehead on his knees. The other engineers were nearly as distraught, and though Terry was, from a technical standpoint, unable to fully comprehend the magnitude of the destruction, he knew he was witnessing something awful.

Seeing Colonel Goethals standing alone by the rail, Terry walked over beside him. "Excuse me, Colonel," he said, "but what is it? What has everyone so upset? Surely the floodwaters will recede?"

"Oh, yes. That shouldn't take more than two or three days," the officer replied.

"It's more than the water, isn't it?"

Colonel Goethals lit a new cigarette from the still-burning stub of his old one, then flipped the used butt into the brown, swirling water. The tiny white cylinder was caught in the wake of the boat and swept away. Still staring out over the side, he replied, "Mr. Perkins, the French began excavating this canal in 1881. The Americans took it over in 1903. In twenty-seven years, we have removed fifty million tons of dirt."

"I believe Major Gaillard told me it would fill a train

stretching all the way across the Atlantic Ocean," Terry said.

"Yes, quite. It would fill a train spanning the ocean. But if you will, Mr. Perkins, I want you to imagine another train. You are from St. Louis, I believe?"

"Yes, sir, I am."

"I was once assigned to the Mississippi River levee project," Goethals remarked, "so I'm familiar with your part of the country. Now, I want you to imagine a train stretching from St. Louis to Memphis. That's a distance of about three hundred miles, isn't it?"

"Yes, it is," Terry agreed, wondering where Goethals was headed with this.

"Now, imagine that train was loaded with rock and dirt, and suppose it came down to dump its entire contents back into the channel we have dug."

"Is that what happened?" Terry asked quietly.

"That's what happened," Goethals replied. "And if you'll just look out there—not at the water, but at what you can see—you'll notice the signs."

Terry looked out at the water. At first it looked like a huge, placid lake. Then he saw, here and there, rocks and mounds of dirt that poked, almost obscenely, through the surface of the water.

"I think I can see what you're talking about. How much of that slid back into the cut?" Terry asked.

"About five million tons," Goethals answered.

Terry gasped. "*Five million tons?* My God, that's ten percent of everything that's been taken out in the whole twenty-seven years!"

"Yes," Goethals replied. "In a matter of a few hours, we lost at least a year's work."

Terry looked over at the second-in-command. "No wonder Major Gaillard is so distraught," he said.

Goethals nodded, then walked over to stand by his assistant. Gaillard looked up at him, and when he did, Terry saw tears in the major's eyes.

"George," Gaillard asked of Goethals, "what are we going to do? What on earth are we going to do?"

"Well, hell, David. We're going to dig it back out," Goethals said calmly.

Anna Rosenstein threw a handful of bread crumbs onto the pond, and a swan glided toward them.

"Look at him," Anna said. "Isn't he beautiful?"

"Yes," David Gelbman agreed.

"More beautiful than anything you have in St. Louis?"

"Well, yes," David said. "But I didn't have to come to the Stadtpark to feed the swans just to find something more beautiful than anything we have in St. Louis. Or perhaps I should say, *someone* more beautiful than anyone we have in St. Louis." David put his hand on Anna's neck, and she tilted her head to hold it there. But after a moment she flushed guiltily, and gently, though resolutely, she pushed his hand away.

"David, someone will see."

"Let them see," David said, grinning. "Everyone!" he called out in English. "Come and see the most beautiful girl in all of Vienna!"

"David!" Anna scolded. "Please, you are making a scene."

But despite her obvious embarrassment, David was pleased to see that she couldn't help but smile at his antics. "Oh, you don't want me to tell everyone you are the most beautiful girl in Vienna?" he teased.

"No."

"Everyone!" I was mistaken! She is *not* the most beautiful girl in Vienna!" David yelled, again in English.

Anna laughed out loud. "You are crazy," she said.

"Yes . . . yes I am, actually. Quite mad, in fact," David said. "But it's your fault, you know. You've driven me mad with your smoldering beauty and your Zionist zeal." David made a face and lunged at her as if he were deranged. A middle-aged couple strolling nearby saw the way he was carrying on and quickly altered their route.

"Even the strollers think I'm mad," David said,

laughing when he saw that they were walking away from him.

Anna laughed too. "They'll probably feel sorry for me and send the police out to rescue me."

"It's all right. I'll tell them I am an American. Everyone knows that Americans are crazy anyway."

"That is the truth."

"And how about you, Anna Rosenstein? Do you still think me the upstart American cousin who came to Vienna to save the day with his miracles?"

"I do not think that anymore," Anna said. "Now I *know* it. You have worked miracles, David. No one else could have taken over a store that was losing money and turned it into a profitable business. In the market and at the synagogue everyone talks about you."

"They do, do they? And what do they say?"

"They say that you are a genius. And already the *shadchan* has been approached by many mothers who are anxious for—" Anna stopped in midsentence and smiled self-consciously. "But of course, you are not supposed to know of such things until the time comes."

"The *shadchan*? Do you mean the matchmaker? Mothers are talking to the matchmaker about me?" David asked, astonished. He then laughed out loud.

"Yes. Why do you laugh?"

"Because it's funny," David said. "To think that a *shadchan* would think she could arrange a marriage for me. Why, I wouldn't even talk to the old crone."

Anna looked away quickly, but not before David saw that her eyes had filled with tears.

"Anna, what is it?" he asked, surprised by the sudden tears. "Why are you crying?"

"I am not crying."

"But you are. There are tears in your eyes. Why should there be tears?"

"When you mock the *shadchan*, you mock everything about us," Anna said. "You mock our faith."

"No!" David said. "How can you say I mock the faith? I am of the faith."

"Are you really? I must tell you that amidst all the

words praising you, there are also words of condemnation, for you do not come to *shul*."

"That doesn't mean I don't believe," David said.

"Then why do you stay away?"

"Anna, I can't come," David said. "I am very uncomfortable around the others. They make me too aware of the differences between us. Their faith is my faith but when I go to temple here, it is like seeing things through a distorting mirror. The language is different, the clothes are different, the customs are different."

"Like the custom of the *shadchan*?"

"Yes."

"But these are not customs of just Austrian Jews, they are customs of the Jewish people, and they should be the same anywhere in the world. Can you not adapt yourself to the customs?"

"Some of them, perhaps. But I find the custom of a matchmaker particularly distasteful."

"Why?"

"Because I am a man capable of making up my own mind about whom I might love and whom I might marry. And when that time comes, I want no one speaking to my bride-to-be on my behalf, nor will I allow anyone to speak to me on behalf of my bride-to-be."

"But marriages have been arranged in such a way for thousands of years," Anna protested. "Surely the wisdom of thousands of years is greater than the impulses and urges of a young man or a young woman?"

"Times change," David countered. "Even if a thing has been done a certain way for hundreds of generations, it doesn't mean it should always be done that way. Why, if everyone thought that, there would be no such thing as the automobile, the train, or the telephone."

"I could never marry anyone without the assistance of a *shadchan*." Anna's tone was soft yet insistent.

"But Anna, surely you—"

"I think perhaps it is time for us to go home now," she said flatly.

David looked at her for a long moment, thinking that never was she more beautiful than she was right now, when he realized that he was on the verge of losing her—losing her before she was even his to lose.

"Yes, perhaps you are right," he said.

It was late, perhaps as late as two o'clock in the morning, and David was still unable to get to sleep. He had been awake for hours, thinking about the conversation in the park.

Anna had said that she would never marry anyone unless it were arranged by a matchmaker. So what? What difference did that make? Why was he so concerned with it? He wasn't going to marry her anyway. He couldn't marry her, for if he did, it would mean he would never go back to the United States. Oh, he could, of course, for as his wife Anna would have no choice but to "lodge where he lodged." But he knew that her strength and spirit came from her traditions, and since those traditions would be in jeopardy in America, her strength and spirit could be destroyed. Without her strength and spirit, Anna would be just the shell of the woman he had come to appreciate. And love.

The house was very quiet, and David was sure everyone else had fallen asleep hours ago. He wished he could. But sleep would elude him unless he could put Anna out of his mind. He sighed and fluffed up his pillow, trying to find a more comfortable position.

It didn't work. Within a moment the position was uncomfortable again, and the pillow had grown hard. He sighed again, fluffed the pillow once more, and repositioned himself. But still sleep would not come.

Finally he sat up. A bar of moonlight streamed in through the window, painting a dappled shadow on the wall. Getting out of bed, David walked over to the window and looked outside.

The dappled shadow came from a large Austrian pine that grew in the garden beside the house. Its branches swayed in the gentle night breeze, breaking the moonlight into bursts of silver. The moon was so bright that David could see the profusion of flowers in the garden, and he felt as if he could make out their colors.

On impulse David put on his robe, then, barefooted, stepped cautiously out of his room. The hall was thickly carpeted, and the carpet's rich texture cradled his feet as he walked silently down the length of the corridor. As he passed the various closed bedroom doors—Sarah's, the grandparents', Anna's, then the younger children's—he could hear snoring or soft, even breathing. He was apparently the only one awake.

The house was dark, but a splash of moonlight coming in through a front window guided him down the stairs. When he reached the bottom of the stairs, he was startled by a sudden clicking noise, followed by a whirring sound.

Dong! Dong!

It was the hall clock announcing the time.

David walked through the moonlit house, and then he stepped through the side door and out into the garden. The grass felt soft and cool, and he could hear frogs calling to each other from their secret places throughout the garden. The gentle breeze carried with it the aromatic perfume of all the garden flowers. It was odd, he thought. He'd visited the garden many times before, but never before had he been as aware of the scent of the flowers as he was now.

A fish pond was in the middle of the garden, and David went over to sit on the grass beside it. It felt so comfortable that he decided if he couldn't sleep, he'd just spend the night right here, enjoying the cool breeze, the smell of the flowers, and the songs of the frogs and insects.

"I heard you walk past my bedroom."

David was startled by the sudden, unexpected voice, and he looked around to see Anna standing behind him. Unlike him, she had not put on a robe, and the soft breeze pressed her nightgown against her body in such a way that the nipples of her breasts stood out in bold relief. A part of him was embarrassed for her, and he wanted to look away. But an even stronger part of him appreciated the view, and he stared openly.

"Aren't you . . . aren't you going to ask me to sit down?" she asked.

"Yes. Yes, of course." David patted the ground beside him. "Join me."

"I haven't made a nighttime visit to the garden since I was a young girl," Anna said.

"You've made such visits before?"

Anna chuckled. "Oh, yes. When I was thirteen or fourteen. I had a lot of questions and disquieting thoughts at that age. I would often come out here in the middle of the night and just sit here, listening to the frogs, sometimes counting the stars. It was so peaceful, and I felt so tiny in a world so large that any problems I might be experiencing in growing up seemed insignificant by comparison."

When Anna sat beside David, she pulled her knees up, and as she did so, her gown fell back to expose her legs. They looked white in the silver light. She made no effort to cover them, but wrapped her arms around them and rested her chin on her knees.

"I'm sorry about this afternoon," she said. "About accusing you of mocking our customs. I should realize that there is a difference between questioning and mocking."

"I should also apologize," David responded. "Sometimes my questions are insensitive."

"I do not think you could ever be insensitive." Anna glanced into his eyes, and their gaze held for a long moment. Then David made an inarticulate sound deep in his throat and moved close to her. Hesitantly, he put his hand to her face, let his fingers linger for a moment, and then pulled her into his arms, pressing his lips against hers.

Anna surrendered easily to his kiss, and when he bent her body backward, she didn't resist. His lips traveled from her mouth down along her throat to the top button of her nightgown. She allowed him to do what he wished, totally submissive to his will and bending to his bidding like a slender reed in a strong spring breeze.

David's fingers opened the buttons that fastened her nightgown, and when he folded the material back, her breasts shone like alabaster in the moonlight. He couldn't keep himself from moving his hand across her skin, cupping her breast, tenderly stroking the nipple with his thumb.

Suddenly he realized what he was doing. He had been carried this far by his own passion and by a desire stronger than any emotion he'd ever before experienced. If he was going to stop, he would have to stop now. With every ounce of willpower in his body, he pulled his fingers away and, with trembling hands, started to close the buttons.

"No, David, please, do not stop. I want to! I want to!"

Inflamed by desire and emboldened by her invitation, David slipped out of his robe and began undressing, even as she wriggled out of her nightgown. Spreading out his robe on the grass for them to use as bedding, he then dropped to one knee beside her and placed a hand lightly on the inside of her thigh.

"Anna," he whispered huskily, "are you sure?"

"David, someday you will return to America, and I will go to the Jewish homeland," she replied. "When that happens, we will never see each other again. By sharing ourselves now we will always have a part of each other."

David moved his body over hers and began to enter her, then felt her wince. He stopped, but she put her arms on his shoulders and pulled him to her.

"No, it's all right," she said firmly.

As he continued, he abandoned all thought of right and wrong, all thought of what might lie in their future. He knew only the pleasure of the moment and knew that she was feeling the same thing, for she rose up against him, giving him all that was hers to give.

"Oh, David!" she whispered in a sharp, rising voice. "Oh, David, it's . . . it's wonderful!" she gasped.

Then it started for David, a tiny, tingling sensation

that began deep inside him and pinwheeled out, spinning faster and faster until every part of his body was caught up in a whirlpool of pleasure.

They lay side by side afterward, Anna's head resting on David's shoulder. Finally she raised herself up onto her elbow and looked into his face.

"Promise me we won't speak of this—not even with our eyes," she said.

"Why not? Didn't you like it?" David asked.

"Like it?" Anna chuckled. "David, for the first time in my life I know what all those poets are raving about when they write of love. I could go to a deserted island in the middle of the ocean and spend the rest of my life with you, living off dates and fish and . . . and this." With a ribald smile, she boldly grabbed him. "But that is only a dream, you see—a wonderful, impossible dream. And since I can't have the dream, I want nothing to remind me of it."

"Why can't we have the dream?"

Anna looked at him for a long moment. At first her eyes glowed brightly, as if she were considering his question. Then the glow dimmed, replaced by a veil.

"We had better get back into the house now," she said, reaching for her nightgown and pulling it over her head.

"I'm serious," David said as he pulled on his pajama bottoms. "Why can't we have the dream? Anna, I want you to marry me."

"David, please," she said, kissing him lightly, then pulling away before he could grab her. "Let us not speak of the impossible. It will only bring about more pain." She turned from him then and ran quickly across the lawn, her bare feet whispering on the grass.

As David watched her leave, he knew it would be impossible for him to ever love another woman as much as he loved this one.

"*Herr* Gelbman?"

David looked up from his desk, tearing his mind

away from the events of the night before, to see his assistant manager, Hans Vogel. "Yes, *Herr* Vogel?"

"You wanted to meet the young man who was trying to sell the paintings?"

"Oh, yes, yes indeed. Is he here?"

"Yes, with another batch of paintings. His name is Kubizek."

"Kubizek. Well, send *Herr* Kubizek in, would you, please?"

Vogel disappeared, and moments later a rather stout young man with blond hair and blue eyes knocked tentatively on the door frame. "You wanted to see me, sir?" the young man said, his voice hesitant.

"Uh, yes," David said. He stroked his chin. "You are Kubizek?" he asked, slightly puzzled.

"Yes, sir. Is there some problem, sir?" Kubizek asked.

"No, no problem," David replied. "It's just that you aren't whom I thought you would be."

"I beg your pardon, sir? Have we met?"

"No," David said. "But the paintings you sold us last week of the opera house, the museum, the parliament building . . . Well, I thought I might know you, you see, because I met a young artist when I first arrived in the city, and those are the sort of pictures I imagined he would paint."

"Where did you meet him, *Herr* Gelbman?"

"First at the railroad station. He carried my bags. Then I saw him again at the opera. He was about your age or maybe slightly younger. He was quite thin, with blue eyes and brown hair." David chuckled. "He seemed to have trouble keeping his hair out of his eyes."

The young man smiled broadly. "Yes, sir, that's him, all right," he said. "He's the artist of these pictures."

"You didn't paint them?" David asked.

"Oh, no, sir. I just sell them. The fellow I share a room with paints them."

"And what's his name?"

"Adi," Kubizek said. "I mean, that's what we at the house call him. His real name is Adolf. Adolf Hitler. Do you like his paintings, *Herr* Gelbman? Do you want more?"

David smiled. "Well, I'll tell you the truth, *Herr* Kubizek. The answer is no and yes. No, I don't like the paintings . . . they seem to lack something that I can't explain exactly, but then Professor Avery, my art professor back at Jefferson University, could never explain it either. Anyway, I now think I know what he was talking about." He held up his hands. "However, even though I don't like the paintings, I do want to buy some more, because I have discovered that the picture frames in the store sell better when something is inside them. So, if you think *Herr* Hitler would be willing to supply his artwork for such a mundane purpose, then I would be willing to buy a few more."

"Is that what you did with the others?" Kubizek asked. "Used them merely to sell picture frames?"

"Yes."

Kubizek smiled. "I will sell the pictures to you, sir, because we need the money. But if Adi comes to the store, you must pretend that you are selling the paintings and not the frames. Otherwise, he might get very angry . . . and, believe me, he is not a pleasant person to be around when he is angry."

David laughed. "The temperamental artist, eh? Well, I understand. Very well, *Herr* Kubizek, you supply the paintings, I will sell the frames, and *Herr* Hitler will be none the wiser for our little subterfuge."

"Yes, sir," Kubizek said. "Thank you, sir. Thank you very much."

Shortly after Kubizek left, Hans Vogel stuck his head into the office again. "Excuse me, *Herr* Gelbman, but an old lady is waiting to speak with you." Vogel scratched his head and looked back outside with a puzzled expression on his face. "I told her you were much too busy, but she insisted that you had sent for her."

"An, yes, yes indeed," David said, smiling broadly. "She would be the matchmaker. Send her in, Vogel. Send her in."

• • •

In his office in the Chronicle Building in St. Louis, Thomas Petzold was going over the circulation figures and the total inches of advertising his paper had run during the previous week. He was just about to enter them on a chart he was keeping when a quiet knock sounded on his door.

"Come in," he called without looking up from his chart.

The door opened, but no one came in. Petzold continued to work with his figures. Then, becoming aware that whoever had knocked still hadn't entered, he looked up to see why. Gerald Fitzhugh was standing just inside the door. To Petzold's surprise, there were tears in his receptionist's eyes.

"Fitzhugh?" Petzold said, standing quickly and starting toward him. "Fitzhugh, what is it, man?"

"This . . . this cable, sir," Fitzhugh said softly. "It has just arrived from the Panama Canal."

"From Terry?"

Fitzhugh didn't answer. Instead he blinked, then pinched the bridge of his nose. Tears flowed freely down his cheeks. "Remember, sir?" the secretary murmured. "Remember the silly disagreement Mr. Perkins and I had on the day he was hired? If only I could call that day back. If only I had known then what a fine man he would turn out to be."

Still puzzled by Fitzhugh's odd behavior, Petzold took the cablegram and began to read:

TO: THOMAS PETZOLD, EDITOR, ST. LOUIS CHRONICLE. SIR, IT IS WITH GREAT REGRET THAT I INFORM YOU OF THE DEATH OF YOUR REPORTER, TERRY PERKINS. MR. PERKINS CONTRACTED YELLOW FEVER ON MONDAY LAST AND SUCCUMBED AT FOUR A.M. TODAY. DETAILS TO FOLLOW IN LETTER. PLEASE EXTEND OUR CONDOLENCES TO HIS FAMILY. SINCERELY, COLONEL GEORGE WASHINGTON GOETHALS.

"Is there anything I should do? Anyone I should notify?" Fitzhugh asked.

"I will take care of it," Petzold replied quietly, turning and sinking heavily into his chair. "Please, go now. Go and leave me alone for a while."

"Yes, sir." Fitzhugh stepped out of the room and closed the door behind him.

Petzold stared at the cable for a long moment, then at a photograph of the young reporter that was on the wall of his office along with the photographs of the rest of his staff. He pulled his gaze away. Taking off his glasses, he laid his head on his desk and wept.

CHAPTER
SEVENTEEN

The Buffalo Bill Wild West Show was spending its final night in Baltimore, where it was the featured attraction at the Del-Mar-Va Fair for three weeks in late August. But because the troupe shared Patterson Park with the fair's midway, rides, and shows, they had less space than they normally occupied. The acts themselves—the runaway stagecoach, the chuck-wagon race, the Indian battle, the shooting exhibitions, even Eric's "wild-bull" act—needed a good deal of room, so in order to have a large enough arena to present them, the living space had to be restricted. Nearly half the housing tents had been left on the train, forcing the performers to crowd in together.

Eric was in a tent with the drovers, nearly a dozen men in all. The tent was so small and the conditions so crowded that even the collapsible cots had to be sacrificed, and the men spread out bedrolls on the ground anywhere they could find space.

357

"Well, what do you know? We have a great hero staying with us, gents," came a spate of bitingly sarcastic words when Eric stepped through the tent flap. "What an honor it is to have Eric Twainbough, who, every night, saves the women and children from a half-blind old steer. 'Course, the women and children don't know it's a half-blind old steer. They think it's a rampaging bull, and sometimes I think Twainbough believes that as well."

The man who had spoken made no effort to conceal his brooding anger. His name was Bodine and he loathed Eric, even though the youth had tried from the very first day to make friends with him. Initially, Eric didn't know why Bodine was so disagreeable; then one of the drovers explained it to him. Bodine had developed an act, "The Great Train Robbery," and he had just about talked Buffalo Bill into putting it in the show, with Bodine as the hero. But before the act could be implemented, Eric came along. The fresh young kid out of nowhere had roped a steer that got away, which suddenly became a regular act—given a featured position at the expense of Bodine's own act.

So instead of becoming a featured performer himself, Bodine was stuck in his job as the concealed driver inside the stage during the runaway-stagecoach act. He strongly resented his lost chance, and he took it out on Eric every chance he could.

"So, how does it feel to be living with the working class, Twainbough?" Bodine asked.

"I don't mind sleeping on the ground," Eric replied. He sat down on his bedroll, got his rope out of his tack bag, and began preparing it for his next show.

"Oh, well, aren't we the lucky ones, boys?" Bodine said to the others. "The great Twainbough doesn't mind sleeping on the ground."

"I mean, I've slept in worse places," Eric tried to explain.

"Oh, yeah, we mustn't forget. Twainbough was a cowboy," Bodine said. "A *real* cowboy; he's not playacting like the rest of you bums."

"I've seen these fellas handle all the stock in this show," Eric countered. "I wouldn't exactly call that playacting. They're damn good—the best I've ever seen, in fact."

"Thank you, Mr. Real Cowboy, for telling these men that you approve of them. I'm sure that, coming from you, they're thrilled by it."

Eric sighed, then put his rope down and stood up. "Bodine, you've been digging your spurs into me for the whole time I've been with this show, and I'm sick of it. Now, pull them out, or let's settle this once and for all."

Bodine smiled a small, evil smile. "You want to settle it, do you? Are you challenging me, boy? Because if you are, I don't think you're going to like the way I fight."

A head popped in through the tent flap. "Five minutes till the runaway stagecoach," the man announced. "Five minutes. Places, everybody."

"That's our call, Bodine," one of the other drovers said, getting up from his own bedroll.

"Wait a minute," Bodine said. "The boy and I are having a little discussion here. Aren't we, boy? You said something about settling this once and for all?"

"Come on, Bodine. Leave the kid alone, for God's sake. He ain't done nothin' to you," another drover said. He, too, was in the next act, and he was getting fidgety. "And you know how upset Mr. Cody gets if we miss our marks."

Bodine stared at Eric for a moment longer. Then, pointing his finger like a gun, he said quietly, *"Bang."* Laughing, he followed the others out of the tent.

Nearly all the drovers were involved in the runaway-stage act, so when they left to take their positions, only Ben Priday was left behind. Somewhere around forty, Ben worked only with the show's stock, never appearing in any of the acts, even as an extra. Unlike most of the others, Ben really had been a cowboy at one time. As a result, he and Eric had a lot in common, and Eric liked Ben. Ironically, Bodine had also lived in the West, working as a real stagecoach driver as well as a railroad detective and a deputy sheriff, but that western background hadn't helped at all in his relationship with Eric.

"Don't let Bodine get under her skin, Eric," Ben said. "He can be a mean one."

"Yes," Eric agreed. He sighed. "Well, I've run across a few mean ones before."

Ben chuckled. "I don't doubt that, but you should just forget about him. Nobody else pays him any mind anyway. Hey, I've got an idea. How about after the show tonight me and you go next door and catch the Flying Lady?"

The Flying Lady was one of the many sideshows featured at the fair. A large, gaudily painted sign showed a beautifully formed woman flying through the air from one trapeze to another. In the painting she was dressed in a gossamer costume so thin that all her feminine attributes could be seen under the filmy gauze. Beside the painting was another sign that warned:

Caution: The Flying Lady's costume is designed for her safety. Therefore, those who find the nearly nude female form offensive, or those who are of a prudish nature, are advised to avoid this show.

The sign of course, had exactly the effect the manager wanted—attracting men in such large numbers that there was a constant line for tickets.

"Well, I've see the trapeze arrangement inside the tent," Eric said. "And they're a lot lower and a lot closer together than they're shown on the painting."

"Yeah," Ben answered with a chuckle. "And I've seen the Flying Lady herself. If it's the same one that's on the painting, then the painting must be twenty years old. But, what the hell. I'm going to go see her act anyway. I figure it's a matter of professional courtesy. If we go see her, then maybe she'll come see our show."

"All right, I'll go with you." Eric picked up his rope. "But right now I'd better get ready for the act. I have to save the citizens of Baltimore from old Cephus." Cephus was the "half-blind old steer" Bodine had been talking about.

"I saw some kids petting Cephus this afternoon," Ben said. "I wonder how frightened everyone'd be if they knew the 'wild bull' charging them every evening is as tame as a housecat."

"Well, we mustn't tell them," Eric said. "What is it Mr. Cody says? Oh, yes: 'Let the public have their illusions; they're paying for it.'"

A few minutes later Eric was sitting his horse just outside the entrance into the arena. Inside the tent the stagecoach "rescue" had just occurred, and one group of drovers was leaving from the other side, while another handful of cowboys were preparing to drive a small herd of cattle in from this side of the tent. It was during this drive that Cephus would "escape" and charge into the stands. As he had in St. Louis, Eric would then ride to the rescue, lassoing the "charging beast" at the last possible moment.

The difference was, in St. Louis it had all been spontaneous and real. Now it was carefully rehearsed, and, as Buffalo Bill had promised, an additional safety factor was thrown in. A rope net was always put in place just in front of the stands where Cephus would run. It wasn't obvious to the spectators, for it normally lay on the ground, but if Cephus got too far before Eric dropped a loop around his neck, two drovers would jerk on ropes attached to the net, causing it to spring up just in time to prevent the steer from doing any actual damage. So far it hadn't been necessary to activate the net. For one thing Eric hadn't missed his target, and for another Cephus would never hurt anyone. The animal had learned the trick so well, he expected to get roped. In fact Eric had to hurry to get the rope on him before he came to a complete stop of his own accord and ruined the act, which had happened a couple of times in rehearsal.

From the bandstand on the far side of the arena the musicians played a fanfare. That not only got the crowd's attention, it was also Eric's cue to get ready. The youth rode to his first mark just inside the tent, then stopped.

"Oh, there he is!" a feminine voice squealed, and Eric looked over to see a group of girls, all around fifteen or sixteen, leaning on the railing that separated the arena from the stands and waving their programs at him. "Eric! Eric, may we have your autograph?" they pleaded.

This had been happening more and more lately, and Eric was always embarrassed by all the unexpected attention of the young girls—not only here, but everywhere the show had appeared. Smiling sheepishly, he tipped his hat and told them, "Ladies, I'm afraid I don't have time to sign it right now. But after the act I'll be happy to."

"Oh, isn't he wonderful?" Eric heard one of them ask the others as he moved over to his mark. He was glad his hat hid his blushing cheeks.

Out of the arena a fan-shaped series of megaphones were mounted on a stand. The ringmaster stepped up to them, then leaned forward to shout out his announcement to the crowd.

"And now, ladies and gentlemen and buckaroos of all ages, the Buffalo Bill Wild West Show is proud to bring right here to Baltimore a genuine cattle drive. In the West, cowboys sometimes have to drive the cattle for many miles across mountain cold and desert heat, encountering dangerous Indians and wild animals. Sometimes there might be a stampede, or sometimes a bull might get away to charge the cowboys. And there's one thing the cowboys learn early: If a mad bull charges, get out of the way, because nothing on earth can stop two thousand pounds of muscle and horn!"

Eric tensed his muscles and rose up in the stirrups, waiting for the moment. He readied the rope and watched as the drovers pushed the herd across the sawdust arena.

"There he goes! Stop him! He's getting away!" one of the drovers called after a few moments, and the steer broke free, heading for the stands.

As expected, the crowd screamed. Some had seen an earlier performance, and many had heard about this part of the show, so they knew it was planned. Nevertheless, it was still one of the more exciting aspects of the show, even for them. The others, who had not seen or heard about the act, thought a bull really had escaped. For them the excitement was tinged with real fear.

But as the animal galloped across the arena, Eric suddenly realized that something was horribly wrong. This animal was the same color as Cephus, but it wasn't the steer! It was a bull—much bigger, much stronger, and much more dangerous than Cephus. And this bull really was making a mad dash for the stands!

My God! How did this happen? Eric wondered. It was St. Louis all over again, only worse, because many in the stands who knew this was all an act remained in their seats for a real close-up look at the event.

The bull crossed the arena far faster than Cephus did, and Eric was starting from much farther back than he had when he did this for the first time in St. Louis. As a result, the bull was way ahead of him, and the youth felt a sense of panic because he realized he wasn't going to get to the animal in time.

With a thunderous clattering of hooves, the bull left the arena and hit the boardwalk, a platform of planks laid down in front of the stands that allowed the spectators to reach their seats without having to walk through the horse and cow piles. In every previous show Eric's rope was around Cephus's neck by the time he'd hit these boards; this time Eric wasn't even close enough to throw his rope.

By now the people in the stands who'd seen the show before and expected the animal to be stopped began to realize that something must've gone wrong as the bull kept coming. A few even realized that this was not the tame steer they'd seen in the earlier performance.

The bull crashed through the guard railing and started up the incline. The safety net was in place at the top of the incline and, if activated, it would be able to stop the bull before he could actually get into the stands.

"Pull the net!" Eric shouted, whirling the rope over

his head and leaning forward over the neck of his horse, urging his steed at a full gallop. "Pull the net!"

The net was pulled, and it sprang up in front of the bull. The bull hit it at full speed . . . and kept going. The safety net wasn't anchored at the bottom as it was supposed to be.

By now Eric was close enough to throw his rope, even though it would be the longest toss he had ever made. The rope sailed out. But it had to travel so far that by the time it reached its quarry, the loop that remained was much too small to go over the animal's head.

Fortunately, the loop didn't have to be very large to slip down over one of the bull's horns, and that's just what it did. Eric's well-trained horse dug in its haunches. The bull kept going, jerking Eric out of the saddle and slamming him painfully onto the rough planks of the boardwalk. Rolling and skidding, Eric's face and arm picked up numerous splinters, but he held onto the rope, managing finally to wrap it around a deeply embedded steel pin anchoring the tent's guy lines to tall tent posts. It was a dangerous maneuver, for if the anchoring pin were to pull up, it would not only fail to stop the bull but also bring down the tent.

But the pin held, and the net—which, while not anchored, was still an encumbrance—helped to stop the bull. The animal had managed to climb up three rows before being curbed, but, thankfully, all three rows had been evacuated by hysterical spectators before the bull got there.

By now a number of drovers had realized that this wasn't Cephus, and they reached the animal moments after Eric had halted him. They got more ropes on the bull who, once he was securely restrained and knew it, gave up his wild fighting and turned to go peacefully with the cowboys.

The spectators, realizing that what they had just seen was real, broke into a thunderous ovation. Eric got up to acknowledge their applause; then everything started spinning and he felt himself passing out.

• • •

"How are you feeling?" Buffalo Bill asked.

Eric opened his eyes and looked around. Aware of motion, he realized that he was on a train. In fact, he was on the show train, in Buffalo Bill's private car.

"I don't know," the youth replied. "I feel fine, I guess. But I don't know how I got in here."

Buffalo Bill chuckled. "I don't suppose you *would* know that," he said, "seeing as how you were out cold."

"What happened? I mean, I remember roping the bull, but I don't remember anything after that."

"You got a skull fracture when you were jerked off your horse. It didn't bother you for a few minutes, but when it started bleeding, your brain started swelling up, and you passed out. At least, that's how the doctor explained it to me. But he assured me that all you need's a little rest, and you'll be all right in another week or two."

"A skull fracture," Eric said. He tried to laugh, then winced with pain.

"Something funny about that that I don't know about?"

"No, not really. It's just that I had one of these before. It's not a habit I particularly want to get into." He put his hand to his forehead. "How long has it been?"

"Thirty-six hours," Buffalo Bill said.

"Thirty-six hours! You mean I've been out for that long?"

"You've been in and out—though I'd say more out than in. This is the first time you've been able to talk . . . or I should say make any sense. So I guess you're all right now."

"I feel fine," Eric said.

"Good. Now, since you're conscious, I don't have to put off any longer what I think you have a right to be a witness to."

"A witness? A witness to what?"

"You'll see." Buffalo Bill walked to the door and

opened it. "Go get Bodine," he said to whoever was just outside. "Tell him I want to see him—right now."

The showman closed the door, then came back over and sat down. He looked at Eric. "I have to take some of the blame for what happened to you, son," he said. "You see, when I hired you, I was thinking of the good of the show. I knew that your heroics would play well if we could find some way to manage it. And I thought we had, by letting you rope a tame steer. That way the crowd would be frightened, but there'd be no danger."

"Yes. Only, that wasn't Cephus," Eric said.

"I know it wasn't. And the net wasn't anchored, either. I hate to think what would've happened if you hadn't gotten your rope around him."

"I was lucky."

"Maybe. But you also kept your head, and I've noticed that God sort of pushes a little more luck toward folks who keep their head in a crisis. You know that Bodine caused the trouble, don't you?"

"Bodine?"

"I'm afraid so. I didn't want to believe it at first, but a couple of the drovers told me what happened. By the way, there was another safety net, a second one in place. Did you know that?"

"No, sir."

"Neither did I. It seems Bodine's idea was to let the bull get to the second net before it was stopped. Then, I believe, I was supposed to decide that your act was too dangerous. I would get rid of you and use Bodine in a Great Train Robbery act."

"Ben mentioned that act. What is it exactly?"

"It's Bodine's idea, which he claims is based on a true incident. It seems that a few years back he worked as a private guard for a railroad. One night, when there was a very large shipment of money going through Wyoming, a couple of cowboys tried to rob it. There were three of them, actually. Two of them were killed, but the third one escaped."

Eric's head suddenly began to pound. "And . . .

Bodine was involved in that?" he asked in a small, strained voice.

"That he was. He has the newspaper clippings and the commendation from the railroad to prove it. Oh, I have to confess, a re-creation of the train robbery would be a good show. According to Bodine, he and two of the robbers shot it out. The third robber turned tail and ran."

"Where did this robbery take place?" Eric asked.

"It happened on the Chicago, Burlington, and Quincy Line, just west of Newcastle, Wyoming," a new voice answered, pushing into the conversation. The speaker was Bodine, arriving from his summons. "You wanted to see me, Mr. Cody?" he asked.

"Yes," Buffalo Bill replied. He nodded toward Eric. "As you can see, Mr. Bodine, Eric is recovering."

"Glad to see you're coming out of it all right, Twainbough. Of course, you and I haven't exactly been friends, but that doesn't mean I wish you bad luck."

"Mr. Bodine, I have a few questions I would like to ask you about the performance the other night," Buffalo Bill started. "Why did you—"

"Excuse me, Mr. Cody," Eric interrupted, "but I'd like to know some more about that train robbery."

"Maybe you'd like to read about it in the papers," Bodine said. "I have a scrapbook."

"Where did the reporters get the story?"

"What do you mean?"

"Well, they weren't there, were they? I mean, did they actually see the attempted holdup?"

"No, of course not. But they interviewed me right afterward." He grinned. "I saved a half-million dollars that night. You might say they were more than anxious to talk to me."

"Then you can just tell me the story," Eric said. "Since it came from you anyway."

"Well, there's not much to it, I guess," Bodine said. "But I got word that a gang was going to try and rob the train sometime that very night."

"How did you hear that?"

"Oh, I had my secret sources. Of course, nobody else knew about it, so I realized I was going to be pretty much on my own. I hid myself in the mail car, ever alert to the slightest trouble. Then, when the train came to a stop, I sneaked out the window on the back side of the car."

"The robbers stopped the train?"

"No. They were waiting for it to stop at a water tank. Anyway, I sneaked out the window and climbed onto the top of the car. The robbers pounded on the door till it was opened, then they just started blazing away, shooting at anyone and everyone inside the car. 'Hold it!' I called down to them. 'Throw down your guns!' To my surprise, even though I had the drop on them, they turned their guns on me and started blazing away. I stood up on that car and fired back, even though I could feel the wind of the bullets passing by my head. I got two of them, but the third one got away."

"I see," Eric said, his voice flat. "What kind of gun were you using?"

"A handgun, a Colt .44," Bodine replied. He looked puzzled, then he turned toward Buffalo Bill. "Look here, Mr. Cody, why is Twainbough asking me all these questions? You aren't planning on letting him be a part of my train robbery act, are you?"

"No—"

"I should think not."

"—because you won't be doing a train robbery act," Buffalo Bill went on. "In fact, you won't be doing anything at all for me anymore. You're fired, Mr. Bodine. And if I weren't afraid that the news would be bad for the show, I would have you put in jail for what you did the other night."

"I don't know what you're talking about."

"You changed animals in Eric's act. You took Ce-phus out of the herd and put that bull in. Or are you going to deny that?"

"No, I did that. But I can explain it," Bodine said defensively. "Cephus had eaten some bad feed. His stomach was so swollen up that we couldn't use him. I had to get a substitute. I didn't know the one I got would be that dangerous. Anyway, I did rig up a second safety net, just in case. No one would've been hurt."

"And the first safety net? Why wasn't *it* anchored?"

"Now, I don't know anything about that," Bodine said. "It's not my job to anchor it. That's Ben's job. He's the one you should get on to."

"Ben said he *did* anchor it."

"Ben's a lair."

"You want to call him that to his face?" the showman asked.

"All I know is, it wasn't anchored, was it? And Ben was the one who was supposed to do it."

"You were seen in that area, after Ben anchored the net," Buffalo Bill said, his voice cold.

"I'm part of the show," Bodine protested. "I'm all over the place."

"Not anymore." Buffalo Bill pulled out his watch and looked at it. "This train will stop in Newport News, Virginia, in about nine minutes. You'll be getting off there."

"Newport News? Where the hell is that? I've never even heard of the place."

"No need you should have. It isn't very large."

"It's the middle of the night," Bodine complained. "What am I supposed to do in Newport News, Virginia, in the middle of the night?"

"Mr. Bodine, that is your problem. You now have about eight minutes. If you're planning on taking anything with you, you'd better get started packing right now."

"You can't do this to me, Cody," Bodine yelled. "You can't put me off in the middle of the night, in the middle of nowhere like this."

"Oh, yes I can, and I will. Now you have seven minutes."

Letting out a growl of anger and frustration, Bodine turned and left Buffalo Bill's private car to hurry back to get his things. Buffalo Bill laughed at his speedy departure, then glanced over at Eric. There were tears in Eric's eyes.

"Eric, lad, what is it? What's wrong?"

"Bodine didn't have any advance warning about that train robbery," Eric said. "He lied about that, just the way he lied about everything else. He didn't have any advance warning because not even the train robbers knew they were going to rob it until just before it happened. You see, they didn't know anything about the half-million dollars. They thought they were going to get a couple hundred, that's all. And Bodine wasn't using a handgun, Mr. Cody. He was using a shotgun. And it wasn't a gunfight, at least, not like he said. Bodine was waiting inside the mail car, in the dark, and the moment the door was opened, Bodine opened fire. Without even the slightest warning he started blazing away. Poor old Marcus and Jake never had a chance."

"My God," Buffalo Bill breathed. "You . . . you were there, weren't you?"

"Yes, sir. I was the third robber—the one who ran," Eric admitted.

"Ah, Loomis, there you are," William Bateman said, answering the knock on his front door. "Right on time, I see."

"You said you wanted me to drive you somewhere at two o'clock," Loomis Booker replied, standing slightly aside to allow the chancellor to exit.

"Yes, yes, so I did. But come in first, won't you? There's someone in here I want you to see."

Professor Bateman led Loomis into the living room, and the janitor was pleased to find Bob and Connie Canfield sitting on the sofa. They stood up, and Bob quickly walked over to Loomis.

"Hello, Mr. Booker," Bob said, grinning.

"Hello, Loomis," Connie added.

"Why, Mr. and Mrs. Canfield," Loomis replied, smiling broadly at each of them and then shaking Bob's extended hand. "I didn't know you two were in St. Louis."

"Yes, Connie and I came up for the ceremony."

"The ceremony? Oh, you're referring to the plaque honoring Mr. Perkins, aren't you? What a terrible tragedy, to lose that fine young man that way."

"Yes, it was," Bob agreed, his smile replaced by a look of sadness. "By the way, did you know that *The Chronicle* is endowing a school here at Jefferson, in Terry's memory? It'll be called the Perkins School of Journalism."

"I heard that," Loomis said. "I also know that it will be the only school of journalism in the country. That's quite a honor for Jefferson University, don't you think?"

Professor Bateman chuckled. "Well, we had to put in a new school, you understand, Loomis, just so we could say that we had a course here that you haven't completed."

Loomis grinned. "Maybe I'll get started on it," he suggested.

"No," Professor Bateman said. "No, I don't think you will, Loomis. I'm afraid you're going to find yourself much too busy."

Laughing, Loomis said, "Yes, sir, you're right. With the baby coming on, I expect that the responsibilities of being a father will be taking up a lot more of my time."

The professor smiled knowingly, then said, "Oh, before we go anywhere, why don't we go into the library for a moment?"

Professor Bateman ushered his guests into the library, and Loomis was surprised to find several other people there, including professors from the university, several members of the Board of Regents, and the university glee club. There were also three very distinguished-looking black men whom Loomis had never seen before. He realized that this must be the ceremony honoring Terry Perkins, though he was surprised that it would be held here rather than, as he had thought, in Spengeman Hall. He knew that was where the plaque was actually mounted, because he had personally mounted it.

Everyone fell silent as the professor stepped to a small podium, and Loomis walked over to the side of the room to be out of the way.

"Almost ten years ago," Professor Bateman began, addressing the assemblage, "a young man applied to me for a position on this campus. I thought perhaps he was too young for the job, but there was something about him, even then, that made me decide to give him a chance. I'm certainly glad that I did, for never in the history of this institution has anyone made better use of the time spent on these hallowed grounds. For this young man, in addition to performing all the duties incumbent with his position, began a program of self-study, and without hope of any reward, learning only for the sake of learning, he mastered every course of instruction offered at Jefferson." He turned to look over at Loomis. "Loomis Booker, I do believe you are improperly dressed."

"I beg your pardon, sir," Loomis asked, confused by the professor's address and surprised by the remark addressed directly to him, here in front of all these distinguished guests.

"I said you are improperly dressed," Professor Bateman repeated. "But I think I can take care of that. Pearl? Pearl, would you bring that jacket up here, please?"

Puzzled by his wife's presence, Loomis watched as Pearl came in from one of the other rooms, carrying a blue jacket over her arm.

"Pearl, if you would, just stand here by me for a moment," the chancellor instructed. Focusing on Pearl's face, Loomis saw that she was beaming with more happiness and pride than he had ever seen. He began to get a funny feeling in his stomach.

"Loomis Booker," Professor Bateman went on. "By authority of the Board of Regents, and in response to a petition circulated in your behalf and signed by every faculty member and every student as well as a significant percentage of the alumni of this university, I hearby confer upon you the degree of Litterarum Humaniorum Doctor—Doctor of Humanities. The courses you have taken on your own have now been officially entered into the school's records, to be reflected there for all time. By this act you are entitled to be addressed by the title accompanying said degree and hereafter shall be accorded all the respect, rights, and privileges so attendant. Congratulations, Dr. Booker. Now, Pearl, if you will kindly get our newest L.H.D. properly dressed . . ."

Pearl walked over to her husband and held out the garment she had been carrying—the school blazer with the gold-embroidered crest. Loomis took off his jacket and slipped into this one, and as he did so, the glee club began singing "Golden Leaves on Jefferson Ground."

Loomis's eyes began to burn, and a lump rose in his throat. Looking at the floor, he blinked several times. Pearl put her arms around him and he pulled her close to him. Her mouth was right beside his ear when she whispered, "Don't be embarrassed about crying, baby. Look around you. There's isn't a dry eye in this room."

At the conclusion of the music everyone applauded; then they formed a long line in order to file by and offer their congratulations. As each person shook his hand, Loomis saw that Pearl was right: Nearly everyone had red-rimmed eyes filmy with tears. It wasn't until the line had completely passed that Loomis learned who the three Negro men were and why they were here.

"Dr. Booker," one of the men explained, "I am Felix Turner, and these are my associates, Troy Hampton and Dion Robinson. We are here on behalf of Lincoln University. Have you heard of our school?"

"Yes, I have," Loomis said. "It's a Negro university in Jefferson City."

"That is correct. How would you like to teach there, Dr. Booker? We could put you on our staff with a full professorship, starting with the fall term."

"A *full professorship?*" Loomis looked over at Professor Bateman. "Sir, did you hear that?"

"Yes, I did hear it . . . Professor Booker."

"How about it, Dr. Booker?" Turner asked.

Loomis looked at Pearl, and Pearl—tears of happiness streaking down her face—was nodding yes. Loomis smiled broadly and stuck out his hand toward the three men.

"Gentlemen," he said, "you have just hired a new professor. Oh, by the way, what will I be teaching?"

Turner, Hampton, and Robinson looked at each other, then laughed.

"Why, Professor Booker," Turner said, "from what I hear about you, it doesn't really matter, does it?"

"Not a bit," Loomis answered, laughing with them. "Not one little bit."

"I'm so pleased that the school finally recognized Mr."—Bob corrected himself—"that is, *Dr*. Booker. I didn't think the Board of Regents would ever go along with it." Bob, Connie, and Professor Bateman were alone in the professor's parlor later that evening. It had been a full day, beginning with Loomis Booker's special graduation ceremony and ending with the dedication of the plaque to Terry Perkins's memory. The visitors, including the three emissaries from Lincoln University, were gone, and once again the chancellor's home was quiet.

"Well, the board would have never allowed Loomis to graduate with a class," Professor Bateman said. "But it doesn't matter. The degree is just as valid, whether he walked through with one hundred and fifty other students or even had it mailed to him. I just hope Lincoln University knows what a good man they're getting."

"If they don't, they'll soon find out," Bob said.

"I wonder if they could use another person on their staff," Professor Bateman mused. He lit his pipe and began puffing until his head was encircled by a wreath of blue, aromatic smoke.

"Who do you have in mind?" Connie asked.

"Me."

"You? But, Daddy, why?"

The professor puffed quietly for a moment before he answered. "You see, everything we did today was a sham. Oh, I don't mean granting Loomis his degree was a sham—that was real enough, all right. But the rest of it, installing a plaque to honor Terry Perkins and accepting a grant for a school of journalism . . . that was all for naught. I'm not even sure I can open the doors when the fall terms starts next month."

"Daddy!"

"Why do you say that, Professor?" Bob asked.

"Quite simply, we are out of money."

Bob laughed. "You're always out of money. I seem to remember there was even some question as to whether *my* class was going to graduate."

"This time we really are out of money," Professor Bateman said.

"But I thought you were going to make it," Connie said. "Enrollment is starting to come back up, isn't it?"

"Oh, yes," Professor Bateman agreed. "Yes, it is. And I think we could have made it, if we hadn't been robbed."

"Robbed?"

Professor Bateman told them of the mismanagement and embezzlement of Jefferson University's funds, describing in great, agonizing detail how that had sealed the school's doom.

"I tried," he went on. "I robbed from Peter to pay Paul, sometimes from Paul to pay Peter, and sometimes I didn't pay at all. By using every trick in the book, I've managed to keep the doors open, but unless we get a lot of money from somewhere, we won't be able to open them next year. That's why I'm particularly glad we were able to give Loomis his degree now. All his study and work would be lost anywhere else. We were uniquely positioned to understand what he had accomplished and to afford him an opportunity to capitalize on his efforts."

"How much would it take to keep the school open?" Bob asked.

"It's not just keeping it open, Bob. It's having enough funds to survive. I can open it on the money we received from advance tuition, but that wouldn't last as far as Christmas. No, to open the doors and really survive we would need at least one and a half million dollars."

Bob gave a low whistle. "That's a lot of money," he said. "But then, who am I to talk? I need three quarters of a million myself."

"Oh? I thought your crisis was over," Professor Bateman said. "I thought you had decided to drain just a few acres at a time."

"Yes," Bob said, grimacing. "But Boyd McMullen has added a new twist. He's buying up all the land he can, and he's starting his own drainage system. Unfortunately, he's designing it in such a way that it will completely alter the water flow of the entire bootheel. The other landowners will be forced to either sell their land to him or use his network of canals to drain their own land. That not only means paying him a tariff, it also means he can cut anyone off anytime he wants to. No, I'm afraid I have no choice now. I have to come up with enough money to put the entire network in, all at once."

"Have you tried any of the other banks?"

"Yes. You see, the drainage system I devised takes into consideration the natural flow of water, which means that everyone would be able to connect with it. At least one of the natural streams—the Little River, Wolfhole Creek, and St. John's Bayou—touches every section of land in the bootheel. I thought I might be able to use that as a point in my favor when I borrowed money, but it didn't work. I still don't have enough drained land to use for leverage."

"What about the Puritex company?" Professor Bateman asked. "Oh, by the way, you'll be pleased to know that I am now eating Corn Toasties for my breakfast. They're on the shelves in nearly all the groceries in St. Louis."

Bob smiled. "If they were on the shelves in all the stores in places like Chicago, Denver, and New York as well, we wouldn't be having a problem. Right now we can't afford to advertise, and Corn Toasties is still pretty

much a local item. And as for borrowing against Puritex,
the company's building and equipment is already mort-
gaged to the hilt. I couldn't get another cent on it
without facing the danger of having the operation completely closed down. I can't take that chance. I made a
promise to the men who work there, who depend upon
it for their livelihood, that I'd keep the plant going. No,
Professor Bateman, I'm afraid I'm going to have to find
some other way to come up with the money."

Professor Bateman smiled. "I'll tell you what I'll do,
Bob. Instead of trying to raise one and a half million, I'll
try to raise three. You know what they say The first
million is the hardest. Once I have that, two more
should be easy."

"Right," Bob said. "I'll do the same thing. Hell, why
don't we just skip the first million and start with the
second?"

Though the feeling was bittersweet, all three of
them laughed.

"David, are you absolutely certain that this is what you
want?" Anna Rosenstein asked.

"Are you trying to change your mind now?" David
Gelbman asked back. "Because if you are, I want to
know about it. After all, I paid good money to have the
matchmaker arrange this marriage for me, so if you're
trying to call it off, I'll just go see her and ask for my
money back. And not only that, I've hired musicians and
a *badchen*."

"You've hired a merrymaker?" Anna said, clapping
and laughing with delight. "David, no, you didn't, did
you?"

"And why not? If I'm to reacquaint myself with all
the ancient customs of my people, would I leave out
something so delightful as hiring a merrymaker for my
wedding?"

"Oh, David, what a wonderful, wonderful surprise,"
Anna said. Putting her arms around his neck, she kissed
him on both cheeks and then on the lips. But when he

began to return her kiss, she pulled away from him and looked up at him with laughing, dancing eyes. "No, no, no," she said. "There will be time for that later. Now we have many things to do to prepare for the wedding."

"All right. I'll let you get away with it this time. But next time you kiss, you had better be prepared to be kissed back," David warned.

"I love you, David," Anna said. "And I thank you for letting me have the marriage under a canopy."

"Anna, Jews in America also get married under a canopy," David said. "What do you think, that we're savages?"

"Well, it is good to know that not all the traditions are broken. I would like to think that when I go there, I will see something that I recognize."

David smiled. He had not yet told Anna that they wouldn't be returning to America. He had also not told his father.

CHAPTER EIGHTEEN

The words CUNARD LINES, PORT OF NEW YORK were painted in huge white letters on the sides of the Cunard Building that jutted into the Hudson River. The sign was visible not only to ships plying the waterway, but also to anyone on Twelfth Avenue, the cobblestone street that ran parallel to the river. Also visible from Twelfth was the huge black stern of a ship moored in Cunard's slip Pier 51. The name LUSITANIA arched across the curving stern and, just above the name, rippling in the breeze, flew the red, blue, and white Union Jack of Great Britain.

It was the middle of October, and the Buffalo Bill Wild West Show had completed its final engagement of the season last night. This morning Buffalo Bill had borrowed a car from the ticket agent at Madison Square Garden to drive Eric Twainbough uptown to the pier. Now, reaching the docks, he stopped the engine and pulled on the hand brake with a series of metallic clicks.

"Well, my boy, we are here," the showman said,

pointing to the ship. He pulled out his watch, checking the time. "And it's only nine-thirty. We're a half hour early."

"Better early than late," Eric replied.

Buffalo Bill chuckled. "You know, Wild Bill Hickok always used to say that. He was early for everything, and he once said that the only thing he ever wanted to be late for was his own funeral." The showman smiled sadly, then added, "It turned out he was early for that, too."

"The ship is big, isn't it?" Eric observed after a moment, looking up at the looming wall of steel that rose from the pier.

"Well, according to what they're saying, it's the biggest ship in the world," Buffalo Bill said. He smiled, adding, "The reason I know that is I read some of that promotional material you showed me. That's damn fine publicity—though I suppose some might call it hyperbole. I could use that kind of stuff for the show."

In illustrating the size of the ship in the pamphlet, the artist had done a drawing of the *Lusitania* side by side with the Great Pyramid. By comparison the Great Pyramid was small. The pamphlet also proudly proclaimed that the crew of the *Lusitania* consisted of 70 able-bodied seamen, 390 members of the engineering department, 50 cooks, assorted telegraph, telephone, and wireless operators, the band, and 350 stewards.

When the ship sailed from New York later today, the newest steward in that army would be Eric Twainbough.

Though Eric could have easily taken a taxi from the hotel this morning, Buffalo Bill had insisted on getting up early and personally driving him down to the waterfront. Eric knew that the showman was sorry to see him go, and he suspected that part of Buffalo Bill's reason for driving him was the chance to try to talk Eric into staying with the show.

Sure enough, Buffalo Bill began pleading his case. "You know, Eric, if you're getting tired of your act, I'd be more than willing to change it. I hate losing you. A lot of people come to see you perform—especially the young ladies," he quipped. "Wouldn't you like to stay with us? Maybe just one more year?"

"I appreciate the offer, but I have this itch to be moving on," Eric answered. "But, Mr. Cody, I want you to know that I've really enjoyed being with the show. The act was fun, and all the people I worked with were great." He thought of Bodine, then amended his statement. "Almost all the people."

"Yes, Bodine," Buffalo Bill said. "Eric, I hope you don't think that because you told me about what happened in Wyoming that you have any reason to be worried."

"No, no, it isn't that, Mr. Cody," Eric said quickly. "I'm not worried about that at all. If I didn't think I could trust you, I never would've told you about it."

Cody nodded. "Good. Anyway, you aren't the only one with secrets. I've got a few myself. In fact, I guess there aren't many men who'd really want all of their past exposed. But if that's not it, and if you really did enjoy the show and the people, why are you leaving us?"

"It's the adventure of it. I want to go to sea because it's something I've never done before."

"The adventure?" Buffalo Bill frowned. "Son, it seems to me like you've already had more adventure than most men could handle in a lifetime. And you're barely eighteen."

"Maybe so," Eric said. "But think about your own life. You were a Pony Express rider, a soldier, scout, buffalo hunter, Indian fighter, and a showman. I figure if there's anyone in the world who would understand why I have to go, it'd be you."

Buffalo Bill shook his head knowingly, then smiled. "Well, I reckon you've got me pegged right, partner. I always did have a hankering to see what was on the other side of the next mountain." He reached over and took Eric's hand. "Good luck to you, son. And think about me from time to time. I wouldn't want you to forget me."

"Are you kidding? Who could ever forget Buffalo Bill?"

The ship's horn let out a long, deep blast, and Eric

looked at the vessel through the windshield. High up on the deck he could see some men standing, their arms resting casually on the railing, as they looked down at the dock. He felt a little thrill of anticipation, knowing that soon he would be one of those men. He reached into the back of the car for his kit bag.

"I guess I'd better be going," he said. "They're already beginning to board the passengers, and they may need some more help."

"*Vaya con Dios,*" Buffalo Bill said as Eric stepped out of the car.

Eric saluted the old showman, then hurried away from the car. He had already been given directions as to where to go, and he could scarcely contain his excitement as he passed under an arch that read, "Crew Boarding Only." A half-dozen or so other men were ahead of him, and as they stepped up onto the gangplank, an officer checked them aboard.

"This is for crew boarding," the officer said when Eric drew even with him.

"I am crew, sir," Eric said. "I just signed on."

"Did you now? And what would your name be, lad?" the officer asked, turning to another page.

"Twainbough, sir. Eric Twainbough."

"Aye, here's your name. Do you have your seaman's papers and boarding orders?"

"Oh, uh, yes, sir," Eric said, remembering then the papers he was supposed to produce as he boarded. He handed them to the officer.

The man looked at them and smiled. "First time then, is it?"

"Yes, sir."

"Well, you started at the top, my boy. The *Lusitania* is the newest and the finest vessel afloat. When you get aboard, lay aft to the ship's office. They'll give you your assignment. Step to, now, lad. Step to."

When Eric reached the top of the gangplank, he turned to look back toward the parking place where he had been just moments earlier. He was a bit surprised to see that Buffalo Bill was already driving away, only the

back of the car visible as it bounced over the uneven
cobblestones. He waved, and then because he felt a little
sheepish about it, he jerked his hand down and looked
around to make certain no one had seen him. He knew
that Buffalo Bill hadn't seen the wave, but then he hadn't
been waving at Buffalo Bill. He was waving good-bye to
a chapter of his life.

The crew's gangplank was just one boarding ramp onto
the *Lusitania*. Several other long, inclined planes
stretched from great yawning maws in the hull down to
the receiving gates, where the passengers were lined up
for embarkation. The steerage and third-class ramps, not
much different from the crew's access, were narrow,
steep, bare things on which shabbily dressed people
trudged toward the doors that opened into the dark
bowels of the ship. These passengers appeared to be
immigrants returning to the Old Country—some because they missed their homelands too much, some
because they thought they'd be escaping poverty by
coming to America only to find themselves mired even
more deeply into it and so chose to return. The second-
class ramp was only marginally nicer.

However, the first-class ramp hinted at the elegance
to be found on board for those travelers who could
afford it. Much wider than the others, this ramp was
carpeted in red and covered with a long, blue canopy. At
the head of the ramp the passengers stepped into a
well-lighted grand salon sparkling with crystal chandeliers, marble columns, and walls decorated with
lacquered-gold bas-reliefs.

The boarding ramps were striking symbols of the
caste system that would prevail during the Atlantic
crossing—as well as of the shipboard facilities themselves. Ninety percent of the passengers boarded the
ship by way of one of the narrow lower-class ramps,
which, though not very crowded on the ship's eastern
transit, would be packed, barely able to handle the
hundreds of desperate people shoving and shouting and

fighting their way on board when the ship made its journey to America. The first-class ramp, on the other hand, was large enough to handle as many people as all the other ramps combined, though it was used by only a few well-dressed, well-heeled voyagers.

Standing at the foot of the first-class ramp, the purser checked his passage book very carefully as each passenger boarded. As one middle-aged couple stopped in front of him, the purser gave them a practiced and professional smile. He had been in this position for a long time, and he could tell much about a person just by observation.

The man and woman before him now were obviously well off—not rich, but well off. Though he had not yet heard them speak, and though they were dressed like typical affluent Americans, there was something about their appearance—something almost indefinable—that made the purser believe that they had immigrated to this country when they were younger. The man, he thought, had probably arrived a few years before the woman.

In a voice having exactly the right blend of snobbery and subservience, he greeted them, "You are Mr. and Mrs. Gelbman from St. Louis?"

"Yes," Mr. Gelbman answered. "I am Chaim, this is my wife, Golda."

"And your destination, Mr. Gelbman?"

"What? You don't know where this ship is going?"

"Chaim!" Golda scolded.

The purser laughed appreciatively. "Of course I do, sir. This ship will be docking in Southampton in just over five days. I meant your ultimate European destination. Please understand, I am not just being nosy, but if your destination is beyond England, your passport must be placed in the 'pass-through' file."

"Oh, yes. Well, then, from England we will take the boat train to the Continent," Chaim replied. "My wife and I are going to Vienna."

"To the wedding of our son," Golda added proudly. "And to meet the lovely young woman who is to be our daughter-in-law. Our son, David, is American, born in this country. But for now he is managing a fine department store in Vienna—my husband's cousin, who owns the store, has written us, informing us that David has done a very good job—and the girl he is to marry is from there."

"You sound as if you are surprised that David is doing a good job," Chaim remarked. "And why are you telling this officer all this? Did he ask, 'Is your son getting married? Have you met the girl? Does he do well in his job?' No he did not ask. 'Where are you going?' he asked. And I told him we are going to Vienna."

"And what does it hurt to say a few nice things about our son?" Golda wanted to know.

The purser smiled. "I am very pleased to hear of your son's good fortune," he said. "And, on behalf of Cunard Line, I would like to wish you a most pleasant voyage. Please, do call upon me if you have any problems during the trip. And, Mrs. Gelbman, my congratulations to your son."

"Do you see?" Golda said to Chaim as they started up the canopied gangway. "That nice man was very pleased to hear such things."

The *Lusitania*'s voyage was problem free, and veteran ocean travelers insisted that it was the most pleasant crossing in years. The sea was as smooth as a lake, the days were crystal-blue, and the nights were clear and bright. The ship, which was only a month old, was one of the new breed of oceangoing leviathans, exceptionally stable and equipped with a steam-turbine engine capable of record-setting speed.

Chaim and Golda Gelbman docked in Southampton five and one-half days out of New York, then took the boat train, again traveling first class, across the channel and through France, Germany, and finally into Austria. Four days later their train pulled into the Westbahnhof in Vienna.

Waiting for them at the railroad station, David

quickly settled them in the carriage he had brought and asked, "Did you have a good trip, Papa?"

"Yes, although the ship was better than the train," Chaim answered. "On the train, too often the cars suddenly jerked, and we stood on the tracks and waited for sometimes an hour or more—but for what we never knew." He shook his head. "The *Lusitania* is certainly much more comfortable than the small wooden boat I traveled on when first I went to America."

David smiled. "Yes, but you went to America in steerage. You came back first class. Don't you perhaps think that may have made a difference?"

"Of course. But even the steerage passengers today have it far better. Don't even ask about steerage on those little boats."

"David, the purser—such a nice man—sends you his congratulations," Golda said.

"Oh, he does?" David replied. "Well, that's nice."

"And have you forgotten the congratulations of the rest of the ship?" Chaim gently chided. Then to David, "You know your mama, David. She must share her news with everyone. The passengers in the cabin, the walkers on the decks, the waiters in the dining hall even, they all know of your wedding."

"So?" she retorted. "The wedding is not such a wonderful thing that I shouldn't be proud and talk about it?"

David laughed. "Mama, you can tell anyone you want about it."

Suddenly Chaim twisted around in his seat and looked back toward the railroad station, which was receding in the distance. "David, our luggage! We have forgotten it!"

"No, we haven't, Papa. It's being taken care of," David said. "Don't worry. Someone will bring it to Cousin Sarah's house."

"You have paid someone to fetch our bags all the way to the house? Such an expense! I thought you came to Vienna to show Cousin Sarah how she could make and save money, not how she could spend more."

David laughed again. "It isn't costing us anything, Papa. Friends and relatives are taking care of the luggage. It's their way of saying thank you for coming."

"Oh. Yes, this I can understand, and this is a good thing."

"Tell me about St. Louis," David said. "How are things going there?"

"The sad news about your friend, Terry Perkins, you have heard already," Chaim said.

"Yes," David answered, sighing. "I received letters from J.P. and Bob. I couldn't believe it." He shook his head. "No, that's not it. I could believe it— I just didn't want to."

"Such a nice boy," Chaim said. "I remember all those times he came to the house. He was a good writer, too. The stories he wrote, they would make you feel like you were there. It is not only us who will miss your friend, but many others as well. But I have even more sad news, I am afraid. I have heard that Jefferson University may not be able to stay open. It is a miracle that it even opened for the fall term."

"What? But, Papa, the last time I heard, they were doing very well. Enrollment was coming back up and everything. What happened?"

"A crook they hired for a business manager made bad investments and lost a lot of money," Chaim explained. "He then took the rest from the bank and left the country. It has not been reported in the newspapers, but I have heard that when the students go home for the winter break, they may not be able to come back, for there will be nothing to come back to."

"That's awful!" David declared. "Isn't there anything to be done?"

"I have made a donation, as have others who are friends of the university. But a great deal of money is needed. Professor Bateman is trying very hard to save his school, but I am afraid it is all over."

"It would be a sad day for St. Louis if that school closes," David said. "In fact, it would be a sad day for the country. I hope the professor is able to do something."

"This is enough talk of sadness," Golda insisted. "Now you must tell us about Anna, David. Is she beautiful?"

"Mama, she is the most beautiful girl in the whole world," David answered, smiling proudly. "I can't wait until you see her. In fact, I can't wait until *I* see her," he added. "She's been staying in the house of another cousin. We've been kept apart for nearly a week now."

Chaim nodded. "Many used to do that before a wedding. But it is not done so much anymore."

David laughed. "It's still done here, Papa. In fact, many of the old ways are still followed here. I even had a matchmaker make all the arrangements for me."

"A matchmaker, you say! Well, this cannot hurt," Chaim said. "There must be some wisdom in a practice that has lasted for centuries, or it would not have lasted. And tell me, do you also go to synagogue?"

David laughed. "At first I didn't, but now I do. And not only that, Papa, on the sabbath before my wedding I will be reading from the Torah."

"This is good," Chaim said. "The one sadness of my life is that perhaps I have been too busy being the businessman to give you the religious instruction you should have had."

"Don't worry about it, Papa. Believe me, since coming over here I've become very aware of my heritage."

"David, we are very proud of you," his mother said. "And I am sure we will be very proud of the wonderful girl you are marrying. I can hardly wait to show her off to all my friends back in St. Louis. An old-fashioned girl who follows all the traditions and is beautiful besides? I will be the envy of everyone."

David drew a deep breath, as if he were preparing himself to jump into very cold water. "Mama, Papa, there is something I need to tell you," he began. "And I want to tell you now, so that it's over with, and you'll have time to accept it before the wedding."

"Oh?" Chaim said, raising his eyebrows. "What is

this thing that is so terrible that you must tell it to us now, to give us time to accept?"

David took another deep breath. "Mama, I'm afraid you won't be able to introduce Anna to all your friends in St. Louis, because we won't be going back. I've bought half of Blumberg's Department Store from Cousin Sarah. Anna and I will be making our home here, in Vienna."

The air was nicely crisp, the sky was bright blue, and the Jefferson University stadium was filled to near capacity. William Bateman and Bob and Connie Canfield wove through the crowd toward the chancellor's reserved box, looking forward, along with the fifteen thousand other spectators, to the football game between Jefferson University and the University of Illinois.

Everywhere one looked on this beautiful fall afternoon there was color. The trees were ablaze with their most brilliant autumn foliage of reds, oranges, yellows, and browns; the grass on the playing field was still fresh and green; and the uniforms of the football players, who were kicking and throwing footballs to warm up for the game, added their own vivid splash of color. Illinois wore orange and blue, while Jefferson wore red and green, colors reflected throughout the stadium on both sides of the field as supporters of their teams waved pennants and crepe-paper pom-poms. The proximity of the University of Illinois to St. Louis ensured nearly as sizable a contingent of "Illini" supporters as there were "Bear" boosters, so orange and blue were as profuse as red and green.

"Okay, let's have a cheer for Jefferson U!" one of the red-and-green-clad cheerleaders shouted through a megaphone. His amplified voice floated up over the crowd as he led them through:

Victory, victory, is our cry! V-I-C-T-O-R-Y!
Are we in it? Well I guess.
Will we win it? Yes, yes, YES!

A number of the spectators, townspeople as well as students, waved at Professor Bateman as he, Connie, and Bob moved toward their seats. The chancellor waved back, and then the threesome sat down.

"Thank God we have a good football team this year," the professor said to Bob. "We've already won three games, and that brings people to the stadium to watch. They spend money for tickets and at the concession stands . . . money that goes immediately into the general revenue fund. I have to confess that this is what's keeping us going."

"Yes, but that won't last much longer," Bob said. "What will you do when football season ends?"

"I'll have no choice but to close the school." Professor Bateman laughed bitterly. "You remember when we were talking about how the second million would be easy if we could raise the first? Well, it doesn't work that way if all you have are fractions. I learned that I can raise the first three quarters of a million dollars just by borrowing against the buildings and grounds, but I can't get the rest of it."

"Why don't you take the seven hundred and fifty thousand?" Bob asked.

Professor Bateman shook his head. "No," he said. "Our accumulated debts are almost that much now. If I were to take it, it would simply go to pay the debts, leaving us nothing with which to operate. I'm afraid I'm going to have to come up with the entire amount or come up with nothing at all."

"It's ironic," Bob said. "Three quarters of a million is just what *I* need."

"I know. It's too bad that we can't figure out some way for *you* to use that money," the professor mused.

Suddenly, from below, the referee's whistle blew, and all the players except those who'd actually start the game left the field. The University of Illinois lined up to kick off, and Jefferson University deployed their men to receive. Then, just before the kickoff, the Jefferson band played "Hail Columbia," and the crowd of fifteen thousand stood in respectful silence.

The game was a dizzying swirl of action as the teams moved up and down the field. For Jefferson it ended on a satisfying note a couple of hours later, with the student body rushing out onto the field to provide a happy escort for their victorious Bears, while the orange-and-blue-clad Illinois players shuffled off, dejected and alone.

"Well," Professor Bateman said, standing and looking at his companions, "what do you say we have a celebratory dinner? We'll have to go out, of course. Since Pearl moved over to Lincoln University with Loomis, I haven't been able to afford another cook and housekeeper—which means I have to prepare my own meals, and I'm afraid I'm not very good."

"Sure, I think a victory meal is in order," Bob agreed.

By now, most of the crowd immediately around the chancellor's box had thinned out, and Bob and the professor started to leave when Bob suddenly realized that Connie was still seated. Turning, he called, "Come on, Connie."

"What?"

"Come on. We're going to celebrate."

"Celebrate what?"

"The game. We won . . . or didn't you notice?"

"Oh," Connie said distractedly. "Is the game over? I guess I didn't notice. Who won?"

"Connie?" Bob said, laughing and starting back toward her. "What's wrong with you? You've been to football games before. I thought you liked football."

"I do."

"But you sit here after one of the most exciting games in years and ask who won?"

"Honey, is anything wrong?" Professor Bateman asked.

"Nothing's wrong, Daddy," Connie said. She smiled. "I think I've just figured out a way to save Jefferson—*and* get enough money to finish the drainage project."

"Oh, really?" Bob asked with a little chuckle. "Would you mind telling us just where you're going to come up with the two and a quarter million dollars it'll take to do it?"

Connie shook her head. "Uh uh," she corrected. "We only need seven hundred and fifty thousand dollars, and we have that. At least, we can get it by mortgaging the grounds and buildings of the university."

"I'm not following you, Connie," Bob said.

"Sit down," Connie ordered. "Both of you, sit down while I try and explain this. Now, it may sound complicated, but if you think about it, it's really quite simple. Bob, could we make a gift of twenty-five thousand acres of undrained land to the school?"

"Yes, I suppose we could. But what good would that do? Twenty-five thousand acres is only worth just over thirty thousand dollars."

"Yes, now it is. But drained it would be worth almost two million, right?"

"Yes."

"That's more than enough to keep the school going. Now, suppose the university borrowed the three quarters of a million on its buildings and grounds, then loaned us the money so we could drain the land. Not just the land we gave them, but *all* the land. When the land is drained, we could easily repay the loan to the school, plus the school would now have one point eight million dollars' worth of collateral. That would be enough to open the doors again and keep them open."

For a long moment Professor Bateman and Bob just stared at Connie as if they were trying to absorb what she had said. Then Bob looked at his father-in-law.

"I hate to admit it," he said, "but I think she has a good idea."

"I agree."

"Can you really raise that much money on the school?"

"Yes, I'm quite sure I can," Professor Bateman said. "But I think I'd rather not do it here in St. Louis. If we *are* going to be doing that kind of maneuvering, it would probably be better to do it somewhere else."

"How about New York?" Connie asked. "J.P. works

for J. Pierpont Morgan. Maybe he could get us an introduction."

"Us?" Professor Bateman said.

Connie smiled coyly at them, then put her arm through her husband's. "Now, you don't really think I'm going to let the two of you go to New York without me, do you?"

"David Gelbman, are you ready now to sign the *ketubah*?" the rabbi asked.

David looked around the large room where the wedding ceremony and the wedding feast were being held. Nearly three hundred guests were present, and they were all smiling at him. On the far side of the room, sitting on a small throne, dressed in a dazzling white wedding gown, and surrounded by her attendants, Anna waited for him. In the middle of the room was a canopy, which David learned was called a *chupah*.

"Yes, I am ready," he replied.

"Your father and the nearest male relative of the bride have signed their agreement; it is now time for you to sign. You have brought two male witnesses to sign with you, neither of whom is a relative?"

"I have," David replied.

He signed the marriage license, and the two unrelated male witnesses signed as well.

After the signing the rabbi picked up a white handkerchief and held on to one end of it, signaling that David should take hold of the other end. When he did, the rabbi began to speak:

"David, by the traditions of our people, it is now my duty to represent the interests of the bride. And, in her interest, I ask now if you, before God and these witnesses, are willing to be bound by the agreements of the *ketubah*, which you have just signed? If you are, signify by saying, 'I am willing.'"

"I am willing."

The rabbi smiled. "So be it." He put the handkerchief down and made a gesture toward Anna. "And now it is time for you to go to your bride-to-be."

All the attendants, male and female, formed a circle around David and began singing as they escorted him across the great room to where Anna sat waiting for him. When David reached her, their eyes met and held, and suddenly the music, the room, and all the people disappeared. They were lost in each other's eyes and in each other's hearts, as isolated from the rest of the world as they had been on that magical night in the garden when they had first made love.

David stepped up to the throne and put his hands on Anna's veil, which for the moment was raised. Gently, he pulled it down to cover her face, symbolizing his confidence that he was getting the right woman.

His escorts now widened their circle to allow Anna inside, then ushered the couple to the canopy, where the rabbi was waiting. David was led in first by his parents. Once under the canopy he draped the white *kittel* over his shoulders, then turned and waited for Anna. Since her parents were dead, she was led to the canopy by Sarah and by Simon, her nearest male relative, who although a boy of fourteen was a man by virtue of his bar mitzvah. The youth was inordinately proud of the role he was playing today.

Stepping under the canopy, Anna, in accordance with tradition, walked around David seven times, then took her place beside him.

The two men who had witnessed David's signing of the marriage license now stepped forward again, and the rabbi told the groom, "David, in the presence of these witnesses, I call upon you to state if this ring truly belongs to you."

"It does," David answered.

"And is it a ring of true value? It has not been adulterated by false stones?"

"It is a ring of true value."

The rabbi nodded, and David took Anna's hand and placed the plain gold band on her index finger. He softly cleared his throat, then said, "Behold you are consecrated to me with this ring, according to the Law of Moses and Israel."

The rabbi then read the *ketubah* aloud and handed it to David, who gave it to Anna. Raising a cup of wine, the rabbi gave the first of his seven blessings:

"Blessed are You, O Lord our God, King of the universe, Creator of the fruit of the vine."

Finally, after the last blessing, David took a wine glass and smashed it by stamping on it. Almost before the sound of the breaking glass had died away, someone shouted, "*L'Chaim!*" Another added, "*Mazel Tov!*"

To the accompaniment of singing, laughter, and shouts of congratulations, David and his new bride were escorted to the *yichud* chamber, a small room where they were given a few moments of privacy. It was the first time they had been alone together in well over a week.

David stared at Anna. "Just how traditional do you want this wedding to be?" he asked with a baiting smile.

"What do you mean?"

"Well, I've looked up the purpose of the *yichud* chamber. It seems that in biblical times this was when the marriage was consummated through intercourse, and then the bloodstained sheet would be displayed as proof of the bride's virginity." His smile broadened. "Of course, if I can't prove you're a virgin, the marriage is nullified."

"David!" Anna gasped.

"I'll settle for a kiss," he said, laughing.

"Oh? And what makes you think I will?" Anna replied, reaching for the top button of her white gown and smiling at him with as much devilment in her eyes as had been in his a moment earlier.

"Anna!" David gasped, then laughed, realizing he had responded to her just as she had to him. In that moment he knew they were truly one.

CHAPTER NINETEEN

It was the last week in October, and it was cold when Bob and Connie Canfield and William Bateman reached New York. Hailing a cab outside Grand Central Station, they went straight from the terminal to the Hotel Victoria, which they had chosen on J.P. Winthrop's recommendation as "a good hotel at a reasonable price," with the added benefit of being only three blocks from his house. J.P. had instructed that they contact him the moment they checked in, so Bob made the call from the lobby telephone, while Connie and Professor Bateman sorted out the luggage for the bellhop.

"Have you had lunch?" J.P. asked Bob.

"No, we haven't."

"Then why don't you meet me at Sherry's Restaurant? They have the most wonderful food, and we can use the private dining room upstairs. Say, three quarters of an hour?"

"Fine. We'll see you then."

Crossing back to the others, Bob took Connie's arm as the bellhop led them into the elevator, which they took to the fifth floor. They were then ushered down a carpeted hallway to adjoining rooms.

"Forty-five minutes?" Connie complained after the bellhop had pocketed his tip and she and Bob were alone in their room. "Bob, surely you don't expect me to get ready that quickly."

"I promised him we'd make it," Bob said. "What's there to do? A little freshening up is all."

"There's more to it than 'a little freshening up,' Bob Canfield," Connie countered. She walked over to the mirror and gazed critically at herself. "Oh, just look at me! My hair is a mess."

"I think your hair is beautiful. I think *you* are beautiful," Bob said. "And you'll look fine to J.P., too. He always did think you were very pretty."

"Did he now?" Connie said, smiling as she began taking pins out to rearrange her upswept hair. "And I always thought he was handsome—so how did I wind up with you?"

"Just unlucky, I guess." Bob came up behind her and put his arms around her, then leaned down and kissed her on the side of the neck.

"Umm," she cooed, "I thought you wanted to be there in forty-five minutes."

"J.P.'s a romantic sort," Bob replied, smiling. "He'll understand."

"Daddy won't," she said, laughing and twisting away from him. After a moment she murmured, "It's too bad J.P. hasn't gotten married."

"Oh, I think maybe he's just been too busy."

"No, that's not why."

"Oh?" Bob raised an eyebrow. "Well, if you know, perhaps you'll share the reason with me."

"He's still in love with Lucinda Delacroix."

"Lucinda Delacroix? Don't you mean Lady Chetwynd-Dunleigh?"

"She may be Lady Chetwynd-Dunleigh to the rest

of the world, but I'll just bet she's still Lucinda Delacroix to J.P."

A light tap sounded on the door.

"That'll be Daddy," Connie said. "Why don't you go down to the lobby with him and wait for me there? I must at least change this wrinkled dress."

"All right," Bob agreed. "But please try to hurry."

The reunion at Sherry's was a happy one. J.P. embraced both Connie and Bob, shook hands with Professor Bateman, and then they chatted for a few moments about the trip and recent events, including David's wedding.

"The last letter I got from David said he was going to stay over there," J.P. said. "Can you see him in Vienna?"

"Yes," Bob answered. "Yes, I think I can, actually. Perhaps it was his father's influence, but I always did think of David as much more worldly than the average fellow from Missouri."

"My dear boy, *everyone* is much more worldly than the average fellow from Missouri," J.P. quipped. He sighed. "And think of poor Terry, dying from a case of yellow fever. If this had been ten years ago, I might not have been so shocked. But I thought medical science just about had that disease beaten."

"Controlled, perhaps, but not beaten," Bob said. "And the controls don't work if you don't use them. According to his mother, whom I spoke to at the funeral, Terry spent an entire week in Panama before he had the benefit of mosquito netting. During that time, he was evidently bitten by an infected mosquito, and then he didn't get treatment until too late."

J.P. shook his head sadly. After a pause he asked, "And your father? How is he doing?"

"As well as can be expected," Bob answered. "We're thankful he's been with us this long." He chuckled. "He certainly has the right attitude. He says since he figures every day is a gift, he's just going to enjoy life and leave all the work to me—such as raising the financing we need to complete the drainage project."

"Which brings us to why you've come to New York," J.P. said after taking a swallow of wine.

"Yes," Bob said. "Professor Bateman and I have a financial package we'd like to put together, and I'm not sure we could get it done in St. Louis."

J.P.'s face clouded over slightly, and he drummed his fingers on the white-clothed table for a long moment before answering. "I'm not sure you can get it done here, either," he finally said.

"What? But, J.P., when we wrote to you of our plans, you said you were sure that Morgan and Company would be able to arrange it for us."

"Yes, I know I did, and at the time of the letter I'm sure it could have been done. But something has come up, something is happening that . . . well, even I'm not sure what it is. But I do know that Mr. Morgan has been summoned back from the Triennial Episcopal Convention down in Richmond, and he's returning earlier than planned. You don't know the significance of that, because you don't know him as I do."

"I don't know him at all," Bob reminded him.

J.P. smiled. "You should. He's the most amazing man, perhaps the most powerful man in the world. He certainly has no peers in the economic world, anyway. But he does enjoy being with all the bishops, arguing ecclesiastical questions and taking himself out of the mainstream of things for a few days. That's why his coming back early is worrying me. I'm afraid this business with one of the local banks is going to end up being much more severe than anyone thought it would be."

"What's going on?" Professor Bateman asked.

"As you perhaps know, the stock market has been steadily eroding over the last several weeks. Union Pacific tried to float a seventy-five-million-dollar bond issue recently, for example, but they could sell only four million. Money is in short supply, and the economy has been dropping rather dangerously. Mr. Morgan and some other financiers have tried to warn President Roosevelt that we're on the verge of a total economic collapse if proper measures aren't taken—and taken immediately."

"But surely it isn't that bad," Bob said. "I just read that the President was down in Louisiana on a bear-hunting trip. He wouldn't go off on some adventure if there were a real crisis, would he?"

"Roosevelt can't cope with it, so he runs from it," J.P. said. Seeing the shocked look on his companions' faces, he laughed. "I know, listen to me making such pronouncements about the President of the United States and the national economy, when only a few years ago I was a mere schoolboy at dear old Jefferson. Well, what I'm saying isn't the result of my own brilliance, believe me. I'm just repeating what I've heard said by intelligent men in positions of authority, people who know what they are talking about. Then, the day before yesterday, things took a decided turn for the worse."

"What happened?" Connie asked.

"Have you ever heard of Augustus Heinze or Charles Morse?"

"I'm afraid not," she replied.

"I wish I had never heard of them," J.P. said with a sigh. "They're a couple of Wall Street traders . . . more properly, I guess, I should call them Wall Street manipulators. Anyway, with the stock market declining, they thought to take advantage of the situation. Last Wednesday, they tried to get control of United Copper. They missed, but they had a lot of exposure and, in order to meet the calls, they began using money from the Heinze Mercantile Bank. Just before noon they had to issue a call to the clearinghouse for more cash, and when the depositors heard about it, they started withdrawing their money."

"Wait a minute. You mean these two men could just take money from the bank to use however they wished?" Connie asked.

"Yes. You see, Heinze Mercantile isn't an ordinary bank, it's a trust company, and a trust company only has to keep two or three percent of the total deposits on cash reserve. The rest can be invested any way the directors wish. Sometimes it pays off well. Why, a couple of years ago, Morse captured all the ice business in the entire city. That produced fantastic profits. Not only for Morse, but for the bank, too. This time, however, his scheme backfired. His depositors started withdrawing all their money, and yesterday that bank went under." J.P. shook his head. "The fear is that that will have an effect on all the other financial institutions as well. I don't need to tell you, if people start rushing to the banks to take out their money, there's going to be chaos. All the banks will have to scramble to get more money, stocks and bonds will be cashed in at distress rates, lifetime savings and investments will be wiped out, businesses will fail, and then men will be forced out of work."

"My God!" Bob gasped. "How come nobody knows about this?"

Gone now, clearly, was any sense of disappointment Bob, Connie, and Professor Bateman had over their own problems. They were caught up in the same anxiety that J.P. was feeling.

"Well, that's just it. Panic is spreading by word of mouth from depositor to depositor, but we have to stop it here, among a few banks, before it spreads all across the nation. We could be on the verge of a total collapse. With no money or viable economic system to run the government, it could even be the end of the republic!"

"What is to be done about it?" Professor Bateman asked, worry creasing his forehead.

"I don't know, sir. I do know that I have faith in J. Pierpont Morgan. He's due back later today, and if anyone can save us, he can. He's sent out word to round up as many accountants as can be found and have them waiting at his private library, ready for service. Even though I work in his archives department, I can also do accounting, so I'm going over there."

"What about us?" the professor asked. "Our educations have included courses in accounting. Perhaps we, too, could be of service. That is, if you think Mr. Morgan would use us."

"All three of us," Connie added pointedly.

J.P. smiled. "I'm sure we could use additional volunteers. Let's finish lunch, and then come along with me over to the library. We'll wait for his return, and then I'll introduce you to my employer—as well as my distant cousin—J. Pierpont Morgan."

After their meal they walked over to the Morgan mansion, a dwelling that the visitors found hard to believe could be a private residence. Their wait for the great financier turned out to be a short one.

Morgan's entry was dramatic. When he stepped into the silk-lined West Room, two dozen people were on hand to welcome him home, then besiege him with tales of woe. The fear before he arrived had been almost palpable; now, in his presence, everyone seemed to relax, as if they were sure he would take care of things.

Looking at him, Bob decided that there was nothing about Morgan's physical appearance that could be described as appealing. He was stout to the point of being overweight, with a round face and fiercely penetrating eyes, and his most prominent feature was an unattractive one—a large, red nose. But he was a man who positively reeked of authority.

When Morgan saw J.P., he smiled. "Don't tell me my art collection is in danger, too."

"No, sir, not yet," J.P. answered. "Though if this gets out of hand, who's to say how far it might go?" He turned and gestured at the visitors, then looked back at Morgan. "I'd like you to meet some friends of mine from Missouri."

"So, you are from Missouri, are you?" Morgan asked. "It's a beautiful state, isn't it, with a wilderness so full of wild rivers, thickly forested mountains, mysterious caves, and mineral springs. As you undoubtedly know, the Mormons believe that Missouri is where the biblical Garden of Eden was located. Yet in the midst of all that pristine beauty is a modern city like St. Louis. You are quite fortunate to live there."

"Yes, sir, we like it very much," Professor Bateman said.

"What brings you to New York?"

"They're here on personal business, sir," J.P. answered for them. "But more importantly, they are all capable accountants, and they've volunteered to help."

"Can the bank situation be turned around, Mr. Morgan?" Bob asked anxiously.

"We are in no immediate danger until Monday—when the banks reopen and the public will in all likelihood start their run," Morgan answered. "If at that time the depositors insist on destroying the economy of this country, there will be nothing we can do. However, if we can convince them that their money is safe—that there are at least a few safe banks—then we might be able to stop it."

"How do you plan to convince them?"

"It won't be easy, Mr. Canfield. But between now and the time the banks reopen on Monday I am going to keep you and all the other accountants who have gathered here very busy. We're going to examine the books of every financial institution in this city. Those that are risky, we will let fail. They have only themselves to blame for their tenuous position. But what I want to do is find a bank that has consistently practiced sound financial policy. In short, I want to find a bank we can save. Find us a good defensive position, and there we will make our stand."

"Mr. Morgan, when you say go over the books of every financial institution, do you also mean those institutions that we have nothing to do with?" one of the financier's own accountants asked.

"I do indeed."

"But how will we get access to their books?"

"Simple," Morgan said, smiling. "Ask for them."

"And if they refuse?"

"If any bank refuses to show us their books, we will let them fail." Morgan pulled out his watch and looked at it. "It's now three o'clock. We have forty-two hours before the banks open Monday morning. I suggest you get busy." He turned to one of his personal accountants. "Matthew, find a place where these good people can work, and bring them a pile of books."

"Yes, sir," the man addressed replied.

"And now, if you would excuse me," he said to everyone assembled, "I am suffering a terrible cold. I think I'll go to my bedroom and try to get some rest. I had the engineer run the train at full speed all the way up from Richmond, and it was a rather tiring trip."

With that, he excused himself, while the new arrivals were ushered to seats at one of the many large tables in the massive room, joining the more than two dozen other accountants gathered there. J.P., Bob, Connie, and Professor Bateman immediately started going over the books of all the banks in the city to see which would be saved, and which would be allowed to die. It was an awesome responsibility.

"You know, this is quite an overwhelming feeling," Connie said. She, like the others, talked just above a whisper, as if they were present at a funeral. "We are playing God here, do you realize that? We are actually playing God."

"No, my dear," her father countered, glancing at the door through which Morgan had exited, "Mr. Morgan is God. At best we are angels." He sighed. "Whether we are angels of mercy or angels of death is yet to be decided."

Some five hours had passed when, at nearly eight o'clock that evening, the bookkeepers were served a light supper of soup and sandwiches. To ensure the safety of the ledgers, tables were brought in and set up for eating on, though there were not enough for everyone to interrupt work at the same time. Bob remarked that this was probably by design, to make certain that the work went on. Chuckling, J.P. said that perhaps Bob was beginning to get a feel for what Morgan was like.

Taking only catnaps, they worked through Saturday night and all day Sunday. Word came from the financier late Sunday night that everyone could go home for a while, but they were asked to be back by noon on Monday. Bob, Connie, and the professor returned to their hotel to sleep the sleep of the exhausted.

At eight o'clock the next morning, however, Bob was shaking Connie awake.

"What is it?" she asked sleepily. "What do you want?"

"I just went down for breakfast," Bob said, "and I heard that a run had started on the Knickerbocker Bank. Come on, let's go down and see it."

"Oh, Bob, that's like going to the site of a train wreck," Connie protested.

"I know. But I'd probably go see that, too," he admitted. "Are you going with me?"

Slowly sitting up in bed, Connie pushed back her disheveled hair. "I guess I should," she said. "It might give me a greater sense of urgency when we go back to work at noon."

She hurriedly bathed and dressed, then accompanied Bob to the bank several blocks away. Reaching their destination, they drew up short. The prospect of a failing bank had drawn a huge crowd, some by the spectacle of it, most by desperation. People lined the sidewalks, the cream of New York society mingling with the very common folk, all caught up in the same panic. As Bob and Connie stood there with the others, they overheard the conversations of dozens of bystanders. What seemed most incredible to these observers was that this could be happening to the Knickerbocker Trust Company—a showplace with marble walls and elegant furnishings located just across the street from the Waldorf-Astoria.

The Canfields learned that the line, several blocks long, had begun forming before sunup this morning. When the doors finally opened at nine o'clock, men and women ran shouting and screaming across the marble-tiled floor, rushing to the tellers' windows to take out their money, waving their passbooks and bank drafts.

At first the bank officials made a big show of paying, to prove that their bank was sound. Despite the fact that the tellers were paying promptly, the lines continued, even growing longer. A traffic jam developed on Fifth Avenue as numerous bejeweled women and elegantly attired men had their chauffeured automobiles and liveried carriages stop as close as they could to the bank. The occupants then went to stand in line between the ordinary laborer and the housemaid, who waited patiently to withdraw their own funds.

After a while Bob and Connie learned from people coming back out of the bank that the bank officials had suddenly changed their tactics. When they'd realized that prompt payment wasn't going to stop the rush, they instructed the tellers to find as many ways as they could to delay payment. Obeying their orders, the tellers excused themselves at every opportunity to closely examine the books or consult with one of the bank officers about a real or invented problem with an account. When they did pay, they paid in as small bills as possible, because they took longer to count. After that, they counted the money twice, once to themselves and again as they paid it out. Then they insisted that the customer count it again, in front of them. Occasionally they'd knock over a stack of coins and hold up paying until the coins were recounted and restacked.

Interspersed throughout the long lines were kids, would-be entrepreneurs who stood in line until they were close to the teller's cage. Once there, they'd auction off their place in line to the highest bidder, often getting as much as ten dollars for their spot.

As a result of all the stalling tactics, the line moved incredibly slowly. Connie discovered a rather curious way of measuring the progress of the line: Out on the street, still some distance away from the entrance of the bank, she saw a bright flash of color, a woman's hat festooned with three red-silk roses. The hat, or more specifically the poor woman under it, moved slowly, ever so slowly, toward the door. The woman finally disappeared inside the bank just as Bob announced that it was time for them to return to the Morgan library.

The couple picked up Professor Bateman at the hotel on their way. When the threesome returned to J.P. Morgan's house at noon and entered the library, they found the financier, his cigar clenched between his teeth and his eyes full of fire, stalking around the room, looking over everyone's shoulders, firing out instructions. J.P. Winthrop was already there, and when he saw his friends, he came over to greet them.

"We were down at the Knickerbocker Bank," Bob said. "I've never seen a bank panic before—and I hope I never have to see another."

"We just got word that the Knickerbocker closed its doors," J.P. said, shaking his head.

"Closed its doors?" Connie asked.

"Failed," J.P. explained.

"The lady in the hat," Connie said abstractedly. "I wonder if she made it. She waited so long and she looked so desperate."

"I don't know about your lady in the hat, but a lot of people didn't get their money out. And we heard that there's a run under way at the American Trust."

"The American Trust?" Connie's voice was filled with confusion. "But how can that be? That's one of the banks we examined most thoroughly last night. It should be sound."

"No bank is sound if there's an all-out panic," Professor Bateman stated.

"That's true," J.P. said. He then smiled. "But my esteemed cousin has made his decision: We're going to nip the trouble here by backing the American Trust. He's already authorized one transfer of funds, and he's prepared to go as far as he has to. Oakley Thorne, the chairman of the bank, brought over all their securities." He gestured across the room. "They're in those bags and cartons, and it's our job to sort them out."

"Then I guess we have some work to do, don't we?" Bob said.

"I guess we do," J.P. confirmed.

For the next few hours the accountants pored over all the securities, recording their value, then transferring them to Morgan and Company in exchange for funds. Several times during that period new funds were taken over to the bank to help hold off the run. Demands for money kept coming into the library, and Morgan continued to answer the demands, sending over huge sums to keep the bank afloat.

Even the city government of New York faced a crisis when it had to have thirty million dollars immediately, to pay off some short-term bonds. When Mayor McClellan made a personal visit to see if Morgan could help, the financier took a sheet of paper from his desk and, in longhand, wrote out an agreement to furnish thirty million dollars at six percent interest.

The constant transfer of money and securities kept everyone so busy that they worked without interruption, pausing only briefly to eat a quick snack. At one point during the afternoon Bob saw J.P.'s face go white as he read from a sheet of paper someone had handed him.

"J.P., what is it?"

"It's beginning to spread. Stocks are being dumped so fast that there's no longer any cash available for transactions. This is a message to Mr. Morgan from Ransom Thomas, president of the New York Stock Exchange. He's threatening to close the Exchange if money isn't made available immediately."

"My God!" Professor Bateman breathed. "On the heels of the bank failures, that would be an absolute disaster!"

"I guess I'd better take this in to him," J.P. said with a sigh, "although I hate to. He's already invested ten million dollars of his own money, plus underwriting thirty million for the city. I don't know what he can possibly do about this."

"Try this," Bob suggested, showing J.P. what he had been working on. J.P. saw immediately what Bob was referring to and went in to talk to Morgan. He came back a few moments later and ushered Bob into the bedroom to talk to the financier personally.

Morgan was drinking orange juice and shuffling a deck of cards. He didn't rise when they entered, but he did nod in acknowledgment. "J.P. tells me you have an idea that would support the stock market. Let me hear it."

"Yes, sir," Bob replied. He cleared his throat, then handed Morgan the paper he had shown to J.P. "According to what I've been able to ascertain from all the records, the brokerage house of Moore and Schley hold the paper for a company called Tennessee Coal and Iron Company. Now, they've used this Tennessee Coal stock as collateral for some loans—loans that are due, and Moore and Schley have no money. Not only that, Tennessee Coal has no current market, so selling that stock would not only ruin Moore and Schley, it would also ruin everyone else who holds any of the stock as collateral. It could jolt the entire market."

"That's true," Morgan agreed. "But J.P. tells me you have a solution?"

"Yes, sir. Suppose United States Steel were to take over Tennessee Coal. Moore and Schley could then substitute U.S. Steel securities for the Tennessee Coal stock as collateral on their loans. That would save their company, give the banks a legitimate collateral, and U.S. Steel would gain a valuable property."

Morgan looked at the paper for a moment, then smiled broadly. "Young man, you have a nose for business," he said. "That is a wonderful idea." Laying the paper on the table, he slammed his fist against it. "This is it," he announced. "This is where we lick it! J.P., put out a call to all the bankers on the 'financially sound' list. I'm going to come up with twenty-five million dollars of my own money to buy Tennessee Coal, and that will support the stock market. The bankers are going to have to come up with an equal amount to save the banks and trust companies. That's fifty million dollars on top of what we've already spent. That will break the back of the panic for good."

"What should I tell the bankers when I call them?" J.P. asked.

Morgan smiled. "Nothing. Don't tell them a thing. Just tell them that I have a plan to stop this, and I want them over here right now." He chuckled. "Then, by God, we'll lock the doors of the library, and none of them will leave until I have that twenty-five million."

"Sir, you don't mean actually lock the doors, do you?" J.P. asked.

"Why not?"

"Why, you'd be virtually holding them prisoner."

"Yes."

"You would do that?"

"I will do whatever it takes. Whatever it takes."

It was four-thirty in the morning. Though exhausted and though the work was now out of their hands, neither Bob, Connie, the professor, nor J.P. thought even for a moment about leaving. Connie was dozing on the leather couch near the burning fireplace. Professor Bateman was also asleep, slumped in a nearby chair. J.P. had staggered to another unused sofa on the other side of the room where he was sprawled out, also asleep. Only Bob remained awake, and he sat on the sofa, cradling Connie's head in his lap as he watched the fire and listened to the pop and snap of the burning log, squinting to soft-focus the flames.

The presidents of the banks and trusts were all still awake, too, gathered around the long conference table, drinking endless cups of coffee, and filling pages with numbers. Throughout this long night they had argued and ranted in hopeless indecision. They'd been told what was expected of them when they arrived, and one at a time they were summoned before J. P. Morgan. But they hadn't been willing to agree to Morgan's demands.

True to his word, Morgan had locked the doors of the library, as one of the bankers learned when he tried to leave at about three A.M. Seeing that Bob was still awake, the banker had come over to ask Bob to let him out. Bob replied that he didn't have the authority to do so, and, not wishing to make a scene, the banker had gone back to join the others, without telling them that they were now prisoners.

"Here's Morgan now," Bob heard one of the bankers say. Bob was amazed that the financier was awake, for he himself was exhausted, and he was young and healthy. J.P. Morgan was an old man, further weakened by a cold, and yet here he was, still going strong. Morgan stood over by the conference table, gazing intently at the bankers. Most had removed their jackets and loosened their ties, a few had even taken off their collars, and some had rolled up their shirtsleeves. Stubble was beginning to form on those who were normally clean-shaven, and everyone's eyes were puffy and tired look-ing.

By contrast, Morgan's jacket was buttoned, his collar was crisp, his tie was knotted tightly at his neck, he was freshly shaven, and his eyes were bright. If he was tired, his tiredness had robbed him of none of his dignity or intensity.

The financier began to speak, and as Bob knew that Morgan was running out of patience with the bankers, he expected to hear thunder. To his surprise there was no thunder. Instead, Morgan's voice was pleasant and warm, as if he were talking to children, and not in a patronizing way, but in a kindly, grandfatherly way.

"Gentlemen, I have talked with each of you indi-vidually, and now I put it to all of you again. I have guaranteed thirty million dollars to the City of New York; I have supported the American Trust Company with more millions; and I have personally raised twenty-five million dollars to save Moore and Schley, thereby supporting the stock market. What I need from you . . . no, what this *nation* needs from you —indeed, what civilization as we know it needs from you . . . is a matching twenty-five million dollars to be available for the trust companies."

Morgan's voice hardened slightly. "Gentlemen, no doubt you truly believe that you are doing right by your shareholders, that by stubbornly refusing to guarantee this money, you are protecting their interests as they have entrusted you to do and have elected you to do. 'How can I be so cavalier with such great sums?' you are asking yourselves. 'How can I risk money that isn't mine?' Well, gentlemen, with all due respect to your integrity and your acumen, I assure you that should you continue in this vein, you will be personally responsible for this country's certain economic collapse."

Morgan waited a moment for the point to sink in, then walked over to Ed King, the leader of the trust company committee. Putting a subscription form in front of the banker, he said, "There's the place to sign, King. And here's the pen."

King hesitated but finally took the proffered pen and signed. Then another banker signed and then another, until at last every banker present had signed the agreement, pledging that they would raise twenty-five million dollars. It was just after five A.M. when Morgan signaled that the library door could be unlocked.

"Gentlemen, you look tired," he said. "Go home and get some rest. But don't forget to be in your offices by nine o'clock. You have much work to do."

Their spirits clearly raised now by the fact that a decision had finally been made and definite action taken to end the crisis, the bankers began to file out, each in turn stopping to shake J. Pierpont Morgan's hand.

Remaining on the sofa by the fire, Connie's head still resting in his lap, Bob looked across the great, dimly lit room at Morgan, and he felt as he believed he would have had he been looking into the face of George Washington or Abraham Lincoln or perhaps, even, Moses. He had never felt a greater sense of awe, respect, and pride in his life than he felt at this moment.

A gas pocket in one of the logs popped loudly, and Morgan, who now stood alone at the door, turned toward the fireplace and obviously just then noticed, with some surprise, that Bob was awake. The financier walked across the big room, smiling.

"So, you are the watchman?" he asked.

"Yes, sir, I guess I am," Bob replied.

Unexpectedly, Morgan began to sing softly:

> Watchman, tell us of the night,
> What its signs of promise are
> Traveler, o'er yon mountain's height,
> See that glory-beaming star.

"That's a pretty song," Bob said.

"It's an old Episcopal hymn."

"Oh? Well, it's too bad Connie isn't awake. She's Episcopalian. She'd probably recognize it."

Morgan gazed at Connie for a long moment, then, unexpectedly, reached down and stroked her hair. His eyes were big and shining and seemed to have greater depth than any eyes Bob had ever looked into.

"Son, I don't want you to get the wrong idea about me," Morgan said

"I beg your pardon?" Bob asked.

"I'm not a hero."

"How did you—" Bob interrupted himself in midquestion. He was about to ask how Morgan knew what he had been thinking, but it was obvious how Morgan knew. It was on Bob's face. Instead Bob said, "But you *are* a hero. You saved the entire economy of the United States tonight. They'll be reading about you in the history books in the next century the way we read about people like Washington and Jefferson and Lincoln now."

"I suppose they will," Morgan said. "And if they are honest about it, well, I'm willing to accept their judgment. I just don't want history to put me down as a neither-nor."

"I don't know what you mean."

"I'm neither a hero nor a great robber baron. And while it's true that we've probably saved the banking system and the stock market by what we did here, it should not go unnoticed that I have also managed to turn it to my own advantage—due in no small measure to your efforts, I might note." He grinned. "Yes, indeed, Tennessee Coal and Iron is going to be an extremely valuable property over the next few decades." Chuckling, he added, "Longer than I have left, that's for certain."

Folding his arms across his ample chest, Morgan glanced over at J.P., still sleeping on the other sofa, then looked back at Bob. Finally he said, "My weary young cousin over there has told me that I may be able to help you with a problem of your own."

"I sincerely hope so," Bob replied.

"Tell me about it."

Briefly, Bob explained his idea of draining the swamps to recover the nutrient-rich agricultural land that lay underneath. He also told the financier about Jefferson University's monetary problems.

"You obviously have some plan in mind," Morgan said, "or you wouldn't have come here."

"Yes, sir, we do have an idea," Bob confirmed, then told how the school wanted to borrow against its buildings and grounds and then lend that money to Bob against a pledge of twenty-five thousand acres. With that money, Bob would drain all the land, making the twenty-five thousand acres valuable enough to guarantee a loan to the school for one and a half million dollars.

Morgan pulled out a cigar and lit it while he listened attentively to the problem and to Bob's recommended solution. When Bob had finished, Morgan studied him for a long moment over the end of his cigar, squinting through the smoke that curled up from the tip.

"All right," he said. "I'll finance the entire proposal at six percent interest. And you don't have to wait until the twenty-five thousand acres are drained for me to underwrite the university's participation. All I want is a second mortgage against the property."

Bob cleared his throat. "Uh, Mr. Morgan, that's two and a quarter million dollars."

"Yes, I guess it is," Morgan said. He smiled broadly. "But son, with all the money we've come up with this night, I wouldn't be surprised if you didn't find that much just lying around in a corner somewhere."

Bob grinned with pleasure.

"By the way," Morgan continued, "your idea of cross-collateralization between the school and your farm is a brilliant one. You should be congratulated for that."

"That was my idea," Connie suddenly spoke up, not opening her eyes.

"Your idea?" Morgan asked.

"Yes," Bob admitted. "I have to confess that it was." He looked down at Connie. "I didn't know you were awake."

"So you were going to take the credit, were you?" she asked, her smile showing that she was only teasing. She sat up and smoothed her skirt, then addressed the financier. "Mr. Morgan, I want to thank you for your help. I'm afraid my husband and my father were about at their wit's end."

"Young lady," Morgan said, "I find it very difficult to believe that you would ever be at your wit's end."

"Oh, I wasn't, Mr. Morgan. I said my husband and my father were."

Connie smiled triumphantly, and Bob and Morgan laughed loudly. Both J.P. and the professor awoke with a start, each of them sleepily wanting to know what was so amusing.

Morgan smiled at the just-roused pair. Gesturing toward the dining room, he told them, "Let's see if we can find something for breakfast, and your companions can tell you while we eat. We've earned a delicious reward, for we've done a good piece of work this night."

"Yes, sir, we have," Bob agreed, standing and then helping Connie up. "We've closed the door on a disastrous week."

"And opened it to a bright future," Connie added.

Though the train ride back to St. Louis was as long as the one to New York had been, it was decidedly more pleasant, for having accomplished more than their fondest hopes, the travelers enjoyed a tremendous sense of well-being. Professor William T. Bateman had raised the money he needed to save the university, Bob and Connie Canfield had raised the money needed to drain their land, and together the threesome had helped avert a national economic disaster of major proportions.

Still euphoric, they congratulated one another often during the small celebration dinner they had enjoyed with J. P. Winthrop before leaving New York and during the trip back. Despite their triumphs, they weren't quite prepared for what greeted them when, just after dark, the horse-drawn cab they had hired at the train depot turned onto the street that led to the chancellor's house.

"Driver, wait a minute," Professor Bateman called, sticking his head out and noticing a huge gathering farther up the block. "What is going on up there, do you know?"

"No, sir," the driver replied, pulling the team up. "Would you like me to go some other way?"

"There *is* no other way," the professor pointed out. "That crowd of people seems to be right in front of my home."

"Look, several of them are carrying torches," Connie said, leaning out the window. "Oh, and I can hear the band! It sounds like some sort of a rally."

At first, only the deep thump of the bass drum and tubas could be heard; then the sound of the bells wafted their way and then the music itself.

Professor Bateman smiled broadly. "Why, of course! We must have beaten the University of Chicago. Yes, that's it. We beat them in the game last Saturday."

"No," Bob said. "I saw the score in the New York paper. We lost."

"Then maybe it's a pep rally for the game *this* Saturday," Connie suggested.

"Well, let's find out," Professor Bateman said. "Driver, please proceed."

"Yes, sir," the driver answered, snapping the reins against the backs of the horses.

The hired carriage rolled up the street, and when it reached the fringe of the crowd, some of those gathered spotted the occupants and started cheering. The crowd parted enough to let the cab through before it closed in on it again, cheering even more loudly. The driver didn't have to worry about controlling his team, for a couple of students grabbed the horses by the bridles and led them in.

"Look!" Connie said, pointing to the front of her father's house.

Spread all across the front yard, lighted by a dozen flickering torches, was a long banner, stating: PROFESSOR WILLIAM T. BATEMAN, HERO OF THE HOUR!

As soon as the carriage had stopped, several young men helped the professor out. To the cheers of the hundreds amassed there, they lifted him to their shoulders, then carried him up to the front porch. The school band played one of Jefferson's fight songs, and a number of students began throwing green and red confetti.

"Three cheers for the professor!"

"Hip, hip!"

"HOORAY!"

"Hip, hip!"

"HOORAY!"

"Hip, hip!"

"HOORAY!"

"Speech! Speech! Speech!" the students began chanting, until the senior-class president held up his hands, calling for silence. When the throng did grow quiet, their leader looked over at the chancellor.

"Professor Bateman, on behalf of the student body of Jefferson University, I would like to extend to you our utmost appreciation and admiration for a job well done. Although you bore the weight of our problems on your shoulders, we all had a huge stake in the outcome of your mission. Your success in saving this school means that our beloved institution will be here for our children and our children's children." He grinned. "And now, sir, we'd like to give you a cheer that's most often heard when one of our boys scores a goal—for this was the greatest goal ever accomplished at Jefferson." He turned to the crowd. "Okay, fellow students, let's hear it for the man who makes our university go. BATEMAN!" the young man shouted, and the crowd shouted with him, "BATEMAN, BATEMAN, YEA, BATEMAN! HOORAY!"

The students again called for a speech, and this time Professor Bateman acquiesced. He stepped to the edge of the porch and held out his hands. The crowd grew quiet, gathering closer so that they could hear him, their intense and eager young faces bathed in the flickering gold of a hundred or more hand-held torches.

"I think you did the cheer very well," Professor Bateman began, his voice ironic, "considering how few touchdowns our boys have made this year."

The crowd laughed.

"But I am not the man who makes this university go," he continued. "I am, at best, the man who is merely keeping watch. Neither am I the savior of this institution. In fact, I was about to bestow that credit upon Bob Canfield, whose generous donation of land made the financing possible—but in truth, the credit does not belong to him either. Neither does it belong to my daughter, who conceived of the plan, nor to J. Pierpont Morgan, who actually made the funds available.

"I cannot take the credit for saving the university, and I cannot bestow the credit on any of the worthy individuals just mentioned because the very definition of the word *saving* would denote that our mission is finished.

"Well, I want to tell you now, my friends, our mission is not finished, and it never will be. When I assumed the job of keeping watch over this college from our founder and first president, Henry R. Spengeman, I accepted that responsibility with the complete understanding that my work would never be done. It has been my privilege to keep watch through the changing of the centuries . . . ushering out the old and bringing in the new. But it is not a job that I do alone.

"We are all keeping watch, we who belong to this

great institution—whether it be as staff or faculty or students. We are all a part of the great continuum of Jefferson University. Time has no dominion over us, for we are one and the same with those who have come before us and with those who are yet to come. Those young men who matriculated in 1857 are the brothers of each of you, as you are brothers and sisters to those men and women who will graduate in 1957. The spirit that we share was here at the founding of this university, and it will be here on the day the doors finally close.

"I thank each and every one of you for this show of love and support, for it is this spirit, accepted from your predecessors, carried by you, and passed on through the corridors of time, that will be the true savior of Jefferson University."

The hush that had prevailed during the professor's speech continued for several seconds at its conclusion. Then everyone simultaneously cheered and applauded.

Bob felt a lump in his throat and the sting of tears in his eyes. Looking around, he saw that in the sea of faces surrounding him, lighted by the dancing flames of the torches, hundreds of eyes were also glistening with tears.

While the men's glee club formed up under an oak tree and began singing, with a final wave the three weary travelers went inside the house.

"It was a lovely speech," Connie said over the muted, melodious singing that could still be heard in the background.

"Yes, it was," Bob agreed. "And I want you to know that as long as I have the wherewithal to provide it, Jefferson University can always count on me for support."

"Thank you," Professor Bateman replied.

"You love this university, don't you?" Bob asked. "I mean, far more than the love any man would normally have for his vocation. You love this university in a way that's almost palpable."

Professor Bateman walked over to the window and looked out at the eager young faces holding the flickering torches. He was quiet for a long moment, then finally said, "Yes, I love it. I love it so much that on the day I die, my last thought will be of this school." He turned away from the window, smiling. "And after that, if I can make a pact with God, for the rest of the time that this school has left, my spirit will be out on the quadrangle . . . just keeping watch."

The saga continues with

THE AMERICAN CHRONICLES
DECADE TWO

OVER THERE

by Robert Vaughan

Turn the page for an exciting preview of
OVER THERE, on sale in 1992 wherever
Bantam Domain Books are sold.

APRIL 1912, THE NORTH ATLANTIC

The luxury liner plowed remarkably smoothly through the night. That fact was appreciated by the tall, handsome ("arrogantly handsome," an admirer had once called him) man who stood in the middle of the Promenade Deck, his arms resting on the rail and his hands clasped. He had also been appreciative of the fact that from the moment the ship had disembarked from Southampton four days earlier, he had been the target of a half-dozen flirtatious women and the topic of conversation of a dozen more. But as thirty-year-old J.P. Winthrop stood looking out over the North Atlantic Ocean, a cold breeze ruffling his black hair, he was unable to distract his mind from busily replaying the music he had just been listening to—music that brought back bittersweet memories.

After dinner the ship's orchestra had presented a

concert in the *Louis Seize* lounge on the A Deck, and those first-class passengers attending were served coffee at the small tables under the palms as they listened. The concert had ended with a selection from *Les Contes d'Hoffman*, Offenbach's opera about softly lighted Venetian balconies, star-crossed lovers, gliding gondolas, and roisterous students celebrating the joy of youth. By coincidence J.P. had attended the same opera just a month earlier, and now, in mid-ocean, sailing through the darkness under a brilliant vault of stars, this moment seemed like a curtain call. The feeling was heightened by the fact that the woman he loved—his own star-crossed love—was on board this very ship.

He sighed and focused on the water. It was 10:30, the cold night air was clear and sharp, and from this perspective he had a magnificent view. Though there was no moon, the stars were so bright that he could observe the gently rolling sea from horizon to horizon. The dark surface was given texture by whitecaps that flickered like a hundred thousand candle flames when the waves spilled over. Looking down fifty feet to the waterline, he could see phosphorescent fish glowing in the sea.

"Don't tell me the heartthrob of every young maiden on this ship is out here all alone," a woman's voice teased. "Have you been abandoned by your harem, J.P.? Or have you abandoned them?"

Though he felt his heart leap, he laughed easily and turned to face the strikingly beautiful young woman standing behind him. She had just stepped through the door from the first-class lounge.

"Perhaps it's a little of both," he said.

"Well, then you won't mind if I join you?"

"Not at all." With a sweeping gesture of his arm, he indicated the empty Promenade Deck. "There's plenty of room, as you can see."

"It was a lovely concert, wasn't it?"

"Yes," J.P. agreed. "I enjoyed it very much."

"It was sad, though, the lovers coming so close, yet never finding happiness."

This wasn't a chance meeting. J.P. knew the woman far too well to think that. She was Lady Lucinda

Chetwynd-Dunliegh, née Delacroix. Eight years ago her father had arranged a union for her—joining American money and English nobility. The marriage had enriched her husband by one million dollars and provided her with a title. She was now the wife of an English earl and the mother of a six-year-old boy whose own title was bigger than he was. She once joked that it had taken three hundred years of English peerage to make her a lady . . . though her remark had not been very well received by the formal, stiff-necked men and women of her husband's social class.

"Brrr," Lucinda said, shivering and pulling her fur coat tighter around her, "I don't care if it is spring, it's freezing out here." She looked so beautiful and vulnerable that J.P.'s impulse was to reach for her and put his arms around her. But he didn't.

Lucinda was his star-crossed lover. She was the first woman he had ever been intimate with and the only one he had ever truly loved. At one time J.P. had entertained the idea that Lucinda might marry him. But that wasn't to be.

She looked down at the ocean. "It really is quite beautiful, isn't it?"

"Yes, it is."

"Have you seen the ship's wake?" she asked. "I'm always fascinated by the wake, the way it churns and shines so white against the black sea. I have a theory about wakes, you know. Would you like to hear it?"

She looked up at him, and J.P. thought she had never been more beautiful than she was at this very moment. Her blond hair gleamed golden in the light from the wall sconce just behind them, and her green eyes sparkled as she gazed intently at him. He involuntarily shivered. Perhaps it was the power of suggestion or perhaps it was being in her presence—or perhaps it was because he was wearing only the evening clothes he had worn at dinner and no overcoat.

"You're cold, too?" Lucinda asked.

"A little."

"Lean against me," she offered. "You'll get some warmth from my coat."

Obediently, J.P. leaned against her, and found she was right. He did realize some warmth from the fur of her coat. Though he didn't want to admit it, not even to himself, he was also warmed by his proximity to her. Above the smell of the sea he could smell her perfume and the essence of her own sweet scent.

"You didn't answer me," she reminded him. Smiling, she reached up, familiarly brushing back a lock of his hair that had fallen onto his forehead, and J.P. wished that there were but the two of them in the world at this moment. He damned all the accursed bright lights of this ship. "Would you like to know my theory about wakes?" she repeated.

"Yes," he replied, his voice somewhat louder than he had intended. "Yes, of course I would."

"Good. Well, I believe that, like a ship, our lives also leave wakes, and if we could follow that wake backward, very fast—say, in the fastest motorboat, we would see our lives unfolding again. Isn't that an interesting theory?"

J.P. chuckled. "Perhaps it is, but the question remains: How many people would really want to do that? Who would want to go back and have to relive earlier parts of life?"

"I would," Lucinda said, her voice somber. "I would especially like to go back if, in so doing, I could alter the course of my life at a certain, critical juncture." Her large eyes grew deep and serious, and she turned to study him. "I think you know which critical juncture I'm talking about," she added.

J.P. didn't respond, and for a long moment there was no sound except the subdued throb of the ship's engines and the quiet slap of water against the ship's hull. Then a sudden peal of laughter burst forth from the lounge, where a marathon game of bridge was in progress and had been for most of the day and evening.

"Have you nothing to say to me about that, J.P.?"

"Would you really want to change anything, Lucinda?" he asked. "Consider your son."

Lucinda let out a long sigh. "Yes," she finally said. "Yes, of course, one must consider Jimmy. He is a dear child, and I love him so. Still, one must hang on to the memories and the dreams of what might have been. Or else how could one go on?"

There was another exuberant peal of laughter from inside. Lucinda turned away from the rail and looked back toward the light shining through the diamond-shaped, leaded-glass window at the top of the door.

"Listen to them in there," she said. "Dear old Alex must be in rare form tonight, regaling the others around the card table with his ribald tales."

"Sir Alex is a likable man and an entertaining fellow," J.P. said. "In these last few days I have come to consider him my friend."

"Yes, and he considers you his friend as well," Lucinda said. "And, I must confess that I also find him quite charming . . . as a friend." She turned toward J.P. and put her fingers on his cheek. "But you must know that you were more than a friend. Much more." She leaned against him, opening the folds of her coat, and J.P. could feel the soft warmth of her thigh through her silken evening dress. "Dear, dear, J.P. Do you never think of me anymore? Do you never recall that afternoon in my friend's apartment when we—"

J.P. reached up and clutched her wrist, then pulled her hand away from his cheek—not roughly, but firmly. "Lucinda, this is very poor form."

Lucinda laughed. "Ah, yes, and we mustn't forget form, must we? But then it wasn't I who re-entered your life, J.P. It was you who re-entered mine, remember? I was quite happy and content . . . well, at least re-signed to life as the Countess of Dunliegh. I had no idea you would show up last week."

"I told you why I went. When I learned that you and Sir Alex had booked passage on this voyage, I thought it'd be good to come see you and inform you that I, too, would be making the crossing. After all, it's been nearly eight years since we went our separate ways. We've both made new lives for ourselves since then."

"And yet you never married," Lucinda said. It was a statement, not a question.

"No. I never married."

"Why didn't you?"

"I don't know. My work as an art buyer for the J.P. Morgan collection, I suppose. It takes me all over the world, and I'm not sure a wife would appreciate or understand such long separations."

"No," Lucinda countered, "we both know that's not why you never married. You never married because you have never stopped loving me."

"Lucinda, please," J.P. said softly. "This is getting us nowhere."

"If you won't confess it to me, then I'll confess it to you." She put her fingers on his cheek again, and he was amazed at the heat they generated. "I love you, J.P. I have never stopped loving you." She tried to embrace him, but he turned away from her, leaving her arms grasping at empty air.

"No!" he said sharply. "No, I won't let you degrade yourself like this."

Lucinda's long sigh signaled defeat. "Yes," she finally said quietly. She shivered again. "Well, it *is* getting a bit too cold out here at that. Perhaps I had better go back in." She started for the door, then turned back toward him. "You are having breakfast at our table in the morning?"

"Yes, of course," J.P. answered. He smiled. "I promised Jimmy."

"I know. And we mustn't disappoint Jimmy, must we?"

He watched her step through the doorway, then turned back to stare out at the sea. This voyage had been a monumental mistake. He had told himself and others that he chose to make the crossing on the *Titanic* because it was the maiden voyage of the newest, biggest, fastest, most elegant ship afloat, and he wanted to be a part of it. But the truth was much more fundamental than that: He chose to make this passage because he had read in the newspaper that Lord and Lady Alex Purcival Chetwynd-Dunliegh and son would be on board. He thought he would test himself, to see if, after eight years, he could be in such close proximity to Lucinda and not be effected by it. Now even that bit of subterfuge was peeled away for the sham it was. He was on this ship for one reason and one reason only: He had to be close to her. He was still in love with Lucinda, and she had just confessed that she was still in love with him. But she was married to one English lord and was the mother of another.

Star-crossed lovers. J.P. had never been more miserable in his life.

"Good evening, Mr. Winthrop."

Turning, J.P. saw the assistant radio operator, Harold Bride, his white uniform crisp and sparkling, hurrying along the deck. Bride was coming from the direction of the radio shack, where earlier this afternoon J.P. had sent a radiogram to his employer, J. Pierpont Morgan, informing the financier that he had just closed the deal on the Monet he had gone to Europe to buy for Morgan's renowned art collection.

"Good evening, Mr. Bride," J.P. responded, and then he turned back to resume his vigil over the sea.

Harold Bride hurried on to the bridge, where he handed a sheet of paper to William Murdoch, the officer on watch.

"Thank you," Murdoch replied.

Captain E. J. Smith, fifty-nine years old and distinguished looking with white hair and beard, was puffing on a pipe as he studied the chart that marked the ship's progress. He glanced up as the message was passed.

"What is it, Mr. Murdoch?" he asked.

"More warnings of icebergs, Captain," Murdoch answered. "One from the French liner *Touraine* and another from the German ship *Amerika*."

"Were the messages sent specifically to us?" Captain Smith asked.

"Aye, sir, they were. Should I reduce speed?"

Captain Smith stroked his beard for a moment. They had been proceeding at just over twenty-two knots for four days on what promised to be a record crossing. The air was clear, the sea was as calm as a mill pond, and the ship was behaving so beautifully that its motion was barely discernable. "Have we someone aloft?" Smith asked.

"Aye, sir, two men. Seamen Fleet and Lee are in the crow's nest."

"Ah, good, good. I know both of them; they're responsible, sober young men. We'll continue at this speed, but pass the word to all hands to be particularly alert."

"Aye, aye, sir."

Smith knocked out his pipe, then slipped it down into his jacket pocket. "I'll be turning in now."

"Very good, sir," Murdoch replied. "I'll continue heading and speed unless otherwise directed by circumstances."

"In which case I want to be informed," Smith added as he left the bridge on the way to his quarters.

Several decks below the bridge, in the third-class compartment, Karl Tannenhower, a nineteen-year-old immigrant from Germany, sat at a table in the dining hall/recreation lounge, playing chess with Tim O'Leary, an equally young immigrant from Ireland.

Physical opposites—one blond, the other black haired; one burly, the other slim—the two young men had taken to each other immediately on their first day out of Southhampton. Karl was about two inches the shorter though probably forty pounds heavier. The additional weight was all muscle, for he had a bull-like neck, broad shoulders, and very powerful arms as the result of his hobby of lifting weights. Unable to bring his dumbbells due to weight and space restrictions, but wanting to stay fit, Karl had improvised, and the first night out he had startled Tim and the other men sharing his compartment by repeatedly lifting one of the heavy lockers over his head.

Karl and Tim had quickly discovered a shared passion for chess, playing innumerable games since setting sail. This particular game had started shortly after they had eaten supper. Now, with but a moment's deliberation, Karl took Tim's rook.

"Ouch, 'tis a cruel assassin you are," Tim complained.

Karl laughed. "But it was you who put the rook at risk with your bold play," he countered.

"Aye, I am a bit of the bold one now, aren't I?" Tim replied with a good-natured laugh. He studied the pieces silently for a moment, then remarked, "So 'tis to St. Louis you'll be going now, I believe you said."

"Yes," Karl answered.

"Why such a place?"

"My uncle owns a brewery there. Why do you call St. Louis 'such a place?' Do you know of some evil in the city I should avoid?"

"I mean nothing by the remark, for I know nothin' of St. Louis," Tim said. "'Tis Boston for the likes of my kind. 'Tis said that Boston has nearly as many Irish as Dublin itself. Strange, isn't it, how a particular city in a foreign country can attract so many from one place?"

"Yes," Karl agreed. "For Germans it is St. Louis and Milwaukee."

"Tell me, Karl, if your uncle owns a brewery, why is it then that you're not crossin' in second class? Or even first? Surely a man such as your uncle must be wealthy. I'd be thinkin' he'd want his nephew to make the crossin' with all the proper ladies and gentlemen."

Karl laughed. "My uncle *did* send me the money for first-class fare, but I thought that an unnecessary extravagance. Besides, where would I find better people than the friends I have made here?" he asked, taking in the big room with a broad sweep of his large hands. "I would much rather save the money, for I have a feeling I will be needing it when I start school. You see, I am going to attend a university in America. My uncle has written of it. He says it is a fine institution, as fine as the University of Heidelburg."

"And would this find school be Harvard, now?" Tim asked. "Sure and I've heard of Harvard, though few of my countrymen attend, I'm told. But I didn't know Harvard was in St. Louis." He moved one of his chessmen, then looked up at Karl, smiling. "Handle that one, lad," the Irishman challenged.

Karl responded with his own move, then said, "Check."

"Check?" Tim asked, clearly surprised by the sudden turn of events and studying the board intently.

"No, it is not Harvard," Karl said, finally answering Tim's question. "It is Jefferson University. It is named after an American president."

"I've never heard of the place or the man." Tim let out a sigh, then began taking his pieces from the board. "You're too good for me," he said. "Would you like to be gettin' a beer, then, and seein' what the fair lassies are doin'?"

"I think that would be nice," Karl agreed, getting up from the table and draping a casual arm around his companion's shoulder.

It was important that the immigrants at least got along with one another, for sleeping accomodations for those in steerage consisted of compartments comprised solely of multiple tiers of bunks. Located deep in the bowels of the ship, those for the women were way back at the stern, while those for the men were far forward in the bow. When not actually in bed, the men and women congregated in the large, rather sterile dining hall that acted as a boundary between the two sets of compartments. It was also the recreation lounge, and a piano had been provided at one end, though any music the instrument produced would have to come from the passengers themselves. Fortunately there were enough steerage passengers with musical talent that someone was playing all the time. A few passengers even had their own instruments, so that on a few occasions an entire band was formed. The only difficulty seemed to lie in finding music that everyone in this diverse ethnic mix liked: Some of the music appealed to eastern Europeans, some to western Europeans, some to the Irish, some to the Jews, and some was uniquely American. Fortunately, there were always some songs that had broken out of their compartmentalized ethnic origins to become widely enjoyed.

The band performing at the moment was made up of several American college students, returning to the

States after a tour of the Continent. They were playing "Alexander's Ragtime Band," one of those pieces having a universal appeal, and dozens of young men and women from all ethnic groups were dancing to the music.

A smile on his face, Karl stood listening to the music while imagining his future in America—a prospect he greatly looked forward to.

Beneath the party going on in third class, way down in the hold, the men of the "black gang" were stripped to the waist, laboring to keep the fires stoked. Some of the men worked in the coal bunkers, shoveling the gritty black chunks into wheelbarrows. Others, called trimmers, would then push the loaded wheelbarrows from the bunkers to the furnaces, where they'd tip them up at the doors, propelling the coal into the roaring flames.

The ship's engines had a voracious appetite, and nearly one hundred tons of coal were consumed during every watch. Though lighted by dozens of electric lights, the room was nevertheless dark because the air was always thick with coal dust. Occasionally one of the men would be silhouetted against the open mouth of a furnace, looking for all the world like a demon stepping out of the fires of hell itself.

A constant din filled the room: the slap of shovels digging into the coal, the clanging of furnace doors opening and closing, the throb of the reciprocating engines driving the outboard propellers, the hum of the turbine driving the center-line propeller, and the whine of the dynamos generating the ship's electricity. Twenty-four of the twenty-nine boilers were lit, watched over by the officers on duty and tended to by the unrelenting, back-breaking labor of the men of the black gang.

It may have been freezing up on deck, but down in the engine room the men had to be watched closely for signs of heat exhaustion. To prevent that from happening, more than forty fans were spinning, providing much-needed circulation of the air. Despite the grueling conditions, these men were proud to be in service on such a mighty vessel.

• • •

Far above all this, up on the Promenade Deck, J.P. Winthrop finally turned away from the railing and went back inside. Passing through the lounge, he glanced over toward the card game. It had drawn over a dozen spectators, for all the participants were exceptionally skilled as was evidenced by some well-played rubbers. At the other end of the room, the orchestra, its members formally dressed, had returned from the concert in the *Louis Sieze* room and was now playing dance music, currently a waltz. A few couples were gliding around the highly polished dance floor, while others sat in quiet conversation at tables. John Jacob Astor and his wife were seated with several other august passengers, including Sir Cosmos and Lady Duff-Gordon and J. Bruce Ismay, chairman of the White Star Line. Astor waved at J.P. as the younger man walked across the lounge, and J.P. waved back.

Reaching the grand staircase, J.P. climbed it to his deck, then walked down the long carpeted corridor to his cabin and let himself in with his key. He closed the door behind him and was about to turn on the light when he had the certain feeling that someone was in his suite.

"Is someone in here?" he asked anxiously, reaching for the light switch.

"No, leave the light off," a woman said from the darkness.

J.P. immediately recognized the voice. "Lucinda!" he gasped. "What are you doing in here? How did you get in?"

"I bribed one of the stewards," she admitted. "And as for what I'm doing in here . . . well, I suppose that all depends on you, doesn't it?"

The cabin wasn't totally dark because a wedge of light spilled in over the transom. As J.P.'s eyes adjusted to the gloom, he located Lucinda. And when she moved slightly so that she was standing in the ambient light, he knew why she was here. She was totally naked and offering herself to him.

"Lucinda, my God," J.P. whispered.

She didn't respond. Instead, she started toward the bedroom of his suite. She didn't ask him to follow, but it was clear that she knew he would.

"Woman, do you know what you are doing?" J.P. asked in a choked voice.

"Do you want me?"

"Yes, of course, but—"

"Then, please, ask no questions," she implored.

"But you shouldn't be here," he insisted. Even as he spoke the words, he knew he was only paying lip service to his conscience. It had gone too far now, and he wasn't sure he would let her leave even if she suddenly changed her mind.

"Still in your evening clothes? I'm surprised at you, J.P. You've never been known to be improperly dressed for any occasion." She laughed at her own joke.

"If I'm improperly dressed, perhaps I should do something about it," he replied, jerking out the knot in his bow-tie and rapidly unbuttoning his shirt.

"I was sure you would want to be correct," Lucinda quipped.

A moment later he was as naked as she, and when she lay back on his bed holding her arms up toward him in invitation, he went to her quickly.

ABOUT THE AUTHOR

Writing under his own name and 25 pen names, ROBERT VAUGHAN has authored over 200 books in every genre but Science Fiction. He won the 1977 Porgie Award (Best Paperback Original) for *The Power and the Pride*. In 1973 *The Valkyrie Mandate* was nominated by its publisher, Simon & Schuster, for the Pulitzer Prize.

Vaughan is a frequent speaker at seminars and at high schools and colleges. He has also hosted three television talk shows: *Eyewitness Magazine*, on WAVY TV in Portsmouth, Virginia, *Tidewater A.M.*, on WHBQ TV in Hampton, Virginia, and *This Week in Books* on the TEMPO Cable Television Network. In addition, he hosted a cooking show at *Phoenix at Mid-day* on KHPO TV in Phoenix, Arizona.

Vaughan is a retired Army Warrant Officer (CW-3) with three tours in Vietnam where he was awarded the Distinguished Flying Cross, the Air Medal with the V for valor, the Bronze Star, the Distinguished Service Medal, and the Purple Heart. He was a helicopter pilot and a maintenance and supply officer. He was also an instructor and Chief of the Aviation Maintenance Officers' Course at Fort Eustis, Virginia. During his military career, Vaughan was a participant in many of the 20th century's most significant events. For example, he served in Korea immediately after the armistice, he was involved in the Nevada Atomic Bomb tests, he was part of the operation which ensured that James Meredith could attend the University of Mississippi, he was alerted for the Cuban Missile Crisis, he served three years in Europe, and of course, the above-mentioned three tours in Vietnam.

DEAR READER:

I do not regard time as something fixed and linear, but rather as a meandering stream which can bend back upon itself. At any given moment we can dip into this "stream of time" and see things, not as they were, *but as they are*.

I wrote *The American Chronicles* to provide you with access points to this stream of time. When you read the books of this series I hope you won't just *see* the past, you will *experience* it. As the series develops, you will be able to move from decade to decade of this century as easily as you move from room to room in your own home.

To those of you who can remember the earliest decades of this century, reading these books will be more than a nostalgic experience . . . it will be a visit with old friends. Those of you who are younger will see the decades before you were born . . . not as dusty history . . . but as a heretofore unexplored element of your own lives, for you too, are a part of this time stream.

ROBERT VAUGHAN
Sikeston, Missouri